XEL - 3

XEL - SERIES, Volume 3

HIFLUR RAHMAN

Published by HIFLUR RAHMAN, 2024.

This is a work of fiction. Similarities to real people, places, or events are entirely coincidental.

XEL - 3

First edition. December 10, 2024.

ISBN: 979-8227834324

Written by HIFLUR RAHMAN.

Table of Contents

I Dedicate This To All My Friends, Family And Readers For The Love They poured on me.

"The Greatest Of All Time Is Always Not Imagined"

XEL 3: The Vanishing Paradox

Written By Hiflur Rahman

I am beyond excited to share with you the final book of this series, a story I've poured my heart and soul into. Each word, each chapter has been crafted with immense care and love, all with the hope of bringing you something truly special and different. Your unwavering support and affection for my earlier books have meant the world to me, and I can never fully express how deeply grateful I am. I often find myself wondering if I will ever be able to repay the debt of love I owe to each and every one of you.

Yet, instead of trying to pay it all back at once, I've decided to take a different path. I will continue writing stories, hoping that each new tale, each new journey, helps me slowly but surely repay this immeasurable gift of your love. My goal is to create stories that resonate deeply within your hearts, to touch you in a way that makes this shared journey of ours worth every moment.

Thank you, from the bottom of my heart, for being a part of this adventure. Your love and support give me the strength to keep going, and I hope this book reflects all the gratitude and love I feel for you.

Recall

Adrian, Mia, Emma, and George were the only ones who managed to survive the island's terror and dark magic. Yet, as they continue their journey, driven by both curiosity and courage, they ultimately encounter something both astonishing and entirely unexpected, deep within the island's mysteries.

1

The Beginning Of The Echoes

As the sun dipped below the horizon, casting a warm golden glow over the ancient landscape, the four adventurers sat in stunned silence, the weight of their discovery pressing heavily upon them. Before them loomed an ancient machine, resembling a portal, its intricate designs glowing faintly as if pulsating with life. This was the revelation they had never anticipated—a relic of a bygone era, hidden within the heart of Xel Island, shrouded in mystery and power.

Adrian stared intently at the portal, his mind racing. *How could they harness its power? What secrets lay beyond?* His heart raced with a mix of excitement and dread. The struggles they had endured seemed trivial now, dwarfed by the monumental choice before them.

"Mia, what do you think?" Adrian finally broke the silence, turning to her. "Is it even safe to approach this thing?"

Mia, her brow furrowed in contemplation, shifted her gaze from the portal to Adrian. "I can't shake the feeling that this is our only chance," she said, her voice steady yet laced with uncertainty. "We've faced so much already—loss, danger, and the island's dark magic. This... this portal could hold the key to everything."

Emma nodded in agreement, her blue eyes shining with determination. "We've come too far to turn back now. Think about all the sacrifices we've made. If we don't at least try, we might never know what could have been."

George, usually the voice of reason, was unusually quiet, his hands clenched into fists. "But what if it's a trap? We could be walking straight into danger, and we've barely survived the island's wrath as it is."

Mia leaned forward, her voice rising with passion. "George, we're already in danger. Staying here, doing nothing, won't save us. Look at everything we've endured! If we don't take this leap of faith, we risk losing all that we've fought for. Don't you see? This could lead us to answers, to understanding what this island truly is."

Adrian, feeling the tension in the air, took a deep breath. *Could they really do this?* "What if there's a way to control it?" he pondered aloud, glancing at Mia and the others. "What if we can use it to understand the island's history, the civilizations that came before us? Think of the knowledge we could unlock."

Emma's eyes lit up. "Exactly! This portal might not just be a doorway; it could be a bridge to the past. We can't ignore the possibilities."

George sighed, torn between his fear and the hope ignited by their words. "Alright, I'm in. But we have to be careful. No more reckless decisions."

Adrian nodded, feeling the weight of responsibility settle on his shoulders. "Then let's do it together. We've faced the darkness as a team; we can't let fear hold us back now."

They all stood up, a united front against the unknown. As they faced the enigmatic portal, a newfound determination coursed through them. "We are brave enough to enter this portal!" Adrian called out, his voice resonating in the still air. "No matter the dangers, we'll face them together!"

Mia stepped forward, her heart racing with exhilaration. "We will not be deterred! We have overcome so much, and we will conquer whatever lies ahead!"

Emma joined in, her voice strong. "This is our moment! We've fought too hard to back down now. We will step into the unknown and uncover the truth!"

George took a deep breath, his fear mingling with courage. "For our journey, for those we've lost, and for the future we want to shape. Let's step through together."

With the sunlight fading and the last rays of warmth touching their backs, the four adventurers stood together before the ancient portal, a symbol of their courage and unity. They exchanged determined glances, each one silently affirming their commitment to the quest ahead. As they readied themselves to enter the unknown, they knew they were not just stepping into a portal; they were embracing their fate, ready to face whatever challenges awaited them on the other side.

As they stood before the shimmering portal, their hearts racing with anticipation, the atmosphere crackled with tension. Just as they were about to take that fateful step into the unknown, a sudden flash illuminated the darkening sky, followed by a deafening crack of thunder. A bolt of lightning struck the ground mere millimeters from their feet, sending a shockwave that knocked them back, tumbling away from the portal in a chaotic scramble.

"Everyone alright?" Adrian gasped as he pushed himself up, his eyes wide with shock. The air around them was charged, the scent of ozone thick and heady.

Mia shook her head, trying to regain her bearings. "What was that?!"

George quickly rose to his feet, his pulse racing. As he turned to face the portal again, a strange silhouette emerged from the smoke and sparks left in the lightning's wake. The figure was humanoid, but something was distinctly off. The dim light cast eerie shadows across its form, making it hard to discern whether it was friend or foe.

"Stay back!" Emma warned, stepping protectively in front of Mia, her instincts kicking in. But curiosity tugged at George, drawing his gaze to the figure. The more he looked, the more familiar it seemed, as if it was pulling fragments of memory from the depths of his mind.

And then it hit him—a wave of recognition crashing over him like an icy wave. "Wait! That face... it's Victor!" he shouted, the realization slicing through the tension. But this wasn't the Victor they had known; this was a twisted reflection of the man he once was.

"Victor?" Mia echoed, disbelief lacing her voice. "But he was... he was killed! We saw it on the television!"

"Yes," Adrian added, his mind racing. "He was beheaded. There's no way he could be—"

But the figure before them was undeniably Victor, or at least a version of him. He stood tall and imposing, his expression a mix of fury and despair, but with something darker lurking behind his eyes. His skin was pallid, stretched taut over bone, and his mouth curled into a smile that didn't reach his eyes—a haunting, unnatural expression.

"Victor!" George called out, stepping forward hesitantly, each word feeling like a betrayal to the memories of their fallen hero. "What happened to you?"

The figure's head tilted slightly, a glint of recognition flickering in his eyes. "Ah, the brave adventurers return to the island," he said, his voice a low, eerie whisper that seemed to echo through the air. "You've come to face your fate."

The chill that crept down their spines was palpable, and Emma gripped Mia's arm tightly. "This can't be real," she murmured, her heart pounding. "He can't be... alive."

Victor's twisted smile widened, revealing teeth that were unnaturally sharp. "Alive? Or merely existing in the shadows of this cursed place? You think you can unravel its secrets, but it is I who holds the answers now."

"Answers?" Adrian asked, his voice steady despite the fear coursing through him. "What do you know about this portal? What have you become?"

"Oh, my dear Adrian," Victor replied, a hint of mockery in his tone. "You always were the curious one, digging where you shouldn't. But the truth is a double-edged sword. You want to enter the portal? You must first confront the darkness within yourself."

With that, Victor extended an arm, his fingers elongated and twisted, pointing towards the portal that shimmered ominously behind him. "Step forward, if you dare. But know this: the island has changed me, and it will change you too. Your journey has only just begun."

The air thickened with tension as the four adventurers exchanged glances, each feeling the weight of their past decisions pressing down on them. The flickering light from the portal pulsed like a heartbeat, tempting them to step closer, but the figure of Victor loomed as a reminder of the dangers that lay ahead.

Adrian took a deep breath, stepping forward slightly. "We won't be intimidated by you, Victor. You may have once been a curious detective or a hero for all, but you're not the same. We're not afraid."

Victor's laughter echoed, chilling them to the bone. "Fear? You should embrace it! It is the key to survival here. But tell me, what will you do when the portal reveals your darkest fears?"

"Whatever it takes," George declared, his voice rising with determination. "We'll face whatever comes, together!"

Mia nodded, her resolve solidifying. "You may have been our role model once, Victor, but we won't let you stop us now. We're stronger than the darkness you represent!"

With a collective nod, they braced themselves, knowing the path ahead would test their strength, courage, and very souls. The portal shimmered behind Victor, a gateway to the unknown, and as they steeled themselves for the confrontation, they understood that the true battle lay not just with the figure before them, but within their own hearts as well.

"Victor, move aside," Adrian commanded, his voice steady despite the fear churning in his stomach. The flickering light from the portal cast ominous shadows across Victor's face, highlighting the malevolence brewing beneath his surface.

But Victor simply smiled—a twisted, sardonic grin that sent chills down Adrian's spine. "Why would I do that?" he asked, his tone dripping with mockery. "You think I'm going to let you pass so easily? This is my domain now."

As the words left his lips, something shifted within Victor. The air grew thick with an electric tension, a palpable force that made the hairs on the back of their necks stand on end. Adrian felt a surge of dread as he watched Victor's body start to contort, the familiar contours of his former self warping into something darker and more sinister.

"Victor, please!" Mia pleaded, stepping forward. "You don't have to do this! We're here to help you!"

But Victor's laughter echoed around them, low and menacing. His eyes began to cloud over, transforming into a blinding white that seemed to reflect the very essence of rage itself. "Help? You don't understand! This island has awakened something within me, something far beyond your comprehension!"

Adrian took a cautious step back, heart pounding in his chest. "Victor, fight it! Remember who you were!"

Yet, as he spoke, Victor's transformation accelerated. The muscles in his face tightened, and with an agonizing groan, his teeth elongated, becoming sharp and jagged, like the fangs of a predator ready to strike. It was as if the darkness of the island had seeped into him, twisting his humanity into something grotesque.

"Do you see?" Victor roared, his voice now a low growl, barely recognizable. "This power, this rage—it courses through me! I am no longer the man you knew! I am reborn in the shadows!"

"Reborn?" George shot back, anger fueling his words. "You've become a monster! This isn't who you were when you were alive!"

Victor lunged forward, his movements swift and erratic, fueled by a fury that radiated from him like heat from a fire. "You think you can challenge me?" he snarled, his once-familiar features now a mask of wrath. "You have no idea what awaits you beyond this portal!"

Adrian felt a surge of determination welling up inside him. "We don't fear you, Victor!" he shouted, stepping forward to face the twisted reflection of a once great detective. "We're here to stop this madness!"

"Then you'll have to go through me!" Victor hissed, his voice reverberating with an otherworldly echo. "The island has given me power beyond imagination, and I will not let you take it from me!"

In that moment, the air crackled with tension, and the portal behind them pulsed ominously, as if aware of the confrontation unfolding before it. Adrian exchanged glances with Mia and Emma, their resolve solidifying. They couldn't allow fear to dictate their actions; they had come too far and lost too much to turn back now.

"Together!" Adrian called out, rallying his friends. "We face him together, just as we always have!"

With a fierce nod, they positioned themselves side by side, ready to confront the creature that Victor had become. The storm of energy crackled between them, a force that merged their courage and determination.

As Victor charged at them, the air crackled with tension, a storm brewing both within and around them. The figure that had once been their friend was now a formidable foe, transformed by the island's dark magic. The ground trembled beneath his feet as he lunged, a primal roar erupting from his twisted mouth, sending shockwaves through the air.

"Get ready!" Adrian shouted, adrenaline surging through his veins. He raised his arms defensively, instinctively positioning himself between Mia and Victor.

Before they could react, Victor barreled into Adrian, slamming him against the ancient stone wall. The impact rattled Adrian's bones, his vision blurring as he fought to regain his focus. Victor's eyes—those once warm, familiar eyes—now burned with a fierce, otherworldly light, devoid of the humanity he had once known.

"Adrian!" Mia screamed, her voice laced with panic. She rushed forward, her heart racing. In that instant, she saw Victor's monstrous form loom over Adrian, his sharpened teeth glistening ominously.

With a surge of courage, Mia threw herself at Victor, aiming a punch at his side. The blow connected, but Victor barely flinched. He turned to her, fury emanating from his twisted visage. "You think you can stop me?" he growled, shoving Mia aside with a flick of his arm. She tumbled to the ground, but the fire in her eyes only burned brighter.

"Get up!" Emma shouted, her voice a clarion call in the chaos. She dashed toward Mia, helping her to her feet as Adrian wrestled with Victor, trying to regain the upper hand. "We need to stick together!"

George, who had been watching the confrontation unfold, sprang into action. "I'll distract him!" he yelled, rushing forward with an unwavering resolve. He lunged toward Victor, dodging the flailing arms and sharp teeth, aiming to create an opening for his friends. "Hey! Over here, you twisted freak!"

Victor turned, eyes narrowing as he locked onto George. In a blur, he pivoted and launched himself toward him, fangs bared. George barely managed to roll out of the way, feeling the rush of wind as Victor passed overhead. The ground erupted in a shower of dirt and debris, the force of Victor's power shaking the very earth beneath them.

"Now!" Emma shouted, taking advantage of the distraction. She grabbed a nearby stone, its edges sharp, and hurled it at Victor with all her might. The stone struck him in the shoulder, and for a fleeting moment, he staggered back, snarling in rage.

"Nice shot!" Adrian called out, seizing the moment. He lunged at Victor again, fists clenched, aiming to deliver a solid blow. But Victor recovered too quickly, swatting Adrian away like a gnat. Adrian hit the ground hard, a sharp pain radiating through his side.

"Adrian!" Mia cried, rushing to his side. "Get up! We can't let him win!"

Adrian grimaced, pushing himself back to his feet despite the pain. "We have to coordinate! We can't just throw ourselves at him blindly."

As Victor regained his composure, his monstrous form radiated a dark energy that filled the space around them, almost tangible in its malevolence. "You cannot hope to defeat me!" he bellowed, eyes glowing with fury. "I am beyond your understanding!"

"Together!" George shouted, rallying them all. "We can't let him tear us apart!"

In that moment, the four friends formed a tight circle, their backs to one another as they faced the monstrous Victor. Adrian took a deep breath, focusing on the strength of their bond. "Alright, on my count—one, two, three!"

They moved as one, each of them lunging at Victor from different angles. Mia struck low, aiming for his legs, while George went for an uppercut. Adrian targeted Victor's midsection, and Emma circled around to land a blow from behind. The collision was electrifying, the impact reverberating through the air.

But Victor was stronger than they had anticipated. He spun around, catching George with a powerful swing of his arm that sent him crashing to the ground. "Foolish children!" Victor roared, a sinister grin spreading across his face. "You think you can defeat me with mere strength? I have transcended the limits of this world!"

As George struggled to regain his footing, Mia took advantage of Victor's momentary distraction. She grabbed a nearby branch, brandishing it like a sword. "Get away from him!" she shouted, charging at Victor with all her might.

Victor turned to her, eyes flashing with disdain. "You are brave, but bravery alone cannot save you!" he hissed. With a swift motion, he swatted the branch from her hands, sending it flying.

"Let her go!" Adrian shouted, seizing the opportunity to tackle Victor from the side. They fell to the ground in a chaotic tumble, grappling with one another as Adrian struggled to maintain his grip.

Victor's strength was overwhelming, but Adrian could feel the energy of his friends rallying around him. With a surge of determination, he rolled Victor onto his back, pinning him momentarily. "Now!" he shouted, as George and Emma rushed forward to help him restrain Victor.

"Hold him!" Emma cried, trying to pin Victor's arms.

But Victor roared with fury, thrashing beneath them, his body twisting in ways that defied logic. "You think you can contain me?" he growled, his voice a guttural snarl. "I will break free! I will consume you all!"

Adrian felt the weight of Victor's power pushing against him, and for a moment, despair threatened to overtake him. But then he heard Mia's voice, a steady anchor in the storm. "We have to believe in each other! Together, we're stronger!"

With renewed resolve, they pushed harder, forcing Victor down. They were four against one, and if they combined their strength and will, they could bring him back from the brink. "On three!" Adrian yelled again, feeling the adrenaline course through his veins.

"One! Two! Three!"

In a final surge of energy, they pressed down on Victor with all their weight. The ground shook as they struggled, Victor's screams reverberating in the air. The portal behind them pulsed ominously, reacting to the chaos unfolding before it.

With one last effort, they managed to restrain Victor, forcing him to the ground. "You will not win this battle!" Adrian shouted, his voice fierce and unwavering.

Victor's eyes, once filled with rage, flickered momentarily, as if the man they had known was trying to break through. "Adrian... help me," he whispered, his voice a haunting echo.

But in that moment of vulnerability, the darkness surged once more, and Victor's monstrous facade returned, eyes blazing with fury. "You cannot save what is lost!" he roared, throwing them off him in a single powerful motion.

They stumbled back, hearts pounding, realizing the fight was far from over. But they refused to give in to despair. They stood together, ready to face whatever came next, knowing that their strength lay in their unity. With a fierce determination, they prepared for the next onslaught, the battle for Victor's soul—and their own—had only just begun.

The fight was far from over. As Victor regained his footing, his once human form seemed to pulse with dark energy, his eyes glowing white-hot with rage. His twisted, elongated figure stood tall before them, an unrelenting force driven by a power none of them fully understood. Adrian, Mia, George, and Emma braced themselves, their breaths coming in ragged gasps as they prepared for another wave of Victor's assault.

"He's stronger than we thought!" George shouted, wiping the sweat from his brow. His voice held an edge of fear, but there was determination there too. They had come too far to back down now.

"Don't lose focus!" Adrian yelled back, his mind racing. His body ached from the earlier hits, but he couldn't afford to slow down. Not now.

Victor bared his teeth in a grotesque grin, his monstrous fangs gleaming in the dim light. "You think your unity makes you strong? You're only delaying the inevitable."

Before anyone could react, Victor surged forward with terrifying speed, his hands curling into claws as he lashed out at Mia. She barely had time to duck, feeling the rush of air as his claws sliced the space where her head had been.

"Damn it, he's too fast!" Mia gasped, scrambling to her feet. Panic was threatening to overtake her, but she pushed it down. She couldn't afford to freeze now.

Emma darted forward, her heart pounding, and swung a thick branch she had grabbed from the ground. She aimed for Victor's torso, hoping to land a solid hit, but as the wood connected with his skin, there was no impact. It was as if she had struck stone. Victor turned his head slowly towards her, his eyes gleaming with amusement.

"Nice try, Emma," he hissed, his voice dripping with mockery. "But you'll have to do better than that."

Without warning, he reached out and grabbed her wrist, squeezing hard. Emma winced in pain but refused to cry out. "Let go!" she demanded, trying to wrench herself free, but Victor's grip was iron-tight.

Adrian saw what was happening and, without hesitation, rushed toward Victor, slamming his shoulder into him with all his strength. The impact caused Victor to stumble slightly, loosening his grip just enough for Emma to pull free.

"Thanks," Emma panted, rubbing her wrist, the red marks of Victor's claws still visible.

"No time for thanks," Adrian replied breathlessly. "We need to find a way to take him down."

George, keeping his distance from Victor, scanned the surroundings frantically. His eyes landed on a patch of thorns nearby—long, sharp thorns growing wild and thick against the stone wall. "Adrian! Mia! Over here!" George called out, his voice filled with urgency. "We can use these!"

They rushed over to him, and George pointed to the thorns. "Maybe if we pierce him with these, we can slow him down, or at least injure him. It's worth a shot."

Mia didn't hesitate, grabbing a handful of the jagged thorns, ignoring the sting as they pricked her palms. "We have to try something," she said, her voice filled with grim determination. She turned to Victor, who was already regaining his footing after Adrian's strike. "This ends now!"

With a fierce yell, Mia charged at Victor, her hands clutching the sharp thorns. She aimed for his torso, thrusting the thorny branches toward him with all her might. The thorns sank into Victor's skin, but to her horror, they didn't have the effect she expected. Instead of wounding him, his skin seemed to stitch itself back together the moment the thorns punctured his flesh. There was no blood, no sign of injury—just smooth, impenetrable skin.

"What...?" Mia gasped, stepping back in shock. "It's not working!"

Victor laughed, a deep, menacing sound that sent chills down their spines. "Foolish girl," he growled, ripping the thorns from his body as if they were nothing more than mere annoyances. "Did you really think you could harm me? I am beyond pain now."

Adrian, watching in disbelief, felt a wave of frustration and dread crash over him. "That can't be possible!" he muttered under his breath, his mind racing for answers. They had faced impossible odds before, but this... Victor seemed invincible. How could they stop him?

Emma, undeterred, grabbed a larger branch of thorns and tried again, this time aiming for Victor's side. She threw herself into the attack, adrenaline coursing through her veins. The thorns pierced his flesh, but just as before, Victor's skin closed around the wounds, healing instantly, leaving no trace of injury.

"It's like his body is repairing itself!" George shouted, frustration clear in his voice. He grabbed a thorny branch and swung at Victor's arm, but the same thing happened. The thorns merely grazed his skin before it healed itself in an instant.

"We're running out of options!" Emma cried, her voice shaking with exhaustion.

Victor's smile widened as he swatted Emma away again, sending her sprawling into the dirt. He turned his attention back to Adrian and Mia, his eyes burning with white-hot fury. "You can't defeat me," he sneered. "This island has granted me power beyond your understanding. I am untouchable."

Adrian gritted his teeth, his fists clenching. "There has to be a way," he whispered fiercely to himself. He wouldn't let Victor win, not after everything they'd been through. He looked at Mia, who was breathing heavily beside him, and then at George and Emma, both of them battered and bruised but still standing strong.

"Adrian," Mia said softly, wiping the sweat from her brow, "what do we do now?"

Adrian's mind raced. The thorns weren't working. Their punches, their attacks—nothing seemed to faze Victor for more than a moment. They were running out of time and energy, but they couldn't give up now.

"There has to be something," Adrian muttered, his eyes darting back to the portal that pulsed behind Victor. The portal itself seemed to vibrate with a strange energy, almost as if it was beckoning them, calling them forward.

Victor stepped toward them, his eyes flashing dangerously. "It's over," he said, his voice cold. "You've lost. Accept it."

"No!" Mia shouted, her voice fierce. She grabbed another handful of thorns and hurled them at Victor, but they did nothing. Her desperation was mounting, her breaths coming faster. "We won't give up!"

Victor tilted his head, almost amused by their defiance. "Then you will die trying."

"Adrian, we have to do something!" George shouted, his voice edged with panic as he glanced between Victor and the portal.

"I know!" Adrian snapped, his mind whirling. He took a deep breath, trying to focus, trying to find some angle they hadn't yet considered. His eyes flicked to the portal again, and something inside him clicked.

"The portal," he whispered, more to himself than anyone else. "What if...?"

"What?" Emma asked breathlessly, dragging herself to her feet.

Adrian's gaze hardened as he looked at his friends. "We need to get him into the portal," he said. "The portal has power—maybe enough to stop him. If we can force him through it, we might be able to sever whatever connection the island has to him."

Victor, hearing Adrian's words, laughed darkly. "You think the portal will save you? You truly know nothing."

Adrian ignored him, turning to the others. "It's our only shot," he said urgently. "We can't beat him with brute force, but maybe we can use the portal to trap him or weaken him. We need to get him close enough and push him in."

Mia's eyes widened in understanding, and a spark of hope ignited in her chest. "It's risky, but it could work."

"Better than being ripped apart," George muttered grimly.

"Then let's do this," Adrian said, his voice steely. He turned back to Victor, determination blazing in his eyes. "Come on!" he yelled, stepping forward, ready for the final fight.

With renewed purpose, the four of them prepared for the next round, knowing they had one last chance to turn the tide. Their strength was fading, but their resolve was unwavering.

Victor, sensing the shift in their stance, narrowed his eyes. "You can try," he growled, his voice laced with venom. "But you will fail."

The battle was far from over, but Adrian, Mia, Emma, and George knew they had one final move to play, and they would see it through to the end—no matter the cost.

As the battle raged on, exhaustion clung to their bodies like a heavy weight, each of them battered and bruised from the relentless onslaught. Victor was more powerful than they had ever imagined—stronger, faster, and nearly impossible to injure. But Adrian's plan was their last hope, and they clung to it with everything they had.

"We need to push him toward the portal!" Adrian yelled over the sound of their labored breaths, his eyes fixed on the shimmering gateway that stood ominously behind Victor. Every part of him screamed for rest, but he pushed through the pain. This had to work.

Mia, George, and Emma moved in tandem, their movements slower now but still fueled by determination. They circled Victor, carefully herding him back toward the portal. But Victor, always one step ahead, seemed to sense their plan. He roared in defiance, lunging forward, slashing at the air with his clawed hands.

"You think you can trick me?" Victor growled, his voice vibrating with rage. His monstrous form towered over them, casting a long shadow. "I will not be bound by your pathetic tactics!"

Mia barely dodged his strike, her heart pounding in her chest. "Keep pushing him back!" she shouted. "We're almost there!"

But just as Victor was nearing the edge of the portal's swirling energy, Adrian hesitated. Something gnawed at him, a deep instinct that pulled him away from the original plan. His eyes locked onto Victor's twisted form, watching how the dark energy swirled around him, healing him, protecting him from every injury they inflicted.

"No," Adrian muttered, shaking his head. A sudden realization washed over him, the plan to trap Victor in the portal now seeming too uncertain, too dangerous. What if the portal made him even stronger? What if it unleashed something even worse?

"Wait!" Adrian called out, his voice sharp with urgency. "Forget the portal! We need to strike now—together!"

Mia and the others turned to him, their confusion clear. "What do you mean?" George panted, keeping his distance from Victor's swiping claws.

"He's too powerful," Adrian continued, his eyes blazing with newfound clarity. "We need to overwhelm him all at once. If we strike together, we might be able to stop his body from healing."

Emma's breath caught in her throat as she realized what Adrian was saying. "You think if we stab him at the same time, his body won't be able to recover?"

Adrian nodded grimly. "It's the only way. His healing is tied to the island's dark energy, but if we hit him simultaneously, we might disrupt it."

Victor, hearing their plan, let out a low, menacing laugh. "You can try," he sneered, his teeth gleaming in the dim light. "But I am beyond your reach now."

"Do it now!" Adrian shouted, ignoring Victor's taunts. "All at once!"

Mia grabbed a thorny branch with both hands, her knuckles turning white from the grip. George and Emma did the same, their faces grim with determination. This was their only shot, and they couldn't afford to miss.

With a fierce battle cry, the three of them lunged at Victor from all sides, thorns aimed for his body. The world seemed to slow as the thorns pierced Victor's flesh at the same time, driving deep into his torso, his arms, his back.

For a brief, agonizing moment, nothing happened.

Then, all at once, Victor let out a guttural scream, his body convulsing violently. His eyes, once glowing with rage and power, widened in shock as dark, inky blood began to seep from the wounds. The black liquid oozed from his body, staining the ground beneath him.

"No..." Victor whispered, his voice now trembling, weak. His body twitched as he fell to his knees, his hands clawing at the air, trying to stop the bleeding. But the thorns had done their work, and his body—once so strong, so invincible—was now crumbling under its own weight.

Adrian, standing a few feet away, watched in stunned silence as Victor collapsed fully onto the ground, his face twisted in pain and disbelief. The black blood flowed freely now, pooling around his broken form.

Victor's eyes flickered, the light in them fading. "This... this isn't... possible," he rasped, his voice barely above a whisper.

"It's over," Adrian said, his voice low but firm. His heart pounded in his chest, but he knew they had finally done it.

Victor's once formidable figure now lay crumpled before them, his body shaking as the dark magic that had kept him alive began to unravel. The island's grip on him was loosening, the power he had claimed now betraying him.

Mia stepped forward, her breath shaky as she watched the black blood spread across the earth. "Is it... is it really over?"

Adrian nodded, though his gaze remained fixed on Victor's still form. "It's over."

Victor's body twitched one last time, and then went still. The once-menacing figure of their friend-turned-monster had finally fallen. The dark magic that had sustained him could no longer heal the damage they had inflicted.

A heavy silence fell over the group, the weight of the battle settling onto their shoulders. It was over, but the cost was heavy. They stood over Victor's body, their hearts filled with a strange mix of relief and sorrow.

Just as the group began to catch their breath, believing the battle to be over, a faint, raspy voice shattered the silence.

"You think... this is the end?"

Adrian froze, his heart skipping a beat. He turned to see Victor's body, still lying in a pool of dark blood, twitching slightly. Victor's eyes, clouded with death, flickered open once more. But something was different—his voice no longer carried the menace it had before. It was weaker, hollow, as if it were coming from a distant place.

Mia stepped back, eyes wide in disbelief. "No... this can't be happening. You're... you're dead."

Victor coughed, dark blood spilling from his lips, yet there was no pain in his expression. Instead, a twisted smile formed on his face. "Dead? Oh, yes... the real Victor died long ago. What you see before you... I am merely an echo."

"An echo?" George whispered, his voice trembling with confusion and dread. "What are you talking about?"

Victor's body convulsed again, the dark blood bubbling up from his wounds, but his voice remained steady. "I am not the man you once knew. I am but a shadow, a reflection of what was. Xel has power—dark, ancient power that reaches into the minds of those who dare to step foot on this cursed land. It keeps the memories of those it has touched... and twists them."

Adrian, still clutching a bloodied thorn, narrowed his eyes. "You're saying... you're not the real Victor?"

Victor's eerie smile grew wider. "No. I am an echo, a mere fragment of his soul, twisted by the island's magic. The real Victor is long dead—beheaded, as you know. But Xel... Xel holds onto those who think of it, those who seek its secrets, and turns them into shadows, echoes of their former selves."

Emma's breath caught in her throat, the horror of the revelation sinking in. "But... that means... there could be more of you?"

Victor nodded, his movements slow and unnatural, as though every word cost him great effort. "Yes... there will be more echoes. Not just of me... but of everyone who ever thought about Xel, who ever dreamed of uncovering its mysteries. It feeds on thoughts, on memories. As long as someone remembers, as long as someone seeks its secrets... the echoes will live on."

Mia's eyes filled with dread. "You're saying there are more like you? More twisted versions of people who came here? People who thought about this island?"

Victor's voice grew softer, weaker, as if it were fading into the darkness. "Yes. You think you've won... but this... this is only the beginning. Xel never truly lets go... not of me, not of you, not of anyone who dares to think about it. You are marked now, each of you. The island knows your names... and it will not forget."

Adrian felt his stomach drop, a cold chill running through his veins. "We're marked?"

Victor let out a low, chilling laugh, his body convulsing once more. "Oh, yes. The island... it's in your minds now. Your thoughts, your fears, your memories... they will become part of Xel. And one day... when you least expect it... there will be echoes of you all too."

George's face drained of color. "They'll be... like us?"

Victor's eyes, now almost lifeless, flickered one last time. "Yes. And when the time comes... the island will call others like you back. Just like it did to me. Just like it has for so many others."

With those final words, Victor's body slumped, his breath leaving him in a long, eerie sigh. The twisted figure that had once been their friend was no more—just a lifeless husk, a vessel for the island's dark magic. But his final words lingered in the air, chilling them to the bone.

Adrian, Mia, Emma, and George stood in silence, the weight of what they had just heard pressing down on them like a suffocating blanket. The realization hit them all at once—they had won this battle, but the war was far from over. The island's grip on them was stronger than ever.

Mia swallowed hard, her voice barely a whisper. "This isn't the end, is it?"

Adrian shook his head, his expression grim. "No... it's only the beginning."

The island, silent and foreboding, seemed to watch them, the whispers of its ancient power echoing in the wind. And as they stood there, surrounded by the darkness of Xel, they knew one thing for certain: the island would never truly let them go.

As the eerie silence settled over Victor's lifeless body, the group stood frozen, their minds reeling from the terrifying revelation. The weight of Victor's final words hung in the air, each of them trying to process the dark truth that they were now marked by the island. The thought alone was suffocating, an invisible chain binding them to Xel forever.

But before they could catch their breath or make sense of their situation, a sound cut through the stillness—a faint rustling in the distance, coming from deep within the forest.

Adrian's body tensed immediately, every nerve on high alert. He exchanged a quick glance with Mia, whose wide eyes mirrored his own fear. "Did you hear that?" Mia whispered, her voice trembling with uncertainty.

"I heard it," Adrian replied, his voice low, his eyes scanning the darkened treeline beyond. The wind had picked up slightly, causing the leaves to rustle, but this sound was different. It was rhythmic, deliberate—footsteps. And not just a few.

Emma's face went pale as she turned toward the sound. "It's getting closer," she muttered, her hand instinctively tightening around the thorny branch she still held. "There's a lot of them."

George stepped forward, his posture tense as he peered into the thick forest. "How many do you think? A group?" His voice was calm, but there was an edge of dread beneath the question.

The rustling grew louder, more distinct, like the crunching of dry leaves under heavy boots. The unmistakable sound of many footsteps moving in unison. The air around them thickened with tension, a growing sense of dread. And yet, they could see nothing—just shadows shifting among the trees, concealed by the darkness of the forest.

"They're coming straight for us," Mia whispered, her heart pounding in her chest. "But we don't even know who—or what—they are."

Adrian's mind raced. The island had already thrown so much at them—dark magic, monstrous echoes, a twisted version of their friend. Now this? "We can't wait to find out," he said, taking a step back from the tree line. "We need to be ready for whatever this is."

Emma nodded, her knuckles white as she gripped her weapon. "They could be more echoes, more versions of people who thought about Xel... or something worse."

The noise grew louder, closer—there was no mistaking it now. The group exchanged panicked glances, their breaths quickening as the tension mounted. Whatever was coming, it wasn't small. The sheer volume of the footsteps suggested a large group, moving fast and with purpose.

"Everyone stay together," Adrian ordered, his voice tight with urgency. He positioned himself in front of Mia, protecting her, while George and Emma flanked either side of the group. They had no idea what was coming, but they knew they couldn't afford to be caught off guard.

The shadows in the forest began to move, faint outlines appearing between the trees. The figures were still too far away to make out clearly, but their shapes were unmistakably human. Dozens of them, at least. A wave of fear washed over the group as the realization hit them: whoever—or whatever—these people were, they were heading directly toward them.

"They're not stopping," George muttered, his grip tightening on the thorned branch in his hand. "They're coming right for us."

Adrian's mind raced. His heart pounded in his chest as the figures drew closer. "Do we run?" Mia asked, her voice barely above a whisper.

Adrian hesitated. Running seemed like the logical choice, but there was something about the way these figures moved—calm, almost deliberate—that unnerved him. "No," he said finally, his voice firm. "We don't run. We face whatever this is, together."

"They might not be hostile," Emma said, though her tone lacked conviction. "But we can't take that chance."

The figures were closer now, still shrouded in darkness, but their numbers were staggering. Adrian could hear them breathing, the rustle of their clothes, the soft whispers of conversation that carried through the trees.

Then, suddenly, the group emerged from the shadows. They stepped into the clearing where Adrian, Mia, George, and Emma stood waiting, their eyes wide with fear and uncertainty. The figures were human—dozens of men and women, dressed in old, tattered clothes that looked like they had been worn for centuries. Their faces were pale, gaunt, and their eyes... their eyes were blank, empty.

Mia gasped, taking a step back. "Who... who are they?"

Adrian's heart dropped into his stomach as he realized the truth. "They're not alive," he whispered, his voice filled with dread.

The group of figures continued their slow march toward them, their faces devoid of emotion. There was something eerily familiar about them, like ghosts of the past, lost souls wandering the island. And then it hit Adrian—their faces. He recognized some of them.

"Oh my God," Emma breathed, her hand flying to her mouth. "They're... echoes."

Adrian nodded, his face pale. "These are the echoes Victor was talking about."

Mia's eyes darted from one figure to the next, her heart hammering in her chest. "These are the people who thought about Xel... who came here before us."

George gritted his teeth, his muscles tensing as the crowd continued to move closer. "Then what the hell do they want from us?"

Adrian swallowed hard, the weight of the situation pressing down on him. "I don't know," he admitted, his voice barely audible. "But we can't let them surround us."

The echoes moved as one, their eyes fixed on the group, their pace slow but relentless. There was no emotion in their expressions, no sign of malice or fear. They were simply there, existing as remnants of people who had once ventured onto the island.

"They're not attacking," Emma said cautiously, though her grip on the thorned branch remained tight. "But I don't trust this."

Adrian's mind raced, the echoes closing in on them from all sides. There was no time to plan, no time to think—just pure instinct. "Everyone, stay close!" he ordered, his voice steady despite the fear coursing through him. "We don't know what they're capable of."

The echoes stopped just a few feet from the group, standing in an eerie silence. Their blank eyes bore into them, their faces emotionless. And then, without warning, one of the echoes—a man with a hollowed-out face and sunken eyes—took a step forward.

"What do you want?" Adrian demanded, his voice firm but trembling. "Why are you here?"

The echo said nothing, his gaze fixed on Adrian. The silence stretched, thick and suffocating. And then, slowly, the echo lifted his hand, pointing directly at the portal behind them

"The portal," Mia whispered, her voice filled with dread. "They're pointing at the portal."

Adrian's stomach clenched as he followed the echo's gaze. The portal behind them shimmered, its surface swirling with dark energy. "They want us to go through," he realized, his blood running cold.

Emma shook her head, panic rising in her chest. "No... no way. We don't even know what's on the other side."

"They've been waiting," George said grimly, his eyes locked on the echoes. "They've been waiting for someone to go through."

Adrian clenched his jaw, his heart pounding in his ears. The echoes didn't move, their eyes still fixed on the portal, their silent command hanging in the air. The island wanted them to enter, to cross the threshold into whatever awaited on the other side.

And they had no choice but to decide.

Adrian's heart raced as the eerie silence stretched out between them and the unmoving echoes, their cold, empty eyes locked on the portal. The hairs on the back of his neck stood on end, and every fiber of his being screamed that this was wrong. There was something sinister in their stillness, something far more dangerous than what Victor had become. These echoes weren't just lost souls—they were a force, waiting to strike.

"We're not going through that portal," Adrian said, his voice steady but tight with tension. "We fight."

Mia looked at him, fear flashing in her eyes. "Fight them? Are you sure that's a good idea?"

"They don't seem aggressive," Emma murmured, her gaze flicking nervously to the nearest echo—a woman with sunken cheeks and hollow eyes. "Maybe we can—"

"They're not attacking yet, but something's off," Adrian interrupted, his hand tightening around the thorny branch. "I don't trust them. We need to strike before they have the chance."

George nodded, determination hardening his features. "I'm with you. Let's take them out before they take us."

Mia swallowed hard, her heart pounding. She could feel the tension crackling in the air like a storm about to break. "What if... what if they're too strong?"

Adrian glanced at her, his expression fierce. "We don't have a choice."

Without waiting for further debate, he lunged forward, his thorn-covered branch raised high as he aimed for the closest echo. The thorny wood connected with the figure's chest, sinking deep into its body. For a split second, there was silence—no reaction, no sound. And then, to their horror, the echo's skin seemed to swallow the thorns, absorbing them into its body. It didn't even flinch.

Adrian staggered back, his eyes wide with disbelief. "No... that's not possible."

"They're not like Victor's Echo!" Mia gasped, watching as the echo stepped forward, unbothered by the thorns piercing its flesh.

Before they could react, the echoes surged forward all at once, their movements slow but powerful, an unstoppable force advancing upon the four of them. Adrian barely had time to block an incoming strike as one of the echoes slammed into him, sending him crashing into the ground. Pain exploded in his ribs, and he coughed, trying to suck in air.

"Adrian!" Emma screamed, swinging her branch wildly at one of the echoes, but just like before, it didn't work. The thorns that had injured Victor were useless here. The echoes' skin closed over the wounds instantly, as if they were made of something more than flesh—something indestructible.

Mia slashed at another echo, her movements desperate, but her weapon was equally ineffective. "We can't hurt them!" she shouted, panic rising in her voice.

The echo grabbed her by the wrist, squeezing hard. Mia let out a cry of pain, feeling the bones in her hand bend under the pressure. She twisted, trying to break free, but the echo's grip was like iron.

"Help her!" George yelled, rushing toward Mia, but another echo blocked his path, its gaunt face expressionless as it backhanded him across the face. The force of the blow sent George sprawling, blood splattering from his mouth.

Emma, breathing heavily, swung again and again at the echo in front of her, but the creature didn't even blink. Its dead, soulless eyes remained fixed on her as it grabbed her arm, twisting it violently until Emma screamed in agony. The sound echoed in the clearing, blending with the crunching of bones and the sharp intakes of breath from the others.

Adrian, clutching his side, tried to get up, but an echo was already on him, its skeletal hand wrapping around his throat. The grip tightened, cutting off his air as the echo lifted him off the ground, its strength terrifyingly unnatural. Adrian kicked and struggled, gasping for breath as spots of darkness clouded his vision.

"This... can't... be happening," he choked out, clawing at the echo's arm. But there was no escape. The creature's strength was absolute, and Adrian's own limbs felt weak in comparison, as if he were fighting the island itself.

"Adrian!" Mia screamed, wrenching herself free from the echo holding her and diving toward him. She grabbed the branch she had dropped, thrusting it into the side of the echo's neck in a desperate attempt to free Adrian. But the branch splintered on impact, and the echo didn't even flinch.

"They're too strong!" Emma cried out, her voice filled with terror as the echo holding her twisted her arm further, the pain almost unbearable.

George, still on the ground, wiped the blood from his mouth, his vision blurred. "We have to retreat!" he shouted, trying to get back to his feet. "We can't fight them head-on!"

But the echoes didn't give them time. Another came at George, kicking him in the chest with brutal force, sending him flying backward. He hit the ground hard, coughing up more blood as pain radiated through his torso.

Adrian's vision was fading fast, the echo's grip on his throat cutting off his air completely. He clawed at its hand, but his strength was draining. The sound of his friends' struggles echoed around him, the pain in their voices piercing through the fog clouding his mind. They were losing. Fast.

"Adrian!" Mia screamed again, but her voice sounded distant, muffled by the blood pounding in his ears. He couldn't hold on much longer. The echo's eyes—those blank, soulless eyes—bored into his own, as if the creature were staring straight into his soul.

With a final, desperate push, Adrian swung wildly at the echo's face, but his blow barely made contact before his arm fell limp. He was losing consciousness, the world around him growing darker by the second.

Mia, fueled by terror, charged at the echo holding Adrian, hitting it with everything she had left. But it was like hitting a stone wall. The echo didn't even acknowledge her attack.

"No!" Mia screamed, tears streaming down her face. "No, this can't be happening!"

Emma let out a cry of pain as the echo twisted her arm again, this time snapping it with a sickening crack. She fell to the ground, clutching her broken limb, her face contorted in agony. George, still struggling to stand, could barely breathe, each movement sending waves of pain through his bruised ribs.

They had fought monsters, endured the island's dark magic, and survived horrors that would break anyone's spirit. But this—these echoes—were beyond anything they could handle.

The echoes loomed over them, their hollow eyes watching, waiting for the fight to drain from their bodies.

Adrian's eyes fluttered shut as darkness claimed him, the last sound he heard being Mia's desperate screams.

The scene was chaos—desperation thick in the air as the echoes closed in, their cold, lifeless eyes betraying no emotion, no hesitation. Adrian's vision blurred, his consciousness hanging by a thread as the echo's grip on his throat tightened further, squeezing the life out of him. His hands, weak and trembling, fought to pry the creature's iron-like fingers from his neck, but it was no use. Every breath was a battle, every second an eternity.

Mia's heart pounded, adrenaline surging through her veins as she watched Adrian's struggle. Her mind raced, panic clawing at her every thought. "Adrian! Hold on!" she screamed, her voice breaking. She knew they were losing—knew that if they didn't do something now, they would all die here. The island would swallow them whole, just like it had so many others before.

"Get away from him!" Mia shouted, swinging another branch with all her strength. The wood splintered uselessly against the echo's back, the force doing nothing to deter the relentless creature. She could feel her energy draining, but she couldn't stop. She wouldn't let Adrian die.

Emma, clutching her broken arm, staggered toward Mia, her face pale and sweat-drenched. “Mia, we can’t win like this!” she gasped, her voice thick with pain. “They’re too strong!”

Mia ignored her, desperation burning through her exhaustion. “We have to keep fighting! We can’t just let them take us!”

But even as she spoke, another echo closed in on her, its movements slow and deliberate, like death itself creeping toward her. Mia’s chest tightened with dread as she swung the branch again, but the echo caught it mid-air, ripping it from her hands with terrifying ease. Before she could react, the echo grabbed her wrist, twisting it sharply. A scream tore from her throat as she felt her bones crack under the pressure, agony shooting up her arm.

“Mia!” George, blood still trickling from his mouth, struggled to his feet, his body battered and broken. He tried to rush toward her, but another echo blocked his path, shoving him back with brutal force. George landed hard on the ground, groaning in pain as the breath was knocked from his lungs.

“They’re everywhere,” George gasped, his vision swimming. “We... we can’t fight them.”

Emma’s knees buckled under her, tears of pain and frustration blurring her vision. She looked at the echo in front of her, at the emotionless face staring back. There was no soul behind those eyes—just emptiness, like the island itself was staring at them through these creatures.

“We need... a plan,” Emma gasped through gritted teeth. But what plan? What strategy could work against an enemy that seemed invincible?

Adrian’s vision darkened, his mind fading in and out of consciousness as the echo continued to strangle him. The life was draining from him faster than he could fight it, his body too weak, too bruised, to mount a defense. A single thought drifted through the fog in his mind: *This can’t be how it ends. Not like this.*

Summoning every ounce of strength left in his battered body, Adrian clawed at the echo's face. His fingers scraped against its cold skin, but it didn't flinch. His attacks felt like nothing more than a nuisance. Desperation surged through him, but his body was betraying him, his limbs going limp as the darkness swallowed him whole.

Then, suddenly, Mia's voice pierced through the haze, a scream of pure, raw emotion. "No! I won't lose you!"

With a surge of adrenaline, Mia twisted in the echo's grip, ignoring the searing pain in her broken wrist. She used her free hand to grab a rock from the ground and slammed it into the side of the echo's head with everything she had. The impact reverberated through her, the sharp pain in her wrist flaring up as she hit the echo again and again, her strikes growing weaker with every blow. But the echo didn't falter—it barely acknowledged her assault. The stone seemed useless against its unnatural strength.

Mia's breaths were ragged, her body trembling from exhaustion. She could feel the tears stinging her eyes, the crushing realization sinking in. "Why won't you die?!" she screamed, her voice breaking. "Why can't we stop you?!"

Adrian's world was fading fast, the edges of his vision dark and blurred, but Mia's voice reached him. He couldn't leave her—not like this. Not when they had come so far. His heart pounded one last time, the adrenaline pumping through him for what felt like the final surge of life. *No...* he thought fiercely. *Not yet.*

With one last, desperate effort, Adrian raised his knee and slammed it into the echo's chest. It wasn't much, but it was enough. The echo loosened its grip for a split second—just long enough for Adrian to gasp in a single breath of air. He tore free, collapsing to the ground, coughing and gagging as air flooded back into his lungs.

"Adrian!" Mia cried, dropping beside him, her hands shaking as she tried to help him up. "Are you okay?"

Adrian coughed, pain rippling through his entire body. "I'm... alive," he rasped, his throat raw. But as he looked up at the echo that had nearly killed him, his stomach twisted. They had barely survived—*barely*. And the echoes were still coming.

The one that had been strangling Adrian took a step forward, its eyes still locked on him. There was no anger, no emotion—just the same relentless drive to finish what it had started. And now it was coming for Mia.

"No," Adrian croaked, his voice weak but filled with resolve. He wouldn't let her suffer the same fate.

Mia grabbed the nearest thorn branch, her hands shaking. "Stay back!" she warned the echo, her voice trembling. But the creature continued forward, undeterred, its blank eyes fixed on her.

George, still struggling to his feet, saw the echo moving toward Mia. "We have to get out of here!" he shouted, spitting blood. "They're going to kill us if we stay!"

"We can't outrun them!" Emma shouted, holding her broken arm close to her body, her face a mask of pain.

The echoes surrounded them now, their slow, deliberate movements terrifying in their inevitability. The group was out of options, out of strength. The realization that they were fighting an unstoppable force weighed heavily on them, sinking into their bones like cold dread.

Adrian, still gasping for breath, looked at Mia, Emma, and George—his friends, his family. They had come so far together, survived the island's darkness, and yet here they were, broken and bleeding. The island had marked them, and now it was closing in for the final strike.

"Adrian, what do we do?" Mia whispered, her voice barely audible over the sound of her own frantic heartbeat.

Adrian looked at the echoes, then at the portal behind them. His mind raced, trying to find a way out. There had to be something. They couldn't just die here—not after everything they had sacrificed.

But as the echoes closed in, their slow, unstoppable march sealing off every escape route, Adrian felt the crushing weight of despair settle over him. He didn't have an answer. They were out of time.

And for the first time since stepping foot on the island, Adrian felt truly powerless.

"Adrian," Mia whispered again, tears streaming down her face. "I don't want to die."

His heart broke at the sound of her words. He didn't want to lose her—didn't want to lose any of them. But the echoes were merciless, and they were already broken.

As the first echo reached out for Mia, its cold, skeletal fingers brushing against her skin, Adrian let out a scream, pure instinct and fear driving him forward.

But deep down, he knew... there was nothing they could do.

The world felt like it was closing in on them, shadows darkening the sky as the echoes advanced with that same slow, inevitable force. Every breath was a battle, every movement seemed futile, but Adrian refused to let it end like this. His mind raced, desperate to find a way out, even as his body screamed in agony.

"Mia!" Adrian shouted, his voice hoarse, but full of command. "We need to move—now!"

Mia, tears staining her cheeks, turned to Adrian, her eyes wide with fear and confusion. "Where can we go? They're everywhere!"

"Opposite the portal!" Adrian barked, staggering to his feet with a groan. "We can't go through it, but we can outrun them!"

Emma, clutching her broken arm, looked over her shoulder at the glowing portal behind them and then at the echoes, who were closing in. Their pale, lifeless eyes fixed on the group like predators cornering prey. "But the forest—there's nowhere to hide!" she said, her voice cracking.

"Anywhere is better than here!" George growled, wincing as he forced himself to stand, his body battered but still determined. "We're dead if we stay!"

With adrenaline pounding through his veins, Adrian shoved Mia forward, and she stumbled before catching her balance. "Go!" he ordered, his voice filled with a mixture of fear and urgency.

The echoes were almost upon them. One of them reached out, its cold hand brushing Mia's arm, but she yanked herself free with a sharp scream. "Move! Run!" Adrian bellowed, grabbing Emma by the arm as she gasped in pain. They had no choice now—they had to run.

Without another second of hesitation, they turned and bolted away from the portal, racing toward the opposite side of the clearing, where the forest loomed dark and ominous. The echoes followed, their steps eerily silent yet relentless.

Adrian's heart pounded in his chest, a desperate rhythm matching his frantic footsteps as he ran. His legs screamed with pain, every step sending a jolt of agony through his battered body, but he couldn't stop. He couldn't slow down. Not when the echoes were right behind them.

"Don't look back!" George shouted, his voice strained as he pushed his legs to their limit. He could feel the hot breath of fear down his neck, knowing they were being chased by something that didn't tire, didn't feel, didn't stop.

Mia was ahead of him, her breath coming in sharp gasps, her face pale as she sprinted through the uneven ground of the forest. Emma was struggling, every jolt causing her broken arm to throb with unbearable pain, but she kept moving, her face a mask of determination. Adrian stayed close to her, his hand gripping her good arm, helping her stay on her feet.

The echoes were faster than they appeared, gaining ground with every step, their pale, skeletal forms gliding through the trees with terrifying grace. Adrian glanced over his shoulder and saw them—dozens of them, their lifeless eyes locked on the group as they moved in perfect unison, like a swarm of shadows.

"They're too fast!" Emma gasped, her face twisted in pain as she stumbled over a root, nearly falling.

Adrian caught her, pulling her up as quickly as he could. "Keep going!" he urged, though his voice was raw, his throat burning from the effort.

The forest closed in around them, the trees growing denser, the branches reaching out like skeletal hands. The underbrush thickened, slowing them down as they tripped over roots and pushed through thorny bushes. But the echoes didn't slow. They moved through the forest like phantoms, gliding effortlessly over obstacles, their empty eyes never blinking, never losing sight of their prey.

"They're still gaining!" George shouted from behind, his voice filled with frustration and exhaustion. "We can't outrun them for long!"

Adrian's mind raced. He knew George was right. They couldn't keep this pace up forever—the echoes were too fast, too persistent. And they were already exhausted, their bodies pushed to the breaking point. But he refused to let them die here. He refused to give up.

"There's a clearing ahead!" Mia yelled, her voice breathless as she pointed through the trees.

Adrian squinted, his eyes catching a glimpse of the faint light filtering through the trees. It wasn't far, but it wasn't enough. The echoes would catch them before they could reach it. His heart pounded in his chest, panic setting in as he realized they had no plan, no way out. Just desperation driving them forward.

The echoes were closing in fast now, the sound of their pursuit growing louder. Adrian could hear their footsteps crunching through the underbrush, the rustle of leaves as they glided effortlessly through the forest. He could feel them getting closer, their presence pressing down on him like a weight.

And then, without warning, one of the echoes lunged forward, its skeletal hand wrapping around George's ankle. George let out a scream of surprise as he stumbled, crashing to the ground.

"George!" Mia screamed, skidding to a halt and turning back, her eyes wide with terror.

Adrian's heart clenched as he saw George struggling to free himself, the echo's grip tightening like a vice. "Go!" George shouted, his voice strained as he kicked at the echo with his free leg. "Keep going!"

Adrian didn't hesitate. He rushed back, grabbing a thick branch from the ground and swinging it at the echo with all the strength he had left. The branch connected with a sickening thud, but the echo didn't react. It didn't feel pain. It didn't flinch. It just kept pulling George closer, its grip tightening like death itself.

"No!" Adrian screamed, swinging again, this time smashing the branch down on the echo's arm. The wood cracked, splintering from the force, but the echo still didn't let go. It was as if the creature were made of stone, unbreakable, unstoppable.

George's face twisted in pain as the echo's grip tightened further, but he fought through it, using every bit of strength he had left to kick the creature in the chest. The blow knocked the echo back just enough for him to yank his leg free. He scrambled to his feet, his breath ragged as he stumbled forward.

"We have to keep moving!" George gasped, his face pale as he limped toward the clearing. "They're not going to stop!"

Adrian nodded, his heart racing as he looked back at the approaching echoes. They were relentless—silent, emotionless, and terrifyingly fast. They had barely managed to escape this time, but the echoes weren't done. They would keep coming until there was nothing left of them to chase.

"Come on!" Adrian shouted, pulling Mia and Emma forward as they ran toward the clearing.

The light of the clearing beckoned them, a thin hope in the overwhelming darkness. But Adrian knew—deep in his gut—that the echoes wouldn't stop. Not now. Not ever. The island had marked them, and there was no escaping it.

As they broke through the tree line and into the clearing, they collapsed onto the ground, their bodies heaving with exhaustion. But the echoes were still there, lingering at the edge of the forest, watching, waiting.

They were not done yet.

The group lay sprawled in the clearing, their bodies trembling with exhaustion and fear. The light of the clearing offered a momentary refuge from the encroaching darkness of the forest, but they knew it was only temporary. The echoes lingered just beyond the tree line, their forms shifting silently, waiting for the right moment to strike again.

Adrian pushed himself up into a seated position, wiping the sweat and dirt from his forehead. The events of the last few moments played back in his mind like a haunting echo, and the adrenaline that had fueled their escape was now giving way to a heavy weariness. He looked at Mia, Emma, and George, their faces pale and drawn.

"What do we do now?" he asked, his voice hoarse but steady. The weight of their predicament pressed down on him, and he could see the fear reflected in his friends' eyes.

Mia hugged her knees to her chest, glancing toward the forest where the echoes stood just out of sight. "We can't stay here. They'll come for us again."

Emma shifted next to her, cradling her broken arm. "But if we leave the clearing, we're vulnerable again. We need a plan."

George, breathing heavily, leaned against a nearby tree for support. "We need to get to the sea," he said, his voice low. "If we can reach the shoreline, maybe we can find a boat or something to help us escape this place."

"The shoreline is right there," Adrian said, pointing toward the distant horizon. He could see the shimmering water, its waves lapping gently against the shore. "It's not far. We can make it."

"But it feels so far away," Mia replied, her brow furrowed with worry. "What if we can't reach it? What if it's a trick?"

Adrian shook his head, trying to banish the doubt creeping into his mind. "We have to try. We can't just wait here to be taken by the echoes. We've fought too hard to give up now."

Emma nodded slowly, determination flashing in her eyes. "We walk slowly and carefully. If we can keep quiet, maybe we can avoid attracting their attention."

Adrian took a deep breath, the salty air from the ocean beckoning him like a siren's call. "Alright. Let's move. Stay close together, and keep your voices low."

They pushed themselves to their feet, muscles aching, but they had no time to dwell on their fatigue. Together, they started toward the shoreline, moving cautiously through the clearing and into the dense trees beyond. The underbrush crackled softly beneath their feet, and every sound seemed amplified in the eerie stillness.

As they walked, the horizon shimmered with the promise of escape, the ocean glistening under the fading sunlight. But with each step they took, the distance to the shore seemed to stretch further away, mocking them.

Minutes passed as they made their way through the forest, every second feeling like an eternity. The rhythmic sound of waves crashing on the shore grew louder, yet the shoreline never seemed to get closer. Adrian glanced back, but the echoes remained at the edge of the trees, their presence an ever-watchful shadow, just out of sight.

"Why isn't it getting any closer?" George muttered, frustration creeping into his voice. "We've been walking forever!"

"Maybe the island is playing tricks on us," Emma suggested, glancing around nervously. "It's like it doesn't want us to leave."

Adrian clenched his jaw, determination fueling his resolve. "We can't let it keep us here. We have to focus. One foot in front of the other."

Mia's brow knitted in concern as she walked beside Adrian. "Do you think there's a way to break whatever hold this place has on us? We can't keep walking forever."

"I don't know," Adrian admitted, his mind racing. "But we can't stop. We need to find a way out."

As they continued forward, the shoreline remained tantalizingly close yet frustratingly far. The salty breeze carried the sound of the waves crashing against the shore, and the sun began to dip lower in the sky, painting the horizon with shades of pink and orange. It felt like a cruel joke—so close, yet so far.

"Adrian," Mia said softly, her voice laced with worry. "What if we're stuck here? What if we can't leave the island?"

Adrian paused, looking into Mia's eyes. He could see the fear bubbling just beneath the surface. "We won't be stuck here," he said firmly, though uncertainty gnawed at him. "We'll find a way."

But as they pressed on, the distance to the shore seemed to stretch into infinity, the beautiful sight growing increasingly elusive. They stumbled over roots and rocks, the forest around them growing denser, as if the trees themselves were trying to hold them back.

"This isn't right," George muttered, frustration building within him. "We should have reached the water by now."

Adrian glanced back at the distant horizon. "We have to keep moving. Focus on the goal."

With renewed determination, they pushed forward, yet the shoreline felt like a mirage, flickering in and out of reach. Each step they took seemed to lead them further into a maze of trees, and every sound made them jump, anxiety gnawing at their insides.

Just as despair threatened to overtake them, they entered a small clearing, and the ocean came into view once more. The waves crashed rhythmically against the shore, the salty scent of the sea filling their lungs. But to their horror, the shore still seemed far away, as if the island was playing a cruel game, warping their perceptions.

"We're so close!" Mia exclaimed, hope igniting in her chest as she pointed. But then her face fell as she looked around. "But why does it still feel so far?"

Adrian's heart sank as he realized they were still nowhere near the water. It felt like an illusion, a taunting vision that they could never quite reach. "We need to keep going," he urged, though his voice trembled with uncertainty.

As they moved forward again, they stumbled upon a small ridge, and Adrian felt his heart drop. They had crossed it, but it only revealed more trees ahead.

"We have to find another way," Emma said, her voice tinged with desperation. "This isn't working."

But Adrian shook his head, resolve hardening within him. "No! We can't stop now. We have to find a way through."

With every ounce of determination, they pressed on. The echoes might have faded from sight, but their presence was still felt in the very air around them, heavy and oppressive. Adrian could almost hear them whispering through the trees, taunting him as they continued to walk, the shoreline still beckoning just out of reach.

After what felt like an eternity, they rounded another tree, and this time the ocean appeared before them, closer than ever before. Hope surged in their chests as they saw the water, its waves crashing against the shore, the salty breeze lifting their spirits.

"Look!" George shouted, pointing. "There! We're finally here!"

But as they rushed forward, a sudden wave of panic washed over Adrian. The shoreline was no longer the promise of escape; it felt like an open maw, waiting to swallow them whole. "Wait!" he called, grabbing Mia's arm. "We need to be careful!"

The echoes appeared again, emerging from the shadows of the trees, their forms gliding effortlessly towards them. They hadn't been far behind, biding their time as the group lost hope.

"No!" Mia screamed, dread washing over her as she looked back at the encroaching figures. "We can't let them catch us!"

Adrian felt a surge of panic, his heart racing. "We'll make it to the shore!" he shouted, pushing forward, ignoring the pain in his legs as they sprinted toward the water.

But the echoes were relentless, their cold hands reaching out as the group reached the edge of the ocean. Adrian could feel the water lapping at his feet, the waves crashing over the sand, but the echoes were closing in.

"This is it!" he yelled, grabbing Mia's hand as he pulled her toward the water. "We need to get in!"

The four of them plunged into the waves, the cold saltwater crashing around them. It felt like a weight lifted, as if the water was washing away the darkness that clung to them. They waded deeper, gasping as the ocean engulfed them, the waves crashing over their heads.

"Keep moving!" George shouted, fighting against the current. "We have to get further out!"

But as they swam, Adrian looked back at the shore, watching as the echoes stood at the water's edge, their empty eyes fixed on them. They couldn't cross the water. The group was safe, for now.

As they swam, the weight of the island's darkness began to lift, the salty air filling their lungs. Together, they pushed forward, desperate to escape the horrors that lay behind them, knowing that as long as they stayed together, they would find a way to break free from the island's grip.

Adrian swam harder, each stroke carrying them further from the shoreline and the echoes that haunted them. The ocean stretched endlessly before them, a new beginning waiting just beyond the horizon.

As they swam frantically in the ocean, the horizon glimmered with the promise of escape, each stroke fueled by adrenaline and the desperate hope of freedom. Adrian, Mia, Emma, and George pressed forward, the waves crashing around them, each one a reminder that they were finally leaving the horrors of the island behind.

But just as they felt they might be free, the ocean began to shift. The waves that had felt so liberating turned ominous, the water churning beneath them like a restless beast. Adrian glanced back, and his heart dropped as he saw it—a massive wave, towering high above the surface, growing larger with every passing second.

"Adrian! Look out!" Mia shouted, her voice filled with panic.

"Swim! We have to get to shore!" he yelled back, fear coursing through him. They were still too close to the island, and the water swirled with a dark energy that sent chills down his spine.

The wave loomed, a monstrous wall of water ready to crash down on them, and before they could react, it surged forward with terrifying speed. Adrian felt the world shift beneath him, the water pulling him down as the wave broke over them with ferocious force.

"Hold your breath!" Emma cried, but it was too late. The wave slammed into them, pulling them under, the roar of the ocean drowning out their screams.

Adrian felt the water engulf him, a cold, suffocating embrace. Panic surged as he was tossed violently in the depths, the power of the wave pinning him down, dragging him deeper into the ocean's grasp. Every instinct screamed at him to fight, to swim upward, but the water was relentless, pushing him further from the surface.

For a moment, time stood still. The pressure of the water pressed against him, and he could barely see anything—only darkness, swirling shadows as he struggled against the tide. He kicked and clawed at the water, desperation fueling his movements, but the current was too strong.

Then, just as suddenly, he was released, thrust forward by the wave's powerful force. He broke the surface, gasping for air as he was hurled back toward the shore, the familiar sight of the island looming ahead.

"Adrian!" Mia's voice pierced through the chaos, but he couldn't see her. He felt himself being pulled along, the waves tossing him about like a rag doll. The shore was rushing at him, and in an instant, he was thrown onto the sand with a bone-jarring impact.

Adrian rolled onto his back, gasping for breath, but the air felt heavy in his lungs. He blinked, trying to focus as the world swam around him, but all he could see was the sky above, dark and turbulent. He felt weak, drained of all energy, as if the island had siphoned the very strength from his body.

"Mia! Emma! George!" he croaked, forcing himself to sit up. The effort made his head spin, and he fell back onto the sand, panting heavily.

One by one, his friends washed ashore, collapsing beside him in similar states of exhaustion. Emma crawled closer, her broken arm cradled against her chest, her face pale and streaked with saltwater. "Adrian... what just happened?" she gasped, her voice a whisper.

Mia lay a few feet away, her chest heaving as she struggled to catch her breath. "We were so close," she said, her eyes wide with disbelief. "How did this happen?"

George, struggling to sit up, looked at them, his face pale and strained. "The wave... it just came out of nowhere. It was like the island didn't want us to leave."

Adrian could feel the weight of those words sinking in, the realization hitting him like a cold slap. The island had turned against them once again. It wasn't just a place; it was a living entity, and it had absorbed their strength, leaving them weak and vulnerable.

"It's not over," Adrian muttered, feeling the crushing weight of despair settling over him. "We can't let it win. We have to get up, keep moving."

But as he tried to push himself up, a wave of fatigue washed over him, and he collapsed back onto the sand, his body refusing to cooperate. "I... I can't," he admitted, feeling utterly defeated.

Mia lay back against the ground, her breathing heavy. "None of us can. It's like we've lost everything," she said, her voice trembling with exhaustion.

"Why won't it let us go?" Emma whispered, tears welling in her eyes. "Why does it keep doing this?"

Adrian glanced around, the ominous forest looming behind them, the echoes still lingering in the shadows. "Because it wants us. We're marked by this place, and it knows it."

He felt the darkness close in, not just from the island but from within himself. The exhaustion was overwhelming, threatening to pull him under once again. The echoes were like a dark cloud hovering over them, waiting for the right moment to strike.

"Get up!" George said, a spark of determination igniting within him. "We can't just lie here and wait for it to finish us off. We need to regroup, find shelter, and figure out our next move."

Adrian took a deep breath, trying to shake off the fog of despair. "George is right. If we stay here, we're sitting ducks. We need to find a way to fight back, to break whatever hold this island has over us."

Mia pushed herself up to a seated position, her resolve returning. "We can't let the echoes win. We can't let this island take us. We need to find something—anything—that can help us."

Adrian nodded, determination slowly replacing the weariness in his bones. “We’ll figure it out together. We always have.”

With great effort, they all slowly began to rise, pushing against the sand, the weight of their fatigue still heavy but not impossible to bear. The horizon shimmered, the waves crashing against the shore, and as they stood together, they formed a united front against the darkness that threatened to consume them.

The echoes had come close to claiming them, but they weren’t finished yet. The island had absorbed their strength, but it hadn’t taken their will to survive.

Adrian took a deep breath, the salty air filling his lungs, and felt a flicker of hope ignite within him. They would not be defeated. Not now, not ever.

As they lay on the sandy shore, the weight of despair pressing down on them, Adrian’s heart raced. The echoes that had haunted them felt distant now, yet the fear remained—a constant reminder of the darkness lurking just beyond the trees. They were all exhausted, physically and emotionally drained, but they knew they couldn’t afford to rest for long.

Mia curled up on the ground, her cheek pressed against the cool sand, closing her eyes as she fought against the overwhelming fatigue. “What now?” she murmured, her voice barely audible, filled with hopelessness

“I don’t know,” Adrian admitted, glancing at Emma and George, both slumped against a rock, trying to catch their breath. “We have to find a way to protect ourselves, to—”

Suddenly, a familiar voice cut through the stillness, a sound they never thought they’d hear again. “What are you doing lying there? You need to get up!”

Adrian’s heart skipped a beat as he turned to see Wren standing a few feet away, his expression a mix of concern and urgency. “Wren?” Adrian exclaimed, disbelief flooding through him. “Is it really you?”

Wren stepped closer, and Adrian could see the bruises and cuts scattered across his skin, evidence of the struggle he must have endured. "Of course it's me! Now come on, we don't have much time!"

2

Entrance Into A New World

Mia shot up, her eyes wide with disbelief and joy. "Wren! You're alive!" She rushed toward him, wrapping her arms around him in a tight embrace, relief washing over her like a tidal wave.

Wren smiled weakly, but there was urgency in his eyes. "I am, but we need to go. The echoes are still out there, and they'll be coming for you soon."

Emma pushed herself up, a mix of confusion and hope flickering across her face. "What do you mean? We thought you were gone!"

"I was," Wren said, glancing back toward the treeline, his voice growing serious. "After you left, I regained consciousness. Something unnatural happened—like a force pushed me back to life, and I found myself alone in the forest, wounded but alive. It took hours, but I managed to rest and recover."

George narrowed his eyes, skepticism etched on his face. "How do we know you're really you? What if it's another trick?"

Wren reached out, pulling up his shirt to reveal the bruises and scars etched into his skin. "I swear it's me. I've been through hell out here. The island is alive in a way I can't fully explain. I barely made it out, but I know how to get to a safe area."

Adrian stepped closer, feeling a rush of emotions—relief, anger, and confusion all mixed together. "A safe area? Why didn't you come for us earlier?"

"I was recovering, trying to regain my strength. And trust me, I didn't want to lose sight of you guys again," Wren replied, urgency returning to his voice. "But the longer we stay here, the more vulnerable we become. The echoes are drawn to us—they can sense our fear."

Mia glanced back at the forest, her heart racing. "What if they find us?"

"They won't if we move quickly," Wren urged, determination burning in his eyes. "I know a place deeper in the island where the echoes can't follow. You'll be safe there."

Adrian's heart raced as he weighed the options. He had nearly lost Wren once; he couldn't let that happen again. "Alright. We'll follow you," he said, steeling himself against the dread that gripped his heart. "But we have to move fast."

"Good," Wren said, relief flooding his features. "We can't waste any more time. Follow me!"

With adrenaline surging, they pushed themselves to their feet, their bodies protesting against the movement, but they forced themselves onward. Wren led them away from the shoreline and into the dense forest, his movements sure and steady as he guided them through the underbrush.

As they moved deeper into the trees, Adrian's mind raced with questions. "Wren, what did you see? What happened after we thought you were gone?"

Wren glanced back at him, his expression serious. "I'm not sure how to explain it. It was as if the island itself was alive—whispers echoing in the wind, shadows lurking in the trees. I felt drawn to it, like something was calling me. But then the echoes found me, and I had to fight to survive."

"Did they... did they hurt you?" Emma asked, her voice trembling.

Wren nodded, his eyes darkening. "Yes. They're stronger than you can imagine. They don't just want to harm you—they want to absorb you, to turn echo just like you. It's what the island does; it preys on fear and despair."

The forest closed in around them, thick and oppressive, but they pushed through, each step feeling more urgent than the last. The shadows seemed to stretch toward them, whispers of danger lingering in the air. Adrian could feel the weight of the island pressing down on them, but Wren's presence ignited a flicker of hope.

"Wren," Mia said softly, her voice filled with concern. "What if we can't escape? What if the island keeps us here?"

"It's a part of us now," Wren replied, his voice firm yet reassuring. "But it doesn't have to define us. We have to confront it, face whatever darkness lies ahead. Together."

Adrian felt a sense of unity surge through him as they moved, a reminder that they were not alone in this fight. They were stronger together, and with Wren back by their side, they had a fighting chance.

Suddenly, they broke through the trees into a small clearing, the sunlight pouring down like a beacon of hope. The sound of waves crashing could still be heard in the distance, but the forest around them felt strangely calm, almost protective.

"There!" Wren pointed to a cave opening nestled against the cliffside. "We can take shelter inside until it's safe to move again."

Adrian nodded, urging everyone forward. "Let's go!" They rushed toward the cave, the cool shadows offering a temporary refuge from the oppressive weight of the island.

Once inside, they collapsed against the walls, panting heavily as relief washed over them. The cave was dark, but they could still see the outline of Wren's bruised form, the evidence of his struggle clear in the dim light.

"How long do you think we can stay here?" George asked, his voice tinged with anxiety.

Wren shook his head, his expression grim. "Not long. The echoes won't give up easily. They'll search for us, and we need to stay alert. But for now, we can rest and regroup."

Adrian took a deep breath, the weight of their ordeal crashing over him in waves. He glanced at his friends—Mia, Emma, and George—all of them battered but still together. And then there was Wren, alive and strong, a flicker of hope amid the darkness.

"Thank you for finding us," Adrian said, his voice filled with gratitude. "We thought we lost you."

Wren met his gaze, a faint smile crossing his lips. "I wouldn't leave you behind. You're my family. We'll get through this together."

In that moment, a renewed sense of determination filled the cave. The island might have taken so much from them, but it hadn't taken their bond. Together, they would face the echoes, the darkness, and whatever else the island threw their way.

As they sat together, the shadows of the cave seemed to fade, and for the first time in what felt like ages, Adrian allowed himself to hope. But just as he felt that flicker of hope ignite, the ground trembled beneath them, a low rumble echoing through the cave like a warning. The walls shook slightly, causing loose stones to tumble from above.

"What was that?" Mia asked, her eyes wide with alarm.

Adrian's heart raced again. "We need to stay focused. The island is shifting, it won't let us rest."

Wren nodded, his expression serious. "We have to be ready. If the echoes find us here, we won't stand a chance."

Adrian took a deep breath, steeling himself against the rising panic. They had fought too hard to let fear take hold now. "Okay, everyone, stay alert. If we hear anything, we need to be ready to move. We can't let the island take us again."

The group fell into a tense silence, each of them straining to hear any sounds that might signal the approach of danger. The air was thick with anticipation, and Adrian could feel the energy in the cave shift, a palpable tension settling around them.

Wren looked around, his brows furrowed in concentration. "If we're going to make it out of here, we need to come up with a plan," he said. "We have to use the darkness to our advantage."

"But how?" George asked, his voice low, tinged with worry. "We barely made it this far."

"We can't give in to despair," Adrian urged, determination flickering to life within him again. "We need to think clearly. We've been through too much together to lose hope now. We can fight back."

Mia nodded slowly, her expression fierce. "What if we create a diversion? Something to draw the echoes away from us?"

Wren considered this for a moment, then nodded. "That could work. If we can lure them away, we might have a chance to escape while they're distracted."

"Alright," Adrian said, feeling the plan solidify in his mind. "We'll need something loud, something to get their attention. The rocks at the entrance could be our best bet."

Emma, her face pale but resolute, said, "I can help with that. I'll gather some rocks and make a noise."

"I'll go with you," George added, determination in his eyes. "I'm not letting you go out there alone."

"No!" Adrian said firmly, shaking his head. "If you both go, there won't be enough of us here to defend against the echoes if they come. Wren and I will stay here. You two go."

Mia's voice trembled. "What if the echoes find you while we're gone?"

"We'll be ready," Adrian reassured her, meeting her gaze. "We've faced worse together. Just be quick. Make as much noise as you can, and we'll move as soon as we can."

With a determined nod, Emma and George slipped out of the cave, leaving Adrian and Wren behind, tension thick in the air.

"Are you sure about this?" Wren asked, his eyes scanning the cave entrance. "It's dangerous."

Adrian took a deep breath, feeling the weight of responsibility pressing down on him. "We can't let fear dictate our actions. We're stronger than that. And we owe it to Mia and everyone else to fight back."

The minutes felt like hours as they waited, their hearts pounding in their chests. Each sound from outside sent shivers down Adrian's spine, a reminder that danger lurked just beyond the safety of the cave walls. But they stayed alert, ready to defend their friends if needed.

Finally, a loud clattering sound echoed through the forest, followed by a chorus of crashing rocks and shouts from Emma and George. Adrian's heart raced. "That's it! They're drawing the echoes away!"

"Let's go!" Wren said, his voice steady as they rushed toward the cave entrance, adrenaline surging through them.

As they stepped out, they could see the echoes in the distance, drawn toward the noise, their pale forms moving quickly through the trees. It was now or never.

"Go!" Adrian urged, sprinting ahead as they made their way down the forest path. The adrenaline coursed through their veins, propelling them forward as they navigated through the trees, the echoes' attention fully drawn away.

"We can't stop now!" Wren called, glancing back to see if the echoes were following. "Keep moving!"

With renewed determination, they pushed through the forest, adrenaline fueling every step as they raced away from the danger that had haunted them for so long. The thrill of hope surged within them as they dodged branches and roots, their bodies moving as one.

"Just a little further!" Adrian shouted, pushing them all forward. "We'll find a way out!"

They burst into another clearing, and the shimmering shoreline lay before them, inviting and serene. The ocean glistened under the moonlight, waves crashing rhythmically against the rocks.

As they reached the edge of the water, Adrian turned back, seeing the echoes still in the distance, searching for them. "We did it! We made it!"

But then he paused, sensing something in the air—the tension was still palpable. The island had not relinquished its hold completely. "Stay alert!" he warned, gripping Wren's arm as they stood at the shoreline.

"We need to find a boat or something to help us leave," Wren said, scanning the beach for any signs of escape.

Adrian nodded, determination flooding his veins once again. "Let's search for anything we can use. We can't let the island keep us here any longer."

And so, under the darkening sky, they began their search, driven by the desire to escape the island's grasp once and for all. Together, they faced the waves of uncertainty, their hearts united in the belief that freedom was within reach.

As the group stood at the water's edge, hope flickered within them like a dying ember. They searched frantically along the shoreline, scanning for any sign of a boat or a way off the island. The rhythmic crash of the waves against the rocks filled the air, mingling with their labored breaths as they combed through the sand and debris.

"Over here!" George shouted, pointing to a tattered piece of driftwood. Adrian's heart raced, but as they approached, the reality set in. It was nothing but a broken remnant, too small and flimsy to serve any purpose. Disappointment washed over them like the tide, and they continued their search, but the shoreline yielded no boats, no life rafts—nothing but sand and shadows.

"What if we're stuck here?" Emma's voice trembled as she picked through the debris, her face pale with exhaustion. "What if there's no way out?"

Adrian clenched his jaw, fighting against the despair that threatened to take hold. "There has to be something! We can't give up!" He looked at each of his friends, their faces drawn and weary, the weight of their situation pressing down on them. "We've made it this far; we can't let this island break us now."

They searched for what felt like hours, combing every inch of the beach, but the reality settled heavily upon them. Each passing moment chipped away at their hope, leaving behind only fatigue and despair. Finally, as the sun dipped below the horizon, casting long shadows across the sand, Adrian stopped and looked around at his friends.

"There's nothing here," he admitted, his voice heavy with defeat. "We need to go back to the cave. It's safer there, at least for tonight."

Mia nodded, her eyes filled with exhaustion. "I don't want to go back, but we can't stay here without a plan." She glanced at the forest, a shiver running down her spine. "The echoes will be looking for us, and we need to regroup."

With a heavy heart, they turned away from the shoreline, retracing their steps back through the trees. The darkness of the forest enveloped them once more, but this time it felt different. It was a familiar weight, one they had grown accustomed to, even if they didn't fully understand it.

As they navigated through the underbrush, each step felt laborious, their bodies heavy with fatigue. The echoes, though they couldn't see them, felt ever-present, lurking just beyond the shadows. The air was thick with anticipation, and every rustle of leaves sent a jolt of fear through Adrian's heart.

"Do you think they'll follow us?" Emma asked quietly, her voice barely above a whisper.

"I don't know," Adrian replied, glancing around warily. "But we can't let fear paralyze us. We need to rest and come up with a plan."

When they finally reached the cave, the cool darkness welcomed them, a refuge from the oppressive forest. They collapsed onto the ground, exhaustion washing over them like a tide. The echoes, for now, were at bay, and the cave felt like a shield against the island's horrors.

Adrian leaned against the wall, closing his eyes as fatigue claimed him. The events of the day replayed in his mind—the battles they fought, the darkness they faced, and the hope that had flickered and waned like a candle in the wind.

"Are you guys okay?" Mia's voice broke through his thoughts, pulling him back to the present.

"I'm fine," he lied, though the weariness etched into his face said otherwise. "Just tired."

Wren, seated against the opposite wall, sighed deeply. "We've all been through so much. Let's take a moment to breathe."

Emma wrapped her arms around her knees, leaning her head back against the rock. "I don't want to sleep, but I know we need to. We can't think straight if we don't rest."

"Just a few hours," George agreed, yawning deeply. "We need to gather our strength. We can figure out a plan in the morning."

Adrian nodded, feeling the weight of his eyelids growing heavier. "Let's rest then. But we need to stay alert. The island is still out there."

As darkness enveloped them, the echoes of the past echoed in Adrian's mind—memories of laughter, friendship, and the warmth of their bond. Despite the island's attempts to tear them apart, they were still together. And for now, that was enough.

Adrian closed his eyes, allowing sleep to wash over him, but as he drifted into unconsciousness, a nagging thought lingered at the back of his mind. They had come so far, faced so many dangers, and yet the island was still holding on to them, as if it were feeding off their fear and despair.

In the stillness of the cave, as they lay huddled together, a sense of unity formed. They might be exhausted, but they were still a team—a family. And no matter what the island threw at them next, they would face it together.

As darkness enveloped them, the world outside faded, the sounds of the forest giving way to the soft whisper of the ocean. For the first time in days, Adrian felt a flicker of hope amid the darkness.

In the stillness of the cave, where shadows danced softly along the walls, Emma stirred from her restless slumber. The weight of exhaustion hung heavily on her eyelids, but a deeper urge pulled her toward Wren, who lay a short distance away. She blinked against the darkness, taking a moment to collect her thoughts, the chaos of the day still echoing in her mind.

With a gentle determination, Emma crawled across the cool ground, her heart fluttering with a mix of hope and nervousness. Wren lay with his back against the cave wall, his chest rising and falling steadily in sleep, bruises still visible across his skin, remnants of his struggle to survive.

As she reached him, she hesitated, her breath catching in her throat. The memories of their last moments together played back vividly, the fear and uncertainty that had threatened to pull them apart. But here he was, alive and breathing, the flickering light from the entrance illuminating his familiar features.

"Wren," she whispered, her voice barely audible as she leaned closer. She gently shook his shoulder, feeling her heart race. "Wren, wake up."

His eyes fluttered open, revealing a mix of surprise and warmth. "Emma?" He rubbed his eyes, the weariness still evident in his expression. "Is it really you?"

She nodded, her heart swelling with emotion. Without another word, she leaned in closer, the world around them fading into nothingness. Their lips met softly, the kiss igniting a spark between them. It was tentative at first, a gentle exploration, but soon deepened into something more fervent, a release of the tension that had built up in both of them.

Wren pulled back slightly, searching her eyes for understanding. "I thought I lost you," he murmured, his voice thick with emotion. "When I woke up, I didn't know if I'd ever see you again.

"I was scared too," Emma confessed, her heart racing as she brushed a strand of hair behind her ear. "But I never stopped hoping."

Wren smiled, a genuine, radiant smile that lit up his face. "You're so brave. I don't know how you do it, but you give me strength."

The connection between them deepened, the shared moments of fear and uncertainty melting away as they sank into the warmth of each other's presence. "We're in this together," Emma said softly, her voice barely above a whisper. "No matter what the island throws at us, we'll face it together."

Wren nodded, his eyes locked onto hers, filled with a mix of admiration and affection. "Together," he echoed, the word heavy with promise.

Emma felt a surge of warmth course through her, knowing they could rely on each other even in the darkest of times. "I'm so glad you're here," she said, her heart swelling. "I was terrified I'd never see you again."

"You're my anchor," Wren replied, his voice earnest and steady. "You always have been."

They leaned in again, sharing another tender kiss, a sweet moment that felt like a fragile sanctuary amidst the chaos. This connection was a lifeline, a reminder that even in the face of overwhelming darkness, love could still flourish.

As they pulled away, Emma sighed contentedly, feeling the weight of the world lift just a little. "We should probably try to get some more sleep," she suggested, though her heart was still racing from their kiss.

"Yeah," Wren agreed, his gaze softening. "But can I just... hold you for a moment?"

"Of course," she replied, smiling as she shifted closer, resting her head against his shoulder. He wrapped his arm around her, pulling her close.

In the sanctuary of the cave, surrounded by the echoes of their friends and the distant sounds of the forest, they felt safe together. The warmth of Wren's embrace wrapped around her like a cocoon, soothing her fears and exhaustion.

"Goodnight, Emma," he murmured, his breath warm against her ear.

"Goodnight, Wren," she replied, her eyes fluttering shut as she nestled against him.

As sleep began to reclaim her, Emma felt a sense of peace wash over her, knowing that whatever awaited them in the darkness, they would face it together.

Before drifting off, they shared one last kiss, sealing their promise to each other—a promise that love could endure even in the most trying of times, a vow to stand together against whatever challenges lay ahead on the haunted shores of the island.

Among them, Adrian drifted into an uneasy sleep, the exhaustion of the day finally catching up with him. But instead of the peaceful rest he craved, his dreams quickly morphed into a vivid nightmare, pulling him into a realm of shadows and uncertainty.

He found himself in a darkened version of the cave, the familiar surroundings twisted into something sinister. The air was thick with tension, the shadows around him shifting and writhing like living entities. A sense of foreboding hung heavy, making his heart race.

"Wren?" he called, his voice echoing into the void. But there was no response, only an oppressive silence that swallowed him whole. The cave walls seemed to close in on him, and a chill ran down his spine.

He took a step forward, and the ground beneath him felt unstable, shifting like sand. With each step, he sensed an unseen presence watching him, lurking just out of sight. Panic bubbled within him, and he called out again, "Mia? Emma? George?"

Then he saw it—a figure standing in the shadows, just beyond the reach of the dim light. The outline was familiar, yet the features remained obscured, hidden behind a veil of darkness. Adrian felt a wave of dread wash over him as he strained to see who it was. "Who are you?" he demanded, his voice trembling.

The figure stepped closer, but the face remained shrouded, an indistinct blur that sent chills down Adrian's spine. "You shouldn't have come here," it said, its voice low and haunting, echoing in the cavernous space.

"Why? What do you want?" Adrian asked, desperation creeping into his voice.

"You'll see," the figure replied cryptically, a chilling smile forming in the darkness. "Trust will be your downfall."

Adrian's heart raced as fear coiled tightly in his chest. "What do you mean?" he pressed, but the figure only laughed—a sound that echoed ominously throughout the cave, filling him with dread.

Suddenly, the scene shifted. Adrian found himself standing on the shores of the island, the ocean a roiling mass of dark water, crashing violently against the rocks. The air was heavy with the scent of salt and fear, and he could feel the presence of the echoes lurking just beyond the waves, their shadowy forms watching, waiting.

He turned back toward the cave, desperate to escape, but the figure was there again, blocking his path. "You will betray them," it hissed, the voice echoing with sinister certainty. "You will lose everything you hold dear."

"No!" Adrian shouted, shaking his head violently. "I would never betray my friends!"

The figure stepped forward, and for the first time, Adrian caught a glimpse of its eyes—cold, empty, devoid of humanity. A deep sense of betrayal washed over him, and he felt an overwhelming urge to flee. But the figure raised a hand, pointing toward the shore. "You can't escape your fate. They will turn on you when you need them the most."

As the words sank in, Adrian's heart raced with fear and confusion. Images flooded his mind—Mia, Wren, Emma, George—all of them turning away, their faces twisted in anger, betrayal etched into their features. "No!" he cried out, trying to push the visions away, but they only grew stronger, overwhelming him.

Adrian stumbled back, his breath coming in quick gasps. "This can't be true! They're my friends!"

But the figure only laughed again, a low, mocking sound that echoed through the stormy night. "Friends are fleeting, Adrian. When darkness falls, trust becomes a weapon. You'll see who your true allies are."

As he stood on the shore, the echoes began to emerge from the water, their forms shifting and morphing, faces contorted into expressions of rage and betrayal. They closed in on him, and Adrian felt a chill grip his heart as he realized the truth—the nightmare was more than just a dream. It was a premonition of the darkness that lay ahead, a warning of the treachery that could tear them apart.

"No!" he screamed, desperation flooding his voice as he stumbled back, trying to escape. But the waves surged forward, crashing against him, pulling him into the depths of the ocean, drowning him in a tide of despair.

Adrian awoke with a gasp, sitting up in the cave, drenched in sweat. The darkness of the cave surrounded him, and for a moment, he felt disoriented, the remnants of the nightmare clinging to him like shadows.

"Adrian?" Mia's voice pierced through the fog of his fear. She looked at him with concern, her features softening in the dim light. "What's wrong?"

He shook his head, trying to shake off the dread that lingered in his chest. "Just a nightmare," he whispered, but even as he spoke, the images flashed in his mind—the figure, the betrayal, the echoes. "It felt... real."

Wren sat up, concern etched on his face. "What did you see?"

Adrian hesitated, the weight of his nightmare pressing heavily on him. "It was about us. About trust... and betrayal."

Mia's brow furrowed, and she scooted closer. "What do you mean?"

"It was a figure," he said slowly, trying to articulate the darkness that had gripped him. "It said that friends are fleeting, and that we would betray each other when darkness falls."

Emma, who had been listening intently, looked alarmed. "You think that could happen? That we could turn on each other?"

"I don't know," Adrian replied, his heart racing. "But it felt like a warning. I can't shake the feeling that something is coming, something that could tear us apart."

Wren exchanged a glance with Mia, a frown on his face. "We've been through so much together. We can't let fear dictate our actions. We have to stay united."

"But what if the island is trying to manipulate us?" Emma said, her voice trembling. "What if it knows our fears and uses them against us?"

Adrian took a deep breath, trying to gather his thoughts. "We can't give in to that fear. We need to trust each other, now more than ever. But we have to be cautious."

Mia reached for Adrian's hand, squeezing it tightly. "We'll get through this together. No matter what."

The weight of their situation settled around them, but Adrian felt a flicker of hope ignite within him. They had survived so much already; they could face this too. Together, they would find a way to break free from the island's grasp and keep the darkness at bay.

As Emma drifted back to sleep, exhaustion pulling her under like an anchor into the depths of a still ocean, her mind became a canvas where the island's darkness painted its cruelest thoughts. At first, her dreams were soft—familiar and peaceful. She stood on the beach again, the setting sun casting warm hues of orange and gold across the horizon. The waves lapped gently at the shore, their rhythmic sound soothing her soul after so much chaos. She breathed in deeply, feeling a moment of serenity.

But a lingering unease fluttered at the edges of her mind, an undercurrent she couldn't quite shake. Something was... wrong.

Suddenly, Adrian appeared beside her, his familiar figure emerging from the soft light. He smiled at her, that kind, reassuring smile she had come to rely on during their journey. But there was something off, something in his eyes that made Emma's heart skip—a flicker of shadow, as though the sunlight could not fully reach him.

"Adrian?" she asked, her voice uncertain as she glanced at him. There was a strange intimacy in his gaze, one that hadn't been there before. Her stomach twisted.

He nodded, stepping closer, his eyes never leaving hers. "It's over, Emma. We're safe now," he said, his voice soft yet somehow hollow. "You don't have to fight anymore."

Emma felt the weight of the last few days melt away at his words. For a moment, she wanted to believe him, to let go of all the fear and exhaustion. But something held her back. She looked into Adrian's eyes again, that same flicker of darkness reflecting in the depths. She tried to push the unease aside.

Without warning, Adrian reached for her, pulling her into an embrace. Emma stiffened, her body reacting with confusion. She loved Wren. Her heart belonged to him, not Adrian. But for some reason, in this dream, her body did not resist. His arms wrapped around her tightly, and her breath caught in her throat.

She tried to speak, tried to voice the conflict that stirred inside her, but no words came. Her thoughts were a jumbled mess, as though the island itself had fogged her mind. Then, in one swift movement, Adrian leaned in, his lips pressing against hers.

Emma froze. Her heart pounded in her chest, not with love, but with a rising sense of wrongness. She shouldn't be here. She shouldn't be doing this. This wasn't Wren. She loved Wren. But she couldn't pull away—her body was paralyzed, locked in the moment, while her mind screamed.

The kiss deepened, but with it came an unsettling change. The warmth of Adrian's lips began to fade, replaced by a coldness that seeped into her bones. His grip on her tightened, no longer tender but possessive, almost suffocating. Emma's eyes fluttered open in panic, but the scene around her had shifted. The peaceful sunset beach was gone, replaced by a sky swirling with dark clouds, tinged red as though the sun had bled into the horizon. The ocean, once calm, now churned violently, waves crashing angrily against jagged rocks that seemed to rise from the depths like monstrous teeth.

"Adrian, stop!" Emma tried to say, but her voice was trapped in her throat, strangled by fear.

She tried to pull away from him, her body trembling with the effort, but his hands clamped down on her wrists, holding her in place. And then, her blood ran cold as she saw it. His eyes—once warm, filled with the compassion she knew—had turned completely black, void of life. His skin darkened and cracked, a sickening transformation spreading across his face like a creeping infection.

"Adrian?" Her voice trembled as she finally managed to speak. But the thing standing before her was no longer Adrian.

The corners of his mouth twisted into a grotesque grin, revealing sharp, jagged teeth. His skin peeled away, revealing a scaled, monstrous texture beneath, and his hands—no longer human—grew into twisted claws, digging into her skin.

"Emma," the creature hissed, its voice a guttural mockery of Adrian's. "You thought you could escape me?"

"No... no..." Emma gasped, struggling to break free. Panic surged through her veins as her mind spun with horror. She had to wake up. This wasn't real. It couldn't be.

But the creature only tightened its grip, pulling her closer, its breath hot against her face. "You'll never escape. You belong to me now," it whispered, its voice slithering into her mind like poison.

Emma screamed, thrashing against the creature with all her strength, but its claws sank deeper into her arms, the pain searing through her like fire. Her vision blurred as tears welled in her eyes, her mind reeling in terror. She tried to kick, to break free, but her body was weak, as though the island itself was draining her strength.

With a violent snarl, the demon-Adrian dragged her toward the rocks. The sand beneath her feet turned to sharp, jagged stone, cutting into her skin as she stumbled, her heart hammering in her chest.

"Please... stop..." Emma whimpered, her voice barely audible. She looked into the creature's eyes, desperately searching for a trace of the real Adrian, but there was nothing—only darkness and cruelty.

The demon grinned wider, relishing her fear. "You thought you could trust him?" it sneered. "He will betray you. They all will."

"No!" Emma screamed, shaking her head violently. "That's not true!"

But the demon's claws dug deeper, and with a swift, brutal motion, it slashed across her chest. A sharp, blinding pain erupted in her body, and Emma cried out, her knees buckling beneath her. Blood poured from the wound, staining the rocks beneath her. She felt her strength slipping away, her vision dimming.

"Help me..." she whispered, her voice a broken plea, but no one came. The sky above her twisted further into chaos, lightning crackling across the blood-red horizon.

The demon loomed over her, its black eyes gleaming with triumph. "There's no one left, Emma. No one to save you now."

With one final, horrifying motion, the demon raised its clawed hand again, ready to strike the killing blow. Emma's world tilted, the pain unbearable, and as the creature's hand came down, she screamed—

And woke up.

Emma bolted upright, gasping for air, her heart racing in her chest. Her body was drenched in sweat, her hands trembling violently as she tried to steady her breathing. The cold, dark cave surrounded her, but the nightmare still clung to her like a shadow. Her skin crawled with the memory of the demon's claws, the phantom pain still fresh in her mind.

"Emma?" Wren's voice cut through the haze of terror. He sat up beside her, his eyes filled with concern as he reached out to touch her arm. "What happened? Are you okay?"

Her breath came in ragged gasps, and she stared at him, her mind struggling to separate dream from reality. It took her a moment to realize she was safe, that Wren was here, not the demon. "I... I had a nightmare," she whispered, her voice trembling.

Wren pulled her into his arms, his touch warm and reassuring. "It's okay," he murmured, gently stroking her hair. "You're safe now. I'm here."

Emma clung to him, her body still shaking. "It was Adrian," she said, her voice barely audible. "He... he turned into a monster and... and killed me."

Wren frowned, his arms tightening around her protectively. "The island is getting into your head, trying to mess with you. It's not real, Emma. You know Adrian would never hurt you."

"I know," she whispered, but the fear still clung to her like a cold fog. "But it felt so real. The island... it's twisting everything."

Wren kissed the top of her head, his voice soft but steady. "It's trying to break us. But we won't let it. We're stronger than this."

Emma nodded, though the lingering horror of the dream gnawed at her. She knew Wren was right. The island was manipulating them, trying to turn them against each other, to weaken their trust. But she couldn't shake the image of Adrian's twisted, demonic face, the feeling of betrayal and terror that had coursed through her in the nightmare.

"Just hold me," she whispered, burying her face against Wren's chest. "Please."

"I'm not going anywhere," he promised, holding her close. "We'll get through this, together."

As she lay in his arms, the steady beat of his heart against her ear, Emma's body finally began to relax. But the nightmare still lingered at the edges of her mind, a reminder of the island's dark power and the constant battle they were fighting—not just against the echoes, but against the island's grip on their minds.

Sleep wouldn't come easily again, and Emma knew the island wasn't done with them yet. But for now, in Wren's embrace, she felt a flicker of peace, even as the darkness loomed ever closer.

As dawn began to break, a soft, muted light crept into the cave, casting long shadows on the rough stone walls. The air was cool and still, carrying with it the lingering tension of the night before. The group had managed to sleep, though it was a restless, uneasy slumber filled with nightmares and the constant awareness of the island's dark presence surrounding them.

Adrian was the first to wake, his body stiff from sleeping on the hard cave floor. He sat up slowly, wincing as his muscles protested. The remnants of the dreadful nightmare still clung to him, the faceless figure from his dream haunting the edges of his mind. He glanced around the cave, his eyes falling on his friends. Mia lay curled up near him, her breathing steady but her face drawn in tension even as she slept. Wren was beside Emma, their closeness a source of quiet comfort in the midst of the island's torment. Emma's face, however, showed the traces of fear, her brow furrowed as if the nightmares hadn't fully let her go.

Adrian let out a long breath, running a hand through his hair. They couldn't stay here. They had survived the night, but the island wasn't done with them. The echoes, the twisted magic, the looming threat—they were always lurking just beyond sight, waiting for them to let their guard down.

Slowly, he stood, careful not to disturb the others. He stretched his arms above his head, feeling the tightness in his back ease just a little. As he gazed out of the cave's entrance, he noticed how the early morning light barely pierced through the thick canopy of trees. It was a reminder that, even with daylight, the island was a place where shadows ruled. They had to move. The echoes would find them if they stayed too long in one place.

Mia stirred next, blinking groggily as she sat up, her eyes finding Adrian almost immediately. "You're up early," she mumbled, rubbing her eyes. "How long have you been awake?"

"Not long," Adrian replied, his voice low so as not to wake the others. "I couldn't sleep much. The nightmare I had last night..." He trailed off, not wanting to dredge up the fear again. He wasn't sure if he should tell them about the faceless figure—the warning about betrayal.

Mia nodded knowingly. "I had one too," she admitted, her voice tinged with exhaustion. "I think we all did."

Adrian glanced over at Emma and Wren, both still asleep but visibly troubled. "Yeah, I think you're right." He sighed, lowering his voice even more. "I don't think we can stay here. The longer we stay in one spot, the more vulnerable we are."

Mia nodded in agreement, looking toward the cave's entrance with a mixture of dread and determination. "I feel it too," she said softly. "Like the island's closing in on us. We need to move."

Adrian stood, looking over at Wren and Emma, still asleep in each other's arms. He didn't want to wake them, but time was of the essence. "I'll wake them," he said quietly, walking toward the pair. He knelt down beside them, gently shaking Wren's shoulder. "Hey, it's time to get up."

Wren stirred, his eyes fluttering open. He looked disoriented at first, then his expression sharpened with awareness as he remembered where they were. "Is it morning already?" he asked, his voice rough with sleep.

"Yeah," Adrian replied, standing up again. "We need to get moving. It's not safe to stay in one place for too long."

Wren nodded and sat up slowly, careful not to disturb Emma. She shifted in her sleep, her brow furrowing, and Wren gently brushed a strand of hair away from her face. "Emma," he whispered, his voice soft. "Wake up, it's morning."

Emma stirred, blinking as she woke. For a moment, she looked confused, her eyes darting around the cave as if trying to piece together where she was. Then, as the reality of the island settled in again, her expression hardened. "Already?" she asked, sitting up beside Wren. The unease from the nightmare was still evident on her face, her lips pressed into a thin line.

"Yeah," Mia said gently, her eyes soft with understanding. "We can't stay here. We need to keep moving."

Emma nodded in agreement, though her body still felt heavy with exhaustion. The nightmare had shaken her more than she wanted to admit. She could still see the image of demon-Adrian in her mind, his monstrous face contorted into a sinister grin. She cast a glance toward Adrian, guilt twisting in her stomach. It wasn't real. He wasn't like that. But the fear clung to her.

Wren, noticing the tension in Emma's face, reached for her hand and gave it a comforting squeeze. "We'll be okay," he reassured her, though there was a flicker of uncertainty in his voice. "We just need to keep moving. Stick together."

Adrian turned toward George, who had just started to stir, his eyes blinking open groggily. "We're heading out, George," Adrian said, offering a hand to help him up. "We don't have time to rest any longer."

George groaned as he sat up, rubbing his neck. "Yeah, I figured," he mumbled, accepting Adrian's hand and getting to his feet. "I don't know how much longer we can keep doing this."

"We don't have a choice," Adrian replied, his voice firm. "We move, we survive. That's the only way."

The group gathered what little they had—mostly the thorny branches they had used as weapons and a few pieces of cloth they had salvaged. As they prepared to leave the cave, the weight of the island's presence pressed down on them once more. Every rustling leaf and distant sound felt like a warning, a reminder that they were never truly alone.

Before they stepped out, Adrian looked back at his friends, taking in their weary faces. Despite the exhaustion, despite the nightmares that plagued them all, there was still a sense of unity among them—a determination to survive.

"Listen," Adrian said, his voice steady but low. "We have to stay sharp. The island is trying to wear us down. It's messing with our minds, our dreams. We can't let it get to us. Whatever happens, we stick together, and we keep moving."

Mia nodded, her expression resolute. "We've made it this far. We're not giving up now."

Emma swallowed hard, her fingers still laced with Wren's. She felt the lingering fear from her nightmare, but she forced herself to push it aside. "We'll make it," she said, though the words felt heavy in her mouth. "We just have to keep going."

George let out a tired sigh, running a hand through his hair. "Let's just hope the next place we find is safer than this one."

Wren, always the steady one, glanced at Adrian with a faint smile. "Lead the way, Adrian. We'll follow."

Adrian nodded, taking the first step out of the cave and into the forest beyond. The morning light barely filtered through the dense canopy above, casting long shadows over the path ahead. Every step felt deliberate, cautious, as if the island itself were waiting for them to make a mistake.

They moved slowly but steadily, each of them on high alert, the weight of their situation pressing down like a physical force. The echoes were still out there somewhere, and the island's dark magic twisted the air around them, making every sound feel amplified, every movement a potential threat.

As they navigated through the forest, Adrian's mind wandered back to his nightmare—the faceless figure, the warning of betrayal. He couldn't shake the feeling that it had meant something, that it was more than just a figment of his imagination. But who? And why? He glanced at each of his friends—Mia, George, Wren, and

Emma—and felt a pang of guilt. They had been through so much together. Could he really let doubt creep in?

But the island was a place of shadows and deceit. He couldn't afford to dismiss anything, no matter how unsettling. His instincts told him to stay alert, to trust his gut, but his heart ached at the thought of doubting the very people he was trying to protect.

As they moved deeper into the forest, the trees thickened, their branches twisting overhead like skeletal arms reaching out to entangle them. The air grew cooler, and the oppressive atmosphere weighed heavier with each step. Every now and then, Adrian would hear a rustle behind them, but when he turned to look, nothing was there. It was as if the island itself was playing games with them, testing their resolve.

"We need to find higher ground," Wren said, his voice breaking the silence. "We'll be safer if we can see more of what's around us."

Adrian nodded in agreement. "Let's head toward that ridge up ahead," he pointed, spotting a slight incline in the distance. "We'll get a better view and decide what to do from there."

The group moved forward, but the weight of the nightmares still hung over them like an unspoken cloud. They were together, but each of them carried their own private fears—the echoes of the night still fresh in their minds.

As they pressed on, the tension among them simmered, unspoken but present. They were survivors, but the island hadn't finished with them yet. And deep down, each of them knew that the real battle was only just beginning.

The dense underbrush crunched underfoot as they ascended the ridge, the sound echoing in the stillness of the forest. Each step felt heavier than the last, and Adrian could sense the tension simmering just beneath the surface. The weight of their recent nightmares hung over them, a shadow that wouldn't lift.

As they reached the top of the ridge, they paused to catch their breath, the view unfolding before them. The landscape stretched out like a living painting—lush greens and browns melded with the blues of the distant ocean. But it was also a deceptive beauty, an illusion that masked the dangers lurking within the island's depths.

"Wow," Mia breathed, her eyes widening at the breathtaking sight. "It's beautiful up here."

"Yeah, but it's also a little too quiet," George added, glancing around nervously. He stepped closer to the edge, peering down into the valleys below. "Where are the echoes? It doesn't feel right."

Adrian nodded, feeling the same uneasy sensation prickling at the back of his mind. "We should stay alert. Just because we can't see them doesn't mean they aren't around." He scanned the surrounding area, taking in the dense foliage, the shadows playing tricks on his eyes. There was an unsettling stillness, as if the very island was holding its breath.

Emma leaned against a tree, trying to steady her breathing. "I don't like this place," she murmured. "It feels like we're being watched."

"Maybe we are," Wren said, crossing his arms as he surveyed the landscape. "But we can't let fear control us. We have to keep moving. If we linger here, we're sitting ducks."

The group exchanged glances, the unspoken agreement passing between them. They needed to find a safe place, somewhere to regroup and plan their next move.

"Let's keep going," Adrian said, his voice firm. "We'll find another way down and keep an eye out for any signs of danger."

With that, they continued along the ridge, navigating the rocky terrain carefully. The path was steep, and the further they went, the more the air thickened with tension. Shadows darted in their peripheral vision, but whenever they turned to look, nothing was there—just the rustling of leaves in the breeze, taunting them with uncertainty.

As they made their way down the other side of the ridge, a sudden rustling from the bushes caught Adrian's attention. His heart raced as he turned, instinctively reaching for the thorny branch at his side. "Did you hear that?" he whispered, his voice low and urgent.

Everyone halted, their eyes wide with fear as they listened intently. The rustling continued, closer now, and then a figure burst forth from the underbrush.

Adrian's breath caught in his throat as the silhouette emerged, a gaunt face with hollow eyes that reflected the light. The figure stumbled forward, and for a moment, Adrian thought it was one of the echoes. But as it came into focus, he realized with a mixture of shock and relief that it was a person—a man, disheveled and wild-eyed.

"Help me!" the man gasped, his voice raw and filled with desperation. "Please!"

Adrian exchanged wary glances with the group. "Who are you?" he asked, keeping his voice steady, even as his heart raced.

"I'm a survivor," the man said, collapsing to his knees. "I've been hiding from the echoes for days. They... they know I'm here." His eyes darted around, panic evident in his gaze. "You have to help me! We can't stay here!"

"What do you mean they know you're here?" Wren asked, stepping forward. "Are you one of the lost ones? The echoes?"

"No! I'm not one of them!" the man exclaimed, his voice shaking. "They're everywhere. They come out at night, and they'll take you if they find you!"

Adrian felt the tension rise in the air. "What do you know about the echoes?" he pressed, trying to gauge the man's truthfulness. "How do we fight them?"

The man's breath hitched, and he glanced nervously at the trees. "There's no fighting them! They can't be killed—they're shadows, echoes of those who came before us. They feed on fear and despair. The more afraid you are, the stronger they become."

A chill ran down Adrian's spine. He had felt it—the echoes had preyed on their fear since the moment they set foot on this island. "What do we do, then?" he asked, desperation creeping into his voice.

"You have to leave this place," the man said urgently, looking up at Adrian with wild eyes. "There's a safe haven, a place where the echoes can't reach you. But you have to hurry! They'll sense you soon, and once they do..."

Before he could finish, the sound of rustling intensified, and suddenly, shadows began to shift in the trees. A wave of panic coursed through Adrian's veins, and he turned to see the silhouettes of the echoes emerging from the underbrush, their pale faces twisted in malicious glee.

"Run!" Adrian shouted, adrenaline surging as the group instinctively fell into motion. They bolted back up the ridge, fear propelling them forward. The echoes were close behind, their presence palpable, as if the very darkness was alive, reaching out to claim them.

They raced down the path, the world blurring around them. Adrian's heart pounded in his chest, each beat echoing the urgency of their flight. They needed to escape, to reach the safe haven the man had spoken of before it was too late.

"Keep moving!" Wren shouted, pushing Mia forward as they navigated the rocky terrain. "We can't let them catch us!"

Adrian glanced back, seeing the echoes gaining ground, their movements fluid and predatory. "They're coming!" he yelled, pushing himself harder, determination fueling his every step.

As they neared the ridge, Adrian could feel the air shift, the whispers of the echoes swirling around him, trying to seep into his mind. "Stay focused!" he shouted to the group. "Don't let them get to you!"

Mia stumbled slightly, but Wren caught her, pulling her close. "We're almost there! Just a bit further!" he urged, his voice filled with unwavering resolve.

With each step, the echoes drew closer, their laughter echoing in the air like a chilling melody. The shadows enveloped them, clawing at their sanity, trying to pry them apart.

Just as Adrian thought they might be overwhelmed, they burst into a small clearing on the other side of the ridge, the open space providing a brief moment of respite. The echoes halted at the edge, their forms swirling and flickering in the light.

"Now what?" George panted, looking around for any signs of escape.

"We need to find a way through!" Adrian shouted, scanning the area for any possible paths. "There has to be something!"

In the distance, a glimmer of light caught his eye. "Over there!" he pointed, noticing a narrow path winding through the trees on the opposite side of the clearing. "We can head that way!"

Without hesitation, they sprinted toward the light, but the echoes were relentless, their laughter growing louder, echoing through the clearing as they surged forward. Adrian could feel the darkness closing in around them, the echoes hungry for their despair.

As they reached the narrow path, Adrian felt a rush of hope. "Go! Now!" he urged, pushing everyone ahead of him. They squeezed through the trees, the branches scratching at their arms as they plunged into the dense underbrush.

But the echoes followed, their voices echoing in the darkness, taunting them as they fled deeper into the woods. "You can't escape!

You will belong to us!" the shadows taunted, their voices a chilling reminder of their relentless pursuit.

Adrian could feel the fear clinging to him, but he pushed it aside, focusing on the path ahead. They had come too far to turn back now. "Keep going!" he shouted, his voice rising above the cacophony. "We have to get to that safe place!"

As they ran, the trees began to thin out, revealing another clearing bathed in soft, dappled light. Hope surged within Adrian's chest as he caught sight of the open space. "There!" he called, urging the group forward.

They burst into the clearing, and for a moment, the echoes hesitated at the edge, the sunlight seemingly repelling their shadowy forms. Adrian glanced back, catching his breath as the whispers of the echoes faded just beyond the trees.

"We made it," Wren panted, looking around as they slowed to a halt. "But where are we?"

Adrian surveyed the clearing, noting the wildflowers and the bright, sunlit meadow that stretched out before them. In the center stood a large, ancient tree, its gnarled branches spreading wide as if offering protection. "I don't know," he admitted, "but it feels... different. Safer."

Emma looked up at the tree, her eyes filled with uncertainty. "Do you think it can protect us from the echoes?"

"It has to," Adrian said, hope mingling with desperation. "If we can reach the tree, maybe we can find some way to shield ourselves from the island's dark magic."

With renewed determination, they moved toward the tree, the sunlight warming their skin as they stepped into the meadow. The air felt lighter here, a stark contrast to the oppressive atmosphere they had just escaped.

As they reached the tree, they pressed their backs against the sturdy trunk, feeling its strength grounding them. They took a moment to catch their breath, the tension in their shoulders easing slightly.

"What now?" Mia asked, glancing around at her friends. "Are we safe here?"

"For now, yes," Adrian replied, his heart still racing. "But we need to figure out our next move. We can't stay here forever."

As they caught their breath, the reality of their situation settled over them once more. They had faced the echoes, but the island was far from defeated. They needed a plan, a way to regain their strength and find a permanent escape from the darkness that had engulfed them.

Adrian took a deep breath, looking around at his friends—Mia, Emma, George, and Wren. "Together, we can do this. We just need to stay focused and stick together. No matter what."

The group nodded, a sense of unity forming among them once again. The echoes may have haunted them, but they would face whatever lay ahead as one. And as the sun continued to rise, casting its warm light over the clearing, they began to formulate their plan—a beacon of hope amid the island's darkness.

The sunlight filtering through the leaves above bathed the clearing in a warm glow, giving the group a momentary sense of safety as they pressed their backs against the ancient tree. It felt like a sanctuary, a refuge from the darkness that had pursued them. But even as they caught their breath and tried to gather their thoughts, a gnawing sense of unease lingered in the air.

Adrian glanced around, scanning the perimeter of the clearing. "We need to keep watch. I don't trust this place," he said, his voice low but firm.

Wren nodded, his expression serious. "I agree. The echoes could be lurking nearby, just waiting for us to lower our guard."

Mia looked up at the towering tree, its gnarled branches swaying slightly in the breeze. "It feels safe here, though," she said, her voice tinged with uncertainty. "Can't we at least take a moment to regroup?"

Emma leaned against the tree, her body still recovering from the stress of the past days. "We've been running for so long. We need to come up with a plan. If we can't figure out our next move, we'll be stuck."

Adrian sighed, feeling the weight of their situation pressing down on him. "Alright, let's take a moment to catch our breath, but we need to be vigilant. I don't want any surprises."

As they settled in the clearing, the atmosphere felt deceptively calm. The birds sang in the distance, and the sunlight danced across the ground. But in the back of Adrian's mind, an unsettling feeling gnawed at him—a whisper of doubt that wouldn't leave him alone.

They spent a few moments discussing their options, but the tension in the air remained thick. Just as they were about to take action, the peaceful atmosphere shattered.

A low, menacing growl echoed through the trees, followed by the rustling of leaves. Adrian's heart dropped as he turned toward the sound, his instincts screaming that something was very wrong.

"Get ready!" he shouted, scrambling to his feet. "They're here!"

Before he could say another word, the echoes surged into the clearing, a wave of darkness descending upon them like a storm. Their forms flickered in and out of existence, a grotesque display of shadows with twisted, snarling faces.

"Run!" Emma yelled, but it was too late. The echoes descended upon them with terrifying speed, their claws glinting in the dappled sunlight as they lunged forward.

Adrian barely had time to react. An echo grabbed him from behind, its cold hands wrapping around his throat. He felt a sharp pain as its grip tightened, cutting off his breath. He fought back, twisting and kicking, but the echo was unyielding, its strength far greater than he could have imagined.

“Adrian!” Wren shouted, trying to reach him, but another echo tackled him to the ground, pinning him with overwhelming force.

Mia and Emma were quickly surrounded, the echoes swarming them like a relentless tide. Adrian could hear the frantic cries of his friends, the sound of flesh meeting flesh, the sickening thud of bodies colliding with the ground.

“Get off me!” Mia screamed, struggling against the echoes that clawed at her. But one of them was on top of her, its face twisted into a hideous grin as it struck her repeatedly.

Adrian fought against his captor, his mind racing. “Let her go!” he shouted, desperation rising within him. But his words fell on deaf ears. The echoes were relentless, fueled by the fear and chaos they thrived on.

“Stop fighting! You cannot escape!” one of the echoes taunted, its voice a chilling blend of laughter and menace.

As the echoes closed in, the clearing erupted into chaos. Adrian felt the strength drain from his body as he struggled against the echo that held him. It was a losing battle, and he could see his friends falling one by one, unable to withstand the onslaught.

Wren grunted as he tried to shove the echo off him, but it was no use. The shadows swarmed him, pummeling him with brutal blows. Adrian’s heart raced as he watched Wren being beaten mercilessly, his cries mingling with Mia’s and Emma’s as they fought against the darkness.

“No!” Adrian screamed, his voice cracking as he twisted violently in the grip of the echo. “Get off them!”

But the echoes were merciless, their laughter ringing in his ears as they struck again and again. Adrian could barely breathe, his vision darkening as panic surged within him. He had to do something, but the shadows held him tight, their strength unyielding.

Just when he thought he might lose consciousness, the grip around his throat loosened slightly, allowing him to gasp for air. He took a deep breath, adrenaline surging through his veins as he pushed against the echo with all his might.

With a sudden burst of strength, he managed to shove the echo away, scrambling to his feet. The chaos around him was disorienting. He saw Mia on the ground, blood trickling from her mouth as she struggled against another echo, while Wren was still grappling with his own captor, the shadows looming over him like a dark cloud.

"Wren!" Adrian shouted, lunging toward him, but the echo that had held him back now blocked his path. Adrian swung a fist, connecting with the echo's face, but it only seemed to anger the creature. It lunged at him, knocking him to the ground.

He hit the ground hard, the air escaping his lungs as the echo bore down on him. Just as the darkness threatened to close in, he heard Emma's voice cutting through the chaos.

"Adrian! Look out!"

Adrian turned just in time to see another echo charging at him from the side. He rolled to the side, narrowly avoiding the impact, and scrambled to his feet again. But the echoes were everywhere, surrounding them, their twisted forms flickering like shadows in the fading light.

"We have to fight back!" he yelled, trying to rally his friends. "We can't let them take us!"

Wren, still struggling against his echo, managed to shout back, "I'm trying! But they're too strong!"

The battle raged on, the air thick with desperation and fear. Adrian felt the weight of despair press down on him, the echoes attacking with a relentless fury. He saw Mia staggering to her feet, a bruised expression on her face, while Emma was cornered against the tree, struggling to evade the grasp of two echoes.

Adrian lunged toward Emma, but before he could reach her, an echo grabbed him from behind, dragging him back into the fray.

"You're not going anywhere!" it hissed, its breath cold against his neck.

"No!" Adrian roared, thrashing against the creature. He could see Emma's eyes wide with fear, tears streaking down her face as she faced the shadows.

In that moment, everything shifted. The echoes intensified their attack, closing in on Adrian and his friends with overwhelming force. They were being beaten down, the echoes reveling in their despair, their laughter echoing in Adrian's ears like a twisted melody.

He felt a blow land hard against his side, sending him crashing to the ground. The pain was sharp and immediate, but it only fueled his determination. He couldn't let them win.

With every ounce of strength he had left, he pushed himself up, adrenaline coursing through his veins. "Get away from them!" he shouted, launching himself at the nearest echo. He struck with everything he had, his fist connecting with the creature's face.

But the echo barely flinched, the blow barely registering. It turned, eyes burning with rage, and lunged at him, knocking him back again. Adrian stumbled but quickly regained his footing, fear and desperation propelling him forward.

Wren managed to break free from his captor momentarily, rushing to Mia's side as she struggled against two echoes. "Mia, hold on!" he shouted, grabbing one of the echoes and attempting to pull it away from her.

But the echoes were relentless, their strength insurmountable. Mia cried out as they struck her, blood spilling from her lip as she fought to keep her head above water.

Adrian couldn't take it anymore. With a roar of defiance, he charged toward Mia, launching himself at the echo holding her down. He tackled it to the ground, fury blinding him as he fought to free her.

"Get off her!" he yelled, striking with everything he had, fueled by desperation and rage. He could feel the adrenaline coursing through him, drowning out the pain of his own injuries.

Mia gasped as the echo fell back, giving her a moment to breathe. "Adrian, thank you!" she cried, scrambling to her feet.

But the moment was fleeting. Another echo appeared, and Adrian barely had time to react as it lunged for him. He felt its claws rake across his arm, a searing pain igniting in his flesh.

"No!" he screamed, fury boiling within him. He couldn't let them take his friends. He couldn't let them win.

With a surge of strength, he pushed himself up, adrenaline driving him as he faced the echo. He fought with everything he had, fueled by the fear of losing his friends, the fear of the darkness swallowing them whole.

"Fight back!" he urged, glancing at Wren and Emma. "We can't let them beat us!"

Wren nodded, his face a mask of determination as he charged at the nearest echo, striking it with a powerful blow. "We're not going down without a fight!"

The battle raged on, each of them pushing back against the shadows that threatened to consume them. But despite their efforts, the echoes were relentless, striking with brutal efficiency. Adrian felt the sting of pain again and again, each blow making him weaker.

"Mia! Get out of here!" Wren shouted as he struggled to hold back another echo. "We'll cover you!"

"No! I'm not leaving you!" she cried, determination flooding her voice.

The echoes continued to close in, the sounds of their laughter blending with the cries of Adrian's friends. But as despair threatened to take hold, Adrian felt a flicker of hope ignite within him.

"We can do this!" he shouted, trying to rally his friends. "We have to fight together!"

With a final surge of strength, they pushed back against the echoes, each blow a testament to their resolve. They fought for each other, refusing to let the darkness win. But the battle was far from over, and as the shadows pressed in around them, Adrian knew they would have to dig deep to survive.

"Stay together!" he shouted, rallying them as they formed a circle, fighting off the echoes that surrounded them. They could do this. They had to believe that they could find a way out of the darkness.

And so, with every ounce of strength they had left, they stood against the shadows, united in their fight for survival, refusing to let the island claim them.

The battle against the echoes raged on, each moment stretching into an eternity. Adrian felt his body wear down, the strikes against him growing stronger, but the determination within him surged like a wildfire. He could feel the weight of his friends around him, their collective will fueling his own resolve.

"Don't give up!" he shouted, his voice hoarse but filled with fire. "We're stronger together!"

Wren and Mia, still fighting back-to-back, exchanged determined glances. With every strike, they pushed against the encroaching darkness, but the echoes were relentless. Adrian could see their faces—twisted and taunting, hungry for despair. But they weren't going to let the island win. Not like this.

"Wren!" Adrian yelled, trying to reach his friend as he struggled against an echo that had managed to get the upper hand. "We need to regroup! We can't let them surround us!"

"I know! I'm trying!" Wren grunted, shoving the echo away momentarily, but another quickly took its place, striking him hard across the ribs. Wren gasped, but he quickly recovered, a look of fierce determination igniting in his eyes.

"Mia! Emma! We have to move!" Adrian urged, fighting off another echo with a desperate shove. "We can't stay here! There's no victory in this place!"

Emma, panting heavily, nodded, her expression resolute. "You're right! We need to find a way out!"

With renewed purpose, they pushed forward, trying to make their way toward the edge of the clearing. The echoes hissed and growled behind them, their forms shifting and swirling like smoke. Adrian could feel the cold breath of fear on his neck, but he fought it back with every ounce of strength he had left.

"Run!" he shouted, breaking into a sprint toward the treeline. The group followed, their hearts racing as they moved as one, dodging and weaving through the trees.

The forest opened up before them, and Adrian could feel the echoes faltering behind them. "This way!" he shouted, veering to the left. They raced deeper into the woods, adrenaline coursing through their veins, propelling them forward.

Just as they thought they were safe, they broke through the trees and stumbled upon an ancient stone pathway, overgrown with moss and vines. At the end of the path loomed a massive structure—an ancient temple, its weathered stones rising up like a sentinel from a forgotten age.

Adrian skidded to a halt, his heart pounding as they all caught their breath. "What is this place?" he whispered, staring at the temple in awe and trepidation.

"I don't know," Wren replied, glancing around. "But it looks old—like it's been here for centuries. We might find something inside that can help us."

"But what if it's a trap?" Mia interjected, her voice tinged with fear. "We don't know what's waiting for us in there."

Adrian stepped closer to the entrance, peering into the darkness beyond. The temple loomed over them, shadows dancing at its threshold. He could feel the weight of its history pressing down on him, a sensation both compelling and terrifying. "We can't stay out here," he urged. "The echoes will find us if we linger too long."

Emma, standing a few paces behind, shifted nervously. "What if there's something worse inside? We've been through so much already. I don't want to risk it."

Wren stepped forward, his brow furrowing in thought. "We need to make a decision. This place could hold answers—or it could provide us the shelter we desperately need."

Adrian nodded, feeling the tension building among them. "But we can't let fear control us. We've fought too hard to back down now." He turned to the group, seeking to inspire courage in their hearts. "Whatever is inside, we face it together. That's the only way we'll survive."

Mia took a deep breath, glancing between Adrian and the temple's dark entrance. "If we go in, we stick together. No one gets left behind, no matter what happens."

"That's right," Adrian affirmed, determination flooding his voice. "We're in this together. We have to trust each other."

As they moved closer to the temple, Adrian could feel the atmosphere shift. The air was thick with anticipation, and a sense of foreboding settled over them. He reached for the heavy stone door, its surface cold and rough beneath his fingertips.

But just as he was about to push it open, he hesitated, his instincts flaring. "Wait," he said, glancing back at his friends. "Are we sure about this? We don't know what's waiting for us inside."

Wren looked at him, his eyes filled with a mix of fear and determination. "If we don't go in, we risk being caught outside by the echoes. They won't stop until they find us."

Adrian took a deep breath, his heart racing as he weighed their options. The temple was daunting, but staying outside was even more dangerous. He could feel the echoes drawing closer, their whispers slithering through the trees like a haunting melody.

"Alright," he said finally, pushing the doubt aside. "We go in. But we stick together, and we stay alert."

The group exchanged resolute nods, the shared determination uniting them as they approached the entrance once more.

"Let's do this," Mia said, her voice steadying with each passing moment.

Adrian pushed the door open with a deep groan, the heavy stone moving reluctantly. A rush of cool air met them as they stepped inside, darkness enveloping them like a shroud. The scent of ancient stone and damp earth filled their nostrils, and the sound of their footsteps echoed eerily in the silence.

As they crossed the threshold, a sense of unease settled within the temple's walls, wrapping around them like a warning. The shadows danced in the corners, and the distant sound of dripping water echoed through the vast chamber.

"Stay close," Adrian urged, his voice low and steady as he peered into the darkness. They moved as one, their hearts pounding in unison as they ventured deeper into the ancient structure.

The air grew heavier, charged with an energy that sent shivers down their spines. Each step felt like a journey into the unknown, and as they moved further into the temple, the darkness threatened to swallow them whole.

But even as uncertainty clung to them, Adrian felt a flicker of hope. Perhaps within these ancient stones lay the key to their survival, a way to overcome the darkness of the island that threatened to consume them.

They had come this far together, and they would face whatever awaited them inside the temple as a united front. The battle against the echoes was far from over, but perhaps within these ancient walls, they would find the strength to continue the fight.

As they stepped inside the ancient temple, the atmosphere shifted dramatically, the cool air wrapping around them like a damp embrace. The light from the entrance quickly faded, leaving them surrounded by shadows that danced eerily across the stone walls. The air felt thick with age and mystery, each breath heavy with the scent of damp earth and stone.

"Stay close," Adrian whispered, his voice barely cutting through the oppressive silence. They moved deeper into the chamber, the darkness gradually revealing more of their surroundings. The stone walls were intricately carved, adorned with strange symbols that glowed faintly, pulsing with a rhythmic energy as if they were alive.

Mia gasped, her eyes widening as she traced the patterns with her fingertips. "What are these?" she murmured, stepping closer to the wall. The symbols seemed to shimmer under her touch, revealing subtle hues of blue and green that intertwined like a living tapestry.

Adrian moved closer, his breath catching as he recognized some of the shapes. "These aren't just random markings," he said, intrigued. "They seem to tell a story."

The first symbol depicted a spiral entwined with a serpent, its body coiling tightly around itself. This emblem exuded a sense of renewal and eternity, as if it represented the cycle of life, death, and rebirth.

"The serpent," Wren said thoughtfully, "it could symbolize knowledge or transformation. In many cultures, serpents are seen as guardians of wisdom."

Further along the wall, another symbol caught Adrian's eye. It was a series of interlocking triangles, forming a star-like shape at the center. This symbol radiated a feeling of balance, representing the union of opposing forces—light and dark, earth and sky. It seemed to pulse with energy, drawing their gaze in an almost hypnotic fashion.

"What do you think it means?" Emma asked, her curiosity piqued as she leaned closer to the symbol.

"Perhaps it signifies harmony," Adrian replied. "Or a call to find balance in our struggles."

Nearby, a series of curved lines flowed like water, interspersed with small circles that resembled ripples. This symbol, almost fluid in nature, seemed to represent movement and change. "This one feels dynamic," Mia said, her voice filled with awe. "Like it's reminding us that everything is in constant flux."

Adrian nodded, the pieces of the puzzle beginning to fit together in his mind. "The echoes are trying to pull us down, to drown us in despair," he said, looking at his friends. "But these symbols—they seem to suggest that we can rise above it. That we can find a way to navigate through the darkness."

As they continued exploring the symbols, they came across a large, circular emblem etched into the floor at the center of the chamber. This symbol was unlike the others—a depiction of a radiant sun surrounded by twelve smaller celestial bodies, each representing the phases of the moon. The sunlight and moonlight intertwined within the design, radiating warmth and illuminating the cold stone around it.

"This is incredible," Wren breathed, kneeling to examine it closely. "It's almost like a cosmic map."

Adrian felt a sense of wonder as he looked at the symbol, the intertwining celestial bodies reflecting the duality of light and dark, hope and despair. "This could be a key to understanding the island," he said. "Perhaps it holds the answers we've been searching for."

"What if we could harness this power?" Mia suggested, her eyes shining with excitement. "What if these symbols are a way to protect ourselves from the echoes?"

Emma nodded, her expression determined. "We have to decipher them. There must be something here that can help us break free from this place."

Suddenly, the ground trembled beneath their feet, the vibrations resonating through the air like a distant warning. Adrian's heart raced as he looked around, sensing an unseen presence lurking just outside their line of sight. The symbols on the walls pulsed in response, their light flickering ominously.

"We need to hurry," he said, urgency creeping into his voice. "Whatever is protecting this temple might not hold for long."

They gathered around the central symbol, their hearts pounding as they placed their hands on its surface. The moment they touched it, a surge of energy coursed through them—a warm, enveloping light that connected them in a shared purpose.

Adrian felt the whispers of the echoes receding, the darkness lingering at the edges of the temple like a ghostly memory. "This is it," he whispered, a spark of hope igniting within him. "This is our chance."

But before they could gather their thoughts, a low growl echoed from the entrance, sending a shiver down Adrian's spine. The echoes were drawing near, and the temple's protective energy was wavering.

"Let's find out what these symbols mean, and quickly!" Adrian urged, desperation lacing his words.

They began to examine the symbols further, hoping to unlock their secrets before the darkness overwhelmed them completely. Each symbol held the potential for understanding, a pathway toward harnessing the strength they needed to escape the island's clutches.

But the tension in the air was palpable, and the shadows were creeping closer. They knew they had little time left to decipher the mysteries of the temple before the echoes descended upon them once again.

As they focused on the symbols, the air crackled with energy, anticipation mingling with dread. They could feel the weight of their situation bearing down on them, the echoes on their heels.

Adrian's heart raced as he prepared to delve deeper into the ancient knowledge that surrounded them. The battle was far from over, and the echoes were waiting for their moment to strike. They had to act fast.

And so, they stood united before the ancient symbols, a flicker of hope in the face of impending darkness, ready to unravel the secrets that could lead them to salvation.

After the first symbol, a **serpent entwined with a spiral**, coiled around itself, its scales glistening faintly in the low light. Nearby, a series of **interlocking triangles** formed a star-like shape, their sharp edges casting shadows that seemed to flicker with a life of their own. The next symbol caught their attention—a fluid design of curved lines and small circles, flowing like water, each circle appearing like ripples expanding outward. In the center of the room, a large, circular emblem depicted a **radiant sun surrounded by twelve smaller celestial bodies**, each representing phases of the moon, all woven into a cosmic tapestry.

Adrian felt his pulse quicken as he took in another symbol—a **double helix intertwining with a pair of wings**, its design both complex and captivating. The last symbol they noticed was **an ancient key, half-buried under layers of dust**, its intricate teeth and guard suggesting that it held the secrets to something monumental.

The air around them seemed to vibrate with potential, but the meanings of these symbols eluded them, wrapping them in a shroud of uncertainty.

As they stood in awe, the shadows danced along the stone walls, and the whispers of the echoes outside grew louder. Time was slipping away, but the symbols held the promise of knowledge, their meanings tantalizingly just out of reach.

Adrian exchanged glances with his friends, the weight of their predicament pressing down on them as they contemplated their next move. The enigmatic symbols loomed before them like silent sentinels, each one a cryptic puzzle waiting to be deciphered. The air was heavy with mystery, and the shadows danced along the stone walls, adding an eerie ambiance that made every whisper feel amplified.

"What do you think they mean?" Mia asked, breaking the silence that hung in the air like a thick fog. She brushed her fingers lightly over the surface of the serpent and spiral symbol, feeling the grooves beneath her touch. "They all seem so... connected, yet I can't make sense of it."

Adrian, still trying to catch his breath from their earlier escape, stepped closer to the symbols, his brow furrowed in thought. "I don't know," he admitted, glancing at the interlocking triangles. "They seem to tell a story, but the meaning isn't clear." He could feel a flicker of frustration rising within him. They had faced so much, and now they stood in front of what could be their salvation, yet the knowledge remained tantalizingly out of reach.

"Maybe it's a map," Wren suggested, his eyes narrowing as he focused on the circular emblem depicting the radiant sun and the celestial bodies. "The sun and moons are often used in navigation, right? It could be a way to find our path."

Emma crossed her arms, her expression skeptical. "But to what? The island? Or somewhere else? If we don't know what these symbols are guiding us to, how can we trust them?"

"They might be connected to the echoes," Adrian chimed in, trying to keep the conversation constructive. "What if they hold the key to understanding what we're up against? The serpent, for instance—it could symbolize something like knowledge or transformation, as Wren said earlier."

"Or perhaps danger," Mia interjected, her eyes reflecting the uncertainty of the moment. "After all, snakes are often associated with treachery in folklore. What if it's warning us against something?"

"Maybe," Wren said thoughtfully, "but we can't just assume the worst. Look at this one—the double helix intertwined with wings. That could represent growth and freedom, right? It could be saying we have the power to break free from whatever binds us here."

"That's a hopeful interpretation," Emma replied, her skepticism softening slightly. "But hope won't save us if we misinterpret these symbols. We have to think about the possibility that they could also be traps. Ancient defenses left behind to deter those who seek to unlock their secrets."

Adrian nodded, feeling the weight of responsibility settle on his shoulders. "We have to approach this carefully. If we dive in headfirst without understanding what we're dealing with, we might end up worse off."

"What about the key?" Mia pointed to the ancient key half-buried in dust. "It looks significant. It has to mean something."

Adrian knelt down, brushing away the dust to get a better look at the key's intricate design. "It does look important. Perhaps it's meant to unlock something within this temple? Or maybe it's a metaphorical key—something we need to figure out to unlock our own potential."

"What if it's a key to open our minds?" Wren suggested, his eyes brightening with excitement. "Maybe we're meant to interpret these symbols in a way that helps us understand our own journey, our own fears."

Mia considered this for a moment, her brow furrowed in concentration. "That makes sense. Each of us has faced different fears on this island, and we've come together to fight them. What if these symbols reflect that journey? Our struggles, our victories, and the wisdom we gain along the way?"

Adrian looked up at his friends, feeling a surge of determination. "We can't let fear dictate our actions. We need to embrace the unknown. The island may be dark, but we have each other. And if these symbols can guide us, we'll find a way to harness their power."

Emma nodded slowly, a spark of hope igniting in her eyes. "So, what do we do next? Do we try to decode the symbols, or is there something else we should focus on first?"

Adrian thought for a moment, looking at the ancient symbols once more. "We can't just guess. We need to study them, see if there's a pattern or something that connects them. Maybe we can find a common thread that leads us to their meaning."

"Or a way to make them work for us," Wren added, standing up and glancing at the entrance. "But we should also keep an eye on the outside. We don't know if the echoes will follow us in here."

With renewed determination, they began to study the symbols more closely, their fingers tracing the intricate designs as they exchanged ideas. The atmosphere grew charged with energy as they delved deeper into the mystery.

"I wonder if we can make a connection between the symbols," Mia said, stepping back to take a broader view of the wall. "Look at the way the spiral and the serpent intersect. It's almost like they're intertwined. What if they represent different stages of our journey?"

"Like how we grow and evolve through each challenge?" Adrian suggested, stepping closer. "Yes! That could make sense! The more we learn, the stronger we become."

"And that growth comes with pain," Emma added, a hint of sadness creeping into her voice. "Every time we face a challenge, we bear scars. But we also gain wisdom."

They all fell silent for a moment, contemplating the weight of Emma's words. The shadows around them felt heavier, but within that heaviness was a profound sense of understanding. They had faced pain and loss, and it was their collective strength that had brought them this far.

"What about the celestial bodies?" Wren pointed at the sun and moons in the central emblem. "They could signify the balance of light and dark. They are both crucial to our survival, just as we have to embrace both hope and fear."

"That balance is so important," Mia replied, her voice tinged with awe. "Without light, we can't see. Without darkness, we can't appreciate the light. It's a cycle."

Adrian nodded, feeling a sense of clarity settling within him. "If we can harness that balance, we might find a way to overcome the darkness of the island and the echoes that threaten us."

As they continued to discuss the symbols, the urgency of their situation began to settle back into their minds. Adrian's heart raced as he remembered the echoes lurking just outside. "We can't lose track of time," he said, glancing toward the entrance. "We have to decide what to do, and quickly."

Mia stepped closer to the entrance, peering out into the dense foliage. "It's quiet for now," she said, her voice tinged with uncertainty. "But that doesn't mean they won't come looking for us."

"Then we need to prepare ourselves," Wren said firmly. "If we're going to face the echoes again, we need to be armed with the knowledge we've gained here."

Adrian felt a surge of determination. "We'll use what we've learned from these symbols to give us strength. They can guide us in our next steps."

Mia nodded, her face resolute. "Then let's gather everything we've discussed and create a plan. We can't just leave this temple without harnessing its knowledge."

As they rallied together, sharing thoughts and ideas, the sense of urgency transformed into something powerful—an unwavering resolve to uncover the truth behind the ancient symbols and harness their power.

The temple felt like a living entity, its walls imbued with the energy of their collective determination. They could feel it pulsing around them, encouraging them to push forward, to find the answers that lay hidden within its depths.

"Okay," Adrian said, standing tall as he faced his friends. "We'll study the symbols, find their connections, and use that knowledge to strengthen our resolve. But we have to remain vigilant."

Just as he spoke, a low rumble echoed through the temple, sending a shiver down Adrian's spine. The ground trembled beneath their feet, and the air grew heavy with tension.

"What was that?" Emma whispered, her eyes wide with alarm.

Adrian glanced toward the entrance, the sense of impending danger creeping back in. "I don't know, but we need to stay alert. We can't let our guard down, not now."

They exchanged anxious glances, and in that moment, the weight of their decision settled heavily upon them. Whatever lay ahead, they would face it together, armed with the knowledge they hoped to gain from the symbols and the strength of their unbreakable bond.

With a final nod of determination, they stepped deeper into the heart of the temple, ready to uncover the secrets it held and face the darkness that awaited them beyond its walls.

As they ventured deeper into the temple, the atmosphere grew increasingly oppressive, the air thick with a sense of foreboding. The flickering shadows cast by their movements seemed to stretch and twist, creating the illusion of lurking figures in the corners of their vision. The further they went, the more the stone walls began to close in on them, as if the temple itself was alive, watching their every move.

"Do you feel that?" Mia whispered, glancing around nervously. "It's like the air is charged with something."

"Yeah," Adrian replied, his heart racing as they pressed on. "It's almost like the temple is responding to us." He glanced at Wren, who was scanning the space ahead, a furrow of concern etched across his brow. "We need to stay sharp. There's no telling what we might encounter in here."

Suddenly, as they rounded a corner, the narrow passage opened into a vast chamber. The sight that greeted them took their breath away—a massive sculpture loomed in the center of the room, dominating the space with its formidable presence. The stone figure depicted a grotesque demon, its features twisted in a permanent snarl, eyes carved deep into the stone that seemed to gleam with an otherworldly light.

"By the gods..." Emma breathed, her voice barely above a whisper as she stepped forward, drawn to the figure. "What is that?"

"It looks ancient," Wren said, his voice laced with both awe and fear. "But it feels alive somehow."

Adrian felt a chill creep up his spine as he approached the sculpture. "It's terrifying," he murmured, the weight of its gaze feeling almost suffocating. The demon's wings were spread wide, intricately detailed and appearing as if they might take flight at any moment. Its claws were poised as though ready to strike, and the jagged teeth of its maw were a stark reminder of the danger they faced.

"What do you think it represents?" Mia asked, her eyes wide with a mixture of fear and fascination.

"Maybe it's a guardian of sorts," Wren suggested, stepping closer to inspect the base of the statue. "Or a warning. Something that symbolizes the darkness we're up against."

Adrian nodded, his gaze locked on the demon's piercing eyes. "It could be a representation of the echoes—the embodiment of the fear and despair we're fighting against." He took a step back, glancing around the chamber for any other symbols or inscriptions that might provide context. "We need to be careful. If this temple is meant to protect us, we don't want to provoke whatever this is."

Emma approached the statue cautiously, her fingers brushing against the rough stone surface. "It's so detailed," she marveled. "It's like they captured its essence. But it's unsettling... I can almost feel its anger."

"Maybe it's just a statue," Wren said, trying to ease the tension in the air. "It can't hurt us, right? Unless... unless this place has some kind of magic."

"Don't say that," Mia replied, her voice tight. "We don't know what this temple is capable of. We've seen too much already."

Adrian stepped forward, his determination rising. "We need to find out if there's anything here that can help us. Look for inscriptions or anything that might provide answers."

As they spread out around the chamber, Adrian couldn't shake the feeling of being watched. The demon's eyes seemed to follow him as he moved, and an unsettling energy crackled in the air.

"Over here!" Emma called, drawing their attention to a series of carvings etched into the wall beside the statue. They depicted scenes of battle, warriors clashing with shadowy figures that resembled the echoes.

Adrian approached, his heart racing as he examined the images. "These must be stories of the past," he said, tracing the carvings with his fingers. "Perhaps they can teach us something."

Mia joined him, her eyes scanning the wall. "Look at this one," she said, pointing to a depiction of a warrior standing strong against a wave of shadows. "It looks like he's holding something—maybe a weapon?"

"Or a shield," Wren added, stepping closer. "That could symbolize protection against the darkness."

As they studied the wall, Adrian felt a sense of urgency building within him. "Whatever we do, we need to be careful. If this demon statue is indeed a guardian, it might react to our presence."

Just as he spoke, a low rumble echoed through the chamber, shaking the ground beneath them. Adrian's heart raced as he looked up, fear coursing through his veins. The eyes of the demon sculpture seemed to glow brighter, the shadows around it shifting and swirling as if animated by some unseen force.

"Everyone, step back!" Adrian shouted, instinctively moving to shield his friends. The atmosphere grew tense, electricity crackling in the air, as the demon statue began to shift.

"What's happening?" Mia gasped, her eyes wide with fear.

"I don't know!" Adrian shouted over the rumbling noise that filled the chamber. The ground shook again, and the statue's stone form began to crack, deep fissures forming along its surface.

"No! This can't be happening!" Emma exclaimed, taking a step back, panic flashing in her eyes.

"Stay together!" Wren urged, reaching for Mia's arm. "We have to be ready for anything!"

Just then, the demon's mouth opened wide, revealing a dark abyss within—a portal to the unknown. From within the depths of that void, shadows began to swirl, taking shape and coalescing into familiar forms.

"Adrian!" Mia shouted, her voice tinged with panic. "What do we do?"

He felt a surge of fear grip his heart as he realized the shadows were echoing back, not just their fears but also their past. "We can't let them take us!" he shouted, rallying his friends. "We need to stay strong!"

The shadows surged forward, darting toward them like a tidal wave of darkness. Adrian braced himself, instinctively stepping forward, determined to protect his friends.

"Face them!" he shouted, heart pounding as he prepared for the onslaught. "We've come too far to turn back now!"

But as the shadows closed in, a realization washed over him. The statue and the symbols—they were a test, a challenge meant to force them to confront their deepest fears. And if they could withstand this moment, they could harness the power within the temple to defeat the echoes once and for all.

"Don't look away!" he yelled, focusing on the swirling shadows. "We're not afraid! We will not be consumed by you!"

The echoes paused, seemingly caught off guard by Adrian's defiance. In that moment, the demon's eyes glowed brighter, a fiery light illuminating the chamber as if the ancient being was awakened from its slumber.

Adrian turned to his friends, the determination in his voice rising. "Together! We can break through this darkness!"

Just then, the shadows lunged, and chaos erupted in the chamber. The echoes swirled around them, their cold fingers reaching out, but Adrian and his friends stood firm, channeling the energy of the ancient symbols, ready to confront the darkness that threatened to consume them.

As the shadows swirled and the temple shook, a deep, resonant growl emanated from the mouth of the demon sculpture. The stone began to crack and crumble, pieces of debris falling away to reveal a twisted, grotesque face lurking behind the stone façade.

Adrian's heart raced as he watched, his breath quickening in his chest. "What is happening?" he gasped, stepping back instinctively as the demon's features became clearer, its jagged teeth bared in a sinister grin. The glow of its eyes intensified, radiating a malevolent light that pierced the dimness of the temple.

Mia's hand flew to her mouth, stifling a gasp. "This can't be real!" she whispered, her voice shaking. The sight was horrifying—a blend of nightmare and reality, the demon's visage both captivating and repulsive.

Emma trembled beside her, her eyes wide with terror. "It's alive! It's actually alive!" she exclaimed, backing away slowly, the primal instinct to flee clawing at her mind.

Wren felt his stomach churn as he stared at the demon's face, now fully revealed. Its skin was a mottled gray, resembling cracked stone, and deep grooves ran along its cheeks like the ravines of a desolate landscape. "We need to get out of here!" he shouted, but his voice was nearly drowned out by the roar of the awakening creature.

The demon's eyes locked onto Adrian, a predatory glint in its gaze that sent a jolt of fear through him. "You dare trespass in my domain?" it hissed, the voice like grinding stone and crackling flames. "You who would seek to unravel the secrets of the ancients?"

Adrian's heart pounded in his chest, his body frozen in place as terror coursed through him. He could feel his limbs shaking uncontrollably, the weight of fear pressing down like an oppressive shroud. "We didn't mean any harm!" he managed to stammer, trying to regain his composure. "We just want to survive!"

The demon's laughter reverberated through the chamber, a low, rumbling sound that echoed ominously. "Survive? You think you can escape the shadows? I am the embodiment of the darkness you fear!" It leaned closer, its grotesque features contorting in a horrifying display of power.

Mia shivered, stepping back further. "We have to go! We can't fight this!" she cried, glancing desperately toward the exit.

But the way out was now shrouded in darkness, the shadows closing in around them, as if the very temple itself conspired against them.

Emma trembled at the sight of the demon's fearsome grin, the sharp teeth glinting in the dim light. "It's not just a statue anymore," she whispered, her voice barely audible. "It wants to eat us."

Adrian felt the weight of dread settle in his stomach, and he swallowed hard, forcing himself to stand tall despite the overwhelming fear that threatened to engulf him. "We have to face it! We can't let it intimidate us!"

But as the demon loomed larger, its presence oppressive, doubt crept into his mind. The air grew heavy with tension, each heartbeat a reminder of the danger that surrounded them. They were trapped in this ancient temple, and the terrifying reality of their situation began to sink in.

"Stay together!" Wren shouted, though even his voice wavered as he took a step back. "We can't let it divide us!"

Adrian felt his resolve falter as the demon's face twisted in a sinister smirk, the eyes gleaming with malice. "You think you can defy me?" it taunted, its voice echoing ominously. "I will devour your fears, your hopes—your very essence!"

The chamber trembled again, and Adrian could feel the ground beneath him shift. Panic surged within him, threatening to overwhelm his senses. He glanced at his friends, their faces pale with fear, and a cold sweat broke out across his forehead.

"Is this it?" he thought, dread creeping into his heart. "Is this how it ends?"

The demon's gaze intensified, a malevolent force that seemed to penetrate deep into their souls. Adrian shivered, his courage wavering in the face of such darkness. The memories of their struggles flashed before him—each challenge, each battle against the echoes—and he felt the weight of it all crashing down.

With the demon now fully alive and looming before them, they were left standing in the darkness of the temple, feeling the icy grip of fear tighten around them, the walls closing in as the shadows danced hungrily.

As the demon loomed over them, its terrifying features becoming ever more pronounced, a sudden shift occurred in the air around the chamber. The atmosphere crackled with energy, and a low hum reverberated through the walls, sending shivers down Adrian's spine.

"Look!" Mia gasped, pointing behind the demon. The large, gaping mouth of the statue, which had previously been a silent observer, now appeared to pulsate with an eerie light. From within the depths of that shadowy void, the portal they had seen earlier in the island, began to materialize, glowing with a brilliant, ethereal energy.

"What is happening?" Wren shouted, his voice strained with confusion. "Why is the portal activating here and now?"

Adrian's heart raced as he turned to face the swirling vortex. The soft, beckoning light contrasted sharply against the dark menace of the demon. "It looks like it's being drawn to the demon," he said, the realization sending chills through him. "But why?"

The demon turned its attention toward the portal, its eyes narrowing as the light intensified. "Foolish mortals!" it bellowed, its voice a mix of rage and amusement. "You think you can escape through that portal? It is merely a passage to greater darkness!"

The whispers of fear began to fill the air, echoing the very sentiments of the demon. Adrian felt his resolve start to waver as the portal flickered enticingly, promising an escape from the horrors before them. "We need to make a choice," he said, his voice steady despite the turmoil within. "Do we try to confront the demon, or do we take the chance and enter the portal?"

"What if it's a trap?" Emma replied, her eyes wide with uncertainty. "What if the portal leads to something worse?"

"It could be a chance to escape," Wren countered, glancing between the demon and the portal. "We can't fight this creature without knowing what it's capable of. The portal could lead us to safety."

Mia shook her head, fear etched across her face. "But what if it's worse? We've seen so much already. What if we're running into a trap?"

Adrian felt the weight of their indecision pressing down on him. The demon watched them with a sinister grin, clearly reveling in their uncertainty. "Make your choice, mortals!" it taunted, its voice laced with mockery. "Choose wisely, for time is running out!"

The portal flickered again, casting shifting patterns of light against the stone walls. Adrian could feel the pull of the unknown, a tantalizing whisper that urged him to take that leap of faith. "What if the portal holds the answers we need?" he said, trying to rally their spirits. "What if it leads us to the knowledge we've been searching for? We've come this far—we can't let fear dictate our choices!"

Wren stepped closer to the portal, his expression a mix of determination and fear. "I think we should go for it," he said, looking back at the group. "We've faced the darkness together, and if we're going to keep fighting, we need to take risks. We can't let the demon control our fate."

Adrian could see the conflict in Mia's eyes, the fear battling against the hope of escape. "But what if it's too dangerous? What if we're not ready?" she pleaded.

"Sometimes, we have to face the danger head-on," Wren replied, his voice steady. "We can't let fear paralyze us. The portal may be our only chance to turn the tide against the echoes and whatever this demon represents."

Emma took a deep breath, her gaze shifting between the demon and the glowing portal. "I trust you all," she said, her voice firm despite her trembling hands. "If we decide to go through, we do it together. We face whatever is on the other side as one."

Adrian felt a surge of courage wash over him at her words. "Together," he echoed, glancing at each of his friends. "We can do this. We can't let the darkness define our fate."

Just then, the demon roared in frustration, its form shifting ominously as it blocked their view of the portal. "You cannot escape!" it thundered, the ground trembling beneath their feet. "You will face your fears here, in my domain!"

The air grew thick with tension, and Adrian felt his heart pound in his chest. The choice lay before them, the portal shimmering with possibility, yet the demon stood as a towering wall of darkness, a reminder of the very fears they were trying to escape.

"Now!" Adrian shouted, his instincts kicking in as he turned toward the portal. "We need to go! If we hesitate, we'll lose our chance!"

Mia hesitated, glancing back at the demon. "What if we get separated?" she asked, fear creeping into her voice.

"We won't!" Wren replied urgently, reaching for her hand. "Just hold on tight!"

Adrian grasped Emma's hand, and they formed a tight circle, feeling the warmth of each other's presence as they faced the portal. "On three," he said, glancing at each of his friends, their eyes reflecting a mix of determination and trepidation. "One... two... three!"

With a shared cry, they leaped toward the portal, the swirling light engulfing them as they crossed the threshold. For a brief moment, they were suspended in a realm of brilliant color and blinding light, the sensation of weightlessness surrounding them.

But as quickly as it began, the brightness faded, and they found themselves tumbling through darkness, the sounds of the temple and the demon's furious roar fading away behind them.

As they stumbled through the swirling light of the portal, time seemed to stretch, bending reality around them. The blinding radiance began to fade, and slowly, they landed on solid ground, the impact jarring them as they struggled to regain their balance. As they had landed on soft grass, they felt cool and refreshing beneath their feet.

They took a moment to catch their breath, blinking against the remnants of the light as their surroundings came into focus. What lay before them was nothing short of breathtaking.

The sky above was an ethereal canvas, painted with swirling shades of blue and violet, reminiscent of a twilight that lingered just past dusk. Larger and brighter stars twinkled overhead, their light shimmering like diamonds scattered across velvet. Some were clustered tightly together, forming shapes that felt both familiar and alien, while others hung solitary, casting a gentle glow on the landscape below.

Adrian gasped, his eyes wide with wonder. "Look at the stars," he whispered, captivated by their brilliance. "I've never seen anything like this."

Mia stood beside him, her expression mirroring his awe. "It's beautiful," she breathed, the colors above seeming to dance and pulse in harmony with the soft wind that brushed against their skin. "It's like we've stepped into a dream."

Wren, shaking off the disorientation of their travel, gazed around, taking in the vast expanse that stretched before them. The ground beneath their feet was lush and vibrant, with tall grasses swaying gently, creating a soothing rustling sound. Distant hills rolled gently in the landscape, dotted with luminescent flowers that glowed with an inner light, casting a surreal illumination across the scene.

"Is this real?" Emma asked, her voice filled with a mixture of disbelief and hope. She stepped forward, reaching out to touch a nearby flower. Its petals were soft, a vivid blend of turquoise and lilac, and it pulsed faintly, as if responding to her touch.

Adrian felt a sense of exhilaration surge within him, the weight of their previous struggles momentarily forgotten. "It has to be real.

We came through the portal, and this is what we found." He stepped closer to the hilltop, eager to see more of this enchanting world.

As they ventured further, the sky deepened in color, the hues of blue and purple mixing like an artist's palette. Stars began to twinkle even brighter, creating constellations that sparkled like a forgotten language waiting to be deciphered. It felt as if they had entered a realm untouched by darkness, a sanctuary far removed from the horrors of the island they had just escaped.

"Do you think we're safe here?" Mia asked, glancing at the vastness around them. There was a glimmer of hope in her voice, but also a trace of caution.

"I don't know," Adrian admitted, his gaze fixed on the horizon, where the land met the sky in a seamless blend of color. "But it feels different. This place... it feels alive in a way that I can't explain."

The gentle breeze carried with it the sweet scent of blooming flowers, mingled with a refreshing coolness that wrapped around them like a comforting embrace. As they walked further into this new world, a sense of peace settled within their hearts, a stark contrast to the chaos they had left behind.

"Look!" Emma exclaimed, pointing toward the distant hills. "What is that?"

In the far distance, nestled between the hills, they could see what appeared to be a structure—tall and majestic, catching the light of the stars. Its architecture was unlike anything they had ever seen, with sweeping arches and intricate designs that shimmered in the twilight. It stood proudly against the vibrant sky, an invitation to explore further.

"Should we go check it out?" Wren suggested, his voice filled with excitement and curiosity.

Adrian nodded, feeling a rush of adrenaline. "Absolutely. This place could hold answers—or at least more wonders."

As they made their way toward the distant structure, the stars above seemed to guide them, illuminating their path. Each step felt lighter, the burdens they had carried slowly lifting as the beauty of this new world enveloped them.

"Whatever happens next, we're in this together," Adrian declared, determination igniting in his chest.

They walked in silence, allowing the sights and sounds of this breathtaking realm to wash over them. The air was filled with the soft hum of nature, a symphony of rustling leaves and distant echoes of creatures unknown.

Adrian felt a flicker of hope blossom within him, the idea that perhaps they had found not just a refuge, but a new beginning. A place where the darkness could not follow.

The journey through the portal had brought them to this magical world, and as they approached the magnificent structure, Adrian couldn't help but wonder what secrets awaited them within. The vibrant sky seemed to pulse in rhythm with their heartbeats, an invitation to embrace whatever lay ahead.

Then, something staggering emerged before them, shimmering with an otherworldly glow that sent chills down their spines. The air crackled with energy, and an unspoken understanding passed among them, igniting a fire of curiosity and apprehension. Without exchanging a word, the four of them instinctively stepped forward, their hearts racing in synchrony, each pulse echoing their shared anticipation of the unknown.

As they approached the majestic structure nestled between the hills, the air buzzed with a mixture of excitement and anxiety. The vibrant colors of the sky illuminated their path, but an undercurrent of dread pulsed through the group, reminding them of the dangers they had narrowly escaped.

"Do you think the echoes followed us through the portal?" Mia asked, her voice barely above a whisper. She glanced over her shoulder, as if expecting to see the familiar, haunting forms emerging from the shadows.

Adrian paused, feeling a knot form in his stomach. "I don't know," he admitted, his brow furrowing. "But if they could, they likely would. The echoes thrive on fear, and we've given them plenty to latch onto."

Wren frowned, considering the implications. "That means we're not safe here," he said grimly. "Even if this place feels different, we could still be vulnerable. The demon's voice, the way it taunted us... it felt personal. Almost like it was aware of us, of our journey."

Emma shivered at the thought, her gaze drifting back to the glowing portal. "What if the echoes are connected to the demon? What if they serve it in some way? They could follow us through the portal, drawn by our fear or by a dark bond that ties them to that thing."

"That's a terrifying thought," Mia replied, her voice laced with apprehension. "If they can track us across dimensions, we might never be truly free. We thought we escaped, but what if we only traded one nightmare for another?"

Adrian shook his head, pushing back against the rising tide of despair. "No, we have to stay focused. We can't let fear dictate our actions. This place may hold the key to understanding what's happening, why the echoes are pursuing us, and how to defeat them."

"But how do we figure that out?" Wren asked, his gaze turning to the enigmatic structure that loomed ahead. "We don't even know what we're dealing with yet. The last thing we want is to walk into another trap."

The group fell silent, each of them lost in thought as they approached the base of the ancient building. The intricate designs adorning the stone walls seemed to whisper secrets, drawing them closer despite their hesitation.

Adrian looked up, studying the structure's towering spires and sweeping arches. "Maybe this place has answers," he said, his voice steadying with conviction. "We just have to be cautious."

As they reached the entrance, a heavy wooden door stood before them, adorned with carvings that mirrored the symbols they had seen in the temple. The air felt charged with energy, and Adrian could sense the anticipation bubbling within his friends.

"What if it's a sanctuary?" Emma suggested, her eyes scanning the entrance. "What if it protects us from the echoes and the demon? Maybe it's a place of knowledge, a way to break free from this cycle of fear."

"That would be ideal," Wren replied, glancing at Adrian. "But we can't assume that. We need to go in prepared, ready for anything."

Adrian nodded, feeling the weight of their situation pressing down on him. "Alright, let's stick together and proceed with caution. If the echoes are here, we need to be vigilant."

With a collective breath, they pushed the heavy door open, its creaking hinges echoing through the vast chamber inside. The moment they stepped across the threshold, the atmosphere shifted, the warmth of the outside world giving way to a cooler, more subdued ambiance.

Inside, the space was expansive, with high ceilings adorned with intricate carvings that seemed to tell stories of their own. Soft, ethereal light illuminated the room, casting gentle shadows that danced along the walls.

"Wow," Mia whispered, her eyes wide as she took in the sights. "This is incredible. It feels... sacred."

Adrian stepped further into the chamber, his gaze roaming over the shelves lined with ancient tomes and artifacts, each one whispering secrets of a time long past. "We have to look for anything that can help us understand the connection between the echoes and the demon," he said, feeling a sense of urgency.

Wren wandered toward a large stone pedestal in the center of the room, where a glowing orb pulsed gently, radiating warmth and light. "What is this?" he murmured, reaching out tentatively.

"Be careful!" Emma warned, her eyes darting around as if expecting something to leap out at them. "We don't know what it does!"

Adrian moved closer, squinting at the orb. "It looks like it could be some sort of power source or artifact," he suggested, feeling the energy emanating from it. "It might be connected to the temple or the symbols we saw."

The air hummed with potential, and as Adrian reached out to touch the orb, a sudden wave of energy surged through the room, making the hairs on his arms stand on end. The orb flared brightly, and for a moment, the world around them dissolved into blinding light.

"Adrian!" Mia shouted, reaching out as the light enveloped him.

He felt a rush of memories flood his mind—visions of battles fought, echoes haunting their steps, and the demon looming in the shadows. The weight of his fears and the pain of their journey pressed in on him, threatening to crush him under the weight of despair.

But then, as quickly as it began, the visions faded, and Adrian found himself standing before the glowing orb, a sense of clarity washing over him. "We need to harness this energy," he said, his voice steady. "If we can connect with it, we might find a way to understand what we're facing."

"I feel it too," Wren replied, stepping back from the pedestal. "There's something about this place—something powerful. It could help us confront the echoes and the demon."

"But how do we use it?" Emma asked, glancing at the orb with a mixture of awe and fear.

Adrian thought for a moment, piecing together their experiences. "The symbols... they're not just warnings. They're a map, a guide to understanding this power. If we can decipher them, we might unlock whatever this orb is meant to do."

"Then we need to figure out what the symbols mean and how they connect to the orb," Mia said, her voice filled with determination. "We can't let the echoes and the demon win."

The tension in the air shifted slightly, a sense of purpose taking hold. They were no longer just survivors—they were a team united against the darkness that threatened to consume them.

With renewed resolve, they gathered around the orb, the flickering light illuminating their faces as they prepared to unravel the mysteries that lay ahead.

But as they stood there, the shadows outside the temple seemed to shift, and Adrian couldn't shake the feeling that the echoes were still lingering nearby, waiting for the right moment to strike.

As they gathered around the glowing orb, the anticipation of discovery filled the air. Yet, as the moments stretched on, the intricacy of the symbols etched in the walls began to feel overwhelming. The once-enigmatic carvings turned into a labyrinth of shapes and lines, each one blending into the next, leaving them feeling confused rather than enlightened.

"This is harder than I thought," Mia sighed, her shoulders slumping as she ran a hand through her hair. She leaned against the pedestal, the warm glow of the orb casting soft light across her features. "How are we supposed to figure out what any of this means?"

Adrian nodded in agreement, his brow furrowing as he traced the outline of a symbol with his finger. "There are too many to decipher at once. I thought the energy from the orb might help us connect the dots, but..." He trailed off, the words falling flat. The excitement that had once filled him began to wane, replaced by a creeping sense of boredom.

Wren stepped back, taking a deep breath as he surveyed the vast chamber. "Maybe we need to take a break," he suggested. "Our minds are racing too much. We won't be able to think clearly if we're exhausted."

Emma leaned against the wall, her gaze drifting to the ceiling where the intricate carvings danced in the shadows. "I agree," she said, her voice softening. "Let's rest for a bit. We've been through so much already."

Adrian glanced around at his friends, recognizing the fatigue in their eyes. They had faced countless trials, fought against the darkness of the echoes and the demon, and now, even in this breathtaking new world, the weight of it all felt heavy. "Alright," he said, trying to infuse his voice with optimism. "Let's take a moment to gather our thoughts and recharge. We can come back to the symbols later."

The group settled down on the cool stone floor, the gentle warmth from the orb casting a comforting glow. Adrian leaned back against the pedestal, closing his eyes for a moment, trying to clear his mind. The sounds of the chamber—the soft hum of the orb and the distant rustling of leaves from outside—created a soothing atmosphere, allowing his thoughts to drift.

"Do you think we'll ever really escape the echoes?" Mia asked quietly, her voice breaking the tranquil silence.

Adrian opened his eyes, glancing at her. "I hope so," he replied. "But we have to keep pushing forward. We can't let fear dictate our choices."

Wren stretched out on the stone floor, letting out a long sigh. "Maybe we just need a change of perspective. We've been so focused on what's behind us that we've forgotten to look ahead."

Emma smiled faintly, trying to lighten the mood. "Well, at least we're not being chased by the echoes right now. That's a win, right?"

"True," Wren chuckled, his eyes sparkling with mischief. "And this place—whatever it is—feels different. It feels... safe, at least for the moment."

The words hung in the air, the concept of safety foreign yet comforting. Adrian let out a breath he didn't realize he was holding. "You're right. We've come far, and we're together. That has to mean something."

They settled into a comfortable silence, each lost in their thoughts. The warmth from the orb and the gentle ambiance of the chamber wrapped around them like a protective cocoon, soothing the weariness etched in their bones.

"Do you think the symbols are trying to tell us something specific?" Mia asked after a moment, her curiosity reigniting as she shifted her position. "Maybe they're not just warnings but a way to communicate with us?"

"I hope so," Adrian said, leaning forward slightly. "If we can understand them, we might find a way to use this place to our advantage. But we need to approach it with fresh minds."

"Maybe we should sketch them out," Wren suggested, sitting up. "Draw what we see, even if it's messy. Sometimes putting it on paper helps us visualize the connections."

"Good idea," Emma agreed, her eyes lighting up. "Let's do that after we rest a bit. A little downtime will help us think clearly."

As they relaxed, the atmosphere shifted slightly, their energy slowly replenishing. Outside, the stars continued to twinkle brightly against the backdrop of the vibrant sky, a reminder of the wonders that surrounded them.

"I wonder what lies beyond this temple," Mia mused, gazing into the depths of the chamber. "What other secrets does this world hold?"

"Let's not forget that whatever we find, we face it together," Adrian replied, his voice steady. "We've been through too much to let anything tear us apart now."

They each nodded, feeling a sense of unity strengthening among them, despite the fatigue that had settled in. After a while, Adrian couldn't help but feel a sense of optimism. Perhaps this new world held the answers they sought, and together, they would uncover the truth.

As the minutes passed, the room gradually filled with a sense of calm, their hearts slowly syncing with the rhythmic pulse of the orb. Whatever lay ahead, they would face it together, their bond unbreakable.

With that thought, Adrian closed his eyes again, allowing the warmth and peace of the chamber to wash over him, feeling hope swell in his chest.

As the gentle warmth of the orb enveloped the chamber, George sat against the cool stone wall, feeling the weight of exhaustion wash over him. He closed his eyes, surrendering to the tranquility of the moment, but as the darkness descended, the peaceful atmosphere quickly morphed into something sinister.

In his mind's eye, he found himself standing in a desolate landscape, where the sky was an oppressive gray, swirling with ominous clouds. The air was thick with a heavy mist that clung to the ground like a shroud, and a bone-chilling wind howled through the barren trees that surrounded him. It felt as if the very earth was alive with despair, and an overwhelming sense of dread settled in his chest.

"Where am I?" George whispered, but the words barely escaped his lips, swallowed by the encroaching darkness. As he took a hesitant step forward, the ground felt uneven beneath his feet, the cracked earth fissuring like an old wound. Shadows danced around him, flickering in and out of existence, whispering words he couldn't quite understand.

A sudden flash of movement caught his eye, and George spun around to find himself face-to-face with a grotesque figure emerging from the mist. Its body was twisted and contorted, a nightmarish reflection of humanity, with hollow eyes that glimmered with a malevolent light. The figure let out a low, guttural growl that echoed in the stillness, sending a jolt of fear racing through George's veins.

"Help me!" a voice cried, distant and distorted. George squinted into the shadows, straining to see the source of the plea. The mist swirled around him, revealing glimpses of familiar faces—his friends, trapped in a whirlwind of despair. They reached out to him, their expressions twisted with terror, but before he could respond, the figures dissolved into the fog, leaving him alone once more.

"No!" George shouted, panic surging within him. "I'm coming! I won't leave you!" But as he turned, the grotesque figure loomed closer, its mouth curling into a twisted grin. It raised a skeletal hand, pointing directly at him, and a wave of fear washed over George.

"You think you can save them?" the figure hissed, its voice dripping with malice. "You're too late. They are already lost!"

The shadows thickened around him, and George felt himself being pulled deeper into the nightmare. He stumbled back, trying to escape, but the ground shifted beneath his feet, swallowing him into a darkness that felt alive.

In the depths of that void, he was suddenly thrust into a series of fragmented images—each one a horrifying scene that tore at the fabric of his sanity. He saw the echoes again, their twisted faces bearing down on his friends, taunting and tormenting them. He watched helplessly as they were dragged into a realm of despair, their cries for help echoing in his ears.

"Stop! Let them go!" he screamed, but his voice was lost in the cacophony of shadows that enveloped him.

The nightmare shifted once more, and he found himself in a dimly lit corridor, the walls lined with grotesque paintings depicting scenes of terror—faces contorted in agony, lost souls trapped in a cycle of despair. Each image felt like a dagger to his heart, and George staggered backward, his breath coming in ragged gasps.

Suddenly, he heard footsteps echoing behind him. He turned, heart racing, and came face to face with a reflection of himself, but twisted and monstrous. The doppelgänger grinned, its eyes glinting with malevolence. "You think you can escape your fate?" it taunted, stepping closer. "You are just like them—lost, powerless, a prisoner of your own fears."

"Get away from me!" George shouted, but the figure lunged forward, and he felt a cold hand grip his throat, choking off his breath. He clawed at its fingers, panic surging through him as darkness closed in.

"Embrace the darkness," the figure hissed, its voice a sinister whisper that echoed in his mind. "You are not a hero. You are nothing!"

Just when George thought he would succumb to the overwhelming despair, the nightmare shifted again. He found himself back in the desolate landscape, but this time, the ground trembled violently, fissures opening up beneath him, threatening to swallow him whole.

He looked around desperately, searching for his friends, but the mist had thickened into a swirling vortex of shadows. "Help!" he cried out again, feeling the cold grip of fear tighten around his chest.

"Join us!" the shadows hissed in unison, their voices a chilling melody of despair. "You cannot fight what you are!"

George stumbled backward, his heart racing, and in that moment of vulnerability, he saw it—the demon's face looming large in the shadows, a twisted grin stretching across its features. It raised its clawed hand, and George felt an icy chill grip his heart as he realized it was summoning the echoes, sending them toward him like a pack of ravenous wolves.

"No!" he shouted, but the words were drowned out by the cacophony of their laughter. The echoes surged forward, their forms shifting and writhing, embodying his worst fears.

As they surrounded him, he felt their cold fingers clutching at his mind, dragging him into a spiral of terror and despair. Images flashed through his mind—his friends being consumed by shadows, the screams of anguish echoing around him, and the demon's laughter ringing in his ears like a death knell.

In the heart of the nightmare, George felt himself being torn apart, his very essence unraveling under the weight of fear and hopelessness. But amidst the chaos, a flicker of defiance ignited within him. "I will not give in!" he roared, fighting against the darkness that threatened to engulf him.

He pushed against the shadows, willing himself to break free from their grasp, but they were relentless, their whispers echoing his doubts. "You're nothing! You can't save them!"

But even as the despair pressed in, he thought of his friends—their laughter, their courage, and the bond they shared. He thought of the journey they had taken together, the challenges they had overcome, and the strength they drew from one another.

"No!" he shouted again, this time with conviction. "I am not alone!"

With that declaration, he felt a surge of energy coursing through him, a warmth that pushed back against the cold tendrils of fear. The shadows hesitated, their grip weakening as he focused on the light that existed within him.

"Together, we can fight this!" he screamed, summoning the memories of their shared battles, the strength they had drawn from one another. The darkness around him began to recede, the echoes faltering as he stood firm in his resolve.

But just as victory seemed within reach, the demon's laughter rang out again, louder and more menacing than before. "You think you can escape? You are nothing but a pawn in this game!"

The ground shook violently beneath him, and as the shadows surged forward once more, George felt himself being pulled back into the depths of despair. The overwhelming sensation of fear closed in around him, the darkness swallowing him whole as he fought against it.

In that moment, he felt himself slipping, the struggle becoming too great. And as the shadows dragged him deeper into their embrace, his consciousness began to fade, leaving only the echoes of his friends' voices lingering in the void.

"George!" they called, but their voices grew distant, echoing in the darkness as the nightmare consumed him completely.

As the last remnants of light faded from his mind, he remained trapped in the clutches of fear, ensnared in a nightmare that would not let him wake.

The nightmare had wrapped itself tightly around George, pulling him deeper into a suffocating darkness. He felt the weight of the echoes' whispers pressing down on him, their voices swirling in a cacophony of despair. But just when it seemed like he would be swallowed whole by the abyss, everything shifted.

The shadows dissolved, and suddenly, he found himself standing in a grand, dimly lit hall. Golden chandeliers hung from the ceiling, casting a soft, warm glow over the polished marble floors. The heavy scent of roses filled the air, and everything felt strangely serene compared to the terror that had plagued him only moments before.

George blinked in confusion, trying to make sense of the abrupt change. His heart still pounded in his chest, but the oppressive weight of the nightmare seemed to have lifted, replaced by an eerie calm.

Then he saw her.

A woman stood at the far end of the hall, her figure bathed in the golden light. She was stunning—radiant, even—with long, flowing hair that shimmered like liquid gold. Her gown was made of delicate, translucent fabric that floated around her like mist, and her eyes sparkled like sapphires, filled with a depth that drew George in, despite the strangeness of the situation.

For a brief moment, George felt an overwhelming sense of peace wash over him, as if the horrors of the nightmare had faded into the background. But as he stepped closer, his sense of unease began to return. There was something off about the scene—something deeply wrong.

It was then that George noticed the man. He stood beside the woman, his face twisted in anger. Without warning, the man struck her across the face with a sharp crack, sending her staggering backward. George's heart leapt into his throat, and without thinking, he started running toward them.

"Hey!" he shouted, his voice filled with fury. "Stop! What are you doing?"

The man ignored him, his hand raised for another strike, his eyes cold and unfeeling. The woman cowered, her face filled with fear, her body trembling as she shrank away from her tormentor. George's protective instincts flared, and he rushed forward, ready to intervene.

As he closed the distance, the world around him seemed to slow. He could hear the woman's soft sobs, see the bruises forming on her delicate skin, and the raw terror in her eyes. Every fiber of his being screamed at him to save her.

When he finally reached them, George shoved the man away with all his strength, sending him stumbling back. "Leave her alone!" he shouted, stepping between them, his fists clenched and ready to defend her.

The woman looked up at George, her eyes wide with gratitude and relief. "Thank you," she whispered, her voice soft and trembling. "You saved me."

George's heart ached as he saw the tears glistening in her eyes. He reached out a hand to comfort her. "It's okay," he said gently. "You're safe now. I won't let him hurt you."

For a moment, it seemed like everything was going to be okay. The man was gone, fading into the shadows, and the woman reached for George's hand, her touch warm and delicate.

But then, without warning, her expression shifted.

The gratitude in her eyes vanished, replaced by something dark and twisted. A cruel smile spread across her lips, and George felt a cold jolt of fear shoot through him. Before he could react, her grip tightened on his hand, unnaturally strong, and she pulled him toward her.

Her once-beautiful face contorted into a grotesque mask of malice, her eyes gleaming with wicked glee. "You think you can save me?" she hissed, her voice dripping with venom. "Fool."

George tried to pull away, but her grip was ironclad, and the warmth of her touch now felt like searing heat. Panic surged through him as he struggled against her, but it was no use.

With a horrifying laugh, she yanked him closer, her other hand transforming into sharp, clawed fingers. Before George could scream, she plunged the claws deep into his chest, the searing pain exploding through his body. He gasped, his breath catching as he felt her claws dig deeper, twisting in his flesh.

The beautiful façade of the woman melted away, revealing a monstrous form—her once-elegant gown tattered and dark, her eyes glowing with malice. Her laughter echoed through the hall, a chilling, manic sound that sent a wave of terror through George.

"Foolish boy," she sneered, her voice low and cruel. "You thought you could play the hero, didn't you?"

George's vision blurred with pain, his knees buckling as blood poured from the wound in his chest. He couldn't breathe, couldn't think. The terror in his heart was overwhelming, and his mind raced, searching for an escape that wasn't there.

The woman leaned closer, her face inches from his as her twisted smile widened. "You were always going to die here," she whispered, her voice soft and mocking. "And you came so willingly."

George's strength ebbed away, his vision darkening as he fell to his knees, the world spinning around him. The woman released her grip on him, letting him collapse to the floor, her laughter echoing through the hall like a chorus of demons.

As he lay there, gasping for breath, the pain unbearable, George looked up at her one last time. Her form had shifted fully into something monstrous, her body looming over him as she reveled in his suffering.

"You should have never come here," she taunted, her voice a cruel whisper. "Now, you're mine."

And with that final, bone-chilling laugh, the darkness swallowed George whole, leaving nothing but the echo of his fading heartbeat in the cold, empty hall.

He remained trapped in the nightmare, his consciousness unable to break free, as the monstrous woman's laughter haunted the depths of his mind.

George lay on the cold, marble floor of the nightmare's hall, gasping for breath. His chest burned from the wound the monstrous woman had inflicted, and the darkness pressed in on him from all sides. Her cruel laughter echoed in his ears, relentless, mocking, never-ending. He felt trapped in an abyss, powerless, his mind spiraling into despair.

But suddenly, a new sound began to filter into the dream—something soft, rhythmic, and strangely out of place. It was faint at first, barely perceptible, like a distant hum. As the monstrous woman's laughter faded into the background, the sound grew clearer, cutting through the oppressive darkness like a lifeline.

A snore.

George blinked, confused. The nightmare's grip seemed to falter for a moment, and the haunting scene of the dark hall began to dissolve. The woman's twisted, mocking face blurred, and the sharp, searing pain in his chest dulled as the shadows retreated.

The snoring grew louder, a steady, almost peaceful rhythm that clashed with the terror that had consumed him moments ago. Slowly, George felt his body relaxing, the sensation of pain and panic slipping away as if being pulled out of a fog.

He blinked again, and when his vision cleared, he was no longer lying in the horrifying, cold hall of his nightmare. Instead, he found himself back in the warm, softly lit chamber of the temple. The orb still glowed with a gentle light, casting a serene glow around the room. The scent of roses was gone, replaced by the familiar earthy aroma of the ancient temple.

George's heart was still pounding in his chest, but the overwhelming fear had vanished. His breathing steadied, and he sat up slowly, the disorienting haze of the nightmare lingering at the edges of his mind. His head throbbed with the intensity of what he'd just experienced, and for a moment, he couldn't believe that he was safe.

Then he heard the snore again—louder, closer this time. He looked around and saw the source of the sound.

His friends were asleep.

Adrian was resting against the pedestal where the glowing orb still pulsed with gentle light, his head tilted back, mouth slightly open as a soft snore escaped him. Wren was lying on the floor with his arms folded behind his head, his chest rising and falling in a steady rhythm, completely at ease. Mia and Emma were both curled up on the floor nearby, their expressions peaceful, the tension of their earlier conversations having faded into the quiet of sleep.

George stared at them, momentarily stunned by the contrast. The nightmare had felt so real, so consuming, and yet here were his friends—safe, asleep, and blissfully unaware of the horrors he had just endured in his dream.

A mix of emotions flooded him. Relief, first and foremost. Relief that it had been just a dream. That the woman, the grotesque figures, the endless terror—none of it had been real. But along with that relief came an unsettling feeling, the vividness of the nightmare still clinging to him like a shadow.

He wiped the cold sweat from his forehead and ran a hand over his chest where the monstrous woman had stabbed him in the dream. There was no wound, no pain—just the ghost of the sensation lingering in his mind. He took a deep breath, trying to steady his racing heart, reminding himself that it had all been in his head. But the memory of that laugh, the way she had taunted him, still echoed in his thoughts.

George leaned back against the stone wall, his eyes drifting between his sleeping friends. For a brief moment, the calm in the room seemed surreal. The oppressive weight of the nightmare had been replaced by a sense of tranquility, but he couldn't shake the unease gnawing at him. What had triggered the dream? Why had it felt so vivid, so personal?

He glanced at the glowing orb at the center of the room, wondering if its energy had somehow fed into his subconscious. Or perhaps the remnants of the echoes' presence still lingered, weaving their way into his mind, even in this seemingly safe place.

Another snore broke the silence—this time from Wren, who shifted slightly in his sleep, muttering something incoherent before settling back into a quiet slumber. George allowed himself a small smile at the normalcy of it all. It was a reminder that, despite the nightmares, they were still together, still fighting, still alive.

"Just a dream," he whispered to himself, exhaling deeply. "It's over now."

He remained sitting there for a while, not quite ready to sleep again, his eyes occasionally drifting to the glowing orb. Despite the nightmare, the room itself felt peaceful. The stars outside the temple still twinkled against the surreal violet-blue sky, and the gentle hum of the orb filled the space with a soft, comforting energy.

George closed his eyes for a moment, listening to the steady breathing of his friends, the calm rhythm helping to ground him. The terror of the nightmare slowly began to fade, replaced by a quiet determination. No matter what darkness awaited them, no matter how deep the nightmares reached, they had each other—and that was what mattered.

For now, he would let them sleep. They would need their strength for whatever challenges lay ahead.

But as he sat there, keeping watch over his friends, the memory of the beautiful maid's twisted smile and the way she had turned on him lingered in his mind, a haunting reminder that even in their moments of rest, the darkness was never far behind.

George leaned against the cold stone pillar, his back pressed into its rough surface as the quiet hum of the temple surrounded him. The soft glow of the orb flickered gently in the center of the room, casting long shadows across the floor. His friends lay peacefully nearby, their soft breathing filling the silence, but sleep did not come for him. The remnants of the nightmare clung to his mind, refusing to let go.

He let out a long sigh, his eyes wandering up to the ceiling where the carvings stretched across the stone, intricate and mysterious. The soft violet-blue glow of the sky beyond the temple spilled in through cracks in the walls, mingling with the warmth of the orb's light. But despite the calm and beauty of this strange world, George couldn't shake the feeling of unease that gnawed at him.

Resting his head back against the pillar, he closed his eyes, but not in search of sleep. He couldn't afford to dream again—not after the nightmare he'd just endured. The image of the maid, her sudden transformation from a figure in need of rescue to a creature of malice, still played over and over in his mind. Her cold, mocking laughter echoed in his thoughts, and the phantom pain of her claws in his chest sent chills through him.

No, he wouldn't risk closing his eyes again. He'd had enough of nightmares for one night.

George's gaze shifted to his friends. Adrian, Mia, Emma, and Wren lay still, their bodies relaxed in slumber, unaware of the horrors George had just faced in his sleep. Part of him felt a deep sense of gratitude that they had found peace, even if only for a short while. The journey had been grueling—physically, mentally, emotionally. They had all been tested beyond what they thought possible. And yet, here they were, resting in the quiet safety of the temple, if only for a moment.

But even in their peaceful slumber, George couldn't shake the responsibility he felt. He was the only one awake, the only one standing guard against whatever might lurk in the shadows. His eyes darted toward the entrance of the temple, the heavy stone door closed but not sealed, as if leaving room for something—or someone—to enter.

"Why won't you let me rest?" he whispered to the room, his voice barely audible. He wasn't sure if he was talking to the echoes, the demons, or the temple itself. There was something about this place—something that felt alive, almost sentient, like the temple had its own consciousness. Maybe it was watching them, waiting for their next move. Or maybe it was just his own paranoia creeping in after the nightmare.

The hours seemed to drag on, each minute stretching longer than the last. George shifted uncomfortably, trying to find a position that would at least allow his body to rest, even if his mind refused to do the same. He could feel the stiffness settling into his muscles, the fatigue weighing down his limbs, but still, he resisted the pull of sleep.

He focused on the soft sounds around him: the gentle hum of the orb, the distant rustling of leaves from outside the temple, the steady rhythm of his friends' breathing. These small sounds grounded him, kept him tethered to the present, far from the nightmare that still lingered at the edges of his consciousness.

At one point, Mia stirred slightly, rolling over in her sleep, her brow furrowing for a moment as if caught in a fleeting dream. George watched her, ready to jump to her side if she showed signs of distress, but she quickly settled back into a deeper sleep. He sighed in relief, grateful that she wasn't plagued by the same tormenting visions that had haunted him.

The sky outside the temple began to shift, the vibrant colors of blue and purple slowly softening into the gentle hues of dawn. It was a strange, otherworldly dawn—unlike anything George had ever seen. The stars didn't fade as they did back home; instead, they seemed to glow brighter, merging with the light of the morning, creating an ethereal blend of night and day. The horizon was painted with soft streaks of pink and lavender, casting a delicate glow over the landscape outside.

George felt the subtle change in the air, the temperature shifting ever so slightly as the dawn broke. It wasn't the harsh light of morning that he was used to, but rather a soft, almost dreamlike transition that made the world feel even more surreal.

He pushed himself up from the pillar, his muscles protesting after hours of stillness. Stretching his arms over his head, he allowed himself a moment to take in the beauty of the dawn, letting it wash over him. Despite the unease that lingered in his chest, there was something calming about this strange world. For now, at least, the horrors of the night were behind them.

Adrian stirred first, rubbing his eyes and blinking groggily as he sat up. He looked over at George, offering a small, tired smile. "You didn't sleep, did you?"

George shook his head, a faint smile tugging at his lips. "No. Didn't feel like it."

Adrian stretched his arms and let out a low groan. "You should've woken me up. I would've taken a turn."

George shrugged. "It's alright. I wasn't tired." A half-truth. His body was exhausted, but his mind... his mind wasn't ready to let go of the night.

One by one, the others began to wake, the soft glow of dawn rousing them from their slumber. Wren yawned loudly, stretching his arms wide, while Emma and Mia slowly sat up, blinking against the morning light.

Mia looked at George, concern etched on her face. "You stayed up all night?"

George nodded. "Yeah. Someone had to keep watch."

Emma frowned slightly. "You should've rested, George. We're all in this together, you know."

"I know," George replied, his tone light. "But I wasn't about to let you all sleep through the night with no one keeping an eye out. Besides," he added with a wry grin, "I wasn't in the mood for nightmares."

Adrian clapped him on the shoulder, his voice full of appreciation. "Thanks, man. We'll get you some proper rest soon."

George nodded, but his thoughts remained elsewhere, lingering on the nightmare that had haunted him through the night. The twisted woman, her mocking laugh, the sensation of helplessness—it was all too vivid. Too real. But as the light of the new day bathed the temple, George allowed himself to push those thoughts aside.

They had survived another night. They were still together. And for now, that was enough.

As the dawn light crept softly through the cracks of the ancient temple, the group gathered, still shaking off the remnants of sleep. The once-vibrant glow of the orb had dimmed, reflecting the soft hues of the violet-blue sky outside, casting an otherworldly glow across the room. The air felt lighter, more charged with possibility, but the weight of uncertainty still hung over them.

George leaned back against the pillar, his body aching from the long night spent awake. Though his friends had rested, he hadn't allowed himself the luxury of sleep. His mind still buzzed with the lingering memories of the nightmare—the twisted, mocking laughter of the woman who had turned on him, and the oppressive darkness that had tried to swallow him whole. But now, with the new day spreading its light, it was time to push forward.

Mia, rubbing the sleep from her eyes, was the first to break the silence. "What now?" she asked softly, looking at the faces around her, all etched with the same mix of fatigue and resolve. "We made it through the night, but what's next? The echoes... the demon... they're still out there."

Adrian ran a hand through his hair, his expression thoughtful. "We can't stay here forever. We've found some peace in this temple, but I don't think it's permanent. Whatever chased us through the portal—those echoes, that demon—they're part of something bigger. We need to figure out what we're dealing with."

Wren, sitting cross-legged on the floor, nodded in agreement. "We're in another world, aren't we? Everything's different here—the sky, the stars, the energy. It's beautiful, sure, but we can't forget what brought us here. We need to understand what this place is and how it connects to everything we've faced so far."

Emma glanced toward the entrance of the temple, where the faint sounds of the outside world drifted in on a soft breeze. "Do you think the echoes can follow us here? I mean, this place... it feels different, but I can't shake the feeling that they're still out there. Waiting."

George, who had remained quiet up until now, shifted slightly and cleared his throat. His voice was calm but laced with the weight of his thoughts. "I don't think we're safe from them," he said, meeting each of their gazes. "I didn't sleep last night. I couldn't." He hesitated for a moment before continuing, his voice low. "I had... a nightmare. But it wasn't like the usual ones. It felt... real. Too real."

Mia's eyes widened in concern. "A nightmare? What happened?"

George sighed, the memory of the dream flashing before his eyes—the woman's cold laughter, the pain in his chest, the helplessness. "It started like I was in some hall—like here but different. There was a woman... she was beautiful, but there was something off about her. She was being hurt by a man, and I tried to save her, but... she turned on me." He paused, clenching his fists as he recalled the chilling feeling of her claws sinking into him. "She killed me... in the dream. And I couldn't wake up."

The room fell silent for a moment, the weight of George's words sinking in. The vividness of the nightmare, the twisted betrayal—it was enough to send a shiver down each of their spines.

Adrian's brow furrowed, his expression serious. "Dreams like that... they're not just dreams. We've seen enough to know that whatever's happening to us, it's affecting more than just our waking moments. These nightmares... they could be another way the echoes are trying to get to us. Or worse, maybe something even more powerful is watching us."

Emma frowned, concern filling her voice. "But how? We're in a different world. How can they reach us here?"

Wren, who had been quietly processing George's story, spoke up. "Maybe it doesn't matter where we are. The echoes and the demon—they're connected to our fears, our deepest anxieties. If they can invade our minds, it doesn't matter where we are physically. We're vulnerable if we let fear in."

George nodded slowly, the truth of Wren's words resonating with him. "Yeah, I felt it in the dream. They feed off fear. That woman... or whatever she was... she wanted me to feel helpless, powerless."

Mia hugged her knees to her chest, her voice soft. "If that's true, then what do we do? We've been fighting for so long, and it feels like no matter what we do, they keep coming."

Adrian's gaze shifted to the glowing orb in the center of the room, its light dimming but still casting a faint glow. "We need answers. We need to understand what this world is, and why we were brought here. The portal wasn't random—it had a purpose. Maybe this place holds the key to defeating the echoes, or at least protecting ourselves from them."

Emma nodded in agreement. "And the symbols... we still haven't figured out what they mean. There has to be a reason why they're here, why they appeared when we arrived."

Wren stood up, brushing the dust off his clothes. "Then let's get to work. We're not going to find any answers sitting around. We need to explore this place, look for more clues, and figure out how to survive."

George pushed himself to his feet, his body still aching from the long night. But there was a fire in his eyes now—a determination that hadn't been there before. "You're right. We're not going to let fear control us. Not anymore."

The group gathered around the orb once more, its faint light illuminating their faces as they shared a moment of solidarity. The nightmares, the echoes, the demon—they were still out there, but they wouldn't be taken down easily. Together, they had already survived so much, and together, they would continue to fight.

"We're not alone in this," Adrian said, his voice filled with quiet confidence. "We have each other. And whatever this place is, whatever challenges come next, we'll face them together."

Mia smiled faintly, the tension in her shoulders easing slightly. "You're right. We've made it this far. We can make it through anything."

With that, the decision was made. They would venture out into the strange new world, seeking the answers they desperately needed. They didn't know what awaited them, but they were ready. Armed with their bond, their resilience, and the hard-earned lessons from their journey so far, they would face whatever came next.

As they gathered their things and prepared to move, George stole one last glance at the soft glow of the orb. The nightmares would come again, he knew that much. But for now, in the light of the new day, he felt stronger. The echoes and the demons had preyed on their fear, but fear could only hold power if they let it.

And George was done letting fear win.

The group gathered their belongings, the air in the temple still charged with the faint energy of the glowing orb. As they stepped into the soft light of dawn, the sky stretched wide above them, painted with streaks of violet and blue, dotted by stars that seemed impossibly bright for morning. The strange beauty of the world they had entered filled them with a sense of wonder, but also a quiet unease. This place was not like anything they had known before—peaceful yet heavy with the unknown.

"We should head out," Adrian said, his voice steady but alert. "If there are answers out there, we need to find them. We've already lost too much time."

The others nodded in agreement, gathering near the entrance of the temple. As they stepped outside, a cool breeze welcomed them, rustling through the strange, glowing flora that dotted the landscape. The air smelled fresh, like dew on grass after a long rain, but beneath the beauty, there was a strange stillness, an eerie quiet that made the hairs on the back of George's neck stand up.

The ground beneath their feet was soft, the grass feeling almost like silk as they walked. In the distance, the hills rolled smoothly, the colors of the land shifting with the light. It all looked so peaceful, so inviting, but something about it felt off—too perfect, like a mirage.

"We should head toward those hills," Wren suggested, pointing in the distance. "There might be something there—another clue, or maybe a way out of this place."

Emma squinted into the horizon, her brow furrowed. "It feels too easy, doesn't it? Like we're being led somewhere."

Adrian nodded but kept moving forward. "We don't have any other choice. Staying in the temple won't get us the answers we need. We have to take a risk."

Mia, who had been walking close to George, glanced around nervously. "What if this place isn't what it seems? What if... it's another trap?"

George looked at her, his eyes filled with understanding. "It might be," he said quietly. "But we can't stay still. We can't let fear paralyze us."

With a shared sense of determination, they moved forward, the temple growing smaller behind them as they headed toward the open landscape. The world seemed to stretch out endlessly before them, the horizon merging with the brilliant sky above. But as they continued their journey, the strange stillness persisted, gnawing at the edges of their minds.

They reached the base of a hill, its incline gentle but noticeable, and as they prepared to ascend, George, who was walking at the front of the group, suddenly stopped in his tracks.

His hand shot out in front of him, as if he had hit something solid, yet nothing was there. His brow furrowed in confusion, and he reached out again, feeling an invisible barrier pressing against his hand.

"What the—" George muttered, stepping back in shock.

Adrian, noticing George's sudden stop, stepped forward and placed his hand where George had reached. His palm met the same invisible force—a solid wall that was completely invisible to the eye. "There's something here," Adrian said, his voice filled with confusion and concern. He ran his fingers along the barrier, searching for any gaps or weaknesses. "It's like... we're trapped."

Emma, eyes wide with disbelief, hurried forward and pressed her hand against the same invisible wall. "What is this?" she asked, her voice tinged with panic. "It's solid, but... there's nothing here."

Wren stepped up beside her, knocking his knuckles against the barrier as if testing its strength. "It's an invisible wall," he said grimly. "We can't get through."

Mia stepped back, her breath catching in her throat. "We're trapped. We're trapped in here."

Adrian took a deep breath, trying to stay calm. He turned to George, who was still staring at the invisible barrier, his mind racing. "Do you think it's magic? Some kind of force field?"

George shook his head, bewildered. "I don't know. It could be. But it's definitely not natural." He took a step back, his heart pounding in his chest. "This wasn't here before."

Adrian pressed his hands flat against the wall, his jaw clenched in frustration. "It's like the whole place is locked down. The portal might have brought us here, but it doesn't look like it's going to let us leave."

Emma slammed her fist against the barrier, her frustration evident. "We have to find a way through! We can't just be stuck here."

Wren examined the invisible wall, his eyes tracing along the edges as if trying to see where it ended. "We need to check the perimeter," he suggested, his tone serious. "There might be a weak point or a way around it."

Adrian nodded. "We'll split up, but we stick close. If anyone finds something, shout."

The group spread out, each person walking along the invisible barrier, hands outstretched as they felt for any gap or opening. But no matter how far they went, the wall stretched endlessly, curving around them like a cage.

George could feel the tension rising within him as they continued searching, the sensation of being trapped tightening around his chest. His nightmare from the previous night resurfaced in his mind—the feeling of helplessness, of being unable to escape. The invisible wall felt all too similar.

Minutes passed, and frustration began to set in. "This can't be it," Wren muttered under his breath as he continued tracing the barrier with his fingers. "There has to be a way out."

But the more they searched, the more futile it seemed. The invisible wall encircled them completely, trapping them within an unseen boundary. It was as if the world itself had decided to imprison them.

Finally, Adrian called out, his voice carrying a mix of exhaustion and frustration. "We've covered all the ground we can. There's no way through."

The group reconvened near where they had first encountered the invisible barrier. Mia's face was pale, her fear creeping back in as the reality of their situation set in. "We're stuck here," she whispered. "We can't get out."

Adrian ran a hand through his hair, trying to think. "There has to be something we're missing," he said, more to himself than to the others. "A key, a switch—something that unlocks this barrier."

Wren kicked the ground in frustration. "Or maybe this world doesn't want us to leave," he said bitterly.

Silence fell over the group as they stood there, the invisible wall looming over them like an unseen force, impenetrable and unyielding. The beauty of the world around them, the glowing sky and soft grass, now felt like a mockery. They had escaped one nightmare, only to find themselves trapped in another.

And as they stood there, helpless and uncertain, the weight of their situation pressed down on them, the invisible wall a constant reminder of the forces at play that they didn't yet understand.

As the group stood in frustrated silence, their thoughts weighed down by the reality of being trapped by the invisible barrier, a low rumble echoed beneath their feet. At first, it was subtle, barely noticeable—just a faint vibration in the ground that they mistook for exhaustion. But within seconds, the rumble intensified, growing louder and more violent.

George was the first to notice the change. His body tensed, eyes darting to the ground as the tremor shook the earth beneath them. "Did you feel that?" he asked, his voice tight with alarm.

Adrian turned toward him, eyes wide. "Yeah... something's not right."

The ground beneath them shuddered again, more violently this time. The grass rippled as if a great force was surging just below the surface, and a deep, ominous cracking sound split the air.

"Get back!" Wren shouted, instinctively stepping away from the center of the tremor. But it was too late.

With a deafening roar, the ground beneath them began to tear apart, splitting down the middle with a force that sent tremors through their legs. The earth opened up like the jaws of a great beast, creating a massive fissure that ran straight through the soft grass and deep into the soil.

Mia screamed as the crack spread faster than they could react, the land beneath them crumbling and giving way. "Move! Move!" Adrian shouted, trying to pull Mia away from the collapsing ground, but the tremor was too powerful, the earth breaking apart beneath their feet.

Before any of them could fully comprehend what was happening, the ground gave way entirely. The fissure widened, swallowing everything in its path.

George's heart raced as he tried to leap toward solid ground, but gravity took hold of him with merciless force. His feet slipped from under him, and suddenly, the earth collapsed beneath him, sending him plummeting into the abyss. He reached out instinctively, his hands grasping at the edges of the crumbling ground, but there was nothing to hold onto.

One by one, they all fell.

Adrian felt the pull of the earth as the ground beneath him disintegrated, his body plunging into the darkness below. He flailed in mid-air, desperately trying to regain control, but the pull was too strong, the abyss too deep.

Mia's scream echoed in the air as she tumbled into the darkness, her hand outstretched toward George, who was falling just ahead of her. "George!" she cried, but her voice was swallowed by the sound of the collapsing earth.

Wren and Emma were the last to fall, the world tilting violently as they were yanked into the massive chasm. Wren's body hit the side of the rocky wall as he fell, the impact knocking the wind out of him as he tumbled into the darkness.

The fall seemed to last forever. The wind howled in their ears, the roar of the earth splitting above them like thunder as they plunged deeper and deeper into the unknown. Their surroundings blurred into a vortex of darkness and chaos, the light from the world above vanishing as they fell farther and farther into the abyss.

George's mind raced, panic flooding his senses as the weightlessness took over. His heart pounded in his chest, adrenaline coursing through his veins. He couldn't see the others, couldn't hear anything but the rush of air and the deep, rumbling growl of the earth collapsing around them.

The cold, dark void wrapped itself around them as they descended, the sensation of freefall both terrifying and disorienting. There was no solid ground beneath them, no light to guide their way—only the endless abyss, pulling them deeper into the unknown.

Time seemed to stretch and warp as they fell, and George's thoughts swirled in a chaotic blur. Where were they falling to? Was this the end? The feeling of helplessness was overwhelming, like being swallowed by the very darkness they had fought so hard to escape.

And then, with a sudden and violent jolt, they hit solid ground.

The impact was brutal, knocking the breath from their lungs and sending shockwaves of pain through their bodies. George felt the hard, uneven surface beneath him as his body crashed into the ground, the air in his chest forced out in a sharp gasp. His vision swam, the world around him spinning as he tried to make sense of what had just happened.

The darkness was thick, suffocating. There was no light, no sound but the faint groans of his friends as they struggled to recover from the fall.

"Is everyone... okay?" Adrian's voice cut through the silence, strained and breathless. He lay a few feet away, his hand clutching at his ribs where he had hit the ground.

"I'm... I'm here," Mia gasped, her voice trembling with pain. She tried to sit up but collapsed back onto the ground, her body aching from the impact.

Wren groaned as he pushed himself onto his hands and knees. “Barely,” he muttered, wincing as he felt the bruise forming along his side.

Emma coughed, her voice weak. “I think... I think I’m okay.” She was lying on her back, staring up into the blackness above them, her heart still pounding in her chest.

George took a shaky breath, his muscles screaming in protest as he slowly rolled onto his side. Every part of him hurt, but they had survived. Somehow, they had survived.

But as his eyes adjusted to the darkness, he realized the danger was far from over.

They were no longer on the surface. The world above, with its vibrant skies and rolling hills, was gone, replaced by the jagged, cold walls of a cavern. The air was damp and heavy, and the oppressive darkness pressed in from all sides, making it impossible to see more than a few feet ahead.

George shuddered, his pulse quickening again as he took in the new surroundings. Whatever had pulled them into this abyss wasn’t finished with them yet.

They had fallen into the depths of the earth.

And now, the true nightmare had begun.

As George slowly regained his senses, the reality of their new surroundings sank in, and with it, a bone-deep terror gripped him. The air was thick and damp, clinging to his skin like a suffocating shroud. The cavern they had fallen into stretched out endlessly, swallowing them in its black embrace. There was no light—only an all-consuming darkness that seemed to pulse with a life of its own.

The ground beneath him was cold, rough, and jagged, littered with sharp stones that dug into his skin as he tried to move. The silence was oppressive, broken only by the faint, distant echoes of dripping water and the occasional groan of the earth far above. Every sound seemed amplified in the stillness, bouncing off the walls of the cavern in eerie, hollow tones that sent shivers down his spine.

The air smelled of rot and decay, a thick, musty odor that lingered with the sour scent of stagnant water. It was as if they had been swallowed by the earth itself, trapped in a tomb that had been sealed for centuries. The deeper George breathed, the more the rancid smell filled his lungs, making it hard to take in a full breath without gagging.

As his eyes adjusted to the dark, he could make out the faintest outlines of the cavern walls—towering cliffs of rough, jagged stone that rose impossibly high, disappearing into the pitch-black void above. The walls were slick with moisture, gleaming faintly in the darkness as if they were covered in a thin, oily film. Thick roots dangled from the ceiling, twisted and gnarled, like skeletal fingers reaching down from the unseen depths above, swaying slightly as if animated by some unseen force.

A low, ominous hum seemed to vibrate through the walls, resonating deep in George's bones. It was faint, barely noticeable at first, but the more he listened, the more it grew—an unsettling, rhythmic pulse that felt like the heartbeat of the cavern itself. It was as if the earth was alive, watching them, waiting for its next move.

The ground beneath them seemed unstable, shifting ever so slightly, like it could give way at any moment and send them plunging even deeper into the abyss. The cold seeped into their bones, a damp, penetrating chill that made their muscles tense and their breath fog in the air, even though there was no wind.

"Where are we?" Mia whispered, her voice trembling with fear. She huddled close to George, her eyes wide as she stared into the void, trying to make sense of the darkness that surrounded them.

"I don't know," George replied, his voice barely above a whisper. He strained to listen, to catch any sound that might indicate they weren't alone in this vast, terrifying space.

The silence was deafening, pressing in on them from all sides. It was a silence that wasn't empty—it was thick with presence, as if the cavern was listening to their every breath, waiting for them to make a move. It felt as though something was watching them from the shadows, lurking just beyond the edge of their vision. The darkness had weight, an oppressive, living entity that wrapped around them, making it impossible to see what lay ahead.

Adrian stood up slowly, wincing from the pain of the fall. "This place feels... wrong," he said, his voice echoing back to them in distorted, hollow whispers. "It's like we've fallen into something we were never meant to find."

Wren, rubbing his sore side, took a step forward, his foot hitting a pool of water that splashed slightly. The sound echoed unnaturally, bouncing off the cavern walls in strange, disjointed rhythms, as though the space itself were bending the noise. "It feels alive down here," he said, his voice unnerved. "Like the ground is moving, breathing even."

Emma shivered, her eyes darting around, trying to make sense of the darkness. "We need to get out of here," she said, her voice shaking. "I don't like this. Something's... something's here. I can feel it."

The dripping water in the distance continued, each drop hitting the ground with a wet slap, echoing through the cavern with a slow, deliberate rhythm. It was as if time had slowed, each sound stretching out longer than it should have, making the already terrifying environment feel surreal, like a nightmare they couldn't wake up from.

George's heart pounded in his chest, his skin crawling with a deep, primal fear. He felt watched—surrounded by a presence he couldn't name but that he knew was there, hidden just beyond the edge of his sight. The darkness pressed against him, threatening to swallow him whole. Every breath he took felt heavy, labored, like the air itself was thick with dread.

Suddenly, a faint noise—something distinct from the echoes—broke through the silence. It was distant but unmistakable: a low, guttural growl that rumbled through the cavern like the sound of an ancient beast stirring from its slumber.

Mia gasped, her hand gripping George's arm tightly. "Did you hear that?" she whispered, her voice shaking.

"I heard it," George replied, his voice low, his pulse quickening. "We're not alone down here."

The growl came again, closer this time, more menacing. It reverberated through the cavern, and the ground beneath them trembled slightly, as if in response to the sound. It was a deep, primal noise, filled with malice and hunger, echoing off the stone walls as it seemed to circle them, moving just out of sight.

The group huddled closer together, their eyes darting around the cavern, searching for any sign of movement. But the darkness was absolute, and whatever was making that sound remained hidden, lurking in the shadows.

"We need to move," Adrian said, his voice urgent. "Now."

George nodded, his throat dry. "Let's go—quietly." He felt the hairs on the back of his neck standing on end, his instincts screaming at him to flee. Whatever was down here with them was dangerous, and they needed to get out before it found them.

As they began to move, their footsteps slow and cautious, the growl echoed again, closer still. The darkness pressed in tighter, suffocating, as the unseen danger stalked them in the shadows.

The cavern was a prison, alive with malevolence, and they were its prey.

As they cautiously navigated the cavern, the oppressive darkness felt even heavier, the air thick with the scent of damp earth and decay. Each step echoed ominously against the cold stone walls, their hearts pounding in unison as they remained acutely aware of the growl that had reverberated through the underground.

But then, as if summoned by their growing tension, another sound broke through the heavy silence—a cacophony of clashing metal and shouts that echoed from somewhere deeper within the cavern. It was a sound that resonated through the very bones of the earth, primal and chaotic, drawing the group toward it like a moth to a flame.

"What is that?" Mia whispered, her eyes wide with a mix of fear and curiosity. She paused, straining to hear over the tumult of noise that seemed to pulse from the depths of the cavern.

"I don't know," Adrian replied, his voice barely above a whisper. "But it sounds like... a battle."

"Should we go check it out?" Wren asked, hesitating as he looked toward the direction of the noise. The urgency in the air felt palpable, but a sense of dread gnawed at him.

Emma shook her head, her expression filled with concern. "What if it's a trap? We've been through enough already. I don't know if I want to get involved in another fight."

George could feel the weight of indecision pressing down on them, but the sounds of war—metal clashing, the cries of warriors, and the roar of something primal—echoed too strongly to ignore. "We need to see what's happening," he urged. "Whatever it is, it might give us insight into this place. We can't afford to miss an opportunity."

With reluctant agreement, they edged closer to the source of the sound, moving cautiously through the dark tunnel that twisted like a serpent. The sounds grew louder, more chaotic, and the air crackled with energy, charged with the raw emotion of conflict.

Finally, they reached a ledge that opened up to a vast underground arena, illuminated by flickering torches that cast dancing shadows against the walls. What lay before them was a breathtaking and horrifying spectacle—a battle raging in the heart of the cavern.

On one side, a group of armored warriors clashed with fierce, shadowy figures that seemed to melt into the darkness itself. The warriors wore intricate armor that glimmered in the torchlight, their faces hidden beneath fearsome helmets. They fought valiantly, their weapons clashing against the dark entities with a symphony of chaos and defiance.

The echoes were everywhere, shifting and writhing, their forms flickering like smoke as they lunged at the warriors, their voices twisted into an unsettling chorus of growls and taunts. "You will fall! You are nothing!" they shrieked, their words filled with malice and mockery.

The sight was both captivating and terrifying. George felt his heart race as he watched, transfixed by the chaos below. The warriors fought with unwavering determination, but the sheer number of echoes was overwhelming. For every shadowy figure that fell, two more seemed to take its place, their malevolent energy feeding off the conflict.

"This is a war," Adrian murmured, his voice filled with awe and fear. "But against what?"

"They're fighting the echoes," Emma replied, her voice barely a whisper. "But look at the shadows—they don't seem to die."

Indeed, as they observed, the fallen echoes dissipated into the darkness, only to reform and charge back into battle, relentless and undying. It was as if they were a force of nature, their presence an insatiable hunger that devoured all in its path.

The air was thick with the scent of sweat, iron, and something darker, something that hinted at the malevolence behind the echoes' relentless attack. The sounds of battle reverberated through the cavern, drowning out the group's thoughts as they stood transfixed by the brutal display of violence.

"We should get out of here," Mia urged, her voice trembling. "This is too dangerous."

But George remained rooted to the spot, a mixture of fear and fascination holding him in place. He felt tired, so utterly fatigued from their journey, and part of him longed to turn away and escape the chaos. Yet, another part of him was drawn to it, yearning for answers, for understanding.

The warriors were fighting for their lives, their movements fluid and precise. They shouted commands to one another, their voices filled with a fierce determination that inspired George. "Push forward!" one of the armored warriors yelled, raising his sword high as he charged into the fray. "For our fallen brothers!"

Each clash of steel against shadow sent shockwaves through the ground, reverberating in George's chest. He couldn't help but admire the bravery of the warriors. They faced insurmountable odds, and yet they pressed on, refusing to surrender to the darkness that threatened to consume them.

But then, amidst the chaos, a chilling sight caught George's eye—a massive shadow emerged from the depths, towering over the battlefield like a storm cloud ready to unleash its fury. The echoes shifted, parting like the sea as the creature stepped forward, its form indistinct but undeniably powerful.

"What is that?" Wren breathed, his voice trembling.

"I don't know," Adrian replied, his eyes wide. "But it can't be good."

The beast raised its arms, summoning a wave of darkness that cascaded over the warriors, engulfing them in shadow. George's heart sank as he watched the echoes surge forward, driving the warriors back as the creature unleashed its power.

"This is a nightmare," Mia murmured, her voice quaking with fear. "We can't stay here. We need to leave!"

But as they turned to flee, the reality of their situation set in—every escape route was blocked by the chaos of the battle. The ground trembled beneath them, and the air crackled with energy, as if the very earth was torn between light and darkness.

George stood at the edge of the ledge, torn between fear and curiosity. They had come seeking answers, and now they were witnessing a conflict that could hold the key to their survival. But at what cost?

As the battle raged on below, the stakes rose, and the weight of their choices pressed down on them. They could turn back, run from the chaos, or they could step into the fray and seek the truth hidden within the darkness.

And with that realization came the understanding that they were about to face their greatest challenge yet, one that would test the very limits of their courage and their bonds.

As George stood at the edge of the ledge, his heart racing from the chaos unfolding before him, he felt the weight of uncertainty pressing down on him. The battle raged below, and the echoes of war filled the cavern with an ominous energy. He couldn't shake the feeling that something monumental was about to happen—something that would change everything.

In an attempt to steady himself, George shifted his weight and accidentally stepped on a branch that lay half-buried in the soft earth. The snap echoed through the cavern like a gunshot, a sharp crack that shattered the tension in the air.

"No!" he gasped, instantly regretting the movement as he watched the eyes of the combatants below shift toward him. The warriors, who had been valiantly fighting against the shadows, suddenly paused. The echoes, too, turned, their twisted forms snapping to attention as they sensed a new target.

"George!" Adrian hissed, his voice filled with urgency. "What have you done?"

Panic surged through George as he took a step back, but it was too late. The moment the branch snapped, the attention of the battlefield had shifted entirely, and the echoes surged forward, their malevolent forms swarming like locusts, driven by an insatiable hunger for fear and chaos.

"Run!" Emma shouted, her voice cutting through the rising tension.

But George stood frozen, the gravity of the situation crashing down around him. "I didn't mean to!" he stammered, the echoes' eyes glinting in the flickering light of the torches, their movements rapid and fluid as they charged toward the ledge.

The warriors below, realizing they were no longer alone in their fight, began to shout orders to one another. "Protect the ledge!" one of them yelled, raising his sword defiantly. But their attention was divided, the chaotic swirl of battle intensifying as the echoes converged on George and his friends.

"Get back!" Wren shouted, pulling Mia back as she instinctively took a step forward, her face etched with fear. "We need to move now!"

The air crackled with energy as the echoes lunged, their forms shifting and writhing in a grotesque dance of shadows. George could feel the heat of their malevolence rising, the oppressive darkness threatening to engulf him.

"Fall back!" Adrian shouted, shoving George to the side. "We can't let them corner us!"

George stumbled, his heart racing as he scrambled to regain his footing. The sight of the charging echoes was enough to send him into a blind panic, and he fought against the instinct to freeze, forcing himself to run back toward the entrance of the cavern.

"Don't look back!" Emma yelled, her voice cutting through the chaos. "Just run!"

They dashed away from the ledge, the sound of their hurried footsteps echoing in the cavern as they fought against the rising tide of darkness. The shadows behind them writhed and hissed, the echoes hot on their heels, eager to seize the chance for chaos and fear.

As they sprinted, George could hear the echoes of war behind him—the clash of metal, the desperate shouts of the warriors, and the guttural growls of the shadows. He felt the weight of dread pressing against his chest, threatening to pull him down. The images of the twisted forms and the sinister grins flooded his mind.

Adrian led the way, his instincts kicking in as he navigated the uneven ground, weaving through the rough terrain. "We need to find cover!" he shouted, scanning the cavern for any place to hide. "Over there!"

He pointed toward a narrow passageway on the side of the cavern, partially hidden by jagged rocks. They veered toward it, adrenaline surging through their veins as they ducked into the shelter. The echoes were relentless, the sound of their pursuit echoing ominously through the cavern.

Breathless, George pressed himself against the cold stone wall, his heart pounding in his chest as he tried to quiet the panic that threatened to take hold. The shadows swirled outside the narrow passage, their forms shifting restlessly as they sought their prey.

"What do we do now?" Mia asked, her voice trembling as she huddled close to George, eyes wide with fear.

Adrian peered cautiously around the edge of the rocks, watching as the echoes prowled outside the passage. "We wait," he said, his voice firm despite the uncertainty in his eyes. "We need to let them pass. We can't let them know we're here."

George nodded, his breath coming in ragged gasps as he pressed himself deeper into the shadows. He could hear the echoes murmuring, their voices a chilling mix of laughter and growls, taunting the warriors who fought valiantly against them. The sounds filled the air like a dark symphony, rising and falling in a haunting cadence.

"Just breathe," George whispered to himself, trying to steady his racing heart. "Just breathe."

The group remained silent, pressed tightly against the stone wall as they listened to the chaos unfolding just beyond their hiding place. The echoes' movements felt palpable, their energy thickening the air around them.

Suddenly, a loud crash resounded from the cavern entrance, and the warriors shouted in alarm. "Hold the line!" a commanding voice rang out, but the chaos was overwhelming, the shadows advancing like a tide, ready to consume everything in their path.

"They're fighting to protect us," Wren murmured, his expression a mixture of fear and admiration. "We can't let their efforts be in vain."

Adrian nodded, his jaw set in determination. "We can't stay hidden forever. We need a plan. If we wait too long, we'll be trapped between the echoes and whatever else is lurking down here."

George felt a surge of resolve. They had come too far, fought too hard to let fear dictate their actions. They couldn't remain passive now; they had to find a way to join the fight. "We have to help them," he said, his voice steadying as he spoke. "We can't just sit here and let them do all the fighting."

Mia exchanged glances with the group, uncertainty etched on her face. "But how? We're not equipped to fight these creatures. We barely survived the last encounter."

"We have to use the shadows to our advantage," Adrian suggested, his eyes narrowing in determination. "If we time our movements right, we can flank the echoes. We need to take them by surprise."

George felt a rush of adrenaline at the idea. "Let's do it. We'll find a way to help. We owe it to the warriors—and to ourselves."

With a newfound sense of purpose, they steeled themselves, ready to make their move. The echoes were fierce, relentless, and deadly, but they wouldn't be pushed aside any longer. United in their resolve, they prepared to step out into the chaos, determined to fight back against the darkness that threatened to consume them all.

As they prepared to join the fray, the tension in the air shifted, and a sense of exhilaration surged through them. The battle was far from over, but together, they would face whatever lay ahead, ready to fight for their survival in a world filled with shadows.

As George and his friends braced themselves to emerge from their hiding place and join the chaotic battle unfolding before them, a sudden flash of movement caught George's eye from the corner of the narrow passage. He turned just in time to see a small figure darting toward them through the shadows, her silhouette barely discernible against the cavern's dark backdrop.

"Who's that?" Emma whispered, her voice barely audible over the sounds of clashing metal and distant cries.

Before anyone could respond, the figure emerged from the darkness—a young girl, no older than twelve, with wild, tangled hair that framed her face. Her wide, bright eyes sparkled with a fierce intensity, and a determined expression set her features as she rushed toward them.

"Come with me!" she exclaimed, her voice urgent yet melodic, cutting through the chaos like a beacon. "You need to get away from here!"

George felt a rush of confusion as he exchanged glances with his friends. "Who are you?" he asked, stepping forward cautiously. "What are you doing here?"

The girl didn't slow down, her energy infectious as she beckoned them with an outstretched hand. "No time for questions! You'll be trapped if you stay! Follow me, quickly!"

Before they could debate, she turned and dashed back into the darkness, her small form moving with surprising agility. George hesitated for only a moment, then felt the pull of urgency. He glanced at Adrian, who gave him a nod, and they all instinctively followed the girl into the shadows.

As they ran, the sounds of battle grew fainter behind them, the growls and clashes gradually swallowed by the distance. The girl led them through a maze of tunnels, her movements swift and confident as she navigated the winding paths of the cavern. George couldn't help but marvel at her grace, her familiarity with the darkness that surrounded them.

"Where are you taking us?" Mia asked, trying to keep up as the girl darted around a corner, her small frame barely breaking stride.

"To safety!" the girl replied, glancing back over her shoulder, her eyes sparkling with determination. "You don't understand how dangerous it is here! The echoes are relentless, and they'll hunt you down if you stay exposed."

George felt a mixture of gratitude and curiosity. "But who are you? How do you know about us?" he pressed, desperate to understand the girl who had appeared so suddenly.

3

The Untold Secrets Of The Bond Between Xel and the Portal's Magic

"My name is Elara," she said, her voice unwavering even as they turned sharply through another passage. "I've been watching. I saw you come through the portal, and I knew you'd need help. I've been living here, hiding from the echoes, and I can help you find a way to fight back."

A spark ignited in George's chest at her words. "You know how to fight them?" he asked, hope blooming within him.

"Yes!" Elara said, her eyes gleaming with enthusiasm. "There's a safe haven deeper in the cavern, a place where the echoes can't reach us. I've set traps and barriers to protect it. If you come with me, we can regroup and plan our next move."

As they continued through the twisting corridors, the atmosphere shifted. The oppressive weight of the darkness began to lighten, and the air felt less thick with malevolence. George couldn't help but feel a sense of camaraderie growing between them and the young girl who led the way. She was small but resolute, her confidence shining through the darkness, guiding them toward safety.

After what felt like an eternity of running, they finally reached a wider chamber, and George caught his breath, his heart racing not just from the exertion but from the thrill of their escape. The chamber was illuminated by a series of bioluminescent plants that clung to the walls, casting a soft, ethereal glow across the rocky surface. It was a stark contrast to the chaos they had just left behind.

"This is it!" Elara announced, a triumphant smile breaking across her face. "Welcome to my sanctuary."

The group stepped into the chamber, relief flooding over them as they took in their new surroundings. The air felt cleaner here, infused with the scent of the glowing plants that emitted a calming light. In the center of the chamber was a small pool of crystal-clear water, its surface shimmering under the soft illumination, surrounded by smooth stones that formed a natural seating area.

"Wow," Mia breathed, her eyes wide as she took in the beauty of the hidden sanctuary. "It's beautiful."

"It's safe," Elara confirmed, her voice filled with pride. "I've set up defenses around the perimeter. The echoes can't breach this space, not while I'm here."

As the group settled into the sanctuary, the initial shock of their escape began to fade, replaced by a sense of cautious optimism. George felt a renewed spark of determination, fueled by the presence of this brave young girl who had led them to safety.

"Thank you, Elara," Adrian said, his voice filled with gratitude. "We owe you everything."

Elara smiled, the light reflecting in her bright eyes. "I just did what anyone would do. You're not the only ones fighting against the darkness. Together, we can find a way to defeat the echoes."

The group exchanged glances, a silent understanding passing between them. They were not alone in their struggle; they had allies now, and with Elara's knowledge of the cavern, they might stand a chance against the horrors that awaited them.

"What's our next move?" George asked, feeling the weight of the moment settle in.

Elara stepped forward, her expression serious. "We regroup and prepare. The echoes may not know where we are, but they won't stop hunting for you. We need to be ready to defend this sanctuary—and ourselves."

As they gathered around the small pool of water, sharing their plans and ideas, a sense of hope blossomed in the sanctuary. In the heart of the cavern, amidst the danger and darkness, they had found a flicker of light. Together, they would fight back against the shadows, armed with newfound determination and the strength of their unity.

As the group settled into the sanctuary, the ambiance shifted from tense uncertainty to a warm camaraderie. The bioluminescent plants cast a soft glow around them, illuminating the faces of George, Adrian, Mia, Emma, Wren, and their newfound ally, Elara. They gathered close to the shimmering pool of water, the air charged with anticipation as they prepared to learn more about the young girl who had saved them.

Elara, sitting cross-legged on a smooth stone, looked around at the group, her eyes sparkling with determination yet shadowed by a hint of sorrow. She took a deep breath, gathering her thoughts as she prepared to share her story.

"I know you have questions," she began, her voice steady but laced with emotion. "And I want you to understand why I've been living down here, hidden from the echoes." She glanced down, her fingers tracing the edge of the stone as she collected her memories.

"I grew up in a village not far from here, a place where people thrived in harmony with nature," she continued, her voice tinged with nostalgia. "My father was a warrior, a protector of our village. He taught me everything I know about fighting, about courage and honor. I admired him more than anything—he was my hero."

George felt a surge of empathy for Elara, understanding the bond she shared with her father. He could see the warmth in her eyes when she spoke of him, but beneath that warmth lay a deep, raw pain.

"As I grew older, I trained alongside my father, learning the ways of combat and strategy. I was proud to be his daughter and dreamed of becoming a warrior like him, defending our home against any threat. But one fateful day, everything changed."

Elara paused, her expression darkening as the memories flooded back. "The echoes had been growing bolder, attacking villages and spreading fear throughout the land. My father and I led a group of warriors to defend our village from an onslaught. We were determined, fierce, ready to protect our home."

The shadows of the past loomed heavy in her words, and George could sense the weight of her recollection. He leaned forward, listening intently as Elara continued.

"The battle was brutal. The echoes came in waves, their twisted forms relentless and horrifying. We fought valiantly, but they were everywhere. In the chaos, I lost sight of my father. I was surrounded by shadows, and all I could hear were the cries of my comrades as they fell one by one. The echoes laughed, their voices taunting us as they surged forward."

Tears glimmered in Elara's eyes, but she held them back, determination flickering in her gaze. "I searched for my father, fighting my way through the darkness, but it was too late. He was gone—lost to the shadows. I felt the world crumble around me. I was terrified and alone, watching everything I loved slip away."

George felt a knot form in his throat as he listened to her recount the loss of her father. He thought of his own family, the weight of loss threatening to crush him under its burden.

"In that moment of despair," Elara continued, her voice gaining strength, "I knew I had to survive. I had to find a way to hide, to protect myself from the echoes that would hunt me down. I retreated into the depths of this cavern, away from the battle, away from the pain."

She looked around at the group, her expression fierce and resolute. "But I didn't just hide. I learned. I studied the echoes, their movements, their weaknesses. I set traps and barriers, built defenses to keep myself safe. I became vigilant, watching over the darkness, waiting for the day I could fight back."

Adrian leaned in, his expression a mix of admiration and sympathy. "You've been alone down here, fighting your own battles. That takes incredible strength."

Elara nodded, her eyes gleaming with determination. "I've had to be strong. I couldn't allow the loss of my father to break me. I promised myself I would find a way to avenge him—to protect others from the fate I suffered. When I saw you arrive through the portal, I knew I couldn't let you fall into the same trap."

Mia spoke up, her voice filled with compassion. "You've done an incredible job, Elara. It takes a lot of courage to survive in a place like this."

"Thank you," Elara replied, a soft smile breaking through her somber expression. "But it's not enough. I need your help. Together, we can be stronger. We can fight against the echoes and reclaim our world from the darkness."

The group exchanged glances, the weight of Elara's story resonating deeply within them. Each of them had faced their own struggles, their own losses, but they also understood the power of unity—the strength that came from standing together against the darkness.

George felt a fire ignite within him, fueled by the stories they all shared, the determination to fight back against the echoes that haunted them. "We're with you," he said firmly, his voice steady. "We've faced our own nightmares, and together, we'll confront whatever comes next."

Elara's expression brightened, hope glimmering in her eyes. "Then we'll prepare. We'll strategize and set our defenses. I've learned much about the echoes, their movements, and their patterns. We can use that knowledge to our advantage."

With that, the atmosphere shifted, transforming from one of sorrow to one of resolve. Elara began to share her strategies, detailing the traps she had set in the cavern, explaining how they could utilize the terrain to their advantage. As she spoke, her passion ignited a fire in the hearts of George and his friends, inspiring them to envision a way forward.

Together, they would forge a plan, harnessing their collective strength to confront the darkness that threatened to engulf them. Elara's story had not only deepened their bond but also illuminated the path ahead. The pain of the past would fuel their determination, and the strength of their unity would guide them as they prepared to face the echoes together.

In the heart of the cavern, amidst the shadows and the uncertainty, they found hope—a flicker of light against the encroaching darkness.

As the air in the sanctuary buzzed with a renewed sense of purpose, Adrian leaned forward, his eyes fixed on Elara. "Can you tell us more about the echoes?" he asked, his tone serious. "What exactly are they, and how do they relate to Xel Island?"

Elara nodded, her expression shifting from determination to a more somber demeanor as she prepared to share the weight of her knowledge. "The echoes are not merely shadows or creatures; they are the souls of the deceased—lost souls who take on the shape and form of those who have fallen. They're remnants of those who have met their end on this island or in the battles that have raged around it. Their existence is tied to the very fabric of this place."

George felt a chill run down his spine at the revelation. The echoes were more than just adversaries; they were the echoes of lives once lived, now twisted and corrupted.

Elara continued, her voice steady yet filled with an underlying sadness. "Many of them were once humans—warriors, villagers, travelers—who came to Xel Island in search of adventure, wealth, or knowledge. But this island has a dark secret. It is a guardian of something far more powerful and dangerous than the echoes themselves."

"What do you mean?" Adrian pressed, intrigued and alarmed by her words.

"The more humans explore Xel Island, the more it weakens," Elara explained. "The island is intertwined with the echoes, feeding off their existence. Every soul that is lost here adds to its strength, but it also creates a cycle of darkness. The island is bound to guard something ancient—something that could unleash chaos if it ever escapes."

Emma frowned, her brow furrowing as she processed this information. "What is it guarding? What could be so powerful that it needs to be kept hidden?"

Elara shook her head, her eyes clouded with worry. "I don't know. There are ancient texts and symbols that hint at it, but no one has ever been able to decipher them completely. The echoes seem to guard that knowledge, just as they guard the island itself. It's as if they are the protectors of a dark secret—one that must never see the light of day."

Wren, who had been listening intently, leaned closer. "So, the more we explore, the stronger the echoes become, and the more dangerous the island grows?"

"Yes," Elara replied, her gaze steady as she met his eyes. "That's why it's so vital that we find a way to fight back. If we let fear dictate our actions, if we allow the echoes to control us, we risk becoming part of that cycle. We could lose ourselves to the darkness."

A heavy silence settled over the group as they absorbed her words. The echoes, once viewed as mere shadows to battle, were now seen as tragic reminders of lives lost and the consequences of exploration. They were tied to the very essence of Xel Island—a guardian over something potentially catastrophic.

"Then we must find a way to weaken the echoes," Adrian said, his voice firm, rallying the group. "If we can understand their connection to the island and what they're guarding, we can take back our power."

Elara smiled, a glimmer of hope returning to her eyes. "Yes. Together, we can devise a plan to unravel the echoes' hold over the island. We can study their movements, set traps, and, most importantly, learn how to protect ourselves and others who might wander here."

George felt a surge of determination course through him. They were no longer just a group of survivors; they were a team bound by a common goal. They would confront the echoes, learn the island's secrets, and find a way to break the cycle of darkness that threatened to consume them all.

As the sun began to rise in the outside world, casting shafts of light through the cavern's openings, George looked around at his friends—Adrian, Mia, Wren, and Emma—each one of them reflecting a fierce resolve. They had faced nightmares and fought through despair, but now they had a purpose. They were connected not just by their struggles but by their shared mission to protect not only themselves but also the souls lost to the echoes.

And with that newfound purpose came the understanding that their journey had only just begun. They would uncover the mysteries of Xel Island, confront the echoes that haunted them, and ultimately face the ancient force that lay hidden beneath the surface. Together, they would stand against the darkness.

Elara looked at each of them, her expression resolute. "Are you ready to take this step with me? We have much to learn, and the echoes will not make it easy."

With unwavering determination, George stepped forward, feeling the weight of their mission settle into his bones. "We're ready. Let's do this."

The others nodded in agreement, their spirits lifted by their shared resolve.

As the group gathered around the shimmering pool, the atmosphere shifted again, and a subtle tension hung in the air. Elara stood at the center, her expression resolute, but suddenly, a slight tremor coursed through her body.

At first, it was almost imperceptible, just a brief shiver that made her shoulders quiver slightly. George noticed it immediately. "Elara?" he asked, his voice laced with concern. "Are you okay?"

She blinked rapidly, shaking her head as if to clear away a fog that had settled in her mind. "I'm fine," she replied, though her voice betrayed a hint of uncertainty. "Just... a chill."

But the shivering intensified, her body quaking slightly as she fought to maintain her composure. George stepped closer, watching her closely. "You're not fine. What's happening?"

Elara took a deep breath, trying to steady herself. "It's just a reaction," she insisted, but another shiver coursed through her, more violent this time. "I think... I think it's the echoes. They sense us. I can feel them stirring."

Mia stepped forward, concern etched across her face. "But nothing's happening. We're safe here, right?"

"I don't know," Elara admitted, her voice trembling slightly. "But I can sense something—like a presence pushing against the barriers I've set. It's as if the echoes are aware of us and are reacting to our presence."

George felt his heart sink at her words. They had only just begun to understand the echoes and their connection to the island, and now it seemed they might be in greater danger than they had realized. He reached out, placing a reassuring hand on Elara's shoulder. "You're not alone in this. We'll face whatever is coming together."

Elara nodded, her eyes narrowing as she concentrated, trying to push past the chilling sensations that threatened to overwhelm her. But despite her resolve, the shivering persisted, her body unable to shake off the feeling of dread that surrounded them.

"Focus on your breathing," Wren suggested, stepping closer. "If you can block it out, we can figure this out together."

As the group surrounded her, George could sense the weight of tension thickening in the air, a palpable reminder of the looming darkness that still hovered just beyond the edges of their sanctuary. They were all aware that the echoes were not just figments of their imagination; they were very real, very dangerous, and somehow aware of their presence.

"Let's keep talking," Adrian suggested, trying to divert attention from Elara's growing unease. "We need to stay focused on our plans and not let fear take hold."

Elara nodded, grateful for the distraction. "You're right," she said, her shivers slowly lessening as she focused on the support of her friends. "We can't let this affect us. The echoes feed on fear. We need to remain strong and united."

As they continued their discussion, Elara's shivering faded, though the sense of unease lingered like a dark cloud hanging over them. The group fell into a rhythm, discussing strategies and ideas for confronting the echoes and understanding the deeper mysteries of Xel Island.

But in the back of George's mind, a whisper of concern remained. He couldn't shake the feeling that something was coming—something powerful that would challenge not just their resolve but the very bonds that held them together.

As the conversation continued, George kept a close eye on Elara. He could see her determination shining through despite the remnants of her earlier fear. She was strong, and her resilience inspired him. They were all in this together, and whatever lay ahead, they would face it as one.

Yet, deep within the shadows of the cavern, the echoes stirred. They were aware. They were watching.

And the true test of their courage was still to come.

As the conversation flowed among the group, the atmosphere grew increasingly tense. Elara's shivers returned with a vengeance, her body trembling as if caught in the grip of a powerful chill. Each wave seemed to surge through her, more intense than the last, threatening to pull her into a vortex of fear.

George noticed her struggle immediately, concern etched on his face. "Elara," he said softly, stepping closer. "Are you sure you're okay? We can stop if you need a moment."

"I'm fine," she insisted, her voice wavering but firm. "I just need to focus. I can feel them stirring. They know we're here."

But the intensity of her shivering made George uneasy. He could see her fighting against something deep within, a battle that was taking a toll on her. The flickering light of the bioluminescent plants around them illuminated her face, highlighting the determination in her eyes even as fear shadowed her features.

"Please, let me help you," George urged, stepping even closer, his heart pounding. He reached out, brushing his fingers gently against her arm, trying to anchor her in the present moment. "You're not alone. We'll face this together."

Elara looked up at him, her eyes searching his, and in that instant, a connection sparked between them. The world around them faded, and the chaos of the cavern fell silent. All that existed was the space between them, charged with an energy that pulsed like a living heartbeat.

"I know I'm not alone," she whispered, her breath catching as she drew closer. "But right now, I feel so lost. I'm scared of what's coming."

Without thinking, she leaned in, closing the distance between them. Their lips met in a soft, tentative kiss, a moment of tenderness amidst the uncertainty. It was a kiss that spoke volumes, conveying the weight of their shared struggles, the fear of the unknown, and the warmth of the bond they were forging.

George's heart raced, his mind swirling with emotions. He kissed her back gently, feeling the warmth of her presence grounding him amidst the storm of chaos that surrounded them. The kiss was a balm for their fears, a reminder that even in the darkest times, there was still light—still connection.

For a brief moment, the shivers that coursed through Elara seemed to dissipate, replaced by the warmth of their shared embrace. She pulled back slightly, searching his eyes for reassurance, and he could see the flicker of strength returning to her gaze.

"Thank you," she said softly, her voice trembling but filled with resolve. "I needed that. We all need to hold onto what we have, even in the face of darkness."

Before George could respond, another wave of shivers struck Elara, more powerful than before, causing her to stagger back slightly. George's heart sank as he watched her fight against the onslaught. "Elara!" he exclaimed, concern flooding his voice.

"I'm okay," she insisted, though the tremors in her body betrayed her words. "It's just... the echoes. They're feeding off my fear." She took a deep breath, trying to steady herself. "But we can't let them win. We have to remain strong."

Adrian stepped closer, his expression serious. "Elara, we're with you. Whatever you're feeling, we'll face it together. You don't have to carry this burden alone."

The rest of the group nodded, their solidarity a powerful reminder of their shared mission. They had faced so much together, and they would continue to fight alongside one another, drawing strength from their unity.

As the tension hung heavy in the air, George reached for Elara's hand, intertwining his fingers with hers. "You're not alone in this," he said firmly. "We'll fight back against the echoes, and we'll do it together."

With that, Elara met his gaze, a spark of determination igniting in her eyes. "Yes," she affirmed, her voice steadying. "We will face whatever comes next, together."

As they stood united in that moment, the weight of the darkness that surrounded them began to feel lighter. Elara's shivers continued, but now there was a sense of hope among them—a reminder that even in the face of fear and uncertainty, they had each other.

With the weight of their shared experiences hanging in the air, the group knew they needed a moment to gather their thoughts and recharge. The flickering bioluminescent plants cast a gentle glow in the sanctuary, creating a comforting atmosphere despite the shadows lurking just beyond.

Elara released George's hand, taking a deep breath as she looked around at the weary faces of her new companions. "Before we face whatever comes next, I think we could all use a break. How about we share some stories?" she suggested, her eyes sparkling with the flicker of hope that always accompanied the telling of tales. "Stories of strength, courage, or even just moments of joy. It could help us bond and remind us of why we're fighting."

Mia smiled faintly, the tension in her shoulders easing slightly at the thought. "I'd like that. We've been through so much, and it might help lift our spirits."

Adrian nodded in agreement. "It's a good idea. We can share a piece of our past—something that reminds us of our humanity."

George settled onto a smooth stone near the shimmering pool, the warm light casting a soft glow on his face. "I'll start," he said, glancing around at his friends. "There was a time when I was just a kid, maybe twelve or so, and my family decided to go on a camping trip in the woods. We didn't have a fancy camper or anything—just a tent and some sleeping bags."

He paused, a small smile creeping onto his face as he recalled the memory. "We set up camp by this beautiful lake, and I remember thinking how magical everything felt. The trees were so tall, and the stars shone so brightly at night. One evening, I wandered off to explore a little and ended up getting lost. I thought I'd never find my way back."

The group leaned in closer, captivated by his story.

"But then I heard laughter. I followed the sound and found my parents and my little sister roasting marshmallows by the campfire, completely unaware I had disappeared. I'll never forget that moment—how relieved I felt when I realized I was safe and that I wasn't alone." He looked at Elara, a connection forming. "Even when we're lost, there's always a way back home, and we can always find our people."

Mia smiled softly, clearly moved by his story. "That's beautiful, George. I think we all need that reminder."

"Okay, I'll go next," Mia said, her tone brightening. "When I was younger, I lived in a small town, and every summer, I used to volunteer at a local animal shelter. One day, we got a call about a litter of abandoned puppies. They were tiny, covered in dirt, and just full of energy. I remember the moment I held one of them in my arms. It snuggled right against me and just fell asleep."

Her eyes twinkled with the memory. "I worked tirelessly to help care for them, and when they were ready for adoption, I was so proud to see them find their forever homes. It taught me the importance of compassion and kindness. It's incredible how something so small can make such a big impact on our lives."

"Wow, that's really sweet, Mia," Emma said, her voice warm. "It's amazing how caring for others can bring us joy."

"I guess it's my turn," Wren chimed in, a hint of mischief dancing in his eyes. "When I was a teenager, I was really into skateboarding. I wanted to be the best, so I spent every waking moment practicing tricks at the local skate park. One day, I decided to try the biggest ramp—way too big for me at the time."

He chuckled at the memory, shaking his head. "I wiped out spectacularly, and everyone was watching. I was so embarrassed, but I got back up and tried again. It took me weeks, but I eventually landed the trick, and when I did, the entire park erupted into cheers."

Wren leaned forward, a grin plastered on his face. "That moment taught me something important: falling down doesn't matter nearly as much as how you get back up. We're all going to face our challenges, but it's our resilience that truly defines us."

"Such great stories!" Emma said, clapping her hands together in excitement. "I've been lucky enough to experience something extraordinary too. When I was sixteen, I traveled with my school for a volunteer project to help restore a historic building. It was an old library that had fallen into disrepair, and we spent the summer painting, cleaning, and fixing it up."

Her eyes brightened as she spoke. "On the last day, the community came together for a grand reopening. I'll never forget the smiles on people's faces when they saw the finished library. They were so grateful, and it made me realize the power of community. We're all connected, and when we work together, we can create something beautiful."

As the stories flowed, a sense of warmth filled the sanctuary, weaving them closer together. Elara listened intently, a soft smile gracing her lips as each tale of courage and connection was shared.

Finally, she spoke, her voice low and steady, yet filled with emotion. "Thank you for sharing those stories. I've felt so alone for so long, but hearing about your lives reminds me that hope exists even in darkness. It's the small moments that build us into who we are and give us strength."

George felt a sense of camaraderie wash over them all. They were no longer just survivors—they were a family forged in the fire of adversity. As their laughter and stories echoed in the sanctuary, the weight of their circumstances began to lift, replaced by a sense of unity that bound them together.

In that moment, they understood that no matter the challenges ahead, they would face them as one. The journey to uncover the mysteries of Xel Island would be fraught with danger, but together, they would find the strength to stand against the darkness.

As the last of the stories faded into the soft glow of the sanctuary, the group settled into a comfortable silence. The warmth of shared memories lingered in the air, easing the tension that had built throughout their journey. One by one, they drifted into a peaceful sleep, the bioluminescent plants casting a gentle light that wrapped them in a sense of calm.

The night passed without incident. The echoes, the darkness, and the dangers of Xel Island seemed to fade into the background, kept at bay by the unity and trust they had built among themselves. It was the first time in days that they had felt truly safe, a rare moment of respite in the midst of uncertainty.

But as dawn approached, the soft light of the cavern began to shift. The bioluminescence dimmed slightly, giving way to a new, natural light that filtered in through unseen cracks in the stone above. The air grew cooler, the slight chill of morning stirring them from their rest.

George was the first to wake. He blinked against the dim light, stretching out his sore muscles as he adjusted to the waking world. His mind was clearer than it had been in days, free from the oppressive weight of fear and exhaustion. He looked around at his

A quiet strength settled over the group, each of them fully committed to the next step of their journey. The tension that had gripped them since they arrived on the island seemed to shift, replaced by a sense of purpose.

"Do you know where the portal is?" Adrian asked, ever practical.

Elara nodded. "I've seen it before, in the heart of the island. It's not far, but it's surrounded by the densest concentration of echoes. They protect it, guard it like it's the source of their power. Reaching it will be dangerous, but I believe we can do it. We just have to stay together."

The gravity of her words settled over the group. They all knew the risks—facing the echoes head-on was a death sentence for anyone unprepared. But with Elara's guidance and the bond they had formed, they believed they could make it.

Wren tapped the side of his head thoughtfully. "So, what's the plan? We can't just stroll in and ask the echoes to let us through."

Elara smiled, the first real smile they had seen from her since the night before. "No, definitely not. But we can use the island's terrain to our advantage. I've set traps throughout the areas we'll need to pass through, and I know where the echoes are weakest. If we're careful, we can make it."

Adrian nodded. "Then we move quickly, strike when we need to, and avoid unnecessary fights. Get to the portal as fast as we can."

Mia's face tightened with resolve. "We'll be ready. We've come too far to give up now."

Elara looked at each of them, her heart swelling with hope. "Thank you," she said, her voice filled with sincerity. "I've been fighting for so long... I didn't realize how much I needed all of you."

George smiled, feeling the weight of their collective determination settle on his shoulders like armor. "We're stronger together. And we'll see this through."

The group stood together, united in their purpose, their bond stronger than ever. With Elara's guidance and the strength of their shared experiences, they were ready to face the final challenge. The portal was their way out, and nothing—not even the echoes—would stand in their way.

As they left the sanctuary, the air grew cooler, a steady breeze sweeping through the tunnels, bringing with it the faint sounds of the island beyond. The group walked in silence at first, the gravity of their mission weighing heavily on their shoulders. George, Adrian, Mia, Wren, Emma, and Elara were bound together now, not just by circumstance but by the shared knowledge that the future—both of this island and their own lives—rested on what they did next.

Elara led the way, her eyes sharp and focused as they moved through the caverns. The path was narrow, the walls pressing in around them, the bioluminescent plants slowly giving way to darker, rougher terrain. The eerie glow that had once bathed the sanctuary in peace was fading, replaced by the harsh reality of the island's looming dangers.

As they moved further from the sanctuary, the sounds of the echoes became more pronounced—distant whispers carried on the wind, the occasional low growl of something far off. It was a reminder of the constant threat lurking just beyond sight, a danger they would soon have to face head-on.

"I can't believe we're actually doing this," Wren muttered under his breath, his voice laced with a mix of awe and dread. "I mean, we're about to walk straight into the lion's den."

Adrian glanced at him, his jaw set in determination. "We've faced worse," he said quietly, though his eyes betrayed a flicker of doubt. "But we have to be smart about this. No unnecessary risks."

Elara, walking slightly ahead, turned her head slightly to address them. "It's not just about being smart—it's about being prepared. The echoes are relentless, and they're growing stronger. They can sense us, feel our presence. They'll do everything in their power to stop us from reaching the portal."

George, keeping pace beside her, could feel the tension radiating off Elara. She had carried this burden for so long, fighting her battles alone in the shadows. But now, as they walked toward the heart of the island, he sensed that something deeper was troubling her.

"What exactly will happen if we don't stop them?" George asked, his voice cutting through the silence. "If the echoes are tied to this island, what happens if they manage to get through the portal? What are we really up against?"

Elara's face darkened at the question, her expression tightening. She hesitated for a moment, her steps slowing as if the weight of the truth she was about to reveal was too heavy to bear. "You need to understand," she began, her voice low and filled with a quiet intensity, "the echoes aren't just mindless shadows. They were once people—warriors, explorers, villagers—who died here. But their spirits were consumed by the island, twisted into something darker, something powerful."

Mia shivered, her arms crossing over her chest as the cold air seemed to seep deeper into her bones. "So they're like... ghosts?"

"Worse," Elara said, shaking her head. "Much worse. The echoes are bound to this island, but if they find a way to break free—to enter the real world through the portal—they will bring destruction unlike anything we've ever seen."

Emma, walking just behind them, frowned. "Destruction? How? They're spirits, right? They can't really hurt people outside of this place, can they?"

Elara stopped walking and turned to face the group, her expression deadly serious. "If the echoes escape, they will be unstoppable. They are fueled by hatred, by the pain of their deaths and the anger they feel at being trapped here for centuries. Imagine an army of vengeful souls, filled with the power of the island, unleashed upon the world."

George felt a chill run down his spine as the gravity of her words settled in. He had seen the echoes up close—felt the malevolence radiating from them. The thought of them breaking free, spreading their darkness beyond the island, was terrifying.

"They won't just haunt people," Elara continued, her voice growing darker. "They will kill. Every single living being they encounter will be consumed by their rage. The echoes are not just souls—they are forces of pure destruction. And if they get through the portal, they will not stop until the entire world is wiped out."

A heavy silence followed her words. The wind howled through the narrow passage, amplifying the tension that hung between them. George's heart pounded in his chest as he struggled to process what Elara had just said.

"If they escape," Adrian said, his voice quiet but firm, "there will be no one left. The entire world will fall."

Elara nodded, her eyes filled with a deep sorrow. "Yes. The echoes will hunt down every last human, every living thing, until there's nothing left. The Earth will become a new planet—empty, lifeless, a wasteland."

Mia gasped, her hand flying to her mouth. "That's... that's horrific."

Emma's face paled as she absorbed the weight of the potential catastrophe. "So, if we fail, it's not just our lives on the line—it's everyone's."

Wren, always the one to crack a joke in tense moments, had nothing to say this time. His usual humor was replaced by a somber expression. "Well, that's... a lot of pressure."

George felt the weight of Elara's words pressing down on him, the realization that the stakes were far greater than he had imagined. This wasn't just about surviving the island or defeating the echoes for their own sake. This was about saving the world from an apocalyptic fate.

"I had no idea it was this bad," George admitted, his voice low. "But now that we know, we can't fail. We can't let those things get through the portal."

Elara nodded, her face etched with a deep resolve. "That's why I've been hiding here for so long. I've seen what the echoes are capable of. I've fought them, studied them, and I know what will happen if they're unleashed on the real world. This island is their prison, and we have to make sure it stays that way."

Adrian clenched his fists, his eyes burning with determination. "Then we'll do whatever it takes to stop them. We've faced impossible odds before, and we'll face them again. But we won't let those echoes escape."

Mia looked between George and Elara, her eyes wide with fear but also filled with resolve. "We can't let them win. We've fought too hard to let the world fall apart now."

Elara's gaze softened, her shivering subsiding slightly as she took a deep breath. "I know it sounds impossible, but I believe in us. The echoes are powerful, but they're not invincible. We can outsmart them, use the traps and the terrain to our advantage."

Wren gave a small nod, though his usual bravado was tinged with a hint of uncertainty. "We've come this far. Might as well go all the way."

Emma spoke up, her voice steady and calm. "We can't let fear stop us. It's like you said, Elara—the echoes feed on fear. If we're going to win, we have to stay strong. We have to believe we can do this."

George couldn't help but feel a surge of pride for his friends. They had been through so much already—faced death, terror, and the unknown—and yet here they were, ready to confront the greatest danger yet, for the sake of the world. He looked at Elara, who had been carrying this burden alone for so long, and knew that they had to do this—for her, for each other, and for everyone waiting in the real world, unaware of the danger that loomed just beyond the portal.

"We'll do it," George said, his voice firm and resolute. "We'll stop the echoes and make sure they stay trapped here. And then we'll get out—together."

Elara's eyes shimmered with gratitude, and she gave a small nod. "Thank you. I've been alone for so long... I wasn't sure if I could ever face this. But now, with all of you, I believe we can do it."

The group began walking again, the conversation settling into a more somber but determined tone. They talked through strategies, discussed the traps Elara had set, and mapped out the best way to reach the portal without drawing too much attention from the echoes.

As they continued down the winding path, George's mind raced with thoughts of what lay ahead. He knew the fight would be brutal. The echoes were unlike any enemy they had faced before—relentless, vengeful, and powerful. But they had each other, and that gave him hope.

The wind howled again, stronger this time, and the faint whispers of the echoes seemed to grow louder, as if they were listening—waiting. The portal was close now, and George could feel the island's energy shifting, tightening around them like a predator watching its prey.

They were walking into the heart of darkness, but they were ready.

No matter the cost, they would make sure the echoes never found their way into the real world.

As they continued their trek through the winding tunnels, the sense of unease grew stronger. The faint echoes of whispers seemed to follow them, a chilling reminder that the island was far from being the peaceful sanctuary they had briefly found in the hidden chamber. Every step carried them closer to the heart of Xel Island, and with it, the danger increased.

George walked alongside Elara, his mind turning over everything she had said. The weight of their mission—to keep the echoes from reaching the real world—pressed heavily on him. But there was something that didn't sit right in his mind, something that nagged at him the more he thought about it.

He glanced over at Elara, her face set in quiet determination, her eyes scanning the path ahead as if searching for any sign of danger. The others walked slightly ahead, discussing strategies and plans to reach the portal without drawing too much attention. But George couldn't let the question forming in his mind go unanswered.

"Elara," he began, his voice low but curious, "I've been thinking about something."

She turned her head slightly, her brow furrowed as she glanced at him. "What is it?"

He hesitated for a moment, unsure how to phrase his thoughts. "You said that the echoes are guarding the portal, right? That they're doing everything they can to keep us from reaching it. But... why?"

Elara slowed her pace, her eyes narrowing slightly as she listened. "What do you mean?"

George gestured around them, the dark cavern walls seeming to close in as he spoke. "I mean, if the echoes are as powerful and dangerous as you say, and if they want to escape so badly... why haven't they already gone through the portal? What's stopping them? They're guarding it like it's their only way out, but why do they need to keep us away from it if they could just leave themselves?"

Elara stopped walking entirely, and the rest of the group, sensing the shift in tone, paused as well, turning to listen. George's question hung in the air, echoing softly against the stone walls.

Adrian stepped closer, his expression thoughtful. "That's a good point. Why haven't they just gone through? What's keeping them tied to the island if they have a way out?"

For a moment, Elara's face darkened, her eyes clouded with something that George couldn't quite place—regret, or perhaps fear. She opened her mouth to speak, then hesitated, as if the truth was something she wasn't sure she wanted to reveal.

Mia, ever intuitive, stepped forward. "Elara? Is there something you haven't told us?"

Elara sighed deeply, her shoulders sagging slightly under the weight of what she was about to say. "It's not that I didn't want to tell you," she began slowly, her voice tinged with sorrow, "but it's something I've tried to forget. Something I didn't want to believe myself."

George's curiosity sharpened. "What is it?"

Elara looked at each of them in turn, her expression grave. "The echoes... can't go through the portal on their own. No matter how powerful they are, no matter how much rage or darkness they carry, they are bound to this island. The portal doesn't work for them—not without a human."

The silence that followed her words was deafening. George's heart sank as the realization hit him, and he saw the same dawning horror reflected in the faces of his friends.

"They need a human to go through?" Wren asked, his voice incredulous. "You mean, they can't escape unless we help them?"

Elara nodded, her eyes filled with sadness. "Yes. The echoes are tied to Xel Island. They are part of its fabric, and they can't break free on their own. They need a living, breathing human to pass through the portal first—someone who can act as a conduit. Once a human goes through, it weakens the portal's barrier and allows them to follow."

Adrian's jaw tightened, his fists clenching at his sides. "So that's why they're guarding it. They're not just keeping us from escaping—they're waiting for us to try. They need one of us to go through first."

George's stomach churned as the full weight of Elara's revelation settled over him. "If we make it to the portal, they'll be right behind us," he said quietly. "They're using us as their way out."

Elara nodded, her face pale. "That's why I've been so careful, why I've stayed hidden for so long. The echoes will do whatever it takes to make sure a human reaches that portal. They want to escape more than anything. But if we go through, we're unleashing them on the world."

Mia's face was drained of color, her eyes wide with fear. "But we have to go through. We can't stay here. What are we supposed to do? If we use the portal, they'll follow, and if we don't... we're trapped."

Emma, usually calm in the face of danger, was visibly shaken. "So, we're damned either way? If we go through, we bring the echoes with us, and if we stay, we're stuck here forever?"

Elara's silence was answer enough.

For a moment, the group stood frozen, the enormity of their situation pressing down on them. The echoes weren't just a threat to them—they were a threat to the entire world. Every step they took toward the portal brought them closer to unleashing a disaster that could wipe out humanity.

Wren, who had been pacing nervously, stopped and ran a hand through his hair. "There's got to be another way," he said, his voice laced with frustration. "There's always another way."

Adrian took a deep breath, his mind clearly racing for a solution. "What about the traps you've set, Elara? Can we weaken the echoes enough to make a run for it? Maybe if we time it right, we can get through the portal before they have a chance to follow."

Elara shook her head. "I wish it were that simple. The echoes aren't just mindless creatures we can outsmart. They're ancient, powerful beings, and they know the island better than anyone. Even with the traps, we'd only be delaying the inevitable. If we go through the portal, they will follow."

Mia's voice cracked slightly as she spoke. "So what do we do? We can't just give up."

George felt the crushing weight of hopelessness settle over him. The realization that their escape could lead to the destruction of the world was almost too much to bear. He wanted to fight, to push forward, but every option felt like a trap.

Elara took a deep breath, her gaze steady. "There might be another way," she said softly, her voice barely above a whisper. "But it's dangerous, and it requires a level of sacrifice I'm not sure any of us are prepared for."

The group turned to her, their expressions a mixture of curiosity and fear.

"What do you mean?" George asked, his heart pounding in his chest.

Elara hesitated, her eyes flickering with a deep sadness. "There are stories—old legends—about how the echoes were first bound to the island. There was a ritual, a way to sever the connection between the island and the echoes. It's said that if the ritual is performed, the echoes will be destroyed, and the portal will remain sealed."

Adrian's eyes narrowed. "What kind of ritual?"

Elara's voice dropped, the weight of her words heavy. "It requires a human sacrifice. Someone has to willingly offer themselves to the island, to sever the bond. Only then will the echoes be destroyed, and the island's hold over the portal broken."

The silence that followed her words was suffocating.

George's heart sank. The idea of someone sacrificing themselves—one of them—was unthinkable. But if that was the only way to save the world from the echoes...

"No," Mia said firmly, her voice filled with emotion. "There has to be another way. We can't just... we can't do that."

Elara's face was filled with sorrow. "I know. I've thought about it for years, hoping there was another way. But the echoes are bound to the island, and the portal is their only escape. If we want to stop them, if we want to save the world, someone has to stay behind."

George felt the weight of her words settle into his bones. The stakes were higher than he had ever imagined. Their mission had transformed from one of survival to one of sacrifice, and the reality of what they were facing was crushing.

Adrian, ever the leader, took a deep breath. "We'll figure it out," he said, his voice steady despite the weight of the situation. "But one thing's for sure—we're not leaving anyone behind. We'll find another way."

Elara nodded, though her expression remained solemn. "I hope you're right."

As they resumed their journey, the echoes' whispers seemed to grow louder, as if they knew that the group was drawing closer to the portal—and to the impossible choice they would have to make.

The path ahead was fraught with danger, and the stakes had never been higher. But George knew one thing for certain: whatever happened, they would face it together.

As they continued down the narrow path, tension thickened the air. George's heart raced, not just from the gravity of Elara's revelation, but from the unmistakable sense that they were being watched. The shadows seemed to stretch unnaturally, flickering at the edges of their vision. The echoes were near—too near.

The whispers grew louder, a twisted chorus of mocking voices that seemed to rise from the depths of the cavern itself. George's stomach clenched as the temperature around them dropped, a chill settling into his bones. The soft sound of shuffling echoed through the tunnel, and it wasn't long before the others noticed it too. Mia stopped abruptly, her eyes wide, and she looked at George, her face pale.

"Do you hear that?" she whispered.

Everyone came to a halt, the cold silence of the tunnel broken only by the distant, ghostly whispers. It was unmistakable now. They weren't alone.

Wren gripped his weapon tightly, scanning the darkness around them. "We're not going to get to the portal without a fight, are we?" he muttered, his voice filled with a mixture of fear and defiance.

Adrian moved forward, stepping between the group and the source of the sound. "Stay sharp," he said, his tone low and commanding. "They're coming."

Suddenly, the faint whispering turned into a cacophony of voices, overlapping and growing louder. The echoes' chilling presence began to materialize—wisps of shadow that moved like liquid through the darkness. George's eyes widened as the echoes took form before them, shifting and flickering like specters drawn from a nightmare.

"They're here," Elara said, her voice steady despite the fear in her eyes. "Get ready."

Before anyone could fully process the situation, the shadows surged toward them. The echoes, twisted and malevolent, came in waves, their once-human forms now distorted into monstrous figures. They had no faces, only dark, empty voids where their eyes should have been, and their bodies seemed to ripple like smoke, darting through the tunnel with a speed that made George's heart pound in his chest.

"Move!" Adrian shouted, unsheathing his weapon just as the first echo lunged toward them. He swung hard, the blade slicing through the air, but the echo moved too quickly, ducking under his attack and reforming behind him. "Damn it!" Adrian cursed, spinning to block another attack.

George's instincts kicked in, and he swung his own weapon at an echo that charged at him. His strike met resistance, cutting through the shadowy figure, but the echo reformed almost instantly, its body coiling and snapping toward him with eerie speed.

"They're not going down!" Mia cried, her voice filled with panic as she struck at an echo with her dagger, only for it to slither away and lunge at her again. The creature's claws grazed her arm, and she gasped in pain, stumbling backward.

Wren swung his axe in a wide arc, trying to keep the echoes at bay. "How the hell do we fight these things?" he shouted, frustration and fear mixing in his voice as the echoes swarmed them.

Elara, standing at the center of the group, her face set in grim determination, shouted over the chaos. "Aim for their core! They're shadows, but they still have a central point where their essence is concentrated! Strike there!"

Her words barely reached George through the noise, but they were enough to give him a moment of clarity. He focused on the echo nearest him, watching its movements closely. As the creature lunged again, he swung his blade at its chest—this time, aiming for the faint, glowing core that pulsed within the shadowy mass.

The blade struck true, and the echo let out a screeching hiss, its form dissolving into a cloud of black mist. George's heart surged with adrenaline as the creature vanished, but there was no time to celebrate. Two more echoes had already replaced the one he had defeated, and they were moving fast.

"They're everywhere!" Emma shouted, ducking as an echo's clawed hand swiped just inches from her face. She spun around, slashing at the creature with her sword, managing to slow it down but not destroy it.

Adrian fought fiercely, his movements precise and calculated. He dodged an echo's attack, then brought his sword down on its core, dispersing the creature in a burst of dark mist. "Stay close! Don't get separated!" he called, his voice steady despite the chaos.

George could feel the weight of the battle pressing down on him. The echoes were relentless, their numbers seemingly endless. Every time one fell, another took its place, surging forward with a fury that sent a wave of dread through him.

Wren gritted his teeth, swinging wildly as echoes closed in from all sides. "This is insane!" he yelled, his voice strained with effort. "There's too many of them!"

Elara moved swiftly through the chaos, her movements sharp and precise. She fought like someone who had been battling these creatures her entire life, each strike of her weapon aimed perfectly at the echoes' cores. But even she was beginning to tire, her breath coming in ragged gasps as the fight dragged on.

"They're trying to overwhelm us!" Elara shouted, cutting down another echo. "We need to get to higher ground, or we won't last much longer!"

Adrian nodded, his eyes scanning the tunnel for an exit. "Up there!" he shouted, pointing to a narrow ledge that ran along the side of the tunnel. "We can make our stand there!"

"Go! I'll cover you!" George yelled, stepping forward to intercept another wave of echoes as the group moved toward the ledge. He swung his weapon in wide arcs, trying to hold the creatures at bay, but it felt like trying to stop an avalanche with his bare hands.

One by one, the group scrambled up to the ledge, their weapons swinging wildly as they fought off the echoes that pursued them. Adrian reached the ledge first, helping Mia up just as an echo lunged at her from behind. With a swift strike, he dispatched the creature, but more were coming.

Wren climbed up next, his face covered in sweat, his chest heaving. "We need a plan," he gasped, his eyes wide with fear. "They're going to keep coming!"

Elara, still fighting below, glanced up at the ledge, her face set with determination. "There's no time for plans! We fight until we can break through!"

George swung his weapon again, cleaving through another echo, but it was a losing battle. The creatures were closing in, and the group was running out of space.

Suddenly, a massive roar filled the tunnel, shaking the very ground beneath them. George's heart skipped a beat as a new figure appeared—larger than any of the echoes they had faced so far. The creature's form was more defined, its body hulking and twisted, with glowing red eyes that burned with rage.

"What the hell is that?" Mia cried, her voice filled with terror.

"It's a commander," Elara said, her voice tight with fear. "One of the stronger echoes. It's come to finish us off."

The creature let out another roar, its massive clawed hands reaching for them as it charged forward. George's heart pounded in his chest as he realized that they were facing something far more dangerous than the echoes they had fought before.

"We can't take that thing down!" Wren shouted, panic rising in his voice.

"We don't have a choice!" Adrian barked, stepping forward to face the creature head-on. "We hold our ground, or we die here!"

The group rallied, their weapons raised as the massive echo charged toward them. George could feel the ground tremble beneath his feet as the creature bore down on them, its red eyes glowing with murderous intent.

With a deafening roar, the creature lunged forward, its massive claws swinging toward George. He barely had time to react, throwing himself to the side as the creature's claws slammed into the ground, sending a shower of stone and debris flying.

Adrian struck first, his blade slashing through the air as he aimed for the creature's core. But the commander was faster than expected, twisting its body to avoid the blow. It swung its massive arm, knocking Adrian back with a force that sent him crashing into the tunnel wall.

"Adrian!" Mia screamed, rushing to his side as the creature turned its attention to the others.

Wren and George moved together, trying to flank the creature from both sides. They swung their weapons in unison, but the commander was too fast. It dodged their attacks effortlessly, its massive claws swiping through the air as it countered.

Emma moved in next, her face set with determination as she aimed for the creature's core. But just as she struck, the commander twisted, catching her with a powerful backhand that sent her sprawling to the ground.

George's heart raced as the creature loomed over Emma, its glowing red eyes fixed on her as it prepared to deliver a killing blow. Without thinking, he rushed forward, swinging his weapon with all his strength. The blade connected with the creature's arm, severing it at the elbow.

The commander let out a roar of rage, its body twisting as dark mist poured from the wound. But even injured, it was far from defeated. It lashed out with its remaining arm, its claws grazing George's side as he dodged out of the way.

"We need to hit its core!" Elara shouted, her voice filled with urgency as she fought off another wave of smaller echoes. "It's the only way to kill it!"

George gritted his teeth, the pain from the creature's attack radiating through his body.

But he knew Elara was right. They couldn't take the commander down through brute force alone. They had to aim for its core, the same way they had with the smaller echoes.

The creature turned its red-eyed gaze on George, its massive form charging toward him with terrifying speed. George's heart pounded in his chest as he prepared for the strike, knowing that this was their only chance.

As the creature lunged, George rolled to the side, dodging its attack and spinning around to face its exposed core. With all his strength, he swung his blade, the metal slicing through the dark mist and plunging deep into the creature's glowing center.

For a moment, time seemed to freeze. The creature let out a guttural roar, its body convulsing as dark mist erupted from the wound. Its form began to disintegrate, the glowing red eyes fading as it collapsed to the ground in a heap of dark mist and shadow.

George stood there, breathing heavily, his heart racing as the creature dissolved into nothingness. The echoes that had surrounded them let out a collective wail, their forms flickering and fading as the commander's death seemed to weaken them.

One by one, the echoes disappeared, leaving the tunnel eerily silent.

George's legs felt weak, and he stumbled back, catching himself against the wall as the adrenaline began to wear off. The others gathered around him, their faces pale but filled with relief.

"We... we did it," Mia gasped, her eyes wide with disbelief.

Adrian, still clutching his side from the impact of the commander's attack, nodded grimly. "For now."

Elara stepped forward, her expression a mix of relief and exhaustion. "That was only the beginning. The echoes will come again, and the portal is still waiting. We can't stop now."

George looked at his friends, their faces etched with determination and exhaustion. The battle had been brutal, and the road ahead was even more dangerous. But they had come too far to turn back now.

With a deep breath, George nodded. "We keep moving. We finish this."

The echoes of their recent battle faded into the distance, but the tension remained, thick in the air as the group moved forward. The tunnel stretched on ahead of them, narrowing in places, then widening again as they wound their way deeper into the heart of Xel Island. The lingering exhaustion from the fight clung to them like a heavy mist, but there was no time to rest. They all knew the urgency of their mission—the portal was waiting, and every second they delayed brought them closer to potential disaster.

George walked near the front of the group, his breathing still uneven from the recent struggle. His side ached from the glancing blow the commander had dealt him, but he ignored the pain. They couldn't afford weakness now. Elara, ever vigilant, led the way, her eyes constantly scanning their surroundings. Adrian, his face tight with focus, remained close behind her, ready for anything.

For a while, the group moved in silence, their footsteps echoing softly against the stone walls of the cavern. The path was winding, twisting in unpredictable directions, as if deliberately designed to confuse and disorient them. Every so often, George would glance behind them, half-expecting to see more echoes creeping out of the shadows. But so far, they were alone—at least for now.

Minutes stretched into an hour, and then another, the group moving steadily forward. But as they walked, a strange sensation began to settle over them—a subtle feeling at first, but one that gradually grew harder to ignore.

"We've been walking for ages," Wren muttered, breaking the silence. His voice was strained, and his brow furrowed in frustration. "How much farther could this place be?"

Elara, still leading, glanced back at him, her face unreadable. "The portal is close. I can feel it. But this island... it doesn't follow the normal rules of space or time. It can stretch distances, warp reality to make things feel longer or shorter than they really are."

Mia, who had been walking quietly beside George, frowned as she looked around. "But it feels like we've been walking in circles," she said, her voice tinged with confusion. "I know it's different, but I swear we've passed this same stretch of tunnel before."

Emma nodded in agreement, her eyes narrowing as she inspected their surroundings. "I was just thinking the same thing. Everything looks different, but it *feels* the same, like we're stuck in a loop."

Adrian stopped walking for a moment, his eyes scanning the dimly lit tunnel. The ground beneath their feet shifted slightly with each step, but there were no landmarks, no signs to tell them how far they had traveled. The walls of the cavern seemed to pulse with a strange energy, making it difficult to keep track of time.

"I don't like this," Adrian said, his voice low. "We've been walking for hours, but it feels like we're not getting anywhere. It's like this world is messing with us."

Elara's expression darkened as she considered his words. "It's possible. The island and this world, both has a way of confusing the mind, especially when we're getting closer to something important. It's a defense mechanism."

"A defense mechanism?" Wren repeated, incredulous. "What are we, mice in a maze?"

George's gaze swept the tunnel, and though everything looked different—the curvature of the walls, the jagged rocks, the shimmering mist that occasionally hung in the air—there was an unsettling sense of familiarity to it all. It was as if they were walking in place, covering ground but getting nowhere. The sensation made his skin crawl.

"We're not lost, are we?" Mia asked, her voice small and uncertain.

"No," Elara said firmly, though there was a flicker of doubt in her eyes. "We're on the right path. But the island... it's trying to disorient us, make us doubt our progress."

Adrian let out a sharp breath, his patience visibly thinning. "Well, it's working. We've been walking for hours, and it feels like we're not making any progress."

George, feeling the growing frustration in the group, spoke up. "Maybe that's the point. If the island can make us doubt ourselves, if it can make us *feel* lost, then it's already winning. We can't give in to that."

Elara nodded, her gaze softening as she looked at George. "You're right. The island feeds off confusion and fear. The more we question what we're doing, the easier it becomes for the echoes to find us."

"But how do we fight something like this?" Emma asked, her voice trembling slightly. "If the island itself is against us, how do we know we're even going in the right direction?"

Elara closed her eyes for a brief moment, as if drawing strength from within herself. When she opened them again, her face was calm, her resolve unshaken. "We follow our instincts. Trust the path we're on. I can still feel the pull of the portal—it's out there, waiting for us. We just have to keep moving, no matter how disorienting it feels."

There was a moment of silence as the group absorbed her words, the weight of their journey pressing down on them more heavily than ever. George could feel the exhaustion settling into his bones, the endless walking and the constant sense of danger draining his energy. But Elara's words rang true. They couldn't let the island break them.

"Let's keep moving," George said, his voice steady. "We'll get there."

They resumed their walk, but the sensation of being trapped in a loop persisted, gnawing at the edges of their minds. Every step felt familiar, even when the scenery changed. The ground sloped downward, then leveled out, the walls of the cavern expanding into larger chambers only to narrow again into tight passages. The more they walked, the more time seemed to blur.

George kept his focus on the path ahead, trying not to think about the strange feeling of repetition. But the deeper they went, the stronger the sensation became. It was as though they were walking through an illusion, moving through a dream where nothing made sense.

Wren broke the silence again, his voice edged with frustration. "I'm telling you, we've passed this same spot three times now."

"We haven't," Elara said, her voice firm but weary. "The island is playing tricks on us. It wants us to believe we're going in circles so we'll give up."

"Well, it's working," Wren muttered under his breath.

Mia, her face drawn with fatigue, sighed heavily. "It feels like we're stuck in some kind of loop, like no matter how far we walk, we're just... nowhere."

George glanced at her, understanding the weariness in her voice. He felt it too, deep in his bones. "We'll get through it," he said quietly, though he wasn't sure if he was trying to reassure her or himself.

Emma's voice was barely above a whisper. "What if this is it? What if this is what the island wants—to trap us here forever?"

"No," Adrian said sharply, his voice cutting through the creeping despair. "We keep moving. No matter what it feels like, we're making progress. We'll get to the portal."

Elara looked over her shoulder at them, her eyes filled with determination. "He's right. The island's trying to break us, but we won't let it. We've come too far to stop now."

They pressed on, step after step, their minds fighting against the growing sense of futility. The island seemed to stretch time and space, making every step feel like a hundred, every moment feel like an eternity. George could feel the weight of it in his chest, the sinking feeling that they were being toyed with by forces beyond their control.

But they kept moving.

The whispers grew louder, swirling around them like a dissonant symphony. George could almost make out words, phrases tangled in the echoing sounds. But they were just out of reach, like voices heard through a thick fog.

"We're close," Elara said suddenly, her voice breaking through the oppressive atmosphere. She stopped, turning to face them. "I can feel it. The portal is near."

George could see the conviction in her eyes, and it reignited a spark of hope in his chest. He didn't know how much longer they would have to walk, or how many more tricks the island would play on them, but they had to believe that they were close. They had to believe that the end was in sight.

Adrian stepped forward, his expression resolute. "Then let's finish this."

With renewed purpose, the group moved forward, determined to break free from the island's illusions. The path twisted and turned, but they no longer questioned it. They walked with purpose, their eyes fixed on the goal ahead.

Even as the island tried to disorient them, tried to make them feel lost, they held onto the one thing it couldn't take from them: their resolve.

The whispers of the echoes faded into the background, and the sensation of walking in circles began to lift. George could feel it in the air, the faint hum of energy that pulsed through the walls of the cavern. The portal was close. They could feel it in their bones.

And as they moved forward, step by step, they knew that they were no longer walking in circles. They were heading toward the heart of the island, toward the portal that would decide the fate of not only their lives, but the world beyond.

They were almost there.

As they continued to walk, the oppressive weight of Xel Island's tricks seemed to lift ever so slightly. George's muscles ached, each step feeling heavier than the last, but a strange new energy hummed in the air around them. The whispering of the echoes had faded into the background, no longer as sharp or threatening, and the path seemed to straighten. It was as if the island itself knew they were nearing something monumental.

Elara led the way, her face focused, determination etched into every feature. She didn't speak, but George could feel her resolve radiating from her. The group followed her, their breaths shallow, their footsteps growing softer as if they knew instinctively that they were approaching something sacred—and dangerous.

The tunnel began to widen, the walls expanding outward until the space around them felt cavernous. The ground beneath their feet flattened, the uneven stones giving way to smoother rock. There was a faint glow ahead, a soft light that flickered like a beacon in the distance.

George's heart began to race. This was it. They were close.

"Elara?" Mia whispered, her voice barely audible in the stillness. "Are we...?"

Elara nodded slowly, her eyes fixed on the distant glow. "Yes," she said quietly. "We're here."

They walked forward, their pace slowing as the tunnel opened up into an enormous chamber, the ceiling so high it disappeared into darkness. The glow they had seen from a distance now flooded the room with a strange, otherworldly light, casting long shadows that danced along the walls.

At the center of the chamber, suspended in the air like something out of a dream, was the portal.

George's breath caught in his throat. It was unlike anything he had ever seen before—beautiful, terrifying, and impossibly powerful. The portal was a swirling vortex of light and magic, its edges crackling with raw energy. The colors were hypnotic—vivid blues and purples blending together in a whirl of shimmering light that pulsed like a heartbeat. It seemed alive, like the very fabric of reality was bending around it, straining to contain the immense power it held.

The light from the portal cast sharp beams throughout the cavern, cutting through the darkness like blades of pure magic. It was both blinding and mesmerizing, filling the air with a hum of energy that vibrated through George's bones.

But as his eyes adjusted to the brilliance of the portal, George's heart sank. They weren't alone.

Surrounding the portal, guarding it like sentinels, were hundreds of twisted echoes.

George's stomach twisted into a knot. The echoes weren't like the ones they had fought before. These were larger, more defined, their bodies grotesquely elongated, with limbs that stretched unnaturally and faces that seemed to ripple with malice. Their forms shifted constantly, twisting and contorting like shadows caught in a violent storm. Dark mist swirled around them, and their eyes—glowing red pinpricks of light—stared unblinking at the portal, as if they were bound to it by some unholy force.

The whispers returned, louder now, filling the air with a discordant chorus of voices that made George's skin crawl. The echoes seemed to pulse in time with the portal's light, their bodies flickering in and out of existence as if tethered to the very magic that powered the portal.

"They're everywhere," Emma breathed, her voice trembling as she took in the sight. "How are we supposed to get past them?"

Adrian's face was grim as he surveyed the scene. "That's... a lot of echoes."

Mia clutched her dagger tightly, her eyes wide with fear. "There's no way we can fight them all. We'll be torn apart."

Wren's face was pale, his usual bravado gone as he stared at the army of twisted creatures guarding the portal. "We're screwed," he muttered, his voice shaking. "There's no way we're getting through that."

Elara stood at the front of the group, her face unreadable as she watched the echoes. Her hands were clenched into fists at her sides, but she didn't move, didn't speak. George could see the conflict in her eyes—the desperate need to reach the portal and the crushing realization that they were hopelessly outnumbered.

"They're waiting," Elara said softly, her voice barely above a whisper. "They know we're here."

George felt his chest tighten. The echoes weren't attacking, not yet. They stood perfectly still, their glowing eyes fixed on the portal, their bodies trembling with barely contained energy. It was as if they were bound to the portal, unable to leave it unguarded but fully aware that the group had come for it.

"They can't leave the portal unprotected," Elara continued, her eyes narrowing. "It's the only thing keeping them here. If we get close enough, they'll have no choice but to attack."

Adrian grimaced, his grip tightening on his sword. "And once they do, it'll be a bloodbath."

George could feel the hopelessness creeping in, the enormity of the task before them crashing down on him like a wave. They had come so far, fought through so much, but now—facing an army of echoes with no clear plan—it felt like the island had outsmarted them. The echoes had been waiting for this moment, and they had the upper hand.

"Is there any other way?" Mia asked, her voice trembling with fear. "Is there a way around them?"

Elara shook her head, her expression grim. "No. The portal is the only way out, and they know it. They'll do whatever it takes to keep us from reaching it."

George's mind raced as he stared at the swirling vortex of light, the portal seeming to beckon them even as the echoes stood between them and escape. His muscles tensed, and a cold sweat broke out on his skin. They couldn't turn back. The portal was their only chance—if they didn't reach it, if they didn't get through and stop the echoes from escaping, everything would be lost.

"We have to find a way," George said quietly, his voice steady despite the fear that gnawed at him. "We can't let them win. We've come too far."

Adrian nodded slowly, his eyes dark with resolve. "We'll find a way."

Elara stepped forward, her gaze fixed on the portal, her voice filled with quiet determination. "There's no going back. We fight."

For a moment, the group stood in silence, the weight of the decision hanging over them like a storm cloud. The echoes stirred, their bodies shifting in the dark mist, but they didn't attack. Not yet. They were waiting, watching, and George knew that the moment they made their move, the battle would begin.

George's heart pounded in his chest as he looked at his friends—Mia, Wren, Emma, Adrian, and Elara. Their faces were etched with fear, but also with a fierce determination. They had survived too much to give up now. They were more than just survivors. They were a team.

"We fight," George said, his voice stronger now, his resolve hardening. "Together."

The others nodded, their weapons at the ready, their eyes fixed on the portal and the army of echoes guarding it.

Elara's gaze softened as she looked at them, a flicker of gratitude in her eyes. "Thank you," she whispered, her voice filled with emotion. "We'll finish this. Together."

And with that, they took their first steps toward the portal.

The echoes, sensing their movement, began to stir. The dark mist thickened, swirling around the creatures as their bodies pulsed with energy. The whispers grew louder, more menacing, as the army of twisted shadows prepared to strike.

The light from the portal grew brighter, the magic within it crackling with power, casting long, sharp shadows across the cavern floor. The hum of energy in the air intensified, vibrating through the ground beneath their feet, as if the very island was coming alive.

They were close now. So close.

But between them and freedom stood an army of nightmares.

As they stood before the portal, the radiant light casting harsh shadows across their faces, the reality of what lay ahead sank in. The echoes, hundreds of them, twisted and monstrous, stood like an army waiting to unleash fury on anything that dared approach. Their red, glowing eyes flickered with malevolent hunger, their bodies rippling like liquid shadows, coiled and ready to strike. Every breath the group took was heavy with tension, but in their eyes, there was no doubt—there was no room for hesitation.

The island had toyed with them, twisted their path, tried to break them down. But now, here, at the brink of escape, it had made its final stand.

George felt the electric charge in the air, the hum of the portal's magic vibrating through his body. His heart pounded against his ribcage, and his hands tightened around his weapon. Every instinct in his body screamed at him to run, to find cover, to hide from the inevitable onslaught, but something deeper urged him forward.

“We’re not hiding,” George said firmly, breaking the tense silence. His voice was steady, though his heart raced with fear and adrenaline. “We’ve come too far for that.”

Adrian stepped forward, his sword gleaming under the sharp light of the portal. His face was grim but resolute. “No more running. No more hiding. We take the fight to them.”

The others nodded in agreement, each of them feeling the same surge of determination that pulsed through George. They had fought too long, too hard to falter now. Hiding would mean giving the echoes the upper hand, and they couldn’t afford that.

Elara, her gaze fixed on the army of echoes, spoke softly but with undeniable conviction. “They’re tied to the portal. If we want to escape, we have to face them. We can’t avoid this. The only way out is through.”

Mia’s knuckles whitened as she gripped her dagger tighter, her breaths shallow but focused. “So we fight. And we win.”

Wren let out a sharp breath, his face pale but determined. “Well, it’s not like we have a better option. Let’s finish this.”

Emma nodded, her eyes scanning the mass of echoes that stood between them and the portal. “We stay together. We fight as one.”

The group moved closer, stepping into formation, their weapons drawn and their hearts pounding. The echoes began to stir more violently, sensing the impending confrontation. Dark mist swirled around them, and their twisted forms seemed to grow more defined, their movements more aggressive. They weren’t just shadows anymore—they were a nightmare made real.

“We hit them hard and fast,” Adrian commanded, his voice strong. “Don’t give them a chance to regroup. We can’t let them surround us.”

George glanced at his friends, feeling the gravity of the moment settle deep in his chest. This wasn’t just a battle for survival—it was a battle for the future, for the real world, for everything they had left behind. The echoes weren't just enemies; they were the embodiment of the island's darkest powers, and if they escaped, they would bring ruin to the world.

"Whatever happens," George said quietly, his eyes meeting each of theirs in turn, "we don't stop. We fight until the end."

Elara's gaze softened as she looked at George, a flicker of admiration crossing her face. "We will fight together," she said firmly, her voice filled with resolve. "We won't let them win."

And then, without another word, they charged.

The echoes surged forward as if the portal itself had given them life, their forms stretching and twisting, red eyes glowing like embers in a storm. The air crackled with tension as the two forces collided—light against shadow, steel against darkness.

Adrian was the first to strike, his sword cutting through the air with precision as he slashed at the nearest echo. The blade met resistance as it sliced through the creature's core, and the echo let out a piercing, inhuman scream before dissolving into mist. But before Adrian could regain his stance, another two echoes lunged at him, their claws sharp and fast.

"Adrian, watch out!" Mia cried, darting forward to intercept one of the echoes. She moved with the speed and grace of a dancer, her dagger flashing in the air as she struck at the creature's chest. The echo hissed as it disintegrated, but more took its place, surging toward her like a tidal wave.

George gritted his teeth, the adrenaline rushing through his veins as he fought his way toward the center of the fray. The echoes were relentless, their forms shifting and reforming almost as quickly as they were struck down. It was like fighting a storm, every swing of his weapon cutting through one, only to have another rise in its place.

"Stay together!" Elara shouted over the roar of the battle. Her own blade moved with deadly accuracy, slicing through the mist-like bodies of the echoes. "They're trying to separate us!"

Wren, who was fending off two echoes at once, grunted in frustration. "They're damn good at it too!"

The echoes were everywhere, a swirling mass of darkness that seemed to press in on them from all sides. They moved with terrifying speed, their claws slashing through the air, their voices a haunting, dissonant chorus that filled the cavern with an overwhelming sense of dread.

But George refused to give in. He swung his sword with all his strength, cleaving through the core of an echo that lunged at him. The creature let out a guttural screech before it evaporated into mist, but George barely had time to catch his breath before another took its place.

"We have to get closer to the portal!" Emma shouted, her voice strained as she fended off two echoes at once. "If we can just reach it—"

"The closer we get," Elara interrupted, her voice tense as she blocked an echo's attack, "the more they'll come. They're tied to it. They'll do everything to stop us."

George could feel the pull of the portal's energy, a strange, humming force that seemed to vibrate in the air around them. The echoes were swarming, their numbers seemingly endless, but he knew they couldn't stop. The portal was their only way out, and they had to reach it.

"Push forward!" Adrian commanded, his voice rising above the chaos. He swung his sword in a wide arc, cutting through two echoes at once before charging ahead. "Don't let them surround us!"

The group moved together, their formation tight, each of them fighting off the echoes with a desperate intensity. George's muscles burned from the constant movement, but he didn't slow down. Every strike, every parry, felt like a battle against time itself. The echoes were relentless, their claws scraping against his skin, their voices echoing in his mind, but he refused to falter.

Beside him, Mia moved with a fierce agility, her dagger flashing in the dim light as she struck down echo after echo. Her movements were fluid, precise, each strike hitting its mark with deadly accuracy. But the effort was taking its toll, and George could see the exhaustion in her eyes, the strain in her posture.

"Are you okay?" George shouted, blocking an echo's attack as he glanced at her.

Mia nodded, her face pale but determined. "I'm fine. Just... keep going!"

Wren, fighting nearby, let out a frustrated growl as he swung his axe in a wide arc, cleaving through an echo's core. "These things just don't stop!"

"They will if we keep pushing," Emma called, her voice filled with a fierce determination. She sliced through another echo, her eyes locked on the swirling vortex of the portal. "We just have to keep going."

The portal loomed ahead of them, its light pulsing with raw magic, but between them and escape stood an army of echoes, their forms shifting and flickering like living nightmares. The battle raged on, each swing of their weapons cutting through the darkness, but the echoes kept coming.

Elara, at the front of the group, fought with a fierce determination, her blade a blur as she cut through the echoes. But even she was starting to tire, her movements slowing as the battle dragged on.

"They're weakening!" Elara shouted, her voice strained but filled with hope. "Keep pushing!"

George could feel the echoes' presence starting to falter, their forms less defined, their attacks less coordinated. But the battle was far from over. They still had a long way to go, and the echoes, though weakening, were still a formidable force.

As they fought, the air around them crackled with energy, the magic from the portal intensifying with every passing moment. The hum of power vibrated through the ground, through their bones, urging them forward even as exhaustion threatened to pull them down.

"We're almost there!" Adrian called, his voice filled with determination. "Just a little more!"

But even as they pushed forward, George knew that the battle wasn't just about reaching the portal. It was about surviving long enough to make it through. The echoes wouldn't stop until they were all dead, or until they had passed through the portal's swirling light.

With a deep breath, George steadied himself, his eyes locked on the portal ahead. They were close—so close. But the echoes were closing in again, their forms flickering with renewed energy.

This battle wasn't over yet.

The battle raged on with the echoes swirling like a storm, their forms twisting and flickering in and out of the misty darkness. Every moment felt like an eternity. Every swing of George's sword was met with the resistance of the shadowy creatures that seemed to multiply with each passing second. The magic from the portal pulsed violently, the air vibrating with an otherworldly hum, pushing them closer to the edge of their endurance.

"We're almost there!" Adrian shouted, his voice rising above the cacophony of the echoes' sinister wails. His sword cut through one of the creatures, sending it screeching into a cloud of dark mist. But before they could press forward, something changed.

The ground beneath their feet began to tremble, shaking violently as though the very island itself had come alive. George stumbled, struggling to keep his footing as the vibrations intensified, sending cracks splintering through the stone floor.

"What's happening?" Mia yelled, panic edging her voice as she swung her dagger, her movements more frantic as the echoes seemed to move in rhythm with the ground.

Before anyone could answer, the ground beneath them exploded with a sudden, violent force.

"Watch out!" Wren screamed, but it was too late.

In one terrifying moment, the ground opened up, and from below, dozens of echoes surged upward like a wave, their claws reaching out to grab them. The force of the eruption sent the group flying backward, their bodies hurled through the air as if they were nothing more than leaves caught in a storm.

George felt the wind rush out of him as he slammed into the ground several feet away, the impact knocking the breath from his lungs. Pain shot through his side, sharp and unforgiving. Dazed, he struggled to push himself up, the world spinning around him as the echoes regrouped, their twisted forms looming over them like predators ready to strike.

Mia was the first to recover, scrambling to her feet with a wince. "They came from underground," she gasped, glancing at George. "They're everywhere now."

The echoes, emboldened by their sudden advantage, closed in with renewed ferocity. They moved with unsettling speed, their bodies coiling and uncoiling like living shadows. Their red eyes glowed menacingly as they converged on the group.

George managed to stand, gritting his teeth against the pain that flared through his ribs. "We have to hold the line!" he shouted, his voice hoarse from exertion. His sword was slick with the dark mist of the echoes he'd already felled, but there were so many more.

Adrian, despite the bruises and cuts that marked his body, regained his stance quickly. "Form up! Don't let them split us!" he ordered, his voice steady, though George could see the fatigue in his eyes.

The group quickly regrouped, though the impact had left them scattered and disoriented. Wren, bloodied but unbroken, growled as he swung his axe in wide arcs, trying to keep the advancing echoes at bay. "These things just don't stop!" he muttered, frustration dripping from his voice as he slammed his axe into another creature's core, turning it into a plume of dark smoke.

Elara, her breathing labored but her focus unwavering, darted through the melee, her blade flashing with deadly precision. She moved like a dancer, cutting down echoes as they lunged toward her. But despite her skill, the relentless attacks from the creatures were beginning to wear her down.

"We have to move forward!" Elara shouted, her voice strained as she blocked an echo's clawed swipe. "The longer we stay here, the more they'll surround us!"

"We're trying!" Emma called back, deflecting an echo that had gotten too close for comfort. "But they're too fast!"

George swung at another echo, cutting through its core just as it lunged at Mia. But before he could regain his footing, the ground trembled again, and another wave of echoes surged from beneath them, their shadowy forms twisting as they emerged from the cracks in the earth.

"They're using the ground to trap us!" Mia shouted, her voice edged with desperation as she fought off another echo. "We can't keep this up!"

Adrian sliced through an echo before turning to Elara. "We need a path! Can you find an opening?"

Elara's eyes darted across the battlefield, searching for any break in the endless waves of creatures. But the echoes were relentless, their numbers seemingly infinite. Her face hardened as she steeled herself for the next move.

And then, in the chaos of the moment, it happened.

Elara, moving swiftly through the fray, made a split-second decision to dodge an attacking echo. She moved to her left, her instincts pushing her away from the creature's clawed swipe. But in doing so, she moved directly into the path of another echo that had been lurking just beyond her line of sight.

"NO!" George screamed, watching in horror as the echo lunged, but it was too late.

The echo shot past Elara, its movement almost too fast to track, and barreled directly into George. He felt its claws rake across his side, tearing through his skin as a searing pain exploded through him. The force of the blow sent him crashing to the ground, his vision swimming as he hit the stone floor with a sickening thud.

"George!" Mia screamed, rushing to his side, but another wave of echoes blocked her path.

Elara's face went pale as she realized what had happened. "No... no, no, no..." she whispered, her voice trembling with shock. She had made the wrong move—she had moved left when she should have gone right—and now George was paying the price.

The echo that had attacked George circled back, its twisted form looming over him like a shadow of death. George, his body wracked with pain, tried to push himself up, but his strength was failing. Blood seeped from the deep gashes in his side, pooling beneath him as the world around him blurred.

Elara's heart pounded in her chest as she fought off the echoes surrounding her, her movements becoming more frantic. She couldn't believe what had just happened—one wrong move, and it had all gone wrong. The weight of her mistake crashed over her like a wave, and she could feel her resolve begin to falter.

"Get to George!" Adrian shouted, his sword cleaving through another echo as he fought his way toward them. "We can't lose him!"

Wren, hearing Adrian's call, swung his axe in a brutal arc, cutting down two echoes that had been pressing him. "Mia! Cover me!" he shouted, charging toward George as the echoes continued to press in from all sides.

Mia nodded, her eyes blazing with determination as she fought off the creatures in their path. She moved with speed and precision, clearing a way for Wren to reach George.

Elara, fighting her way through the swarm of echoes, was consumed with guilt. Her wrong move had cost them—had cost George. But she couldn't let it end here. She wouldn't.

With a surge of adrenaline, Elara pushed forward, her blade flashing in the dim light as she cut through the echoes with renewed fury. She reached George just as Wren did, and together they pulled him to his feet, though George was barely conscious, his face pale and his breathing labored.

"George, stay with us!" Mia cried, her eyes wide with fear as she fended off an attacking echo. "We're almost there!"

George's vision swam, the pain in his side radiating through his entire body. He could feel the warmth of his own blood trickling down his skin, and every breath felt like a battle. But even through the haze of pain, he could hear the urgency in Mia's voice, feel the pressure of Wren's strong grip pulling him up.

"I'm... I'm okay," George rasped, though the words felt like they were slipping from his mouth.

Elara, her face etched with guilt and determination, tightened her grip on her sword. "I'm sorry," she whispered, her voice barely audible over the roar of the battle around them. "I won't make that mistake again."

The echoes surged again, their numbers seemingly endless, but the group held their ground. Despite the chaos, despite the overwhelming odds, they refused to give in. They fought together, as one, every strike, every movement synchronized as they pressed forward.

But the battle was far from over.

The echoes were growing more aggressive, their movements more erratic as the magic of the portal intensified. The light from the swirling vortex pulsed violently, casting sharp beams of light through the cavern, and the air crackled with energy.

This war wasn't just about survival anymore—it was about escape. It was about getting to the portal and making sure the echoes never left this cursed island.

But first, they had to survive.

The battle continued to rage, an unrelenting storm of shadows and light. The echoes seemed to grow more aggressive with every second, their twisted forms lunging with terrifying speed and precision. The air was thick with tension, the magic from the portal crackling violently as the group fought with everything they had. They moved in unison, a desperate, well-coordinated force trying to carve a path toward their only hope of escape.

But the exhaustion was beginning to show. George, still reeling from the injury he'd sustained from Elara's earlier mistake, fought through the pain, his body screaming for rest as blood seeped through his side. He gritted his teeth, forcing his movements to remain sharp despite the agony. Every time an echo lunged, George managed to block, parry, or deflect the strike, but he knew his strength was fading.

Adrian, ever the leader, was at the front, driving the group forward. His sword slashed through the air with deadly accuracy, cutting down echoes as they surged toward him. But even he was beginning to slow, his movements growing heavier with fatigue.

"We're getting closer!" Adrian shouted over the roar of the battle, his voice hoarse but determined. The portal's swirling light pulsed brighter with every step they took, and the energy in the air grew more intense. "Keep pushing!"

Mia moved beside George, her dagger flashing in quick, precise strikes as she took down an echo that had tried to circle behind them.

"We can't let up now!" she called out, her voice filled with fierce determination despite the exhaustion on her face.

Wren, wielding his axe with brute strength, grunted as he cleaved through an echo that had lunged at him. His eyes were wild, his adrenaline surging as he swung his weapon with reckless force, cutting through the echoes in wide, sweeping arcs.

But in the chaos of the moment, something shifted. Wren, caught up in the battle, made a split-second decision that would prove to be disastrous.

An echo darted toward him from the side, and in his haste to block the attack, Wren swung his axe hard—too hard—trying to force the creature back. His movement, though powerful, was mistimed, and the momentum of the swing threw him off balance. He stumbled to the side, his footing slipping on the uneven ground.

"Wren, no!" Emma shouted, her eyes wide as she saw what was about to happen.

Wren's misstep sent him crashing into Adrian, who had been in the middle of parrying a vicious strike from a nearby echo. The force of Wren's body colliding with Adrian knocked him off balance, and before Adrian could recover, the echo's claws slashed across his chest with terrifying speed.

Time seemed to slow.

Adrian let out a sharp, strangled cry as the echo's claws raked through his armor, tearing through flesh and muscle. Blood sprayed into the air, and Adrian staggered backward, his sword slipping from his grasp as he fell to his knees.

"Adrian!" Mia screamed, her voice filled with horror as she rushed toward him.

George's heart plummeted as he saw the blood pouring from Adrian's chest, his body crumpling under the force of the attack. For a moment, it looked like the echo had finished him—like the leader who had carried them through this entire nightmare was about to fall.

"No, no, no!" George shouted, adrenaline surging through him as he fought to get to Adrian, his sword cutting down an echo that stood in his way. "We can't lose him!"

Elara, still reeling from her own earlier mistake, looked horrified as she watched Adrian collapse. She fought her way through the echoes, her movements frantic as she tried to reach him.

Wren, his eyes wide with disbelief and panic, scrambled to his feet, realizing what he had done. "Adrian!" he gasped, his voice shaking as he reached for his friend. "I—I'm sorry! I didn't mean—"

But before Wren could say anything else, an echo lunged at him, its claws slicing through the air with deadly intent. Wren barely managed to deflect the strike, but his face was pale, his body trembling as the weight of his mistake settled over him.

Adrian, clutching his chest where the echo had torn through him, struggled to breathe, his face twisted in pain. Blood poured from the wound, staining the ground beneath him. His vision blurred, and for a moment, he thought it was the end.

But somehow, against all odds, he managed to move.

With a desperate grunt, Adrian forced himself to roll to the side just as another echo lunged at him, its claws missing him by inches. He reached out, his fingers brushing against the hilt of his sword, and with a surge of willpower, he grabbed it, swinging the blade upward in a defensive arc. The echo screeched as the blade connected with its core, dissolving into mist as Adrian gasped for breath.

"Adrian, hang on!" George shouted, his voice thick with fear as he fought his way toward him. His side throbbed painfully from his earlier injury, but he ignored it, focusing only on reaching his friend. "Don't you dare give up!"

Mia reached Adrian first, dropping to her knees beside him as she tried to assess the damage. "Stay with me, Adrian!" she cried, her hands shaking as she pressed them against his chest, trying to stem the flow of blood. "We need you!"

Adrian, his face pale and slick with sweat, managed a weak smile. "I'm not... going anywhere," he rasped, though his voice was strained and barely audible.

Elara reached them next, her eyes wide with panic. "Adrian, I—I'm so sorry, I didn't see—"

"It's not your fault," Adrian grunted, his breath coming in shallow gasps. "We... need to keep moving. The portal... it's right there."

But even as he spoke, the echoes pressed in closer, their forms more aggressive, their attacks more violent. They seemed to sense that Adrian had been wounded, and they moved toward him like sharks drawn to blood.

George, seeing the echoes converging on them, gritted his teeth and swung his sword with renewed fury, determined to keep them at bay. "We need to get him out of here!" he shouted, his voice hoarse from the effort.

Wren, still shaken by what had happened, fought beside George, his face tight with guilt. "This is my fault," he muttered, his voice filled with regret. "If I hadn't—"

"There's no time for that!" George snapped, cutting down another echo as it lunged at them. "We need to focus on keeping him alive!"

Emma, her face pale but determined, fought her way to the group, her sword flashing as she struck down another echo. "We need to get Adrian back on his feet, or we won't make it to the portal!"

Mia, still pressing her hands against Adrian's chest, nodded frantically. "We need to stop the bleeding, or he's not going to make it."

Elara, her face filled with guilt and fear, stepped forward. "I can help. I know a way to stabilize him—just long enough for us to get to the portal."

"Do it!" George urged, slashing at another echo that had come too close. "We don't have much time!"

As Elara knelt beside Adrian, whispering soft incantations that pulsed with a strange magic, the others formed a protective circle around them, fending off the waves of echoes that continued to press in.

Wren, his face twisted with guilt and anger, fought harder than ever, his axe cutting through the echoes with brutal force. "I won't let this be the end," he muttered to himself, his eyes blazing with determination. "Not after everything we've been through."

George fought alongside him, each swing of his sword filled with a fierce intensity. The pain from his earlier wound still throbbed, but it only fueled his resolve. He wasn't about to let Adrian fall—not when they were this close to the portal.

Elara's magic seemed to take hold, and Adrian's breathing steadied, though the wound was still grave. He gave them a weak nod, his voice barely a whisper. "Let's... finish this."

But the echoes weren't done with them yet.

They still stood between the group and the portal, their forms twisting and contorting as they prepared for one final push. The air crackled with tension, and George knew that the next few moments would decide everything.

They were almost there.

As the battle raged on, every swing of the sword, every dodge and block felt like a fight against time itself. George's muscles ached, and the wound in his side throbbed painfully, but he didn't stop. None of them could stop now. The portal loomed just ahead, pulsing with raw, dangerous magic, the swirling light casting eerie shadows across the battlefield. It was their only way out, their only chance to escape Xel Island and the monstrous echoes that swarmed around them.

Adrian, though still weak and pale from the attack that had nearly killed him, was back on his feet, his face determined despite the pain. Elara had stabilized him with her magic, though the strain of it was evident in her trembling hands and the exhaustion that lined her face. But there was no time to rest—no time to recover. The portal was right there, and the echoes were closing in fast.

"They're everywhere!" Mia shouted, her voice filled with panic as she slashed at another echo that lunged toward her. "We can't hold them off much longer!"

George glanced around, his heart racing. The echoes were relentless, their shadowy forms swirling like a storm, their red eyes glowing with malicious intent. More and more of them were emerging from the ground, their claws slashing through the air as they closed in on the group. It was like fighting the tide—no matter how many they cut down, more seemed to take their place.

"We need to go!" Emma yelled, her voice strained as she blocked an echo's attack with her sword. "We won't survive another wave!"

Adrian gritted his teeth, his hand pressed against his chest where blood still seeped from the wound. "We have to make a break for the portal. It's now or never."

Elara's face was pale, her eyes wide as she looked toward the swirling vortex of light. She hesitated for a moment, as though she couldn't quite believe they were so close. The portal, the gateway back to the real world, was right in front of them—but the echoes stood between them and freedom.

George, sensing her hesitation, grabbed her arm. "Elara, we have to go! Now!"

Elara's eyes met his, and for a moment, George saw the fear in her gaze—the fear of what lay on the other side, the uncertainty of the world they were about to step into. But then she nodded, her resolve hardening as she squared her shoulders. "Let's do this," she said, her voice steady despite the chaos around them.

Adrian took the lead, his sword flashing in the dim light as he fought his way toward the portal. "Stay together! Don't stop for anything!"

The group moved as one, their weapons cutting through the air as they fought off the echoes that tried to block their path. The swirling mist and dark forms pressed in from all sides, their attacks more frenzied, more desperate as the group neared the portal. It was as though the echoes knew this was their last chance to stop them.

Wren swung his axe with brutal force, cutting down two echoes that had lunged at him. "Come on! We're almost there!"

George's heart pounded in his chest as they closed the final distance to the portal. The light from the swirling vortex pulsed violently, the air around them crackling with raw energy. He could feel the magic pulling at him, urging him forward, but the echoes were right behind them, their claws slashing through the air with terrifying speed.

"We have to jump!" Mia yelled, her eyes wide as she fought off another echo.

Without another word, Adrian led the charge, diving headfirst into the swirling light of the portal. The instant his body touched the magic, the light seemed to envelop him, pulling him through in a burst of energy.

One by one, the others followed. Emma was next, her sword flashing one last time as she struck down an echo before leaping into the portal. Mia was right behind her, her eyes filled with determination as she threw herself into the light.

George and Elara were the last to move, their backs to the portal as they fought off the echoes that were still trying to close in. "Go!" George shouted, his voice filled with urgency. "I'll cover you!"

Elara hesitated for only a second before nodding, and with a final swing of her sword, she jumped into the portal, the light swallowing her up in a flash.

George turned to face the portal, his heart racing. The echoes were right behind him, their claws slashing through the air, their red eyes burning with fury. He could feel the darkness closing in, the weight of the island's magic pressing down on him.

But just as the echoes lunged, George threw himself into the portal.

For a moment, everything went dark.

The sensation of falling, weightless, as though he had been torn from one world and thrown into another. The magic of the portal surrounded him, pulling him through time and space, twisting reality itself as he was flung toward the unknown.

And then, with a jarring thud, he landed on solid ground.

George gasped, his lungs burning as he sucked in a breath. The air was different here—cooler, fresher, untouched by the malevolent presence of Xel Island. He blinked rapidly, trying to adjust to the sudden change in light and surroundings.

He was no longer in the dark caverns of the magical realm created by Xel Island. They had made it.

Around him, the others were recovering, each of them shaking off the disorienting effects of the portal. Adrian, though still weakened from his injury, was already on his feet, his sword in hand as he scanned their new surroundings. Mia and Emma were close by, their faces pale but filled with relief. Wren, breathing heavily, sat on the ground, his axe resting beside him.

Elara was the last to rise, her face pale as she looked around. "We're... we're here," she whispered, her voice filled with disbelief.

But before anyone could celebrate, the air around them began to shift. The once-still breeze turned sharp, cold, and ominous. George's heart sank as he heard the unmistakable sound of whispering, the same eerie chorus of voices they had heard on Xel Island.

"No," George muttered, his eyes widening in horror as he turned to look behind them.

The echoes had followed them.

The dark, twisted forms of the creatures began to emerge from the swirling light of the portal, their red eyes glowing with malevolent fury. The portal, which had been their escape, had now become a doorway for the echoes to cross into the real world.

"They're here," Adrian said, his voice tight with fear and disbelief. "They followed us."

Elara's face drained of color as she realized the truth. "No... this can't be happening."

But it was happening.

The echoes had escaped.

4

The Horrifying Truths

The relief that had washed over them when they landed on solid ground quickly dissolved into pure horror. George's heart raced as the once-still breeze turned chilling, the familiar, haunting whisper of the echoes filling the air. They had barely escaped Xel Island, but somehow—somehow—the echoes had followed.

Behind them, the portal still swirled with raw, pulsating magic, and from it emerged the nightmarish figures of the echoes. Dozens at first, their red eyes glowing like embers in the dim light, but then more—hundreds, their twisted, shadowy forms coiling and writhing as they moved forward. The army of echoes was closing in fast, their presence turning the air cold and oppressive.

Mia gasped, backing away instinctively. "No... no, this can't be happening!" she cried, her voice filled with desperation. "They're supposed to be trapped on the island!"

Adrian's face paled as he gripped his sword tightly, his eyes scanning the mass of echoes that stood between them and any chance of safety. "They followed us through the portal," he said, his voice tight with disbelief. "How could this happen?"

Wren's eyes were wide with panic, his hands shaking as he lifted his axe. "We didn't just bring ourselves out... we brought them with us. We've unleashed them into the real world!"

Emma, her face a mask of horror, shook her head in disbelief. "How could we have been so stupid? We should've known..."

But George's attention wasn't on the encroaching echoes. It was on Elara.

She stood still, unmoving, her face unreadable as the chaos unfolded around her. George, who had been right beside her as they jumped through the portal, now sensed something deeply wrong. Her silence was deafening in the midst of the terror, and when she finally spoke, it wasn't with the fear or confusion that the rest of them felt.

It was something colder. Something far more unsettling.

"Elara," George began, his voice hesitant, his eyes narrowing as he approached her. "What's going on? What are we going to do now?"

Elara turned slowly to face him, and George's breath caught in his throat. There was something in her eyes—something that had changed, something that hadn't been there before. Her gaze was sharp, calculating, and utterly devoid of the warmth or concern she'd shown earlier.

"Elara?" Mia asked, stepping closer, her voice trembling. "What's happening?"

And then, Elara smiled.

But it wasn't the kind, reassuring smile they had seen from her before. This smile was something else entirely—cold, cruel, and filled with an eerie satisfaction that made George's skin crawl. The air around them seemed to still, the sounds of the echoes momentarily fading as if the entire world was waiting for what was about to unfold.

"You still don't understand, do you?" Elara said softly, her voice dripping with something dark and unfamiliar. "After all this time... you still don't get it."

George felt a cold chill run down his spine. "What do you mean?"

Elara's smile widened, her eyes glinting with a malevolent light that made George take a step back. "The stories I told you," she continued, her voice calm but laced with an underlying cruelty, "everything I said about my past, about the echoes, about needing your help... it was all a lie."

Mia's eyes widened in shock. "What... what are you talking about?"

Elara turned to face the entire group, her gaze sweeping over them like a predator surveying its prey. "Did you really think I needed your help to escape the island?" she asked, her voice filled with mockery. "Did you really think I was just another victim trapped in that cursed place, desperate for freedom?"

Adrian's grip tightened on his sword, his jaw clenched as he took a step toward her. "What are you saying, Elara?"

Her eyes flickered with something dangerous. "I'm not who you think I am," she said, her voice growing colder with every word. "In fact... I'm not even Elara."

George's heart skipped a beat. "What?"

She took a step forward, her smile widening as she spoke. "You've been played, all of you," she said, her voice filled with a dark, twisted glee. "From the moment I found you, from the moment I led you on this path, every step you took was part of my plan."

The echoes behind her grew more restless, their movements synchronized with her words as if they were waiting for her command. George's stomach twisted as the horrifying realization began to sink in.

"Elara..." Emma whispered, her voice barely audible, "what have you done?"

Elara's form seemed to shift slightly, her shadow growing darker, more twisted, as if the truth of her nature was beginning to reveal itself. "I am the leader of the echoes," she said, her voice steady and filled with power. "The strongest among them. I've ruled that world for centuries, feeding off the souls of those foolish enough to set foot in the Xel Island."

George's blood ran cold. "No..."

She laughed softly, the sound sending chills down George's spine. "I told you about the echoes, about how they needed a human to escape that world. That part was true. But what I didn't tell you was that I orchestrated everything—every choice you made, every battle you fought. I led you to the portal because I needed you. I needed all of you."

Adrian's face was a mask of fury and disbelief. "You used us."

Elara nodded, her eyes gleaming with satisfaction. "I needed humans to open the portal, and you were perfect for the job. You were so determined, so noble... so easy to manipulate."

George felt like the ground had been ripped out from under him. "Everything we did... everything we fought for..."

"Was part of my plan," Elara finished, her voice sharp as a blade. "You thought you were saving the world, but all you did was open the door for my army to follow. And now, the echoes are free. They're no longer bound to the island. They will spread through this world like a plague, consuming everything in their path."

Mia's voice cracked with emotion as she stepped forward, her eyes wide with disbelief. "Why would you do this? Why would you betray us like this?"

Elara's smile faded, replaced by a cold, expressionless stare. "Because I am not one of you. I never was. I am a being of darkness, born from the island's magic, and the echoes are my creation. I exist to destroy, to consume. And now, thanks to you, I can do it on a much larger scale."

Adrian stepped forward, his sword raised. "We won't let you do this."

Elara laughed, a sound that echoed through the air like broken glass. "You still don't understand, do you?" she said, her voice filled with scorn. "You can't stop me. You're too late."

As she spoke, her form shifted even further, her body elongating and twisting into something monstrous. Her skin darkened, her eyes glowing a deep, malevolent red as her true form began to emerge. She was no longer the woman they had known. She was a creature of pure darkness, a being of shadow and malice, her presence radiating power and terror.

George took a step back, his heart pounding in his chest. "Elara..."

She sneered at him, her voice dripping with disdain. "Elara was never real. She was just a mask. I am something much worse. And now, I am free."

The echoes behind her surged forward, their red eyes glowing brighter as they awaited her command. The air grew colder, heavier, as the army of twisted shadows surrounded them, ready to unleash chaos.

Adrian, his face pale but determined, raised his sword. "We'll stop you," he said, his voice filled with a fierce resolve. "We'll fight you until our last breath."

Elara's laughter echoed through the air, cruel and mocking. "You can try," she said softly, "but it won't matter. The real battle has just begun."

And with that, the echoes surged forward.

Elara—no, *Catherina*—stood before them, her once-familiar face now fully transformed into something twisted and malevolent, her eyes glowing with a deep red that reflected the darkest depths of her power. Her body, now more s hadow than flesh, radiated a palpable sense of dread that gripped George's heart and made the air itself feel thick and suffocating. The army of echoes loomed behind her, their red eyes flickering like embers, ready to obey her every command.

George, Mia, Wren, Adrian, and Emma stood frozen, the revelation of her true identity weighing heavily on their minds. Everything they thought they knew about Elara—about the mission, the island, the portal—had shattered in an instant. This wasn't just a betrayal. This was something far worse.

Adrian's grip tightened on his sword as he glared at her, fury etched into his every feature. "Catherina," he spat, the name bitter on his tongue. "So that's your real name?"

Catherina—no longer pretending to be the ally they had fought beside—smiled, her voice dripping with satisfaction as she spoke. "Yes. Elara was just a lie, a mask to make you trust me. But now that the portal is open and the echoes have crossed over, I no longer need to hide who I truly am."

Mia, her face pale and stricken with disbelief, stepped forward, her eyes wide with horror. "Why? Why would you do this? We trusted you!"

Catherina's eyes gleamed with a cold, calculated malice. "You trusted me because you were desperate—because you wanted to believe that there was hope, that someone was on your side. But I was never on your side. I never needed your help. I only needed your bodies to open the portal, and now that I've crossed into your world... everything will fall into place."

George's chest tightened with fear and anger, his voice strained as he demanded, "What do you mean by everything? What are you planning?"

Catherina's smile widened, her voice taking on a haunting, almost mocking tone. "You still don't understand, do you? You think the echoes are just here to kill, to feed off your world. But it's so much more than that."

She took a step forward, her form dark and ethereal, as if she were more shadow than substance now. "The echoes are tied to time itself, to the fabric of reality. When they enter a new world, they don't just feed on its people. They feed on its *history*. When echoes cross into the real world, time will begin to collapse."

A stunned silence fell over the group. George felt his heart drop into his stomach as the weight of her words sank in.

"Time?" Adrian said, his voice low, almost as if he were struggling to comprehend the magnitude of what she was saying. "What do you mean, time will collapse?"

Catherina's eyes flickered with dark amusement, as if she were savoring the moment. "As the echoes spread through your world, they will begin to unravel the very essence of time. Anything old, anything tied to the past—buildings, monuments, even memories—will begin to fade. The older something is, the faster it will disappear. Time itself will lose its meaning."

Emma's voice was filled with disbelief. "That's impossible."

"Is it?" Catherina asked, her tone sharp and cutting. "Have you not already felt it? The island played tricks on your mind, bent time to confuse you, to make you doubt what was real. But that was just a taste. When the echoes fully spread, the collapse will be total. Your world will fall into chaos as the past disappears, and all that will remain is... nothing."

Mia let out a shaky breath, her voice barely above a whisper. "You're going to destroy everything."

Catherina's smile grew darker, more sinister. "That's the beauty of it, isn't it? A world without time. A world where the echoes thrive, where everything is in constant flux, and nothing remains for too long. The old will fade, and the new will become the hunting ground for my army."

George could hardly breathe, his mind racing as he tried to grasp the scope of what she was saying. "And all those stories you told us about needing our help... about being trapped on the island... those were lies too?"

Catherina tilted her head, her expression one of cruel amusement. "Of course. I was never a prisoner. I've been the one in control the entire time. Everything you fought for was part of my plan."

Wren, who had been silent up until now, his face twisted in guilt and anger, finally spoke, his voice thick with regret. "We helped you. We opened that portal for you. We... we brought this on ourselves."

Catherina turned her gaze toward him, her smile cold and mocking. "Yes. You did. But don't be too hard on yourself, Wren. You were all so eager to believe in me. You were so desperate for hope that you never questioned whether I might be leading you straight into the trap I'd set."

Adrian stepped forward, his expression filled with fury. "You may have tricked us, but we're not done yet. We'll stop you. We'll close that portal, and we'll destroy every last one of your echoes."

Catherina's laughter echoed through the air, the sound sharp and chilling. "Destroy my echoes?" she mocked. "You couldn't even defeat them on the island, and now you think you'll stop them when they're free in your world? You don't stand a chance."

She took another step closer, her eyes burning with a dangerous, dark energy. "But go ahead, try. Fight me. Fight the echoes. It will make no difference in the end. Time is already unraveling. Your world is already dying."

George's hands clenched into fists at his sides, his heart hammering in his chest. The weight of what they had unleashed pressed down on him like a crushing force. They had trusted her, followed her, believed that they were doing the right thing—and now, they had opened the door to the destruction of everything they knew.

"Why are you doing this?" George asked, his voice filled with a desperate anger. "What do you gain from destroying everything?"

Catherina's smile faded slightly, replaced by something darker, more ancient. "I gain what I was created for—chaos. I was born of the island's magic, of the echoes' hatred and rage. I exist to destroy, to consume. And now, with the real world at my feet, I will reshape it in my image."

Mia's voice trembled as she took a step closer to George, her face pale with fear. "We have to stop her," she whispered, her eyes filled with despair. "We can't let her do this."

Adrian's jaw clenched, his face grim but determined. "We will stop her. We'll find a way."

But as Catherina stood before them, her army of echoes waiting at her back, the sheer weight of the task ahead of them felt impossible. The echoes were no longer bound to the island. Time itself was beginning to unravel, and every second that passed brought them closer to the collapse of everything they knew.

Catherina's voice cut through the air like a knife. "You wanted to be heroes, didn't you? You wanted to save the world. But now, you're nothing more than pawns in a game you don't even understand."

George's heart pounded as he met her gaze, his mind racing. Everything they had fought for, everything they had believed in, had led to this moment.

And now, they were faced with an enemy who had planned every step of the way.

The echoes moved closer, their red eyes glowing with hunger, and George knew one thing for certain: the real battle had only just begun.

The realization of their betrayal hit them like a tidal wave, but there was no time to process it. Catherina—Elara—stood before them, her true form revealed, an army of echoes at her back. Her eyes gleamed with malevolent satisfaction, and the air around them grew colder, thicker, as the echoes surged forward, their red eyes glowing like burning coals. The weight of her words, the sheer enormity of the danger they were now in, sank deep into George's bones. They had been duped, tricked into unleashing the very thing they had tried so hard to stop. And now, they were paying the price.

Adrian was the first to react. "We have to go!" he shouted, his voice cutting through the chaos like a knife. His sword was already raised, though it was clear that staying to fight was suicide. "Now! Into the forest!"

George's legs were already moving before his mind fully caught up. The echoes were advancing, their forms shifting and twisting like living shadows, their claws reaching out for them. "Run!" George yelled, grabbing Mia by the arm and pulling her with him as they sprinted toward the dense trees.

The group scattered into the forest, the twisted branches of the trees looming overhead like skeletal arms. The forest was dark and suffocating, but it was their only hope. Behind them, the echoes howled, a deafening, eerie sound that made George's blood run cold. The ground shook beneath their feet as the creatures chased after them, their unnatural speed making escape feel like a futile effort.

"Keep moving!" Wren shouted, his voice strained with fear as he dodged through the trees. His axe was clutched in his hand, but there was no time to fight—only to flee. "Don't look back!"

George didn't need to be told twice. His heart pounded in his chest as he ran, the trees whipping past him in a blur. He could hear the echoes behind them, their footsteps unnervingly fast, like claws scraping against stone. Every muscle in his body screamed with exertion, but he forced himself to keep going. This was survival now. They had to get away from Catherina—away from the echoes—or they were finished.

"Faster!" Emma cried, darting between the trees with incredible speed. Her breathing was labored, and George could hear the panic in her voice. "We can't let them catch us!"

The forest around them grew thicker, the branches clawing at their clothes and skin as they pushed deeper into the woods. The air was heavy with humidity, the ground uneven and covered in thick roots that threatened to trip them with every step. But there was no stopping now, no slowing down. They could feel the echoes closing in, their dark forms barely visible through the dense underbrush.

Suddenly, George's foot caught on a root, and he stumbled forward, nearly falling face-first into the dirt. He caught himself just in time, his heart pounding as he pushed himself back up, adrenaline surging through his veins. Mia grabbed his arm, helping him to his feet before they continued their desperate flight.

"They're getting closer!" Mia gasped, her voice shaking with fear. "We need to find somewhere to hide!"

Adrian's voice cut through the trees from up ahead. "There's no hiding from them! We have to keep moving!"

The trees became denser, their branches intertwining above like a thick canopy, blotting out what little light remained. The forest was a maze of shadows, and it was impossible to tell if they were running in circles or heading deeper into the unknown. But there was no time to think, no time to plan. All they could do was run.

Wren, who had been bringing up the rear, suddenly shouted in pain as something sharp raked across his back. He stumbled but kept his footing, glancing back with wide eyes. "They're right behind us!" he yelled, his voice filled with terror. "We can't outrun them!"

George's lungs burned, and his legs felt like they were on fire, but he couldn't stop. The echoes were gaining ground, their twisted forms darting through the trees with inhuman speed. Every time George glanced back, he saw their red eyes glowing in the darkness, getting closer, more menacing. The sound of their howling filled the forest, drowning out everything else.

"We need to split up!" Emma cried, her voice strained as she darted through a thicket of thorny bushes. "It's our only chance!"

"No!" Adrian shouted, his voice firm despite the panic. "If we split up, they'll pick us off one by one! We stay together!"

George's mind raced as they ran, his thoughts a blur of fear and exhaustion. His side ached from the earlier injury, and every breath felt like a battle. He didn't know how much longer he could keep running, but he knew stopping wasn't an option.

Ahead, the forest began to slope downward, the ground uneven and treacherous. Adrian led the way, his sword still in hand, though it was clear they couldn't hope to fight off the echoes in their current state. "Watch your step!" he called, his voice echoing through the trees as they began to descend the slope.

The group scrambled down the hill, their footing precarious as the ground became more unstable. Rocks and loose soil slid beneath their feet, and several times George felt himself nearly lose his balance. But the echoes were still behind them, their howls growing louder, closer.

Suddenly, a deafening roar echoed through the forest, and George's heart leapt into his throat. He glanced back just in time to see one of the larger echoes break through the trees, its twisted form looming over the others. Its eyes burned with a furious red light, and its claws were outstretched, ready to strike.

"Move, move, move!" George screamed, panic surging through him as the massive echo barreled toward them.

The group reached the bottom of the slope, their feet skidding across the uneven ground. The forest around them seemed to close in, the trees growing even more tightly packed, their branches casting deep, jagged shadows on the ground. The air felt suffocating, thick with fear and tension.

"There!" Mia shouted, pointing to a small clearing up ahead. "We can make a stand there!"

Adrian shook his head, his face pale with exhaustion. "We can't fight them!"

But there was no time to argue. The echoes were closing in, and they were out of options.

The group reached the clearing, their breaths coming in ragged gasps. The echoes were right behind them, their dark forms closing in from all sides, their red eyes glowing with a terrible hunger. George could feel the ground trembling beneath his feet as the creatures advanced, their claws ready to tear them apart.

"We have to keep moving!" Adrian urged, but there was nowhere left to go.

Suddenly, Wren stepped forward, his axe raised, his face twisted with fear and determination. "I'll hold them off!" he shouted, his voice trembling. "You guys go!"

George's eyes widened in shock. "Wren, no! You can't—"

"I have to!" Wren interrupted, his voice firm despite the fear in his eyes. "It's the only way! Go, now!"

Before George could protest, Wren charged forward, swinging his axe with all his might as the echoes descended on him. The group hesitated for a brief moment, torn between staying to help and running for their lives. But the echoes were too close, too fast.

"We have to go," Adrian said quietly, his voice filled with a grim resolve. "He's buying us time."

George felt a lump rise in his throat, his heart pounding with fear and guilt. But there was no choice. They had to run.

With a final glance at Wren, George turned and sprinted into the forest, Mia, Emma, and Adrian following close behind. The echoes howled in fury as they broke through the clearing, their claws tearing through the air as they chased after them.

They ran and ran, the forest closing in around them, the echoes always just a step behind.

But there was no time to stop. No time to look back.

Only the relentless, desperate race to survive.

As they tore through the dense underbrush, the forest seemed to tighten around them, the twisted branches scraping at their clothes and skin like skeletal hands trying to pull them back. The howls of the echoes still echoed in the distance, chilling and predatory, but louder than anything were the sounds that came from behind—Wren's slashes, his desperate battle cries, and the sickening screeches of the echoes clashing with him.

But the most horrifying sound of all were his screams.

George's heart pounded in his chest, every scream from Wren stabbing him like a knife. His mind raced, torn between the instinct to keep running and the desperate urge to turn back, to go to his friend's side. But he knew—deep down, painfully—that if they stopped, if they hesitated for even a moment, it would be the end of them all.

Mia's breath was ragged beside him, her face pale as she struggled to keep up. "We can't leave him!" she gasped, her voice breaking as Wren's screams grew louder behind them. "George, we can't just—"

"We have to keep going!" Adrian's voice cut through the darkness like a whip, sharp and filled with a grim finality. His own face was tight with anguish, but there was no doubt in his tone. "Wren knew what he was doing. He's giving us a chance. We can't waste it."

Emma's eyes were wide with fear and disbelief as she glanced back, her hands trembling around the hilt of her sword. "He's fighting them alone," she whispered, her voice barely audible over the sound of Wren's desperate battle. "He won't last."

George's stomach twisted painfully, the weight of the situation pressing down on him like a suffocating force. He had known Wren for so long—had fought beside him, laughed with him, survived with him. And now... now he was listening to him die.

"I... I know," George said, his voice thick with emotion, his heart breaking with each of Wren's cries. He wanted to turn back so badly, but the cold, brutal truth gnawed at him. "We can't save him."

Mia's face crumpled as tears welled in her eyes, but she kept running, even as Wren's screams pierced through the trees again. George felt like every scream was a piece of himself being torn away. Each cry, each desperate slash of Wren's axe sent a wave of guilt crashing over him, but he forced his legs to keep moving.

The forest blurred around them, the branches and leaves whipping past as they ran deeper into the unknown. Every step felt like they were fleeing further from safety, further from anything familiar, but it didn't matter. The echoes were still on their heels, and Wren's sacrifice had bought them only a sliver of time.

Then, in the distance behind them, the sounds of battle suddenly shifted.

The slashing of Wren's axe stopped, replaced by a single, gut-wrenching scream of pure agony.

It cut through the air like a blade, sharp and final, echoing through the trees before being swallowed by the suffocating silence of the forest.

George stumbled, his breath catching in his throat as Wren's final scream tore through him like a physical blow. Mia let out a choked sob beside him, her hand covering her mouth as the reality of it hit her. Wren was gone.

There were no more slashes. No more cries of defiance. Just... silence.

Emma slowed for a moment, her shoulders trembling as the full weight of the loss hit her. "He's... he's dead," she whispered, her voice cracking with grief.

Adrian's face was pale, his jaw clenched tightly as he forced himself to keep moving. "We can't stop," he said, though his voice was rough, strained. "We need to get as far away from them as we can."

But George felt frozen in place, his feet slowing as the horror of the situation crashed over him. Wren was dead. One of his closest friends, someone who had been with him through everything, was gone. And it had all happened so fast.

Wren had bought them time. He had saved them. And now he was dead.

"We have to keep going," Adrian said again, more forcefully this time, his voice shaking with barely contained emotion. "If we stop now, his sacrifice will mean nothing. We'll die for nothing."

George swallowed hard, his throat dry and tight. He knew Adrian was right. Wren had given everything for them—for him. To stop now, to turn back, would be to waste that sacrifice. But that didn't make it any easier. The guilt gnawed at him, a deep, aching pit that threatened to consume him as they ran further into the forest.

Mia, still sobbing quietly, wiped at her eyes as she kept moving, her legs trembling with exhaustion and grief. "I... I can't believe he's gone," she whispered, her voice trembling. "He was right there, and now..."

"He did it for us," Emma said, her voice hollow as she stared straight ahead. "He saved us."

The sound of footsteps—heavy, fast, and inhuman—began to echo through the trees once again, breaking the brief silence that had followed Wren's death. The echoes were coming. They had finished with Wren, and now they were coming for them.

George felt his heart tighten as he forced his legs to move again, his body aching with fatigue and grief. "We can't let them catch us," he muttered, more to himself than anyone else. "We can't stop."

Adrian nodded grimly. "We'll make it. We have to."

But as they pushed deeper into the forest, George couldn't shake the feeling that they were being swallowed by the island itself. The trees seemed to close in around them, the darkness growing thicker, the air heavier. The echoes' presence felt like a weight pressing down on them, as though the very island was hunting them now, pulling them into its grasp.

George's legs burned with every step, his lungs screaming for air, but he didn't stop. Wren's screams echoed in his mind, a haunting reminder of what they had lost and what still hunted them. They had to survive. They had to keep moving.

And yet, as they ran, the forest seemed endless, and George couldn't help but wonder how much longer they could last.

How much longer could they keep running before the echoes caught up?

The group continued their desperate flight through the thick, oppressive darkness of the forest. Every breath felt like fire in their lungs, and their bodies screamed in protest from exhaustion and the weight of their grief. George's mind raced, still reeling from Wren's death. The horrifying sound of his final scream echoed in his head like a haunting melody he couldn't escape, but they had to keep moving—there was no time to stop. The echoes would not let them rest.

But then, something flickered in George's memory—a small glimmer of hope buried beneath the overwhelming fear.

"There's... there's a place," he gasped, his voice hoarse as he forced the words out between ragged breaths. "The place where we hid... earlier. With Wren."

Adrian, running just ahead, glanced back at him, his eyes narrowing in understanding. "The shelter. Yes, I remember. It's not far from here."

George nodded, his heart racing. "We can make it there. We... we can rest."

Mia, her face streaked with tears and exhaustion, stumbled slightly as she ran, but she managed to keep pace. "Do you think it's safe?" she asked, her voice filled with both hope and doubt. "I mean... we barely made it out the first time."

"It's the only chance we have right now," Adrian said grimly, his eyes scanning the forest as they ran. "If we keep running like this, we won't last much longer."

Emma, still pale with grief but steady in her resolve, nodded. "We have to try. We need to rest... regroup."

The forest around them seemed to grow darker, more suffocating, as they ran through it, the thick branches reaching out like twisted claws. The echoes were still behind them, their distant howls sending chills down George's spine, but they were far enough away now that the group had a sliver of hope—hope that they might reach the shelter and buy themselves some time.

The path through the forest blurred, but George's feet carried him forward on instinct, remembering the way even through the overwhelming haze of fatigue. The ground beneath them was uneven, the thick roots threatening to trip them at every turn, but they pushed on, their desperation fueling their movements.

Then, finally, through the thick brush and dense shadows, they saw it—the small, hidden clearing where they had once sought refuge with Wren. The memory of that time seemed so distant now, even though it had only been hours ago. So much had happened since then, so much had changed.

And Wren was no longer with them.

They stumbled into the clearing, their breaths coming in sharp, ragged gasps as they collapsed onto the ground. The shelter stood just ahead, a small, makeshift structure hidden beneath the dense foliage. It was quiet—too quiet—but the echoes had not yet found them.

Adrian was the first to reach the shelter, his hand resting on the rough wood as he glanced around warily. "No one's here," he said quietly, his voice filled with both relief and a hint of suspicion. "We should be safe... for now."

Mia dropped to her knees, her body trembling with exhaustion as she buried her face in her hands. "I can't believe Wren's gone," she whispered, her voice breaking. "He was just with us..."

George swallowed hard, his throat tight with emotion. He sat down beside her, placing a gentle hand on her shoulder. "He saved us," he said quietly, his voice filled with both sorrow and gratitude. "He gave us a chance."

Emma sat a little ways off, her back pressed against a tree as she stared blankly into the distance. "It feels wrong... being here without him," she said softly. "Like we've left him behind."

"We had no choice," Adrian said firmly, though his own voice was heavy with grief. "Wren knew what he was doing. He wanted us to survive."

There was a long silence, broken only by the distant, faint howls of the echoes that still hunted them. But for the moment, they were safe. They were alive. And they needed rest.

George leaned his head back against the rough bark of the tree, his body trembling from both the physical strain and the emotional weight pressing down on him. The shelter, though simple and small, felt like the only thing keeping them grounded—keeping them from spiraling into despair. But even in this moment of quiet, Wren's absence was palpable. His laughter, his strength, his presence... all of it felt like a gaping hole that none of them could fill.

"Do you think they'll find us here?" Mia asked quietly, her voice barely above a whisper. Her face was still streaked with tears, her eyes red from crying.

Adrian shook his head, though there was a hint of uncertainty in his expression. “I don’t know,” he admitted. “But we’ll be ready if they do.”

George stared up at the thick canopy of trees above, the twisted branches blotting out what little light remained. His body ached with fatigue, his mind racing with thoughts of what had happened, of what they had lost. The echoes were still out there, hunting them, relentless in their pursuit. And Catherina—now fully revealed as their enemy—was still out there too, orchestrating it all, waiting for the moment to strike.

“We’ll figure out our next move after we rest,” Adrian said, his voice steady despite the uncertainty in his eyes. “We can’t do anything if we’re dead on our feet.”

Mia nodded, though her face was still filled with worry. “Do you think... do you think Wren knew this would happen?” she asked quietly. “That we’d end up here again?”

George’s chest tightened. “I don’t know,” he said softly. “But I know he’d want us to keep fighting. He’d want us to survive.”

There was another long pause, the group sitting in silence as they caught their breath and tried to process everything that had happened. The weight of their situation hung over them like a cloud, dark and heavy, but they were alive. And as long as they were alive, they had a chance.

Finally, Emma spoke, her voice quiet and thoughtful. “We can’t let Catherina win,” she said, her words filled with determination. “No matter what it takes... we can’t let her destroy everything.”

George nodded, his resolve hardening despite the grief that still gripped his heart. “We won’t,” he said quietly, his voice steady. “We’ll stop her. We have to.”

The distant howls of the echoes still echoed through the forest, but for now, they were safe. For now, they had a moment to rest.

But the battle wasn't over yet. And George knew that when the time came, they would have to face Catherina—and the echoes—once again.

The shelter was silent, save for the soft rustling of leaves in the breeze and the faint, distant howls of the echoes that still haunted the forest. The air felt heavy, thick with exhaustion, fear, and something deeper—grief. As the group sat huddled together, their bodies aching and their minds weighed down by everything they had endured, the absence of Wren felt like a crushing void between them.

For a long time, none of them spoke. The sounds of the forest, normally comforting, seemed eerie and distant now. Every creak of a branch, every whisper of wind made George flinch, his body on high alert even though they had found temporary refuge. The tension in his muscles had not eased, and despite the safety of the shelter, he couldn't relax. He couldn't stop thinking about Wren.

His friend. His brother-in-arms.

Gone.

Finally, Mia broke the silence. Her voice was soft, almost hesitant, as though speaking the words would make the loss even more real. "Wren... he shouldn't have had to die like that."

Her words hung in the air, thick with sadness and regret, and George felt his chest tighten. He hadn't wanted to acknowledge it, hadn't wanted to say the words out loud, but there they were. The truth, stark and undeniable.

Wren was dead.

"He was so brave," Emma whispered, her voice trembling as she hugged her knees to her chest. Her eyes glistened with unshed tears as she stared down at the ground, her hands trembling slightly. "He didn't even hesitate. He just... he just threw himself at them to save us."

Adrian, sitting a little distance away, stared into the distance, his face grim and lined with guilt. "It should've been me," he muttered under his breath, his fists clenched tightly at his sides. "I should've been the one to hold them off. Not Wren. Not him."

George shook his head, his throat tight. He couldn't let Adrian blame himself for this. None of them could bear the weight of that guilt. "No, Adrian," George said quietly, his voice thick with emotion. "It wasn't your fault. It wasn't anyone's fault. Wren made that choice because he believed in what he was doing. He wanted to give us a chance. We can't let that be in vain."

Mia wiped at her eyes with the back of her hand, her voice breaking as she spoke. "I just... I just wish there was something we could've done. Something that could've stopped him from making that decision."

Emma nodded, her lip quivering as she tried to hold back her tears. "He was so strong, always so confident. I thought... I thought he'd survive anything."

George felt a lump form in his throat, and he swallowed hard, trying to push down the overwhelming grief that threatened to swallow him whole. Wren had always been the strong one. The one who never backed down, who never gave in to fear. Even in the darkest moments, Wren had been their rock. Their anchor. And now...

Now he was gone.

"I keep thinking about what he said before we left him behind," George said softly, his voice barely above a whisper. "He told us to run. Told us not to look back. He knew what he was doing, and he wasn't afraid. Not once."

Mia let out a small, choked sob. "How could he be so fearless? How could he just... throw himself into that? Into those monsters?"

George took a shaky breath, his mind filled with memories of Wren—the way he used to crack jokes even in the middle of the most dangerous situations, the way he always seemed to know what to say to lighten the mood, the way he had stood tall and unyielding in the face of danger, even when everything around them was falling apart.

"He wasn't fearless," George said quietly. "He was scared, just like the rest of us. But that's what made him brave. He didn't let that fear stop him. He pushed through it because he knew what had to be done."

Adrian, still staring off into the distance, finally spoke, his voice low and filled with regret. "He saved our lives," he said, his jaw clenched tightly. "He sacrificed himself for us, and now... now we're sitting here while he's gone. How are we supposed to make peace with that?"

George looked at Adrian, seeing the pain and guilt etched into his friend's face. He understood it, felt it himself, but he also knew that Wren wouldn't have wanted them to fall apart like this. He wouldn't have wanted them to wallow in guilt and sorrow. Wren had always been about moving forward, about fighting, about survival.

"We don't make peace with it," George said softly. "Not now. Maybe not ever. But what we can do is make sure his sacrifice meant something. We have to keep going. We have to finish what we started."

Mia wiped away more tears, her voice shaking. "I don't know if I can keep going without him," she admitted, her face crumpling with grief. "It feels like there's this hole... this emptiness where he used to be."

Emma reached out, placing a comforting hand on Mia's shoulder. "I feel it too," she whispered. "But George is right. Wren wouldn't want us to stop now. He believed in us, in what we were fighting for. We have to keep moving, for him."

Adrian finally looked up, his face still drawn with sorrow, but there was a flicker of determination in his eyes. "We'll finish this," he said, his voice steady but filled with emotion. "We'll make sure Catherina doesn't win. That's how we honor him."

George nodded, his heart heavy with both grief and resolve. "We owe it to him to fight. To make sure that what he did wasn't for nothing."

They sat in silence for a long while after that, the weight of Wren's absence pressing down on them like a heavy cloak. The shelter felt colder, and emptier, without him there. Every breath, every thought seemed to carry the painful reminder that he was gone, that they would never hear his voice again, never laugh with him or fight alongside him again.

But even in that silence, there was a shared understanding, a mutual grief that bound them together. They had all loved Wren. They had all fought beside him, trusted him, relied on him. And now, they would carry him with them in everything they did.

As the distant howls of the echoes echoed through the trees, growing fainter and fainter, the group knew that their journey wasn't over. They knew that more challenges awaited them, more battles to fight, more sacrifices to be made. But they also knew that Wren's memory would drive them forward.

They couldn't bring him back. They couldn't undo what had happened. But they could fight. They could survive.

For Wren.

For the world they were trying to save.

The shelter fell into a heavy, suffocating silence. The grief that had consumed them was still there, raw and aching, but now the weight of the situation—of what they still had to do—pressed down on them like an iron fist. They had lost Wren. They were battered, exhausted, and running out of options. But the world wasn't going to stop for their pain. Time, as Catherina had said, was collapsing, and the echoes were already spreading. If they didn't come up with a plan—and soon—everything they knew would be wiped away.

But no one knew where to begin.

George leaned back against the rough bark of the tree, staring up at the thick canopy above them. The weight of Wren's sacrifice still lingered, but he tried to push it aside, to focus on what came next. The echoes were out there, Catherina was out there, and time itself was slipping through their fingers. They needed a solution. They needed a way to stop it.

But how?

"We have to do something," Mia said softly, breaking the silence. Her voice trembled slightly, still thick with emotion, but there was a hard edge to her words now—a determination that hadn't been there before. "We can't just sit here. We can't let them win."

Adrian, sitting across from her, let out a frustrated sigh. His face was lined with exhaustion, but his eyes burned with anger and desperation. "We know that, Mia," he said quietly, his voice taut with frustration. "But what can we do? We opened the portal. We let the echoes into the real world. How the hell are we supposed to stop them now?"

Emma hugged her knees to her chest, her brow furrowed in thought. "There has to be something we missed," she said, though her voice lacked its usual confidence. "Some way to reverse it. Maybe we could... I don't know... close the portal?"

Mia shook her head. "Even if we could, what good would that do now? The echoes are already here. They've already started spreading."

"And they don't just kill," George added quietly, his mind racing as he remembered Catherina's words. "They unravel time. Even if we closed the portal, the damage is already being done. Old things are going to start disappearing, collapsing into nothing. The world's history is literally falling apart."

A heavy silence followed his words. The enormity of what they were facing was suffocating. The echoes weren't just monsters to be killed—they were a force of destruction far beyond anything they had faced before. And now that they had crossed into the real world, it felt like there was no way to stop them.

Adrian rubbed his hands over his face, his frustration palpable. "We're running out of time," he muttered, more to himself than anyone else. "If we don't find a solution soon, there won't be a world left to save."

Mia looked around at the group, her eyes pleading. "What if we go back to the island's carvings? Maybe there's something we missed there. Something... some artifact, some power that could stop Catherina and the echoes. There has to be something."

George frowned. The thought of returning to Xel Island made his stomach churn with dread, but Mia had a point. The island was where it had all started—maybe there was something they hadn't uncovered yet. Something that could stop the collapse before it spread any further.

But Adrian was already shaking his head. "The island is a death trap. It's where Catherina's power is strongest. If we go back there, we'll be walking right into her hands. We barely survived the first time."

"So what, then?" Mia asked, her voice rising in frustration. "We just sit here and do nothing? Wait for the world to fall apart around us?"

Adrian clenched his jaw, his eyes hard as he stared into the distance. "I don't know. But we're not going back to the island's carvings. That's suicide."

Emma sighed, rubbing her temples as she tried to think. "Maybe there's another way," she said quietly, though her voice lacked conviction. "Catherina said that time is collapsing because the echoes are spreading. If we can somehow contain them... or stop them from spreading further... maybe we can slow it down."

George glanced at her. "How do we do that?"

Emma bit her lip, her brow furrowed in frustration. "I don't know," she admitted. "But we need to find a way to trap the echoes, or at least stop them from spreading. If they're tied to the portal, maybe there's some way to sever that connection. Cut them off from the source."

Mia shook her head. "We don't even understand how the portal works, let alone how to sever its connection to the echoes. We'd be guessing."

Adrian stood up, pacing the small space in frustration. "We don't have time for guesses," he muttered, his voice filled with barely contained anger. "Every minute we sit here trying to come up with a plan, the echoes are out there, unraveling the world."

George felt the frustration building inside him as well. No matter how hard they thought, no matter how many ideas they tossed around, nothing felt right. Every plan seemed impossible, every solution out of reach. The echoes were too strong, too widespread. Catherina had planned everything perfectly, and now it felt like they were running in circles, grasping at straws.

Mia hugged her knees, her face twisted in despair. "It's hopeless, isn't it?" she whispered, her voice breaking. "No matter what we come up with... it's all too late."

George wanted to say something, to offer some kind of hope, but he couldn't. He didn't have the answers. None of them did. They were fighting against something far bigger than themselves, something that seemed impossible to defeat.

Adrian stopped pacing, his hands clenched into fists at his sides. "There has to be a way," he said through gritted teeth. "We can't just give up. We owe it to Wren—to everyone—to keep fighting."

"But how?" Emma asked, her voice filled with frustration. "We've run out of options, Adrian. We can't go back to the island's carvings, we can't stop the echoes from spreading, and we don't even know how to close the portal."

Silence fell over the group again, heavy and suffocating. The forest around them felt even darker, even more oppressive, as if the weight of their hopelessness was pressing down on them from all sides.

George leaned his head back, closing his eyes as he tried to think. He wanted to believe there was a way out of this, some solution they hadn't thought of yet, but every idea seemed like a dead end. The echoes were too powerful, too widespread. And Catherina...

Catherina was always one step ahead.

"We need to stop thinking like we can win," George said quietly, opening his eyes and staring at the ground. "We can't beat them. Not the way we've been thinking."

The others turned to look at him, confusion and despair etched into their faces.

"What are you saying?" Mia asked, her voice soft, fragile.

George took a deep breath, his chest heavy with the weight of his next words. "I'm saying that maybe this isn't about winning. Maybe it's about buying time. We can't stop the echoes, but maybe we can slow them down. Maybe we can keep them from spreading long enough to find another way."

Adrian frowned. "And how do we do that?"

George shook his head, feeling the weight of uncertainty pressing down on him. "I don't know yet. But I think we need to change the way we're thinking about this. It's not about stopping Catherina outright. It's about survival."

Another long silence followed his words. No one wanted to admit it, but George knew they were all thinking the same thing. The world was unraveling, time was collapsing, and they were running out of options. This wasn't a battle they could win by fighting.

It was a battle they had to survive.

And right now, even survival felt impossible.

The forest around them seemed to close in, the weight of their collective despair heavy like a suffocating blanket. Each of them sat in silence, hearts heavy with grief, frustration, and a gnawing sense of hopelessness. The air felt thick, and every breath was labored, as if the forest itself was squeezing the life out of them. George stared at the ground, replaying Wren's death over and over in his mind, his chest tight with guilt and regret. No matter how hard he tried, no solutions came. Every plan they thought of felt like it was destined to fail before it even began.

Mia let out a deep sigh, her head in her hands. "There's nothing left for us," she whispered, her voice barely audible. "We're running out of time."

Adrian, his jaw clenched tightly, said nothing. His anger was palpable, simmering just beneath the surface, but even he didn't have an answer.

And then, something happened. Something none of them could have predicted.

The ground beneath them began to tremble, just slightly at first, then with more intensity. George snapped his head up, eyes wide with alarm. "What—what's happening?" he asked, his voice tense with fear.

The others quickly stood, their bodies tense and ready for anything, their hands reaching for their weapons instinctively. The forest around them remained eerily still, save for the faint tremors beneath their feet.

Mia's eyes darted around nervously. "Is it the echoes?" she asked, her voice trembling with fear. "Are they—?"

"No," Emma interrupted, her gaze fixed on something in the distance. "It's... something else."

Before anyone could react, the ground in the center of their small clearing began to shift. A soft, glowing light appeared, slowly growing brighter as the earth itself seemed to part, allowing the light to rise up from the ground. The tremors intensified for a brief moment, and then, as suddenly as they had started, the shaking stopped.

The glowing figure continued to rise, its form slowly taking shape—a figure made entirely of light, soft and ethereal, as if it were not bound by the same physical laws as the world around it. It hovered above the ground, its radiance casting long, eerie shadows across the forest floor. The light figure was humanoid in shape but blurred at the edges, almost as if it were a ghost or a memory made real.

George's breath caught in his throat, his heart racing as he stared at the figure in awe and confusion. "What... what is that?"

Adrian stepped forward cautiously, his hand still gripping his sword, though he made no move to draw it. "Who are you?" he demanded, his voice steady but filled with wariness.

The figure said nothing for a long moment, its form pulsing gently with a soft, golden light. And then, finally, it spoke.

Its voice was soft but powerful, echoing through the clearing with a strange reverberation that made it feel as though the words were coming from everywhere and nowhere at once. "Believe in yourselves," the figure said, its words clear and deliberate. "Recall the incidents... and you may conquer the unconquered."

The air around them seemed to hum with energy as the figure's words washed over them. For a moment, the weight of their despair seemed to lift, replaced by a strange sense of clarity, of purpose.

Mia took a step closer, her eyes wide with both fear and curiosity. "What do you mean?" she asked, her voice trembling. "What incidents? How do we...?"

But the figure didn't respond. It simply hovered there, its light growing softer, dimmer, until, in a blink, it vanished. The clearing was left in silence once again, the only sound the faint rustling of leaves in the breeze.

For a moment, no one spoke. The group stood frozen, their minds racing as they tried to make sense of what had just happened.

Adrian was the first to break the silence. "Did... did that just happen?" he asked, his voice low and filled with disbelief. "Or are we losing our minds?"

"It happened," George said quietly, his heart still pounding in his chest. "I... I felt it."

Mia looked at him, her brow furrowed in confusion. "But what does it mean?" she asked, her voice shaky. "Believe in ourselves? Recall the incidents? What incidents?"

George's mind raced, the figure's words echoing in his head. *Believe in yourselves. Recall the incidents. Conquer the unconquered.* It sounded like a riddle, like a message hidden within the words. But what incidents was it talking about? What were they supposed to recall?

Emma let out a frustrated breath, running a hand through her hair. "Great. A cryptic message from a glowing ghost. How is this supposed to help us?"

Adrian frowned, his eyes narrowing as he stared at the ground where the figure had appeared. "It said we need to believe in ourselves," he muttered, more to himself than anyone else. "Maybe... maybe it's not about finding a solution out there. Maybe it's about looking back—at everything we've already done."

Mia's face brightened slightly as she turned to Adrian. "You think... you think the answer is in our past? That we've already done something that could help us?"

Adrian shrugged, though there was a spark of hope in his eyes now. "I don't know. But it's the only thing that makes sense. Maybe we've overlooked something. Maybe the key to stopping Catherina, to stopping the echoes, is something we've already experienced."

George thought back over everything that had happened since they first arrived on Xel Island—the battles, the nightmares, the sacrifices. They had been through so much, had uncovered so many secrets, but could there really be something they had missed? Something buried in their memories that held the key to conquering what seemed unconquerable?

"I don't know if it's enough," Emma said, her voice laced with doubt. "We're dealing with magic that's older than time itself. How are we supposed to believe in ourselves enough to stop something like that?"

Mia shook her head. "We've survived everything so far, haven't we? Wren gave his life to buy us time. We owe it to him to believe we can finish this."

George nodded slowly, the figure's words still lingering in his mind. "We've faced impossible odds before," he said quietly. "And we've made it through. Maybe... maybe that's what this is all about. Trusting that we've learned enough, that we're strong enough, to do what needs to be done."

Adrian's face was still grim, but there was a glint of determination in his eyes now. "We need to think. Go over everything again, every moment, every choice we've made. There's something there—we just have to find it."

George took a deep breath, feeling the weight of the task ahead. They had been given a cryptic message, a thin thread of hope in a world that was collapsing around them. But if the light figure's words meant anything, then there was still a chance. A chance to fight back. A chance to save the world.

"Believe in ourselves," George whispered to himself, feeling a flicker of resolve growing in his chest. "Recall the incidents."

They had been through so much. They had survived. Now, it was time to conquer the unconquered.

The cryptic words of the glowing figure hung over them like a mist, heavy and impenetrable. "Believe in yourselves. Recall the incidents." The message echoed in George's mind, twisting and turning as he tried to make sense of it, but no matter how hard he thought, no matter how deeply he reached into his memories, there was nothing. No revelation. No clear answer.

The group sat in silence, their faces drawn with exhaustion and frustration. The forest around them felt oppressively quiet, as if even the echoes were momentarily holding back, waiting for them to decipher the mysterious message. But with each passing second, the tension grew, and George could feel the weight of time pressing down on them.

"We're missing something," Mia said, her voice thick with frustration. She ran a hand through her tangled hair, letting out a small, exasperated sigh. "There has to be something. Something we're not seeing."

Adrian sat with his back against the rough bark of a tree, his arms resting on his knees, staring blankly ahead. "It's not just about believing in ourselves," he muttered, more to himself than anyone else. "There's something deeper. But what the hell are we supposed to recall?"

Emma, her brows furrowed in concentration, shook her head. "I've been thinking about everything—every moment on that island, every battle, every nightmare... and none of it makes sense. The light said to recall the incidents, but which ones? How do we know what matters?"

George remained silent, his mind racing as he tried to pull something—anything—from the fog of his memories. They had faced so much, gone through so many horrors. But nothing stood out. There was no clear moment, no pivotal event that screamed, *this is it*.

"Nothing," he muttered, frustrated. "I can't think of anything. Everything that's happened... it's all just a blur."

Mia looked at him, her eyes wide with worry. "Same. I keep thinking about all we've been through—Wren, the echoes,

Catherina... and there's nothing. It's like the answer is hiding right in front of us, but we can't see it."

Adrian let out a long breath, rubbing his forehead. "We don't have time for this. We don't have time to sit here and try to remember something vague and impossible. Every second we waste, the echoes are out there unraveling everything. We're running out of time."

Emma's voice wavered slightly as she spoke, her eyes glistening with the weight of their situation. "Maybe... maybe we're not meant to figure it out. Maybe it's just another dead end."

The thought of that made George's stomach churn. They had been given what felt like a lifeline, a clue that could lead them to salvation, but now... it all felt like smoke and mirrors. The more they reached for answers, the further away they seemed.

"We can't give up," George said softly, though even he wasn't sure what they were supposed to do next. "There's got to be something. We just... we're not seeing it yet."

Adrian shook his head, frustration building in his voice. "We've been through hell and back. We've fought every battle, survived every nightmare. How are we supposed to 'recall' something when nothing makes sense?"

Mia sat up straighter, her face pinched with determination. "We have to keep thinking. Maybe we're overcomplicating it. Maybe it's not some grand revelation we're looking for."

"What do you mean?" Emma asked, her brow furrowing.

"Maybe it's not a specific moment we have to remember," Mia continued. "Maybe it's about the bigger picture. The entire journey—everything we've gone through. Not one single incident, but all of it together."

George frowned, trying to piece together what Mia was suggesting. "So, you think it's not one event we need to focus on, but... the sum of everything?"

Mia nodded slowly, though doubt still clouded her expression. "It's possible. Maybe the light meant we should look at the journey as a whole. Every choice we've made, every battle we've fought. There has to be a pattern, something we're not seeing."

Adrian let out a humorless laugh. "A pattern? There's no pattern to any of this, Mia. It's been chaos since the moment we set foot on that island. How do we find a pattern in that?"

George closed his eyes, trying to center himself, to pull any clarity from the overwhelming confusion. The island, the echoes, Catherina... it all seemed like a whirlwind of pain and death, with no rhyme or reason. How could they make sense of it now? How could they hope to piece together something they didn't understand?

"We're wasting time," Emma said, her voice tight with frustration. "We're sitting here, trying to figure out some riddle, and meanwhile, the echoes are tearing everything apart. Maybe we've already lost."

A heavy silence fell over the group. No one wanted to admit it, but Emma's words hung over them like a dark cloud. What if they *had* already lost? What if the figure's words were just a distraction, something to give them false hope while the world crumbled around them?

Mia shook her head, her voice shaking slightly. "We can't think like that. We can't just... give up."

"But what do we do?" George asked, his voice low and defeated. "We've been through every possibility, every memory. And there's nothing. No clue. No answers."

Adrian stood up, his fists clenched at his sides, his face a mask of frustration and exhaustion. "We can't stay here much longer. We need to move. Whether we figure this out or not, we can't just sit here and wait for the echoes to find us."

George knew Adrian was right, but the crushing weight of not knowing—of being so close to a possible answer and yet having no clue how to reach it—felt unbearable. It was as though the light figure had given them a puzzle without all the pieces, and now they were expected to solve it before time ran out.

Mia wiped at her face, her voice thick with emotion. "We've been through so much. Fought so hard. We can't let it all end like this."

George looked at her, the despair in her eyes reflecting his own. "I don't know what else to try, Mia. I don't know how we're supposed to believe in something when everything feels... impossible."

Adrian's jaw clenched as he stared into the distance, the frustration in his eyes mirrored by the others. "Then we keep moving. We keep fighting. Whatever comes next... we face it. That's all we can do."

The group sat in silence, the weight of their uncertainty hanging over them like a heavy shroud. The light figure's words still echoed in their minds, but the meaning remained elusive. They had no answers, no clear path forward.

The distant howls of the echoes grew louder, sharper, cutting through the dense forest like an approaching storm. The eerie wails echoed in the air, sending chills down George's spine. It felt as though the very ground beneath them vibrated with the force of the echoes' presence, as if the creatures were drawing ever closer, tightening their grip on the island and on time itself. The momentary refuge they had found felt like it was collapsing under the weight of their enemies.

"We can't stay here any longer," Adrian whispered, his voice tense as he glanced around the shadowy clearing. His eyes darted toward the thick canopy of trees, listening intently to the growing chorus of haunting cries. "They're getting closer."

Mia, her face pale and streaked with tears, looked up, her hands trembling. "But where do we go? We're running out of places to hide."

George tightened his grip on his sword, though he knew it would do little against the tide of echoes that hunted them. "We keep moving," he said, though his voice was thick with exhaustion and uncertainty. "If we stay here, we're dead. We need to get as far away as possible before they find us."

Adrian nodded, standing up slowly and motioning for the others to do the same. "We move quietly. Slow and steady. They'll be searching this area, so we need to make sure they don't hear or see us. Stay close."

The group gathered what little strength they had left and began to move through the thick underbrush, their footsteps careful and silent as they slipped away from the clearing. The shadows of the forest seemed to stretch around them, the trees looming overhead like ancient guardians. Every breath felt heavy, every movement deliberate, as they crept deeper into the darkness, trying to escape the relentless hunt.

The howls of the echoes followed them, growing louder, closer. The eerie wails echoed through the forest, sending a wave of dread through George's chest. His heart pounded in rhythm with his footsteps, each beat a reminder that time was running out.

They walked in silence, the weight of Wren's absence hanging over them like a ghost. But there was no time to grieve now. Only survival mattered.

As they moved further away from the shelter, George glanced back over his shoulder, his eyes narrowing as the eerie glow of the echoes began to dance in the distance. They were close—too close. The shadows twisted and shifted as the echoes drew nearer, their twisted forms barely visible through the thick trees.

"We need to move faster," George whispered urgently, his voice tight with fear.

Adrian nodded, quickening his pace as they pressed deeper into the forest. The tension in the air was suffocating, every rustle of leaves or snap of a twig sending jolts of panic through them. The echoes were hunting them, their presence like a dark cloud that seemed to close in from all sides.

Suddenly, the eerie howls of the echoes seemed to stop.

The forest grew deathly still.

George froze, his breath catching in his throat as he strained to listen. The silence was oppressive, almost unnatural, and it filled him with a sense of dread. He could feel the tension in the air, thick and heavy, as if something terrible was about to happen.

"What's happening?" Mia whispered, her voice trembling as she looked around, her wide eyes filled with fear.

Adrian held up his hand, signaling for them to stay quiet, his body tense and ready. His eyes scanned the forest, his breathing shallow, as if expecting the worst.

And then, the sound of footsteps—slow, deliberate—approached the clearing they had just left behind.

It was not the echoes this time.

It was Catherina.

The very air around them seemed to grow colder as her presence approached. George could feel it, the oppressive weight of her dark power filling the forest like a fog, choking the very life out of the air. They had escaped her for now, but she was close—so close that he could feel her in the back of his mind, her dark, malevolent energy seeping into every thought, every breath.

They crouched low, hiding behind a thick cluster of trees, as Catherina's shadowy form appeared in the clearing they had just vacated. Her figure was tall and commanding, her presence dominating the space. She moved with a predatory grace, her eyes glowing with a sinister red light as she surveyed the area.

George's heart pounded in his chest as he watched her from the shadows, his body rigid with fear. The air around her seemed to ripple with dark energy, and her form flickered at the edges, as if she was not fully bound to the physical world. She was a creature of shadows, of nightmares—and now, she was hunting them.

Catherina stepped into the center of the clearing, her eyes narrowing as she knelt to the ground. She placed a hand on the earth, her fingers digging into the dirt as if she could sense their presence, as if the very ground whispered their secrets to her.

"They were here," she hissed, her voice a low, guttural growl that sent chills down George's spine.

The echoes, now silent and waiting, hovered in the distance, their red eyes glowing as they awaited her command. But Catherina's attention was fully on the clearing, her eyes scanning the space with a deadly precision.

For a moment, there was only silence. And then, without warning, Catherina threw her head back and let out a scream—a horrifying, blood-curdling scream that echoed through the forest like a banshee's wail. The sound was filled with pure rage, a guttural, terrifying sound that seemed to shake the very trees around them.

George's blood ran cold. The scream was unlike anything he had ever heard before—a sound of pure, unbridled fury and hatred. It tore through the forest, rattling the branches and sending flocks of birds scattering into the sky in terror.

"She knows," Emma whispered, her voice barely audible, her face pale with fear. "She knows we were here."

Catherina's eyes flashed with fury as she rose to her feet, her shadowy form towering over the clearing. The air around her seemed to darken, the ground trembling beneath her feet as she summoned her power. "You think you can hide from me?" she snarled, her voice filled with venom. "You think you can escape me? I will find you. I will tear you apart."

The echoes stirred in the distance, their forms shifting and rippling with dark energy as they responded to her anger.

George's breath came in shallow, quick bursts as he crouched lower, praying that Catherina wouldn't notice them hiding just beyond the clearing. His heart raced in his chest, his body frozen in fear as he watched her.

Adrian motioned for them to stay still, his face tense and pale. They couldn't afford to make a sound, couldn't risk drawing her attention. Not now. Not when they were so close to being caught.

Catherina's eyes scanned the treeline, her face twisted with fury. "I will find you," she growled, her voice low and dangerous. "And when I do, you will wish you had never set foot on my island."

And then, with one final, terrifying scream, she turned and stalked back into the shadows, her army of echoes following in her wake.

The group remained silent for several long moments, their bodies trembling with fear as they listened to the echoes fade into the distance. George let out a shaky breath, his heart still pounding in his chest.

They had escaped—barely.

But Catherina knew.

She was hunting them.

And time was running out.

The group moved slowly, hearts pounding, as they crept through the dense underbrush, leaving the shelter behind. The echoes' howls grew louder, closing in with every passing second. Each footstep was deliberate, their movements careful as they stayed low to avoid detection. Every rustle of leaves made them flinch, the weight of Catherina's fury still hanging in the air from the horrifying scream that had echoed through the forest minutes earlier. They knew she was hunting them. She knew they had been there.

As they moved further away from the clearing, the oppressive silence began to weigh on them. Mia's breath was shallow, her face pale, and George could feel the tension growing with every step they took. No one spoke, but the fear was palpable. It felt like the echoes were everywhere, lurking in the shadows, waiting for the perfect moment to strike.

Adrian, walking slightly ahead, finally broke the silence, his voice low and strained. "We can't outrun them forever. We need to figure out our next move."

Emma glanced around nervously, her eyes darting to the dark shapes in the distance. "What next move? We're running blind."

George, his mind racing, wiped sweat from his brow, his muscles aching from exhaustion. The idea of a plan seemed distant, impossible. They had been running for so long, it was hard to think clearly. But then, a fragment of memory surfaced—something they had seen in the caves back on the island. The symbols.

"Wait," George said suddenly, his voice hushed but urgent. "The icons. The ones we saw in the cave on the island."

Mia turned to him, her face etched with confusion. "Icons? What are you talking about?"

"The symbols," George clarified, his thoughts starting to come together, though still hazy. "When we were in that cave, remember? There were strange markings on the walls—ancient symbols. We never figured out what they meant, but... what if they're important? What if they're part of how we stop all this?"

Adrian stopped in his tracks, his eyes narrowing as he thought back to that moment. "The symbols... I remember them. They were carved deep into the stone. But we didn't have time to decipher them before the echoes attacked."

Emma's brow furrowed in concentration. "Do you think those symbols have something to do with Catherina? Or the echoes?"

"It has to be connected," George said, his voice more confident now. "Xel Island is where all of this started. The echoes, Catherina, the magic—everything. Those symbols weren't random. They must mean something."

Mia crossed her arms, her face still clouded with uncertainty. "But what if they don't help us? We don't even know how to read them. And Catherina—she's getting stronger. We don't have time to waste on things that might not work."

Adrian paced, the weight of the situation pressing down on him as he considered their options. "We don't have time, but we also don't have a choice. We've tried everything else, and nothing's worked. Those symbols might be the key to stopping this madness. If we can figure them out..."

Emma nodded, a flicker of hope in her eyes. "It's better than running blind. And it's tied to the island—that much is clear. We have to at least try."

George took a deep breath, his mind swirling with the implications. The symbols had been buried deep in the island's caves, hidden from the world. They had seemed old—ancient, even—older than anything they had encountered. If the echoes were connected to the island's magic, then it made sense that the symbols might hold the secret to controlling or even defeating them.

"We'll need to get back to the cave," George said, his voice steady. "We need to take a closer look at those symbols. Maybe... maybe we missed something the first time."

Mia glanced nervously toward the distant trees, where the shadows seemed to writhe and twist as if the echoes themselves were watching. "But how do we even get back there? We're in the middle of the island, and Catherina is hunting us. We barely made it out of there alive the last time."

Adrian's jaw tightened as he thought through their options. "We'll have to move carefully, stay off the main paths. If we can get back to the cave without alerting her, we might stand a chance."

"And what if the echoes are already there?" Emma asked, her voice tense. "We're walking into a trap if they are."

Adrian's eyes darkened. "We'll deal with that when we get there. Right now, it's our only lead."

George felt the tension coil tighter in his chest, but he nodded in agreement. "We've come this far. We have to see it through."

With that decision made, the group began moving again, this time with more purpose. The forest remained thick, the shadows pressing in from all sides, but George's mind was fixed on the cave, on those strange symbols that had felt like a puzzle waiting to be solved. The echoes were still out there, their presence palpable in the air, but something told him that the answers they needed were buried in the heart of the island, in those ancient carvings.

They moved quietly, their footsteps nearly silent as they navigated through the dense forest. Every rustle of leaves, every faint echo of movement sent shivers down their spines, but they pressed on, their goal clear now.

As they neared the familiar path leading toward the cave, the eerie stillness of the forest grew heavier. The air felt thick with anticipation, as if the island itself knew they were getting closer to something important. George's pulse quickened, his heart pounding in his chest as they approached the mouth of the road far ahead.

But before they could step inside, a distant sound stopped them cold.

A shriek.

Catherina's voice—furious, blood-curdling—pierced the air, echoing through the trees. George felt a chill crawl down his spine. She knew they were near. She was getting closer.

Adrian glanced back at the group, his expression grim. "We don't have much time. She's going to find us."

George swallowed hard, his gaze fixed on the dark entrance of the cave ahead. "Then we'd better figure out those symbols before she does."

Without another word, they stepped inside the cave, the air immediately cooler and the darkness almost consuming. The walls were lined with the strange symbols, glowing faintly in the dim light. They moved toward the carvings, their hands tracing the ancient markings.

Whatever secrets the island held, they were buried here.

And now, it was a race against time to uncover them.

The cool, damp air of the cave wrapped around them like a suffocating shroud as they entered, the darkness almost absolute except for the faint glow of the ancient symbols on the walls. Every step echoed through the chamber, the sound of their footsteps bouncing off the rock, amplifying the silence that followed them like a shadow. George's heart raced as he moved further into the cave, his eyes scanning the walls, searching for any clue that might help them unravel the mystery that had eluded them.

The symbols were everywhere, etched deep into the stone, glowing faintly in hues of blue and green. They twisted and looped in intricate patterns, some familiar, some alien. The deeper they went into the cave, the more the symbols seemed to pulse with an otherworldly energy, as if they were waiting for something—someone—to unlock their meaning.

Mia's breath was shallow as she ran her fingers across the carvings, her face pale with concentration. "There has to be something here," she whispered, her voice barely audible in the vast chamber. "We missed it the first time, but it's here. I can feel it."

Adrian walked beside her, his eyes sharp, his hand resting on the hilt of his sword. "We need to move fast. Catherina's scream... she's coming. We don't have much time."

George nodded, his pulse quickening. The thought of Catherina closing in on them sent a wave of dread through his body. They had to find whatever it was they were looking for—and fast. But as he scanned the symbols, frustration gnawed at him. They had seen these before, but they had no idea how to read them. What if this was all for nothing?

"What are we looking for, exactly?" Emma asked, her voice tinged with desperation. "There are hundreds of symbols here. We could spend hours trying to figure out what they mean."

George clenched his jaw, his eyes narrowing as he studied the wall before him. "It's not about reading them. It's about finding the right one. The light figure told us to recall the incidents. Maybe we're not supposed to decipher every symbol—just find the one that connects to everything we've been through."

Mia frowned, stepping closer to a cluster of glowing markings. "What if it's the one we missed before? What if it's been right in front of us all along, and we just didn't know how to see it?"

Adrian moved to the far wall, his eyes scanning the highest symbols. "We have to think back. What did we experience that ties all of this together?"

George's mind raced. The island, the echoes, Catherina—they were all tied together in some twisted way. The island had been their prison, but also a key. The echoes weren't just random monsters—they were creations of something ancient and dark. And Catherina—she was more than a leader of the echoes. She was something born from the island's magic itself.

And then, it hit him.

"Time," George said suddenly, his voice startling the others. "It's about time. Catherina said the echoes feed on time. They unravel it. The island... it's connected to time itself. That's what the symbols are about."

Mia's eyes widened in realization. "That's why we kept experiencing those strange time shifts—the moments where things didn't make sense, where we felt like we were walking in circles. The island is warping time. It's using it against us."

Emma stepped closer, her hand tracing the edge of a large symbol that seemed to stand out more than the others. "Then... these symbols might be part of how the island controls time. Maybe they're not just ancient carvings—they're part of the island's magic."

George nodded, his heart racing with new urgency. "That's it. The symbols are a map—maybe even a lock. If we can find the one that controls time, we can use it to stop Catherina and the echoes. We can reverse whatever damage they're doing to the real world."

Adrian's eyes narrowed as he moved closer to the glowing symbol Emma had been studying. "This one," he said, his voice tense. "It's different from the others. Look at the way it's carved—it's deeper, more intricate. Like it's meant to stand out."

The group gathered around the symbol, their eyes locked on its swirling patterns. It glowed brighter than the others, its energy pulsing with an intensity that made George's skin prickle. The symbol itself was a complex spiral, but within the spiral were smaller, interlocking shapes—almost like a clock, ticking endlessly in a loop.

"That has to be it," Mia whispered, her voice trembling with excitement and fear. "It's connected to time. Look at the way it moves—it's like it's counting down."

George reached out, his fingers hovering over the symbol, feeling the warmth of its energy radiating from the stone. His heart pounded in his chest as he felt a pull, an instinct that told him this was what they had been searching for.

"Do it," Adrian said, his voice steady but tense. "We don't have time to waste. If this symbol controls the island's magic, we need to activate it now."

George hesitated for a moment, fear and uncertainty gnawing at him. What if this was the wrong move? What if it made things worse? But deep down, he knew this was their only chance. The symbols had led them here for a reason. This was the key to stopping Catherina.

With a deep breath, George pressed his hand against the symbol.

The cave seemed to come alive the moment his skin touched the stone. The symbols on the walls began to glow brighter, pulsing in unison with the symbol George had activated. The air around them crackled with energy, a low hum filling the chamber as the magic of the island surged to life.

Mia gasped, her eyes wide as the ground beneath them trembled. "What's happening?"

George's breath came in short bursts as the symbol grew hotter beneath his palm. "I think... I think it's unlocking something."

Suddenly, a burst of light shot from the symbol, filling the cave with a blinding glow. The energy surged through the walls, the symbols glowing brighter and brighter until the entire cave was bathed in radiant light.

And then, just as quickly as it had started, the light dimmed, and the cave fell silent.

George pulled his hand away, his heart pounding in his chest as he looked around. The cave was still, the air thick with the weight of the magic they had just unleashed.

Adrian took a cautious step forward, his eyes scanning the now-dimly glowing symbols. "Did it work?"

Before George could respond, the symbols on the wall began to shift, rearranging themselves into a new pattern. The spiraling symbol at the center of the cave glowed brighter, and the air around them grew heavier, as if time itself had been altered.

Mia's eyes were wide with awe. "We did it. We unlocked the island's magic."

George nodded, though his heart was still racing. "Now we need to figure out how to use it."

But as the echoes' howls echoed once again in the distance, closer this time, George knew their time was running out.

Catherina was coming

Adrian's gaze fell upon the walls, where strange, intricate symbols were carved with painstaking precision. He recognized them from his studies of ancient civilizations, their enigmatic elegance captivating and chilling him at once. The cryptic text pulsed with an unearthly energy:

�⋈⋆ ✦⋆�� ��� �� -¦-⋆��ǂ�� �⋈⋆ ⋆✧⋈�⋆�, �� �� -¦-⋆��ǂ�� �⋈⋆ ��ǂ�-¦- ��-¦- ��� �ǂ�������

A shiver ran down his spine as the realization struck him: this was no ordinary graffiti; it was a key to something far greater, perhaps a warning or a prophecy. Confusion washed over him, a wave of uncertainty crashing against the shores of his mind. **What did it mean?** He felt as if he stood on the precipice of an abyss, the weight of the unknown pressing heavily on his chest. Adrian's heart raced, his instincts urging him to decipher the meaning hidden within these symbols. Time seemed to freeze as he grappled with his next move, caught between fear and fascination, wondering if he should delve deeper into this mystery or flee before it ensnared him completely. But he knew he couldn't leave his friends behind in this tangled web of mystery. A sense of loyalty anchored him, compelling him to call out to Emma, who was engrossed in deciphering the meanings of other symbols etched along the wall.

"Emma!" he shouted, his voice echoing in the dim corridor. "You need to see this!"

Her head snapped up, curiosity igniting her eyes as she hurried over to where Adrian stood, a mix of excitement and concern evident on her face. "What did you find?"

He gestured toward the cryptic carvings, his heart racing as he shared the weight of his discovery. "These symbols—they're not just random. I think they're connected to what we're looking for. They might hold the key to understanding everything."

Emma leaned closer, her brow furrowed in concentration. “You’re right. I’ve seen similar markings in the texts we studied. If we can piece this together, it could lead us to the truth.”

Together, they studied the ancient engravings, each symbol revealing fragments of a larger puzzle. The air buzzed with a sense of urgency as they realized they were on the brink of uncovering something profound—something that could change everything for them and their friends.

Suddenly, Emma's eyes widened as a spark of recognition lit up her face. Her mind clicked into place like a lock turning with the right key. She remembered where she’d seen those symbols before—and even more importantly, she recalled the language they belonged to.

“It’s Proto-Eldric!” she whispered, a mixture of awe and excitement in her voice. She glanced at Adrian, her hands trembling slightly. “These symbols—they’re from the lost Eldric civilization. They used a pictographic language, one they believed could hold magic within the shapes themselves.”

Adrian’s eyes narrowed, trying to recall everything he knew about the fabled Eldrics. "Weren’t they supposed to have vanished centuries ago? Left nothing but myths and ruins?”

Emma nodded, her gaze fixed on the ancient text, her mind racing. “Yes, but if these symbols are here, then maybe... just maybe, they left behind more than ruins.” She ran her fingers carefully over the carvings. “This isn’t just a message, Adrian. I think it’s a gateway—a guide, maybe even a warning.”

They exchanged a look, one filled with both fear and wonder, as the weight of Emma's revelation settled between them. They were no longer merely observers of history; they were about to unlock a secret lost to time itself.

Emma turned to the others, her voice carrying a strange mix of dread and urgency as she tried to make sense of the ancient inscription.

"These symbols... they form a sentence," she began, glancing around at her friends, her eyes shadowed with a solemn intensity. "It says something like... 'The universe can be saved from the echoes only by the destruction of all organisms.'"

A heavy silence settled over the group as her words sank in, the air thick with a creeping horror. Adrian's mind reeled as he tried to grasp the implication. *Destruction of all organisms?* It was an unthinkable solution, one that left no room for life, no room for hope. The symbols suddenly seemed to pulse with a menacing energy, as though they were alive with the foreboding message they carried.

"Are they saying we have to... end everything?" one of the others murmured, their voice barely above a whisper.

Emma nodded grimly, her face pale. "If this translation is right, then it's not just a warning—it's a prophecy. Or maybe... a command."

Adrian looked into the shadows beyond the ancient carvings, a chill creeping down his spine. What kind of civilization would inscribe such a message? And could they truly be forced to make an unimaginable choice to protect the universe from whatever the 'echoes' were?

As the weight of the revelation sank in, they realized they were no longer just explorers. They were now keepers of a dangerous secret, one that could shatter worlds—or save them.

George stammered, his mind a whirl of scattered thoughts, unable to string together anything but incoherent sounds. Words seemed to slip through his grasp, reduced to nothing more than blabber, while he stared helplessly at the haunting symbols on the wall.

Meanwhile, Mia stood frozen in sheer bewilderment, her hands clenched at her sides. Her eyes flickered with a strange mixture of fear and awe, her mind racing as the enormity of Emma's translation sank in. She was caught in a state of silent alteration, as if the very core of her beliefs had been shaken and reshaped by the weight of the ancient message.

"Are we really supposed to...?" George managed to mutter, his voice trailing off, thick with disbelief.

Mia finally broke her silence, her voice low but steady. "If this prophecy is true... if these echoes mean what I think they do... then we're facing something far darker than we ever imagined."

They both looked to Emma and Adrian, desperately hoping someone else might offer a way out of this dreadful revelation. But in the solemnity of the dim light, it was clear: they were all grappling with an impossible truth, one that would haunt them from this moment forward.

A collective realization washed over the group as they each remembered the symbols they had encountered before. They had been scattered across ruins, carved into forgotten artifacts, woven into the fabric of mystery surrounding them.

But until now, they hadn't grasped the meaning. The symbols had been mere curiosities, fragments of a distant past they assumed were benign or indecipherable. Now, with Emma's revelation, they realized how dangerously naive they had been.

George's eyes darted between the others, his face pale. "We've seen these symbols before... I thought they were just old decorations, ancient nonsense. But they were warnings. Signs leading us here." He clenched his fists, anger and regret mixing in his voice. "We ignored them."

Mia took a shaky breath, her gaze distant as she recalled the symbols from the earlier encounters. "Every time we saw them, it was like they were calling to us, urging us to see something we couldn't yet understand."

Emma's voice was soft but steady as she filled in the missing pieces. "They weren't just warnings. They were leading us here deliberately, as if something wanted us to understand this choice. Like... it's been waiting for us to arrive at this moment, ready to test our resolve."

The place seemed to close in around them, the shadows growing heavier as the symbols on the wall glinted with an almost predatory gleam.

A sudden, low rumble echoed from behind the walls, making them all jump. It was a deep, resonant sound, like something ancient stirring to life—a presence hidden just beyond the stone, waiting. The noise reverberated, filling the narrow corridor with a menacing hum that vibrated through their bones.

Mia took a cautious step back, her breath quickening. "Did... did anyone else hear that?"

George nodded, swallowing hard as he strained his ears. "It's coming from behind the wall," he whispered, his voice barely audible over the growing rumble. "Almost like... like something's moving back there."

Emma's eyes flicked from the symbols to the wall, fear mingling with fascination. "Maybe our presence here triggered it. These symbols—they weren't just warnings; they were meant to summon something." Her voice trembled as she dared to put her thoughts into words.

Adrian pressed his ear to the cold stone, trying to discern the nature of the noise. It was relentless now, pulsing with an unnatural rhythm, as though a heartbeat were echoing from deep within the walls.

Then, without warning, the sound shifted—a scraping, dragging noise, as though massive gears or ancient machinery were grinding into motion. Dust fell from the ceiling as the vibrations intensified, and the wall before them shuddered, revealing a faint crack down the middle that began to widen.

"Stand back!" Adrian shouted, pulling them away just as the wall split, the hidden entrance slowly sliding open. Behind it loomed a dark passage, and from its depths, a cold, foul-smelling breeze drifted outward, carrying with it the unsettling weight of something forgotten and waiting to be unleashed.

As the wall slid open, the rumbling subsided, replaced by a metallic clink. There, emerging from the shadows, was an ancient machine—a weapon, tarnished yet intimidating. It was a shotgun, unmistakably old but eerily well-preserved, with intricate engravings along the barrel and stock, symbols matching those on the walls. The gun gleamed with a sinister allure, as though it had been waiting through the ages for someone to wield it once more.

But that wasn't the worst of it.

A figure began to materialize from the darkness, as if conjured by the weapon itself. The man's skin was pale, his frame gaunt yet unnervingly steady. His eyes, cold and vacant, flickered with a spectral light as he wrapped his hands around the ancient shotgun, lifting it with a sense of purpose that sent chills down their spines. His grip tightened on the weapon, a silent promise of violence in his touch.

The group stood rooted in shock, unable to tear their gaze away from the apparition before them. George took a shaky step back, his mouth falling open as he struggled to find words, but none came.

Mia's voice broke the silence, a frightened whisper. "Is... is he alive?"

The man's hollow gaze settled on them, unfeeling, as though he were looking through them rather than at them. Slowly, he raised the shotgun, the weight of his presence pressing down like an invisible force, almost tangible in its intensity. His mouth opened, and in a voice that sounded like gravel dragged across metal, he spoke:

"Only death restores the balance."

Emma felt her heart stop as the words echoed around them. They were the final line of the prophecy, the last part of the inscription they had yet to translate. And here it was, spoken by a figure that should have been long dead.

Adrian moved to shield the others, his mind racing for a way out of this nightmare. But the man raised the shotgun with practiced ease, as if centuries of silence had never dulled his skill. The group could feel the weight of every second ticking by, knowing they were standing on the brink of something far beyond their understanding. The ancient weapon gleamed ominously, and they knew—one wrong move, one sound, and that relic of destruction would be unleashed.

The man's voice, rough and unearthly, sliced through the silence, filling the air with an ominous weight.

"This gun... it can destroy the echoes," he rasped, his gaze cold and steady as he looked upon them. "But only if it's fired at... Catherine."

A chill ran through the group, his words sinking in like ice-water. *Catherine?* The name lingered, echoing in their minds as they struggled to understand. Catherine was one of their own—an ally, a friend but now a scary enemy.

Mia's face went pale, and she stepped forward cautiously, voice trembling. "What... what do you mean? Why Catherine?"

The man's eyes flickered with a glimmer of something that might have been sadness or regret, though it was difficult to tell. He held up the shotgun, his bony fingers running along its engraved surface with an almost reverent touch. "The echoes can only be silenced by blood. Catherine's blood... holds the key to binding them. But this weapon—this is no ordinary shotgun. To make it work... you need to find the *gunkey*."

Adrian narrowed his eyes. "Gunkey? What is that?"

The man's grip tightened around the shotgun, his gaze turning distant. "A relic, hidden where only the desperate dare look. Without it, this gun will remain silent, useless. The gunkey is what binds the weapon to its target. Only with it in place... can the final shot be fired."

Emma felt a surge of anger mix with fear as she looked from the weapon to the man. "And where are we supposed to find this gunkey? You're asking us to sacrifice someone—and for what?"

The man's expression darkened, his voice rough as if scraped from the depths of some forgotten hell. "That is for you to discover. But know this... the gunkey was hidden by those who wished to seal away the echoes forever. If you're not willing to go to the depths... then the echoes will continue. And the price will be far greater than one life."

The group fell silent, the weight of the choice looming over them. Somewhere, buried in the darkness, lay the key to this weapon, the only hope they had of stopping the echoes. But was it worth the cost? And could they truly condemn one of their own to save the rest?

Adrian stepped forward, voice steady but filled with urgency. "Where can we find the gunkey? If it's the only way to stop the echoes, we need to know."

The man's hollow eyes shifted to him, a flicker of something ancient and weary in his gaze. "The gunkey... It was hidden long ago, in a place where only those with true purpose might seek it. You'll find it in the *Capitoline Museum*. But as for the exact location..." He shook his head slowly, almost regretfully. "That knowledge was lost to time."

Emma's heart raced as she exchanged a look with the others. "The Capitoline Museum," she murmured, mind racing. "That place is enormous, with endless rooms, exhibits... We could search for days and not find it."

The man's gaze didn't waver. "Those who seek the gunkey must follow more than logic. The echoes will guide you... if you know how to listen." He paused, his voice turning to a chilling whisper. "But be warned—the museum holds more than artifacts. It guards its secrets well, and the gunkey will not reveal itself easily. You will have to prove yourselves."

Mia felt the hairs on the back of her neck stand up. She could feel the weight of the task ahead, the danger lurking in every corner. "Prove ourselves... How?"

But the man gave no answer. His form began to flicker, his grip on the shotgun loosening as though he were fading back into the shadows. His final words echoed in the still air, leaving them more determined—and more afraid—than before.

"Only those who are willing to face the echoes can truly wield the gunkey. Remember that."

And then, with a whisper of cold air, he was gone.

No, he wasn't.

The man remained, moving closer to the wall, where he stood still, his form partially merging with the ancient stone. It was as if he had become one with the very structure, an eerie sentinel of the secrets held within.

Adrian turned to his friends, urgency lacing his voice. "We need to figure out our next steps. The Capitoline Museum could be our only chance to find the gunkey, but without specific directions, we'll be lost."

Mia nodded, her brow furrowed in concentration. "Maybe we should split up and do some research. The museum's history, the artifacts—there has to be something that can point us in the right direction."

George ran a hand through his hair, anxiety evident in his eyes. "But what if we get caught up in something we don't understand? The echoes, this man—he warned us. We don't even know what we're dealing with."

Emma stepped forward, determination etched on her face. "If the echoes can only be stopped by targeting Catherine, we can't afford to hesitate. We need that gunkey. Besides, the longer we wait, the more power they could gain. We must act."

Adrian nodded in agreement, but uncertainty flickered in his eyes. "We should also consider what the man said about proving ourselves. It sounds like there's more to this than just finding a key. We might face challenges in the museum—tests that could reveal our true intentions."

"Then we prepare for that," Mia replied firmly. "We'll gather what we can about the museum and its hidden artifacts. Maybe there are records or myths associated with the gunkey. It might lead us to the location."

As they discussed their options, the man standing against the wall remained a silent, watchful presence. His ethereal form seemed to pulse with an ancient energy, as if the very air around him held its breath, waiting for the group to make their choice.

With a shared sense of purpose, they took a deep breath and began to strategize, knowing the path ahead would test not only their resolve but the bonds of their friendship.

With a renewed sense of urgency, Adrian and his friends left the ancient chamber behind, their hearts pounding as they navigated the dark corridor. The haunting figure of the man merged into the wall lingered in their minds, a reminder of the perilous task that lay ahead. They burst through the heavy stone door and emerged into the cool, crisp air, the evening sky a tapestry of deep blues and purples as the sun dipped below the horizon.

The scent of salt and damp earth filled their lungs as they made their way toward the shores, where the rhythmic sound of waves crashing against the rocks offered a momentary solace from the weight of their mission. Each step took them further from the shadows of the past and closer to the unknown future that awaited them.

As they reached the sandy expanse, the moonlight shimmered on the water's surface, casting an ethereal glow that illuminated their path. The shoreline was serene, the gentle lapping of the waves contrasting sharply with the chaos of thoughts swirling in their minds.

"Do you think we're truly ready for this?" George asked, breaking the silence. His voice was barely a whisper, as if afraid the very air might carry his doubts away. "We're talking about facing something we barely understand."

Mia glanced at him, her expression a mix of determination and concern. "We don't have a choice. The echoes... they're more than just a threat to Catherine. They could tear apart everything we know if we don't stop them." She picked up a pebble and tossed it into the water, watching as the ripples expanded outward, merging with the waves. "We have to be stronger than our fears."

Adrian stood at the water's edge, the moonlight reflecting off his face, illuminating the resolve in his eyes. "Mia's right. The longer we wait, the more dangerous this gets. We need to gather as much information as possible about the Capitoline Museum. If we can figure out how to find the gunkey, we can confront whatever challenges lie ahead."

Emma, gazing out at the horizon, added, "We should consider what the man said about proving ourselves. There's a reason he wanted us to seek the gunkey. Perhaps there's a test waiting for us in the museum, something that will reveal our true intentions and determine whether we're worthy of wielding that power."

The group fell silent, contemplating the weight of her words. The air was thick with anticipation, and the sound of the waves seemed to echo their rising determination. The shoreline was their sanctuary, a momentary pause before the storm they were about to face.

"We need to prepare," Adrian finally said, turning back to his friends. "Let's search for any information we can find about the museum and its artifacts. We should also look into any legends surrounding the gunkey. Maybe we can find clues that will help us."

With a shared sense of purpose, they set off along the beach, the sand soft beneath their feet, their minds buzzing with ideas and strategies. Each step was imbued with a sense of urgency, a reminder of the echoes looming in the shadows, ready to strike.

As they walked, the conversation flowed, each of them contributing thoughts and theories. They discussed historical texts, local legends, and the potential dangers that awaited them at the museum. The camaraderie they shared grew stronger with each shared worry and determination, binding them together as they faced the uncertainty ahead.

The stars began to twinkle overhead, a canvas of light against the darkening sky, as they reached the end of the shoreline. The vast expanse of the ocean stretched out before them, a reminder of the challenges they would soon face. But there was also a sense of hope; they were not alone in this fight. Each of them carried a part of the puzzle, and together, they would forge a path through the darkness.

As they turned away from the shoreline, their hearts were resolute. The Capitoline Museum awaited them, a treasure trove of secrets and challenges, and they were ready to uncover its mysteries. With one last glance at the waves, they made their way inland, prepared to delve into the depths of history and face whatever lay ahead.

After gathering their thoughts along the shores, Adrian and his friends made their way to the nearest port, their determination fueled by the urgency of their mission. The evening had deepened into night, the air crisp and alive with the scent of salt and adventure. They found a small fishing boat bobbing gently in the harbor, its weathered hull reflecting the moonlight as they approached.

Mia, always the resourceful one, negotiated with the elderly fisherman who manned the boat. "We need to reach the nearest island," she explained, her voice firm. "It's important. We have to get there as quickly as possible."

The fisherman squinted at them, his face etched with lines of curiosity and skepticism. "You youngsters are always in a rush. But if you've got the coin, I'll take you."

With a handful of coins exchanged, they boarded the vessel, their hearts racing with the thrill of impending adventure. As the engine roared to life, the boat surged forward, cutting through the waves that glistened like diamonds under the moonlight. The night air whipped around them, filling their lungs with the salty essence of freedom.

As they traveled across the sea, the horizon stretched endlessly before them, a blend of shadows and moonlit water. The waves rocked the boat gently, the rhythmic sound a soothing backdrop to their anxious thoughts. Each of them wrestled with the gravity of their journey, the echoes lurking just out of sight, the gunkey still shrouded in mystery.

"I can't shake the feeling that something awaits us on the other side," Emma said, her voice barely audible over the engine's roar. "The man's words... they felt like a warning."

Adrian nodded, his gaze fixed on the distant horizon. "We'll be ready for whatever comes. We have to be."

The sea air invigorated them, washing away some of the tension that had settled since they left the ruins. As the boat sped over the waves, laughter and shared stories broke the heaviness of their thoughts, a reminder of their shared purpose and the strength they found in one another.

Hours passed, and the darkness deepened, the stars above shining like scattered jewels. Just when weariness began to creep in, a silhouette emerged on the horizon—a landmass breaking the monotony of the sea. The outline grew clearer as they drew closer, revealing jagged cliffs and lush greenery framing the coast.

"Look!" George pointed excitedly. "Land!"

The fisherman steered the boat toward the rocky shore, where the waves crashed with a ferocious welcome. As they approached, the group felt a mixture of anticipation and apprehension. They had no idea what lay ahead on this unfamiliar land.

Once the boat was anchored, they disembarked onto the rocky beach, the ground solid beneath their feet. The sound of the surf filled the air as they took their first steps onto this new territory. They scanned their surroundings, taking in the towering cliffs, dense foliage, and the distant sound of wildlife echoing through the trees.

"What place is this?" Mia asked, her voice laced with wonder and uncertainty.

"I have no idea," Adrian admitted, gazing at the horizon where the cliffs met the sky. "But we need to find out. This could be the key to understanding the gunkey and the echoes."

As they ventured inland, the dense forest enveloped them, the air thick with the scent of earth and vegetation. The trees towered above, their leaves whispering secrets in the gentle breeze. They moved cautiously, acutely aware that they were in uncharted territory, and anything could be lurking within the shadows of the ancient trees.

The path wound deeper into the forest, with the sounds of nature surrounding them. Birds flitted between branches, and the distant rustle of small creatures stirred the underbrush. Despite the beauty of the landscape, an uneasy tension filled the air, as if the very ground they walked on held its breath, waiting for something to unfold.

"What if this land holds the answers we seek?" Emma mused, glancing back at her friends, a spark of hope lighting her eyes. "What if we find something that can lead us to the gunkey?"

The group nodded in agreement, their resolve solidifying. They were ready to face whatever awaited them in this strange land, their mission clear: uncover the mysteries that lay hidden within the depths of the forest and find the gunkey before the echoes could rise again.

With that, they pressed forward, each step echoing with purpose, prepared to confront the challenges that awaited them in this unknown realm.

As they ventured deeper into the forest, the dampness of the air enveloped them like a shroud. The ground squished beneath their feet, evidence of a recent downpour that had transformed the landscape into a lush, vibrant oasis. The rich scent of wet earth mingled with the fragrant aroma of damp leaves and moss, filling their lungs with each breath.

Adrian paused for a moment, looking around at the glistening foliage. "It must have rained heavily earlier. Look at how saturated everything is." Water droplets clung to the leaves like diamonds, sparkling in the filtered sunlight that managed to break through the thick canopy above.

Mia knelt to touch the ground, her fingers sinking slightly into the mud. "It's like a sponge," she said, glancing up with wide eyes. "This forest feels alive. I can't believe how vibrant everything is."

The sound of water trickling through the underbrush filled the air, harmonizing with the distant call of birds that flitted between the branches. Small streams had formed, meandering their way through the roots of trees, their clear waters gliding over smooth stones. The once-dry paths were now transformed into miniature rivers, carving out new routes through the verdant undergrowth.

As they pressed on, the light filtering through the leaves cast a mosaic of shadows and reflections on the ground, creating a kaleidoscope of green and gold. Yet amidst the beauty, a sense of unease lingered. The heavy moisture in the air seemed to amplify the sounds around them—the rustle of leaves, the distant splashes of unseen creatures, and the steady rhythm of their own footsteps.

"Stay alert," Adrian advised, glancing at his friends. "We don't know what could be lurking in this wet terrain. The echoes might have influence here, too."

Emma nodded, her senses heightened. "This place feels... different. Like it's been untouched for a long time, but something has stirred in the shadows. We need to be careful."

As they continued through the forest, the scenery shifted. The towering trees, their trunks thick and ancient, were draped in layers of moss and ferns that thrived in the dampness. Their roots intertwined like gnarled fingers reaching out from the ground, creating natural barriers and hidden paths that seemed to beckon them further into the heart of the woods.

Suddenly, a flash of movement caught George's eye. "Did you see that?" he exclaimed, pointing toward a cluster of ferns where something darted away, vanishing in an instant.

"What was it?" Mia whispered, her pulse quickening.

"I'm not sure," he replied, his voice low. "But it felt like we're not alone here."

Adrian stepped forward, straining to see through the thick vegetation. "We need to keep moving. The longer we stay in one place, the more vulnerable we are."

With a shared look of determination, they pressed on, the wet ground squelching beneath their boots. Each step was a reminder of the urgency of their quest, the whispers of the echoes looming in the back of their minds. The forest, though beautiful, felt like a labyrinth of uncertainty, each twist and turn leading them deeper into the unknown.

As they ventured further, the trees began to thin, revealing a clearing ahead. The sound of rushing water grew louder, and they hurried toward it, drawn by the promise of a stream or waterfall.

When they reached the clearing, they were met with a breathtaking sight. A crystal-clear waterfall cascaded down a rocky cliff, creating a pool of shimmering water below. The surrounding rocks were slick with moisture, and the sunlight caught the droplets as they danced in the air, creating a dazzling display.

"Wow," Mia breathed, awestruck by the beauty before them. "This place is incredible."

Adrian nodded, feeling a wave of relief wash over him. "We should take a moment to rest. We've covered a lot of ground, and this seems like a safe spot."

They settled on the rocky shore, the sound of the waterfall soothing their frayed nerves. Yet even in this moment of tranquility, the weight of their mission hung heavy in the air. They couldn't shake the feeling that the forest held secrets yet to be uncovered, and the quest for the gunkey was far from over.

As they sat, catching their breath and allowing the cool mist from the waterfall to refresh them, the echoes of the past whispered through the trees, urging them onward into the heart of the mystery that lay ahead.

As they sat by the waterfall, taking in the serenity of their surroundings, a sudden rustling in the trees snapped them back to alertness. The underbrush shook violently, leaves quivering as if in response to some unseen force. With hearts racing, they exchanged wary glances, instinctively preparing for whatever might emerge from the shadows.

From the thicket, an old man appeared, his presence both unexpected and commanding. He was draped in a tattered cloak, his long white beard flowing like a waterfall itself, and his eyes sparkled with the wisdom of ages. He looked as if he belonged to the forest, a part of its ancient lore, yet entirely separate from the world outside.

Adrian took a cautious step forward. "Excuse me!" he called out, his voice steady despite the uncertainty that hung in the air. "What city is this?"

The old man paused, turning his gaze toward them with an expression that held both amusement and knowing. "This is Rome," he replied, his voice gravelly yet melodic, as though the very syllables were steeped in history. "Though perhaps not the Rome you've known from maps and stories."

"What do you mean?" Emma asked, curiosity piqued. "Is this... a different version of Rome?"

The old man chuckled softly, a sound like leaves rustling in the wind. "Many Romes exist, dear child. Some are lost to time, hidden within the echoes of memory. Others are found in places like this, where the past breathes alongside the present. But I cannot linger."

Without waiting for further questions, he turned and began to walk away, disappearing into the dense foliage as effortlessly as he had arrived. The sound of his footsteps faded, swallowed by the forest, leaving the group in stunned silence.

"Did he just say this is Rome?" George murmured, still processing the encounter. "What does that even mean?"

Adrian shook his head, his thoughts racing. "It's as if he's suggesting there's more to this place than just the land we recognize. Maybe the echoes have woven this area into a version of Rome we've never encountered before."

Mia frowned, looking after the old man's retreating figure. "But why here? And what does this have to do with our quest for the gunkey?"

Emma stood, her eyes scanning the treetops where the old man had vanished. "Perhaps he knows something about the gunkey or the echoes. We need to find him. He could be a key to unlocking the mysteries of this land."

With renewed purpose, the group decided to follow the path the old man had taken. They navigated through the trees, their footsteps careful and deliberate. The atmosphere felt charged, as if the forest itself were holding its breath, eager to reveal its secrets.

As they moved deeper into the woods, they couldn't shake the feeling that they were being watched, that the forest was alive with hidden eyes observing their every move. They exchanged hushed words, sharing theories about the old man and the peculiar claim that this was Rome.

"Do you think there are other people here?" George asked, glancing around nervously. "What if they're all like him?"

"We need to stay focused on our goal," Adrian reminded them. "Finding the gunkey is our priority. If this place truly is a different version of Rome, it might hold more answers than we realize."

With that, they pressed on, their senses heightened as they ventured further into the heart of the forest, determined to unravel the mysteries that lay ahead. Each step was filled with anticipation, the whispers of the echoes growing louder, guiding them deeper into the enchanted, wet realm of Rome, where past and present intertwined in ways they were only beginning to understand.

As they continued onward, the thick underbrush began to thin, and the trees gradually receded, revealing an open expanse bathed in sunlight. The vibrant greenery of the forest gave way to a breathtaking landscape that stretched out before them—rolling hills, scattered wildflowers, and the distant outline of ancient structures that hinted at civilization.

Adrian paused, a sudden spark of recognition igniting within him. He turned to his friends, his expression shifting from uncertainty to excitement. "Wait a minute. I know this place! This isn't just any forest. It's *that* forest—the one I studied in school!"

The others stopped, curiosity etched on their faces. "What do you mean?" Mia asked, stepping closer. "You've seen this before?"

"Yes!" Adrian exclaimed, a rush of memories flooding back. "In history class, we learned about a forest that was said to be connected to ancient Roman legends. I remember reading that it was believed to hold remnants of forgotten tales and hidden pathways to other realms. I never thought I'd actually find myself here!"

George furrowed his brow, trying to grasp the significance. "So you're saying this place has historical importance? But why is it here? Why did that old man call it Rome?"

"It's possible," Adrian speculated, "that this forest is a gateway to ancient Rome's forgotten history, a place where the lines between reality and legend blur. The stories we learned in school might have roots here, and the echoes we've encountered could be manifestations of those stories."

Emma nodded, her eyes wide with realization. "That makes sense. The echoes might be tied to the history of this place, to the events that shaped its past. If we can uncover what those stories are, it might lead us to the gunkey."

"Exactly," Adrian replied, feeling a surge of hope. "We have to explore further. There could be artifacts or symbols here that connect us to our quest."

With a newfound sense of purpose, they stepped out of the forest and into the open landscape, the warmth of the sun embracing them. As they looked around, the distant ruins beckoned, their crumbling walls hinting at the mysteries waiting to be uncovered. The ground beneath their feet felt charged with energy, as if the very soil carried the weight of history.

Adrian took a deep breath, grounding himself in the moment. "Let's head toward those ruins. If this is a gateway to something greater, we need to see what lies beyond."

As they approached the ancient ruins, the weight of their decision hung in the air. Adrian, sensing a collective hesitation among his friends, paused just a few steps from the threshold of the crumbling structure. "Wait," he said, his voice steady yet thoughtful. "Maybe we shouldn't go in there just yet."

Mia raised an eyebrow, her curiosity piqued. "What do you mean? We could find something important inside."

"I know," Adrian replied, glancing back toward the forest. "But this place feels heavy with history—more than we can handle right now. The old man's warning, the echoes... it all suggests that the answers we seek might not lie within those ruins. Not yet, at least."

George folded his arms, considering Adrian's words. "He's right. If this truly is a significant part of Rome's history, we need to approach it with caution. There might be more at play here than we realize."

Emma nodded in agreement. "And we've been through a lot already. Let's explore the surrounding area first. There could be other clues or paths that we haven't discovered yet."

With a shared sense of understanding, they turned away from the ruins, opting to walk in the opposite direction, away from the beckoning stones and into the wild expanse that lay before them. The ground beneath their feet transformed from the well-trodden soil of the forest to a patchwork of grass and wildflowers, swaying gently in the soft breeze. The vibrant colors danced in the sunlight, a stark contrast to the shadowy depths of the forest they had just exited.

As they walked, the landscape unfolded like a story, revealing rolling hills dotted with ancient trees and the distant sound of a bubbling brook. The air was fragrant with the scent of blooming flowers and fresh earth, invigorating their spirits as they ventured further from the ruins.

Adrian led the way, his mind racing with possibilities. "There has to be something here—some connection to the legends we learned about in school. If this forest is tied to ancient Rome, then surely this landscape is too. We just have to look closely."

Mia picked a wildflower and tucked it behind her ear. "I love how this place feels so alive. It's like nature is welcoming us, giving us the space to breathe and think."

They walked in silence for a moment, each lost in their thoughts, until they reached the crest of a hill. As they ascended, the view opened up before them, revealing a breathtaking panorama of the land stretching out to the horizon. Golden fields rolled away, dotted with patches of dense forest and glimmering streams that wound like silver ribbons through the landscape.

"Wow," George breathed, his eyes wide with wonder. "It's beautiful up here."

Adrian smiled, taking in the scene. "And it's perfect for us to gather our thoughts. We need to strategize about how to approach this journey. We have a lot to figure out, and being out here feels right."

They settled on the grass, the gentle slope of the hill providing a comfortable spot to rest. The sun warmed their backs as they discussed their next steps, the echoes of the forest fading into the background.

"Maybe we should search for other people," Emma suggested, her voice laced with determination. "If this really is an extension of Rome, there might be locals who can help us understand what we're dealing with."

Adrian nodded, feeling a sense of camaraderie with his friends. "That's a good idea. We should also look for any signs—symbols, artifacts, anything that might connect us to the gunkey."

As they laid out their plan, the sun began to dip lower in the sky, casting a warm golden hue over the landscape. They were no longer just wandering through an unfamiliar place; they were adventurers, explorers on the brink of uncovering the secrets of a world steeped in history.

As the sun dipped lower in the sky, casting long shadows across the rolling hills, the group felt a renewed sense of purpose. They gathered their thoughts and decided it was time to seek out the Capitoline Museum, the last known location of the gunkey.

"Alright, let's see if we can find someone who can point us in the right direction," Adrian suggested, scanning the horizon for any signs of life or a nearby village.

As they walked down the hill, the landscape shifted from open fields to a narrow path lined with wildflowers, the vibrant blooms swaying gently in the breeze. The sounds of chirping birds and rustling leaves filled the air, a soothing backdrop to their journey. They kept their eyes peeled for any locals who might provide guidance.

After a short while, they came across an elderly woman tending to a small vegetable garden beside a quaint cottage nestled at the foot of the hill. Her silver hair glimmered in the sunlight, and she wore a warm smile as she noticed the group approaching.

"Excuse me, ma'am," Adrian called out, raising his hand in greeting. "Could you help us? We're looking for directions to the Capitoline Museum."

The woman straightened up, wiping her hands on her apron. "Ah, the Capitoline Museum! A fine place indeed. You're not too far from it. Just follow the path down this way," she said, gesturing toward a narrow dirt road that meandered through the fields. "You'll come to a larger road that will lead you straight there. Can't miss it!"

"Thank you so much!" Mia replied, her eyes shining with gratitude. "Do you know how far it is?"

"It's about a mile from here," the woman said, her voice rich with a gentle accent. "But take your time. There's beauty along the way, and you may find the journey just as rewarding as the destination."

With heartfelt thanks, they waved goodbye and set off down the path she had indicated. As they walked, they exchanged eager glances, anticipation bubbling beneath the surface.

"I can't believe we're actually going to the Capitoline Museum," George said, his enthusiasm infectious. "This is it! The key to our quest might be waiting for us inside."

The road gradually widened, revealing more of the surrounding landscape. The sun continued to sink, casting a golden light that made everything glow, enhancing the sense of magic in the air. The path twisted and turned, leading them through patches of wild grasses and blooming flowers, each step filled with a sense of wonder.

After several minutes of walking, they finally spotted a grand structure rising in the distance. It was an imposing building, with classical columns and intricate carvings that spoke of an ancient past. The entrance gate stood tall, framed by lush greenery, welcoming them as if inviting them into a world of history and mystery.

"There it is!" Adrian exclaimed, pointing excitedly. "The Capitoline Museum!"

As they approached the entrance, their hearts raced with anticipation. The imposing gates, adorned with ornate designs, loomed before them, whispering promises of secrets waiting to be uncovered. They paused for a moment, taking in the beauty of the architecture and the weight of what lay ahead.

"Are we ready for this?" Mia asked, her voice barely above a whisper, filled with both excitement and apprehension.

"Absolutely," Adrian replied, determination shining in his eyes. "Whatever we find in there, we'll face it together. This is the next step in our journey."

With a deep breath, they stepped forward, crossing the threshold into the Capitoline Museum. The grand entrance opened before them like a portal to another time, a gateway to the mysteries of the past that held the potential to change their lives forever. Together, they entered, hearts racing and minds buzzing with possibilities, ready to uncover the truth hidden within those hallowed walls.

As Adrian and his friends crossed the threshold into the Capitoline Museum, they were immediately enveloped in an atmosphere rich with history and artistry. The air felt different here—charged with the whispers of the past and the echoes of countless footsteps that had traversed the same halls over centuries. The entrance was adorned with magnificent marble statues, each one telling a story of ancient Rome's grandeur, capturing the very essence of civilization at its peak.

First Impressions: A Grand Hallway

Stepping through the entrance, they found themselves in a vast atrium, where the high ceilings soared above them like a cathedral of culture. Sunlight streamed through tall, arched windows, illuminating the intricate mosaics that adorned the marble floor beneath their feet. The vibrant colors of the tiles seemed to dance, a beautiful tapestry of scenes depicting mythological stories and historical events, inviting the onlooker to ponder their significance.

To their left, a grand staircase spiraled upward, its steps worn smooth by the passage of time. The banister, carved from dark wood and embellished with gilded details, added an air of elegance to the otherwise imposing structure. As they climbed the staircase, they could hear the soft echoes of their footsteps merging with the faint whispers of visitors who had come before them, adding to the sense of connection to a long-lost world.

The Sculpture Gallery: A Glimpse into the Past

Upon reaching the upper level, they entered the Sculpture Gallery, and it felt as though they had stepped into a living museum of ancient artistry. The room was expansive, filled with statues that loomed over them, each one a masterpiece of its time. Renowned figures from Roman mythology stood tall, their expressions carved with such detail that it seemed they might come to life at any moment.

Adrian's gaze was drawn to a striking statue of the goddess Minerva, her armor glinting in the soft light. She held a shield adorned with an owl, symbolizing wisdom, and her gaze seemed to follow them as they moved, as if she were guarding the secrets of the museum. "Look at the detail," he whispered in awe. "It's incredible how they captured her strength and grace."

As they continued to explore, the shadows of the past loomed over them, and they found themselves lost in the stories behind each statue. They marveled at the colossal busts of emperors, their stern visages reflecting power and authority. Each figure told tales of conquest, tragedy, and triumph, connecting them to a history that felt both distant and intimately familiar.

The Gallery of the Ancient Romans: A Journey Through Time

Venturing deeper into the museum, they discovered the Gallery of the Ancient Romans, where ancient artifacts were carefully displayed in glass cases, each one a testament to the ingenuity of Roman civilization. Gold and silver coins glinted under the museum's soft lighting, telling stories of trade and wealth. Adrian reached out to touch the glass case, feeling a rush of excitement at the thought of the history contained within.

"Can you imagine the people who once held these coins?" Mia mused, her eyes wide. "They were part of a thriving empire!"

As they wandered further, they encountered pottery that had survived the ravages of time, its intricate designs still visible, depicting daily life in ancient Rome. Vases, amphorae, and plates were carefully arranged, each telling its own story of domestic life, commerce, and culture. They stood in awe of a beautifully painted fresco that adorned one wall, vibrant scenes of banquets and celebrations that seemed to come alive before their eyes.

The Room of the Emperors: Where Legends Walked

Next, they entered the Room of the Emperors, a grand hall that felt both majestic and solemn. The walls were lined with portraits of the great leaders of Rome, their painted faces gazing down upon the visitors as if to remind them of the weight of history. The atmosphere shifted, and an air of reverence filled the room, as if they were in the presence of legends.

Adrian felt a chill run down his spine as he stood before a grand portrait of Julius Caesar. The expression on Caesar's face was intense, embodying the ambition and complexity of a man who changed the course of history. "He looks almost alive," he whispered, captivated by the fierce determination captured in the artwork.

"This place is incredible," George said, breaking the silence. "It's like walking through a time machine."

Emma nodded, her eyes sparkling with excitement. "We need to find out more about the gunkey. Maybe there's something here that can help us."

The Garden of the Gods: A Serene Escape

After exploring the indoor exhibits, the group stumbled upon a set of large glass doors that led to an outdoor terrace. They stepped out into the Garden of the Gods, a serene escape from the bustling galleries. The garden was a hidden oasis, bursting with vibrant flowers and lush greenery, offering a breathtaking view of the Roman skyline. The air was fragrant with the scent of blooming jasmine and lavender, filling their senses with tranquility.

In the center of the garden stood a magnificent fountain, its waters glistening in the sunlight as it cascaded down intricately carved stone. Statues of various deities surrounded the fountain, their serene expressions complementing the peaceful ambiance. The sound of water splashing was soothing, creating a perfect backdrop for contemplation.

"This place feels magical," Mia said, closing her eyes and letting the sun warm her face. "I could stay here forever."

Adrian smiled, feeling the weight of their journey momentarily lift. "Let's take a moment to breathe. We've come so far, and we still have a mission ahead of us."

As they sat on a nearby bench, they reflected on their adventure so far, the challenges they had faced, and the mysteries that awaited them in the heart of the museum. With their spirits revitalized, they rose to continue their exploration.

The Hall of Mirrors: Reflections of the Past

They made their way to the Hall of Mirrors, an enchanting space where history and art intertwined. The hall was adorned with mirrors that reflected not only their images but also the grandeur of the museum itself. As they walked through, the reflections created an illusion of infinite space, amplifying the feeling of being part of something much larger than themselves.

"Look at this!" Emma exclaimed, pointing to a stunning mural on the ceiling. It depicted the founding of Rome, with Romulus and Remus suckling from the she-wolf, a powerful symbol of resilience and myth. The colors were vivid, almost pulsating with life, as if the mural were telling the story anew with every glance.

"This is where legends were born," George said, his voice filled with awe. "We're standing where history was made."

The Library of Knowledge: A Final Discovery

As they neared the end of their journey through the museum, they discovered the Library of Knowledge. Shelves lined with ancient texts, scrolls, and manuscripts filled the room, creating an atmosphere of reverence for knowledge and learning. The scent of aged paper and ink wafted through the air, transporting them back to a time when wisdom was revered above all else.

Adrian walked slowly down the aisles, fingers brushing against the spines of books that contained the wisdom of generations. He stopped in front of a large tome, its cover embossed with golden letters. "This could be it—the knowledge we need to find the gunkey," he murmured, entranced by the promise of discovery.

With every step through the museum, they were not only uncovering the past but also forging their own path into the unknown, a journey marked by the intertwining of history and destiny. The Capitoline Museum was not just a repository of artifacts; it was a living testament to the echoes of time, each room a chapter in a story that was far from over.

As they left the library, filled with inspiration and determination, they knew they were one step closer to uncovering the secrets that would ultimately lead them to their goal. The thrill of adventure surged through them as they prepared to delve deeper into the mysteries of this ancient place, ready to embrace whatever awaited them in the depths of the Capitoline Museum.

With renewed determination and a palpable sense of anticipation, Adrian and his friends set off to search for the elusive gunkey within the vast halls of the Capitoline Museum. The weight of history surrounded them, and the excitement of uncovering hidden truths fueled their quest. They had entered this treasure trove of antiquity with the hope that answers lay hidden amongst the relics of a bygone era.

Diving Into the Depths of History

As they moved deeper into the museum, the atmosphere shifted. The intricate artworks and sculptures that once inspired awe now seemed to watch them with silent judgment. Each piece they passed told a story, but none seemed to connect to their immediate goal. Adrian could feel the weight of expectation pressing upon them, but he refused to let it dampen his spirits. "Let's split up and cover more ground," he suggested. "We can meet back here in an hour."

Mia nodded eagerly, her curiosity driving her forward. "I'll check the room with the mosaics. They might have something hidden among the patterns." George was already eyeing a dimly lit hallway that seemed to beckon him. "I'll go this way and see what I can find," he said, motioning down a corridor lined with statues. Emma, ever the diligent researcher, decided to head toward the library once more, believing that perhaps there lay clues buried within the texts.

Adrian, feeling a mix of excitement and anxiety, chose to explore a room that housed ancient weaponry. The walls were adorned with shields and swords, each piece steeped in the stories of battles long past. As he entered, the cool air filled his lungs, and the distinct scent of aged metal and leather enveloped him. He wandered through the displays, each item an artifact of strength and valor, yet none spoke to him about the gunkey.

The Weapons Room: Echoes of Valor

Adrian moved cautiously among the artifacts, his fingers grazing the cool surfaces of the weapons as he examined their intricate designs. Each sword was a testament to the craftsmanship of ancient blacksmiths, while the shields bore the scars of battles fought in the name of honor. He studied a particular sword, its hilt wrapped in leather, the blade shimmering faintly under the museum's soft lights.

"What if the gunkey is a weapon?" he pondered aloud, momentarily distracted. "Could it be disguised as something else?" Yet as he scanned the room for any sign of the fabled object, his heart sank. Nothing seemed out of the ordinary, nothing hinted at the power they sought. The echoes of ancient battles resonated within these walls, but they did not reveal the secrets he needed.

The Mosaic Gallery: Patterns of the Past

Meanwhile, Mia had found her way to the Mosaic Gallery, a breathtaking room filled with intricate floor mosaics that told stories of gods, heroes, and everyday life in ancient Rome. The vibrant colors and intricate patterns mesmerized her, but she was focused on her quest. Kneeling down, she examined a particularly captivating mosaic of Neptune, the god of the sea (according to its particular religion or ethnicity), surrounded by a flurry of marine creatures.

"Could there be something hidden within the art?" she mused, running her fingers along the edges of the stones. She scrutinized the design for anything unusual, any markings that might lead to the gunkey. Hours could be spent deciphering the stories behind each tile, yet her purpose kept her from becoming lost in the beauty around her.

As she shifted her gaze, something caught her attention—a slight anomaly in one corner of the mosaic. A tile that seemed slightly discolored, slightly askew compared to the surrounding stones. Mia's heart raced as she knelt closer, her fingers tracing the edge of the rogue tile. With a gentle push, she attempted to pry it free.

"Come on," she whispered, her breath quickening. "Show me something." But despite her efforts, the tile wouldn't budge, and frustration began to simmer beneath her excitement. She leaned back, studying the surrounding patterns once more, but her initial hope waned.

The Library: Knowledge Hidden Amongst Pages

In the library, Emma stood surrounded by shelves upon shelves of ancient texts, the faint scent of old paper filling the air. She felt like a child in a candy store, yet time was of the essence. "There has to be something here," she murmured, pulling a thick tome from a nearby shelf. Dust motes danced in the shafts of light as she opened it, the pages crackling beneath her fingertips.

The text was in Latin, the script elegant and flowing. She scanned the words quickly, looking for any mention of the gunkey or any artifacts associated with it. Her eyes darted back and forth, but the language was dense and complex, each sentence layered with meaning. She flipped through pages filled with diagrams of ancient machinery, maps of Rome, and historical accounts that felt tangential to her quest.

Hours passed as she delved deeper, searching for connections, but the more she read, the more elusive the gunkey became. "This isn't right," she sighed, feeling the weight of disappointment settle on her shoulders. "There must be a way to decipher this faster."

Lost in the Hallways of Time

Meanwhile, George had ventured into the dimly lit corridor, lined with imposing statues of ancient gods and warriors. Each statue seemed to loom over him, their stone eyes fixed upon his every move. He walked slowly, feeling an odd sense of unease, as if the very air was charged with expectations. "What are you hiding?" he asked the statues, his voice echoing slightly against the stone walls.

As he wandered deeper, he stumbled upon a small alcove that held a collection of relics—smaller items that appeared to be forgotten treasures. Among them were trinkets and baubles, remnants of daily life in ancient Rome. George rifled through the assortment, hoping for a clue or hint that could lead them to the gunkey.

His fingers brushed against a tarnished bronze box, intricately engraved with swirling patterns. Curiosity piqued, he lifted the box, its weight feeling oddly significant. "What have we here?" he wondered aloud, inspecting the item for any hidden compartments. But despite his efforts, it remained stubbornly shut, and after several minutes of fruitless probing, he set it back down, disappointment gnawing at him.

The Convergence of Despair

After the hour passed, the friends reconvened at the atrium, their expressions revealing the frustrations of their fruitless search. Mia, shaking her head, was the first to speak. "I thought for sure I would find something in the mosaics. There's a tile that might be hiding a secret, but I couldn't get it to move."

"I combed through the weaponry room, hoping for some hidden connection," Adrian admitted, his brow furrowed with concern. "But nothing stood out. It's like the gunkey is deliberately eluding us."

Emma sighed heavily, the weight of her research evident in her voice. "The library was filled with knowledge, but none of it pointed to what we're looking for. It's like searching for a ghost."

George, leaning against a marble pillar, ran a hand through his hair. "What if we're not looking in the right places? Maybe the gunkey isn't an artifact at all. What if it's something more conceptual—something we need to interpret rather than physically find?"

The group fell silent, contemplating George's words. The shadows cast by the setting sun loomed longer, heightening the sense of urgency that hung in the air. They had come so far, and yet, the gunkey remained elusive, slipping through their fingers like sand.

A Moment of Clarity

As the tension thickened, Adrian felt a spark of inspiration. "What if the key to finding the gunkey lies in the very stories these artifacts tell? Perhaps it's hidden in the legends, not in the physical items themselves."

Mia's eyes lit up with understanding. "The mosaics, the statues, the texts—they all hold narratives. If we piece those narratives together, maybe we can uncover the truth about the gunkey."

"Yes!" Emma exclaimed, her enthusiasm rekindled. "If we can find a common thread in the stories, we might uncover what we're missing."

George nodded, a newfound sense of hope coursing through him. "Let's do it. We can split up again, but this time, let's focus on the narratives behind the artifacts. We need to think creatively."

Reinvigorated, they set out once more, determined to uncover the gunkey by delving into the heart of the stories the museum had to offer. The echoes of ancient Rome still reverberated through the halls, and they were ready to listen, eager to decode the tales that would lead them to their destiny. With every step, they felt the weight of history behind them, pushing them forward into the depths of the Capitoline Museum, where the secrets of the past awaited their discovery.

As the group dispersed again, a renewed energy buzzed in the air. Adrian meandered through the galleries, his eyes flitting from one artifact to the next, determined to find some hint that would unravel the mystery of the gunkey. The rich textures of the museum enveloped him, and the stories held within each piece seemed to whisper secrets he was only beginning to understand.

As he strolled past a line of ten imposing statues, each one capturing the essence of Roman grandeur, something caught his eye—a subtle oddity that set one statue apart from the others. Standing tall amongst its companions, the statue depicted a stoic figure, his face a mask of strength and wisdom, but it was the forehead that intrigued Adrian.

There, engraved into the stone, was a symbol he had never encountered before: a small, downward-pointing figure resembling a dwarf. It was faint, almost camouflaged against the natural imperfections of the stone, but unmistakably present. Adrian felt a thrill of curiosity. Why was this symbol here? What did it mean?

He stepped closer, studying the engraving. The downward-pointing symbol struck him as unusual—there was something almost ominous about it. In Roman culture, symbols often carried layers of meaning, intertwining with myth and folklore. Yet this particular emblem eluded him, teasing his memory but refusing to reveal its secrets.

Adrian reached out, his fingers grazing the cold surface of the statue's forehead. He could almost feel the weight of history pressing against him, urging him to remember, to connect the dots. "What are you hiding?" he murmured, lost in thought. The other statues stood in silent vigil, their expressions unyielding, as if they too were guardians of the knowledge he sought.

The rest of the museum faded into the background as he focused intently on the dwarf symbol. He recalled fragments of his studies—stories of dwarves in mythology often associated with wisdom, protection, or even mischief, but he couldn't quite place this specific symbol or its relevance to the gunkey.

He stepped back, scanning the other statues, each a representation of valor and virtue, but none bore the same mark. The dwarf symbol seemed out of place, an anomaly amidst the grandeur, and yet it held his attention like a beacon in the darkness.

Adrian knew he needed answers, but with time slipping away and the elusive gunkey still beyond their reach, frustration began to bubble within him. He couldn't help but feel that this symbol was a clue, a part of the puzzle they were desperate to solve.

"Could this be related to the legends?" he thought, pacing in front of the statue. Perhaps understanding the meaning of the dwarf symbol would unlock a new perspective on their quest. His mind raced with possibilities, but the connection remained elusive.

He decided to head back to the atrium, hoping to share his discovery with the others. They needed to work together to decipher the symbol's meaning, to figure out if it had anything to do with the gunkey.

When he reunited with Mia, George, and Emma, he felt a sense of urgency. "I found something," he announced, his excitement bubbling to the surface. "There's a statue with a dwarf symbol engraved on its forehead. I don't know what it means, but I think it's important."

Mia tilted her head, intrigued. "A dwarf symbol? What does it look like?"

"It points downward," Adrian explained, gesturing animatedly. "It's different from the others, almost hidden. I couldn't find anything else like it in the museum."

George frowned thoughtfully. "Maybe it's a marker or a clue about the history of the statue. We should see if there's anything in the library that connects it to the legends or folklore."

Emma nodded in agreement, her eyes shining with interest. "Let's look into it further. If we can understand what the symbol signifies, it might lead us closer to the gunkey."

With a renewed sense of purpose, they set off toward the library once more, determined to uncover the meaning behind the dwarf symbol and its potential connection to their quest. The shadows of the museum loomed around them, each step resonating with the echoes of history, pushing them further into the depths of the unknown.

As Adrian raced through the museum's grand halls, his mind was ablaze with the implications of his discovery. The downward-pointing dwarf symbol etched onto the forehead of the statue lingered in his thoughts, like a whisper echoing through the corridors of his memory. Suddenly, an idea struck him with electrifying clarity—what if the arrow wasn't pointing to a hidden chamber somewhere in the museum but instead indicated something beneath the very feet of the statue itself?

His heart raced at the realization. "The foot of the statue!" he exclaimed, halting abruptly in the middle of the atrium. The others turned to him, curiosity etched on their faces. "What if that symbol is not a warning or a mere decoration? What if it points to something hidden beneath the statue itself?"

Mia's eyes widened with intrigue. "You think there could be something buried there?"

"It makes sense," Adrian pressed on, his excitement palpable. "The downward arrow—it's like a directive, telling us to look below.

Statues often conceal secrets, and this one might be no different. If the dwarf symbol represents something significant, then what if there's a connection to the gunkey right under our noses?"

George, who had been deep in thought, nodded in agreement. "If there's something hidden beneath it, it could lead us to the gunkey or provide more context. We need to check it out right now."

Without another word, the group sprang into action, retracing their steps through the museum's ornate hallways. They moved with urgency, the air thick with anticipation. Each echo of their footsteps seemed to amplify the stakes of their quest. Adrian's mind raced as they approached the statue once more, the towering figure looming above them with an air of authority and mystery.

As they reached the base of the statue, Adrian knelt down, examining the ground closely. Dust and debris collected around the pedestal, but there was no doubt that the symbol was meant to signify something vital. "It has to be here," he murmured, brushing his fingers against the stone. The intricate carvings that adorned the statue's feet seemed to shimmer in the dim light, as if they were hiding secrets of their own.

"Can you see anything?" Mia asked, squatting beside him, her eyes scanning the base with keen interest.

Adrian focused intently, feeling the texture of the stone under his fingertips. "It's just solid stone... or is it?" He squinted, noticing a faint line running along the edge of the pedestal. It wasn't just the smooth base of the statue; it was an edge that suggested a potential mechanism or hidden compartment. He felt a rush of adrenaline as he pressed his palm against it, searching for any sign of movement.

"Help me," he said, looking up at his friends. Together, they pushed against the statue's base, their combined strength straining against the ancient stone. With a low rumble, they felt the pedestal shift slightly, as if responding to their efforts.

“That’s it! Keep going!” George encouraged, excitement surging through him.

With one final heave, the stone began to slide aside, revealing a shallow recess beneath the statue. A musty, cool air wafted from the opening, carrying with it the scent of centuries-old dust and secrets long forgotten. Adrian’s heart raced as they peered into the dark crevice.

“Look!” Emma exclaimed, her voice filled with awe as she pointed into the recess. There, nestled within the shadows, was a small, ornate box, its surface covered in intricate engravings that mirrored the designs they had seen throughout the museum. The dwarf symbol was repeated along the edges, further solidifying its connection to their quest.

Adrian felt a surge of triumph wash over him. “This has to be it—the gunkey or a key to finding it!” He carefully reached into the recess, his fingers trembling with anticipation as he grasped the box. It was surprisingly warm to the touch, as if it had absorbed the energy of the centuries around it.

As he pulled it free, the entire group held their breath, their eyes wide with wonder. The moment felt monumental, a turning point in their journey. Adrian set the box down on the ground, examining its ornate designs and the way it caught the light. This could be the breakthrough they had desperately sought.

“Should we open it?” Mia asked, a mixture of excitement and trepidation in her voice.

“Absolutely,” Adrian replied, the thrill of discovery electrifying the air around them. He examined the box for a latch or a way to unlock it. The surface appeared seamless, with no obvious way to access whatever lay inside.

“This is where the knowledge we’ve gathered comes into play,” Emma suggested. “Maybe it’s a puzzle or requires a specific way to open it. We need to think back to the statues, the stories, and the symbols we've encountered. Perhaps there's something we've missed."

With a renewed sense of purpose, they gathered around the box, their minds racing to connect the dots. The dwarf symbol, the legends, the narratives—they all began to weave together, forming a tapestry of clues that could lead them to the truth.

Adrian felt a surge of determination, ready to unlock the secrets that had been hidden for so long. They were on the cusp of something incredible, and he was certain that the answer they sought was finally within their grasp. As they worked together, piecing together their knowledge and insight, they were united in their quest, ready to unveil the mystery that had eluded them for far too long.

With a soft click that echoed like a heartbeat in the stillness of the museum, the ornate box finally gave way, its lid creaking open to reveal the treasure within. Adrian's breath caught in his throat as he leaned closer, the flickering light casting an ethereal glow over the contents. Nestled inside was the gunkey, a magnificent artifact that seemed to shimmer with a life of its own.

The gunkey was unlike anything they had ever seen. Its surface was crafted from a deep, lustrous metal that glinted like polished obsidian, intricately engraved with symbols that mirrored the dwarf insignia they had encountered earlier. The craftsmanship was exquisite, with each etching telling a story of its own—stories of battles fought, of echoes silenced, and of power harnessed.

As Adrian reached in to lift the gunkey from its resting place, he marveled at the weight of it in his hand. It felt substantial, almost as if it held the essence of the ancient knowledge from which it had been born. The cold metal sent a shiver up his spine, a reminder of the gravity of what they were dealing with.

"It's beautiful," Mia whispered, her eyes wide with awe. "I can't believe we actually found it."

George leaned closer, examining the gunkey's surface. "Look at these engravings," he said, tracing his fingers along the intricate designs. "They look like a combination of different languages. This must be tied to the legends."

Adrian felt an electrifying surge of excitement. "We have to figure out how to use it. This is the key to stopping Catherine and the echoes! If we can unlock its full potential, we might stand a chance."

But as the weight of the gunkey settled into his palm, Adrian was acutely aware of the responsibility it represented. This was not just an ancient artifact; it was a tool that could change the fate of their world. He felt the eyes of history upon him, as if the very essence of those who had wielded such power before was urging him to make the right choice.

"What do you think we should do next?" Emma asked, her voice laced with a mix of enthusiasm and concern. "Do we take it to confront Catherine directly, or should we try to learn more about how it works first?"

Adrian pondered her question, the gunkey weighing heavily in his hand. "We need to understand its purpose fully before confronting her. This gunkey could have unforeseen consequences if we don't know how to wield it properly. The legends might hold the key to its power."

As they stood in a semicircle around the gunkey, a sense of unity and determination surged within the group. The tension of the previous hours seemed to dissipate, replaced by a shared purpose. Together, they had unraveled the mystery of the box and discovered the ancient weapon that could alter the fate of their world.

"Let's return to the library," Adrian suggested, looking at each of his friends in turn. "We need to research the engravings, to decode its meaning and learn how to harness its power. If this gunkey can truly destroy the echoes, we must be prepared."

Mia nodded, a spark of determination igniting in her eyes. "Let's do it. We've come too far to turn back now."

As they carefully placed the gunkey back in its box, the weight of their mission became clearer than ever. Each of them felt the gravity of what lay ahead—the battle against Catherine, the head of the echoes, and the impending showdown that would test not just their courage but their bond as friends.

With renewed vigor, they left the statue behind, the echoes of their footsteps trailing through the museum, a testament to their resolve. The journey was far from over; it was just beginning, and the ancient gunkey was their guide—a beacon of hope in a world overshadowed by darkness. As they moved through the halls once more, the whispers of history seemed to echo around them, urging them forward, toward the unknown challenges that awaited.

With a sense of urgency igniting their determination, Adrian and his friends made a collective decision: they would not return to the library. Instead, the time had come to act on what they had discovered. The gunkey was now in their possession, a powerful artifact that could potentially turn the tide in their favor against Catherine and her echoes.

They exited the museum, the air outside crisp and charged with anticipation. The sun hung low in the sky, casting a warm golden hue over the ancient city of Rome. For a moment, they paused to take in their surroundings, the weight of their journey settling heavily on their shoulders. The museum had been a treasure trove of knowledge, but now it was time to embrace the unknown.

"Let's head to the shore and catch a boat back to XEL Island," Adrian said, glancing at the distant waters glistening under the fading sunlight. "We can regroup there and figure out our next move."

Mia nodded in agreement, her expression resolute. "It's the best option. We'll have time to strategize and understand the gunkey without the pressure of being in the museum."

George glanced around, ensuring that no one was watching too closely. "Let's move quickly, then. The last thing we need is to draw attention to ourselves with this gunkey."

The group hurried to the harbor, their hearts racing with a mixture of excitement and anxiety. They found a small boat bobbing gently in the water, its weathered hull a reminder of the countless journeys it had undertaken. Adrian stepped aboard first, followed closely by his friends, each of them feeling the weight of their newfound responsibility.

As the boat pulled away from the dock, the city of Rome began to recede into the distance, its ancient architecture fading against the horizon. The sun dipped lower, casting fiery reflections on the water's surface, and a tranquil calm enveloped them. For the first time in what felt like ages, they were free from the labyrinthine confines of the museum, unbound and ready to embrace their fate.

The boat glided smoothly across the waves, the gentle rocking creating a rhythm that seemed to resonate with their hearts. The air was filled with the scent of salt and adventure, and as they moved further away from the shore, Adrian felt a sense of liberation wash over him.

"This is it," he said, breaking the comfortable silence. "Once we get to XEL Island, we'll need to find a safe place to analyze the gunkey. I want to understand every detail before we make our next move."

Mia leaned back against the boat's edge, her gaze fixed on the horizon. "We should also consider how to confront Catherine. This gunkey is powerful, but we have to be careful. She's cunning, and we can't underestimate her."

Emma interjected, her voice filled with determination. "If we work together and stay focused, we can figure this out. We've already come so far, and we have the advantage of surprise. Let's not forget that."

George nodded, the gravity of their mission settling in. "Once we reach the island, we should scout for any potential allies as well. We might need all the help we can get when the time comes to face her."

As the boat navigated the waves, the outline of XEL Island emerged from the mist, its rugged cliffs and lush greenery beckoning them closer. The island had always felt like a second home, a sanctuary where they could regroup and plan their next steps.

Adrian's heart swelled with hope as they neared the shore. The familiar landscape was comforting, yet he knew that everything had changed. They were no longer just friends on a simple adventure; they were now guardians of an ancient weapon, tasked with a mission far greater than themselves.

With a sense of purpose guiding them, they docked the boat and disembarked onto the sandy beach, the sound of waves crashing against the shore filling their ears. Each step felt like a declaration of their commitment to the journey ahead. They were ready to confront the challenges that awaited them, armed with the knowledge of the gunkey and the bonds of friendship that had only grown stronger through their trials.

As they made their way inland, they began to formulate a plan. "We need to find a secure location," Adrian suggested, glancing at the dense forest that fringed the beach. "Somewhere we can lay low and study the gunkey."

"Over there," Mia pointed to a cluster of trees, their thick trunks providing ample cover. "That clearing looks perfect. We can set up camp and start examining the engravings right away."

With purpose, they moved toward the clearing, their minds buzzing with possibilities and strategies. The time for action was drawing near, and with each passing moment, they could feel the weight of the gunkey in Adrian's pocket—a tangible reminder of the battle ahead and the stakes that lay before them.

As they settled into their new environment, a shared resolve blossomed among them. They would decipher the mysteries of the gunkey, prepare for the confrontation with Catherine, and stand united against the echoes that threatened their world. The journey was far from over; it was only just beginning, and they were ready to face whatever lay ahead.

As Adrian and his friends ventured deeper into the thick, verdant forest of XEL Island, a palpable mix of fear and curiosity enveloped them. The air was dense with the earthy scent of moss and damp leaves, and the sounds of nature—chirping birds and rustling branches—created a symphony that both calmed and unnerved them. Each step felt weighted with the knowledge of what they carried: the gunkey, a magnificent and ancient artifact that held the potential to alter their fate.

The towering trees loomed overhead, their branches intertwining like the fingers of ancient giants, casting dappled shadows on the forest floor. Sunlight filtered through the leaves, illuminating patches of vibrant green, yet the deeper they went, the darker it became, as if the very forest were alive, watching their every move. Adrian felt a shiver run down his spine, a mix of anticipation and apprehension. What secrets lay hidden within this familiar yet foreboding landscape?

"Stick together," he reminded the group, his voice steady but low. "We don't know what might be lurking in here."

Mia, walking closely beside him, nodded, her expression resolute despite the unease creeping into her heart. "We've faced danger before. This time, we're not alone."

They pressed on, their senses heightened. Every crack of a twig and whisper of the wind seemed amplified, fueling their curiosity about what lay ahead. Adrian's thoughts raced, spiraling around the potential power of the gunkey and the responsibility they had undertaken. Would it truly be enough to confront Catherine?

After what felt like hours, they reached a clearing bathed in soft, golden light, a stark contrast to the dark, looming trees surrounding them. It was a beautiful oasis, filled with wildflowers that danced gently in the breeze. But Adrian couldn't shake the feeling that they were not alone.

"Let's stop here for a moment," he said, glancing around. "This clearing feels safe."

As they gathered in the center, Emma pulled out the gunkey from its ornate box, the intricate engravings catching the light like a beacon. "Now, let's examine this closely. We need to decipher its power and purpose."

They formed a tight circle, leaning in as Emma placed the gunkey on a flat stone, its surface smooth and cool against the warmth of their hands. The engravings shimmered with ancient wisdom, and as they studied them, a sense of connection to the past washed over Adrian.

"I can't help but feel that the people who created this knew we would come one day," he murmured, tracing the intricate designs with his fingertips. "Like they left us a message."

"Or a warning," George added, scanning the surrounding trees with wary eyes. "We need to be careful. The echoes might not be far behind us."

Mia, ever the optimistic voice in their group, leaned closer to the gunkey. "What if it has a key phrase or a command? Something that activates its power? We should think about the legends we've heard."

Adrian felt a surge of inspiration. "The downward dwarf symbol! It must relate to the key phrase or the way we need to handle it."

He straightened, eyes gleaming with newfound determination. "If we can figure out the connection between the symbol and the engravings, it might lead us to understanding how to use the gunkey against Catherine."

As they each studied the engravings closely, a sudden rustle in the bushes nearby caught their attention, causing their hearts to race. They turned instinctively, tension rising as the sound grew louder.

"Did you hear that?" Emma whispered, her eyes wide.

"Stay alert," Adrian instructed, gripping the gunkey tightly. The moment felt electric, charged with the potential for both danger and discovery.

The rustling grew nearer, and before they could react, a figure emerged from the shadows—a small, furry creature darting between the underbrush. Adrian let out a relieved laugh, his heart easing as he recognized a bushy-tailed fox, its bright eyes glinting with curiosity.

"Just a fox," George said, chuckling nervously. "For a second there, I thought we were in for a showdown."

Adrian chuckled as well, but his mind remained focused. "This forest has secrets, just like the gunkey. We have to be vigilant. There's more to discover here."

With the tension easing, they returned to their task, pouring over the engravings with renewed energy. They debated, hypothesized, and shared thoughts, the fear of the unknown turning into excitement at the prospect of unraveling the mysteries before them.

As they worked together, Adrian felt the connections begin to form—a thread weaving through the engravings and the stories they had heard. He closed his eyes for a moment, visualizing the legends that spoke of the echoes and their defeat.

"Maybe we need to speak the words out loud, test the gunkey in some way," he suggested, his voice steady. "What if we chant the names of those who fell to the echoes? It could trigger something."

Mia nodded enthusiastically. "Yes! It's worth a try. We need to honor those who fought before us and connect with their strength."

Gathering in a circle around the gunkey, they took a deep breath, their voices merging into a single chant, reverberating through the clearing as they called upon the names and stories of those lost to the echoes. Each word felt like a pulse of energy, resonating in the air around them.

As they spoke, the air grew still, and the light seemed to shift, enveloping the clearing in a warm glow. Adrian felt a tingling sensation at the tips of his fingers as he reached toward the gunkey, and for a moment, it felt as though the very fabric of time had woven them together with the spirits of the past.

Suddenly, the engravings on the gunkey began to pulse with a radiant light, illuminating their faces in a brilliant glow. Adrian's heart raced as he realized they were onto something monumental.

"Keep going!" he urged, feeling the energy building between them. "We're getting closer!"

The clearing seemed to vibrate with energy as their voices rose, merging with the whispers of the ancient forest around them. Fear was replaced with a sense of purpose, a shared understanding that they were not merely searching for power; they were tapping into the strength of those who had come before, channeling their courage against the darkness that loomed ahead.

As they continued to chant, the light enveloped them, revealing the true power of the gunkey—a connection to the echoes and the strength needed to confront them. The forest, with all its mysteries and fears, had become their ally, and together, they would face the challenges that lay ahead.

AS ADRIAN AND HIS FRIENDS continued their chant, a sudden whispering broke through the serene atmosphere of the clearing. It was soft at first, a barely audible rustle that tickled their ears like the faintest breeze, but it quickly escalated into a series of hushed, urgent voices.

Adrian froze, his heart racing as the whispers coalesced into distinct words. "They're close," he murmured, wide-eyed, glancing at Mia, who was already straining to listen. The others exchanged anxious glances, the gravity of the moment sinking in.

"Who is it?" George asked, his voice barely above a whisper, as he instinctively moved closer to Adrian. They all peered through the thick foliage, their breath caught in their throats, each of them acutely aware of what was at stake.

Then, they saw her: Catherine, the head of the echoes, flanked by several shadowy figures—echoes that seemed to ripple in and out of existence, their forms flickering like flames in a breeze. The malevolent aura surrounding them sent a chill down Adrian's spine, and he felt the primal urge to flee grip him tightly.

Catherine's voice, sharp and commanding, sliced through the whispers. "Search the area thoroughly," she instructed her followers, her eyes glinting with an unsettling confidence. "They were here. I can feel their presence."

"Quick, we need to hide!" Emma hissed, her eyes wide with fear. The group instinctively ducked behind a thicket, the underbrush scratching at their skin as they pressed against the earth, their hearts pounding like war drums.

Adrian's mind raced, thoughts colliding in a frantic rush. They had come so far, uncovered so much, and yet here they were, on the brink of discovery, only to find themselves in the very crosshairs of the enemy. The stakes were higher than ever, and the reality of their situation felt overwhelming.

"Stay quiet," Adrian whispered urgently, peering through the leaves. He could see Catherine scanning the area, her expression one of fierce determination. "We can't let her find us. We have to get away."

Before he could formulate a plan, the echoes began to fan out, their movements eerie and unnatural, searching the shadows with an unsettling precision. The air thickened with a sense of impending danger, and Adrian could feel the weight of the gunkey in his pocket, a reminder of the power they now wielded—but it offered little comfort in the face of such an imminent threat.

"Now!" he whispered fiercely, adrenaline surging through his veins. Without hesitation, the group bolted, instinctively retreating deeper into the forest. Branches whipped against their arms, and the undergrowth crackled beneath their hurried steps. Fear propelled them forward, urging them to escape the looming threat.

As they sprinted, Adrian glanced back, seeing Catherine and the echoes close on their heels. Her voice rose above the rustle of the trees, fierce and commanding. "They won't escape! Find them!"

The urgency in her tone drove them faster, each footfall echoing their desperate flight. The forest seemed to shift around them, the trees closing in as they navigated the twisting paths, adrenaline blurring the lines of their surroundings.

The foliage thinned ahead, revealing a rocky outcrop that overlooked a steep drop into the churning sea below. The wind whipped around them, carrying with it the scent of salt and urgency. Without thinking, they sprinted toward the outcrop, desperate for a vantage point to plan their next move.

"Over here!" Mia shouted, pointing toward a narrow path that snaked down the cliffside. It was treacherous and steep, but it was their only option. They could hear the echoes moving closer, their whispers mixing with the sound of the waves crashing against the rocks below.

Without a second thought, Adrian led the charge down the path, urging his friends to follow. The descent was perilous, the ground unstable underfoot, but fear fueled their determination. They could hear the echoes gaining on them, their voices growing more distinct, more threatening.

"Adrian, hurry!" Emma called, her voice trembling as they navigated the rocky terrain.

"Almost there!" he replied, pushing himself harder. Each step felt like a race against time, and the gunkey rattled in his pocket, a reminder of their mission and the stakes they faced.

Finally, they reached the bottom of the cliff, breathless and disoriented. The sound of the waves crashing against the rocks drowned out the echoes' pursuit, and they ducked behind a large boulder, the salt spray cooling their flushed faces.

Panting, they listened intently as the whispers faded into the distance, the echoes seemingly confused by the abrupt change in their surroundings. Adrian's heart raced as he peeked around the boulder, ensuring they had evaded capture.

"I think we lost them," he whispered, relief flooding his voice.

Mia leaned against the boulder, her chest rising and falling rapidly as she tried to catch her breath. "That was too close," she said, her eyes wide with shock.

"Now we need to regroup and figure out our next steps," Adrian replied, his mind racing. They had the gunkey, but they also had a powerful enemy who was determined to stop them.

As they gathered their composure, a newfound sense of determination replaced the fear. They were not just fleeing from danger; they were strategizing, preparing for the confrontation that lay ahead.

"This isn't over," Adrian declared, his voice steadying with conviction. "We have the gunkey. We know where Catherine is, and we can't let fear dictate our actions. We need to harness the power of the gunkey and confront her on our terms."

Mia and George nodded, their expressions hardening with resolve. They had faced the echoes and lived to tell the tale, and now they were more than just survivors; they were warriors on a mission to reclaim their world from the shadows that threatened to engulf it.

With a final glance at the forest, where the whispers had been silenced, they steeled themselves for the battles yet to come.

As Adrian and his friends huddled behind the boulder, their hearts still pounding from their narrow escape, the sound of crashing waves gradually calmed their racing thoughts. They took a moment to breathe, gazing out at the expanse of the sea that lay before them. The water sparkled under the sun, its surface a mesmerizing dance of light and color. Shades of deep blue merged seamlessly with turquoise, while the frothy white caps of the waves rolled rhythmically toward the shore, creating a tranquil yet powerful backdrop to their turmoil.

Adrian leaned back against the cool stone, allowing himself a moment of reprieve as he absorbed the beauty around him. The salty breeze whipped through his hair, invigorating him and washing away the remnants of fear that had clung to him since their encounter with Catherine.

"Look at that view," Emma said, her voice barely above a whisper. She gestured toward the horizon, where the sky met the sea in a breathtaking display of vibrant oranges and pinks. The clouds were streaked with gold, a masterpiece painted by nature itself. For a moment, the worries of their quest faded into the background, and they found solace in the awe-inspiring landscape.

"It's stunning," George agreed, his eyes scanning the horizon. "But we can't forget why we're here." He shifted uneasily, still feeling the weight of the gunkey in his pocket.

"We'll figure it out," Adrian reassured him, his mind still racing with possibilities. "We just need to gather our strength and think clearly. This moment of beauty is a reminder of what we're fighting for."

As they stood there, lost in thought, the tranquility of the scene was abruptly shattered. A low rumble echoed from the distance, like the growl of a slumbering beast awakening from its long rest. The ground beneath their feet trembled slightly, sending a ripple of alarm through the group. Adrian's gaze shot toward the horizon just as a distant landmass erupted into a cataclysmic explosion of dust and debris, shooting upward like a volcano awakening from centuries of slumber.

"What the—?" Mia gasped, her eyes wide with shock.

The plume of dust ascended rapidly, darkening the sky and obscuring the setting sun, as if the very earth itself were reacting to an unspeakable threat. Time seemed to stretch in that moment, each heartbeat amplifying the shock of what they had just witnessed.

But the moment was quickly eclipsed by a chilling sound—laughter. It was a cruel, mocking sound that sliced through the air, echoing ominously against the waves.

"Catherine," Adrian breathed, his heart sinking. "She's doing this."

They turned toward the source of the laughter, their eyes narrowing as the familiar figure of Catherine emerged from the shadows of the trees above, her presence radiant and malevolent. The chaos of destruction behind her illuminated her silhouette, casting her in an otherworldly glow. Her laughter danced on the wind, sending shivers down Adrian's spine.

"Did you really think you could escape me?" she called, her voice dripping with disdain. "Look at the power I wield! You are nothing but fleeting shadows in my domain."

Adrian clenched his fists, a mix of anger and determination surging within him. The destruction she had unleashed was a stark reminder of the stakes they faced. "We won't let you win!" he shouted back, his voice cutting through the air with defiance.

Emma stepped forward, her resolve hardening in the face of their adversary. "You may have power, Catherine, but we have something you can never take from us—hope and the will to fight!"

The echoes flanking Catherine moved closer, their forms shimmering ominously in the twilight. But even as the darkness threatened to engulf them, Adrian felt a renewed sense of purpose blooming within him.

"This is our fight, and we won't back down," he declared, his eyes blazing with determination. "We have the gunkey, and we will use it!"

As the laughter from Catherine faded into the sound of crashing waves, the gravity of their situation anchored them firmly in reality. The distant land had vanished, and with it, a piece of their world, but they would not let fear dictate their fate. They had come too far and endured too much to allow Catherine to triumph.

The beauty of the sea, once a symbol of peace, now served as a backdrop for their battle. They stood together, a united front against the encroaching darkness, ready to reclaim what was theirs and protect the world from the echoes that threatened to consume it.

"Let's move," Adrian urged, determination propelling them forward. "We need to regroup and find a way to confront her. We'll turn her laughter into a lesson she won't forget."

With the gunkey clutched tightly in hand, they set off along the shoreline, the weight of their mission heavier than ever.

As Adrian and his friends forged ahead, their resolve bolstered by the moment of beauty they had witnessed, a sudden shift in the ground beneath them sent shockwaves of alarm coursing through their bodies.

Without warning, the earth trembled violently, as if it had been stirred by some ancient force. Adrian barely had time to react when a gaping hole erupted beneath them, the ground splitting open with a deafening roar. The world tilted dangerously, and before they could even scream, they were swallowed whole by the darkness that yawned open at their feet.

Mia's startled cry echoed in the air as they plummeted into the abyss, the descent a chaotic whirlwind of flailing limbs and disoriented thoughts. The sensation of falling enveloped them, a chilling reminder of their precarious situation.

As they tumbled through the void, time seemed to stretch infinitely. Adrian felt a rush of panic coursing through him, but it was quickly eclipsed by an instinctive determination to protect his friends. He reached out, grabbing Mia's arm, pulling her closer. "Hold on!" he shouted, his voice barely piercing the overwhelming roar of the wind around them.

In the depths of the chasm, darkness consumed them. The only sounds were their racing hearts and the wind howling past, a ghostly chorus that seemed to mock their plight. Suddenly, the sensation of falling shifted, and they landed with a jarring thud on a hard, uneven surface.

Adrian gasped for breath, his heart pounding in his chest as he blinked against the darkness. The air was damp and cool, a stark contrast to the chaos above. Slowly, he pushed himself up, groaning as he surveyed their surroundings. They were in a vast underground chamber, the walls slick with moisture and the faint scent of earth lingering in the air.

"Everyone okay?" he asked, his voice echoing in the stillness. He turned to see Mia and George pulling themselves to their feet, their expressions a mixture of shock and determination.

"Yeah, I think so," Mia replied, brushing dirt off her clothes. "What just happened?"

"I have no idea," Adrian said, scanning the shadows that flickered at the edges of their vision. "But it's not over. We need to figure out where we are and find a way back."

The gravity of their situation settled heavily upon them as they gathered their bearings. The laughter of Catherine echoed faintly in the distance, a chilling reminder of their adversary still looming above. They were separated from her and her echoes, but for how long? And what lay ahead in this dark, foreboding chamber?

"Look!" George exclaimed, pointing toward the far end of the chamber, where a dim light flickered. "There might be a way out over there!"

Adrian's heart raced with the prospect of escape, but caution crept in. "Let's move carefully," he urged, his instincts on high alert. The last thing they needed was to stumble into another trap.

As they cautiously made their way toward the flickering light, the shadows around them seemed to shift and dance, playing tricks on their eyes. Each step echoed ominously, the sound amplifying the tension that coiled in the air.

"What if this is another trap?" Mia whispered, glancing nervously around. "What if Catherine is waiting for us?"

Adrian shook his head, pushing the fear aside. "We have to keep moving. We can't let her control us. We have the gunkey, and that gives us power."

With renewed determination, they approached the light, the glimmer growing stronger as they neared. As they stepped into the illumination, they found themselves in a narrow passageway that branched off from the chamber. The walls were lined with ancient carvings, symbols that pulsed with a strange energy, and the air hummed with an eerie resonance.

"Look at these!" Mia gasped, running her fingers along the carvings. "These must be connected to the echoes... or even to the gunkey!"

Adrian's eyes widened as he studied the symbols. They were unlike anything he had ever seen, intricate designs that seemed to shift and change under the dim light. "Maybe they can guide us," he suggested, his curiosity piqued. "We need to decipher them."

The urgency of their situation fueled their determination. They couldn't afford to waste any time. They gathered around the carvings, their minds racing as they tried to make sense of the cryptic messages etched into the stone.

As they worked together, piecing together the clues, Adrian felt a sense of hope blossoming within him. They were not defeated; they were merely redirected. The darkness that surrounded them now felt less suffocating, and he could sense a path forward.

"We'll find a way to confront Catherine," Adrian vowed, determination hardening his resolve. "We've come too far to give up now."

With the echoes of laughter still haunting their ears, they pressed onward, the gunkey secure in Adrian's pocket and their spirits ignited by the promise of discovery. They were not just lost in the dark; they were on the brink of uncovering the secrets of the echoes, ready to reclaim their fate from the shadows that sought to ensnare them. Together, they would forge ahead, unraveling the mysteries of this underground realm and preparing for the battle that lay ahead.

As Adrian and his friends stood surrounded by the ancient carvings, their hearts racing with the thrill of discovery, the atmosphere suddenly shifted. A shiver ran down Adrian's spine, as if the very air had thickened with anticipation. Then, from the shadows that clung to the edges of the chamber, a figure emerged.

It was the man they had encountered earlier—the one who had warned them about Catherine and urged them to retrieve the gunkey. His presence was striking, illuminated by the faint glow of the symbols that adorned the walls. He seemed both ethereal and grounded, his eyes piercing and filled with an ancient wisdom that sent chills through Adrian.

"Have you brought the gunkey?" he asked, his voice resonating in the stillness, a gravelly timbre that echoed with authority.

Adrian's heart raced. "Yes, we have it!" he declared, reaching into his pocket and pulling out the magnificent artifact. The gunkey shimmered in the dim light, its intricate designs reflecting the history and power it held. He stepped forward, holding it aloft for the man to see. "We found it hidden beneath the statue. We're ready to confront Catherine."

The man's gaze intensified as he studied the gunkey, and for a moment, silence enveloped the chamber, thick with the weight of expectation. The air hummed with energy, and Adrian could feel the ground beneath him pulse in response to the relic's presence.

"Good," the man said finally, a hint of approval flickering in his eyes. "You have done well to retrieve it, but understand this: the gunkey is more than just a weapon. It holds the power to either save or destroy. You must wield it wisely."

"What do you mean?" Mia asked, her brow furrowed with concern. "How can it save us from Catherine?"

The man stepped closer, his expression shifting from stern to earnest. "The echoes thrive on chaos and fear. They feed on the darkness within us. To confront Catherine, you must not only have the gunkey but also the strength to face the echoes of your own doubts and fears. The weapon will not function if your hearts are clouded by uncertainty."

Adrian felt a swell of determination rise within him. He thought of the trials they had faced—the harrowing encounters, the laughter of Catherine that echoed through their minds. Each challenge had brought them closer together, but it had also tested their resolve. They had faced their fears, but could they truly harness that strength in the face of Catherine's darkness?

"We're ready," Adrian replied, his voice steady. "We've come this far together, and we won't let her win."

The man nodded slowly, as if weighing Adrian's words against an unspoken truth. "Very well. The gunkey is your key to the confrontation, but remember, it is not just the power of the weapon that will define your victory. It is your unity and the bonds you have forged that will carry you through the darkness."

With that, the man stepped back, his form shimmering in the dim light, as if he were a figment of the very shadows that surrounded them. "You must move swiftly. The echoes will not remain dormant for long. When you face Catherine, remember: the strength you need is within you."

Before Adrian could respond, the man's figure began to fade, melding seamlessly with the darkness, leaving behind an air of mystery and urgency.

"Wait!" Adrian called out, but it was too late. The man had vanished, swallowed by the shadows.

"What do we do now?" George asked, his voice tinged with uncertainty.

Adrian turned to his friends, seeing the determination in their eyes mirrored in his own. "We prepare ourselves for the confrontation. We can't let Catherine have the upper hand. We'll use the gunkey, and we'll do it together."

With a collective breath, they gathered around the gunkey, feeling its energy pulse with life. They understood that their journey had led them to this moment—a crucial turning point where they could either fall prey to the echoes or rise to meet their destiny.

"Let's find a way back to the surface," Adrian urged, determination surging through him. "We have a battle to win."

As they moved deeper into the underground passage, their resolve hardened. The echoes may have laughed, but they would soon find that laughter transformed into a fight for survival. United, they would stand against the darkness, armed with hope and the gunkey, ready to reclaim their world from the clutches of the echoes that threatened to consume it. The path ahead was fraught with danger, but together, they would confront the shadows and carve their own destiny.

Adrian's mind raced with questions, the weight of their mission pressing heavily upon him. He turned back to the enigmatic man, his determination resolute. "Where is the shotgun?" he asked, urgency lacing his voice. "We need it to confront Catherine and the echoes."

The man regarded Adrian thoughtfully, his expression serious as if weighing the gravity of the moment. "The shotgun is in the same area where you first encountered it," he replied, his tone grave. "But be warned, you must approach it without drawing attention. The echoes are vigilant and will not hesitate to strike if they sense your presence."

Adrian nodded, understanding the risks that lay ahead. "How do we get there without being seen?" he pressed, feeling the adrenaline coursing through his veins.

The man stepped closer, lowering his voice as though sharing a sacred secret. "The echoes are sensitive to light and sound. Move in silence and keep your surroundings in mind. There are paths in the shadows—use them to your advantage. Remember, you must remain united, for the strength of your bond will protect you as much as any weapon."

"Got it," Mia replied, her voice barely above a whisper. "We'll stick together and stay alert."

"Exactly," the man affirmed, his gaze piercing. "Once you reach the shotgun, it will require a specific action to activate. I cannot tell you what it is, but trust your instincts. They will guide you."

Adrian felt a mix of anticipation and anxiety swelling within him. They were so close, yet the path ahead seemed fraught with danger. "Thank you," he said, genuine gratitude in his voice. "We won't let you down."

With the man's words resonating in their minds, the group turned their attention back to the darkness that surrounded them. The air felt charged with energy, each shadow looming ominously as they began to move.

"Stay close," Adrian instructed, leading the way into the narrow passage. As they navigated through the labyrinthine tunnels, their senses heightened, every creak of the walls and whisper of the wind amplified their tension.

They pressed on, hearts pounding in unison, determined to reach their goal without alerting the echoes that lurked nearby. The flickering light from the ancient carvings provided the only illumination, casting dancing shadows that played tricks on their minds.

Adrian led them through the winding corridors, relying on the fragmented memories of their earlier journey through the museum. He recalled the sense of dread that had settled over him when they first encountered the echoes. That weight now pressed upon him again, a constant reminder of the stakes at hand.

"Over there!" George whispered urgently, pointing to a narrow gap in the stone wall ahead. "It looks like it leads toward the area where we saw the shotgun!"

Adrian nodded, leading them through the opening. The passageway was tight, forcing them to move in single file, the darkness closing in around them like a cloak. Every rustle of fabric felt amplified in the silence, and Adrian could feel the weight of their collective breath as they pressed forward.

As they approached the entrance to the room where the shotgun lay hidden, Adrian's pulse quickened. The dim light spilling from the chamber illuminated the outline of the ancient weapon, its presence a beacon of hope amid the encroaching darkness.

"Okay, we're almost there," he murmured, glancing back at his friends. Their eyes were wide with anticipation, and he could sense the nervous energy pulsing among them.

They slipped into the room, careful to keep their movements deliberate and quiet. The shotgun rested against the wall, its metal surface gleaming ominously in the low light. But something felt off. The air was thick with tension, and Adrian could feel the echoes lurking just beyond the threshold, waiting for an opportunity to pounce.

"Everyone, stay alert," he cautioned, stepping closer to the weapon. "We need to grab it and get out of here before they realize we're here."

As they approached the shotgun, Adrian's mind raced with the weight of their mission. With each passing moment, the echoes loomed larger in his thoughts. They were the embodiment of chaos, feeding off fear and doubt, and they would not easily allow their prey to escape.

With a swift motion, Adrian reached for the shotgun, his hands wrapping around the cool, worn metal. He could feel the energy coursing through it, a silent promise of power and protection. As he lifted it, the air crackled, and for a fleeting moment, the echoes seemed to stir, as if sensing their impending confrontation.

"Let's move!" Adrian urged, his voice urgent yet hushed. They needed to be quick; the echoes were always watching, always waiting.

As they turned to leave the room, the shadows shifted, the very fabric of the darkness seeming to thrum with anticipation. They hurried through the passageway, hearts racing as they fought against the oppressive silence that enveloped them.

But as they neared the exit, the laughter of Catherine echoed in their minds once more, a chilling reminder that they were not yet free.

"Stay together!" Adrian called, fear edging into his tone. They were on the cusp of facing their greatest challenge, armed with the gunkey and the shotgun, but the battle ahead promised to be unlike anything they had ever encountered. They would need every ounce of courage, every shred of their bond, to confront Catherine and the echoes that threatened to consume them.

Adrian and his friends reached the dimly lit chamber, their hearts pounding in anticipation. There, nestled against the wall, stood the ancient shotgun—a relic of power and desperation. It was an imposing sight, its barrel glinting in the muted light, echoing the weight of the mission that had led them here. Yet, to their astonishment, the enigmatic man who had previously guided them was standing there too, a silent guardian of their next step.

The man's presence was a reassuring sight amidst the chaos of their mission. He looked at them with a mix of approval and concern, his eyes reflecting a deep understanding of the challenges they faced. "You've made it," he said, his voice a low rumble that resonated in the stillness of the chamber. "But the task is not yet complete."

"What do you mean?" Adrian asked, his pulse quickening as he stepped closer to the shotgun. "We have the gunkey. We can use it to confront Catherine."

The man nodded, gesturing toward the shotgun with an air of gravitas. "Indeed, but it requires more than just the gunkey. The shotgun is a vessel of ancient power, and it must be ignited with intent. You need to channel your strength into it; your resolve must be unwavering."

With a shared glance of determination, Adrian approached the shotgun. The gunkey gleamed in his hand, a symbol of their journey and the burdens they carried. He felt the weight of his friends' eyes on him, their hopes and fears coalescing into a palpable energy. He took a deep breath, steeling himself for the task ahead.

"Let's do this together," he said, a wave of solidarity washing over them.

As they gathered around the shotgun, Adrian carefully inserted the gunkey into the designated slot, a metallic click echoing through the chamber. The moment the gunkey locked into place, a low hum reverberated through the air, pulsing with energy and life.

A brilliant light erupted from the gunkey, illuminating the chamber with a dazzling glow. The shotgun responded as if awakening from a long slumber, its heavy frame vibrating with newfound vitality. Adrian felt a rush of warmth spread through him, as if the power of the weapon was merging with their collective determination.

The man stepped back, observing with a look of satisfaction. "Focus your intentions. Think of what you are fighting for, and the shotgun will respond."

Adrian closed his eyes, allowing his thoughts to coalesce into a singular vision. He thought of Catherine, of the echoes that had tormented them, and of the lives that depended on their success. He felt the weight of responsibility settle on his shoulders, but alongside it surged a fierce resolve.

"Together," he murmured, and he felt his friends draw closer, their hands resting on the shotgun.

In unison, they channeled their thoughts and emotions into the weapon, their shared strength fueling its power. The air thickened with tension, and the shotgun thrummed in response, pulsing like a living thing, eager to be unleashed.

As the last echoes of energy faded, Adrian took hold of the shotgun. It was heavier than he had anticipated, a tangible reminder of the weight of their mission. He steadied himself, feeling the reassuring grip of the weapon in his hands. "It's time," he said, voice firm despite the trembling excitement coursing through him.

"Are you ready?" Mia asked, her eyes wide with a mixture of fear and determination.

Adrian nodded, meeting her gaze. "We've come too far to turn back now. We have to face Catherine and the echoes. They've tried to break us, but we won't let them win."

The man regarded them with a knowing smile. "Remember, the power of the shotgun is great, but it is not the only weapon you carry. Your courage, your bond, and your willingness to confront the darkness within yourselves are what will truly lead you to victory."

With those words resonating in their hearts, they exchanged a final glance before stepping toward the exit. The weight of the shotgun felt both liberating and daunting, a constant reminder of the confrontation that awaited them.

As they left the chamber, the echoes of laughter danced in the back of Adrian's mind, taunting them with the promise of chaos and despair. But now, armed with the shotgun and the gunkey, they felt a renewed sense of purpose.

They traversed the dark corridors, their steps echoing in the silence, each footfall a declaration of their intent. They would face Catherine, and they would reclaim their world from the shadows.

As they neared the exit, the man called out to them one last time, his voice echoing like a distant bell. "Remember, the echoes may try to sow doubt, but you hold the power to silence them. Stay true to yourselves and to each other."

With those words hanging in the air, Adrian and his friends emerged into the light, ready to confront the darkness that awaited them beyond the walls of the museum. They stepped into the unknown, united and undeterred, prepared to face whatever came next with unwavering resolve.

5

The G.O.A.T Disaster!

As they stepped into the open air, the weight of the journey behind them settled into their bones, an invisible tether connecting them to the ancient corridors they had just escaped. The sky was a quiet, muted grey, casting a soft light over the surroundings, lending a haunting beauty to the otherwise still and deserted world. The museum loomed behind them, an unassuming structure housing secrets and ancient energies that few would ever dare to confront.

Adrian, still holding the shotgun, took a tentative step forward, letting his eyes adjust to the outdoor expanse. The quiet was almost eerie, a thick silence hanging in the air as if the world itself was holding its breath. Every sound seemed amplified, from the distant rustle of leaves to the faint whisper of wind threading through the trees.

His friends gathered close around him, their faces reflecting a blend of exhaustion and wary anticipation. They scanned their surroundings, expecting the shadows to reveal lurking dangers at any moment, but saw nothing. There was no sign of Catherine, no echoes swirling in the distance, no footsteps echoing across the empty streets. The vast silence was both a relief and an unsettling emptiness, an unknown calm after the storm.

Mia took a slow, deep breath, breaking the spell of silence. "It feels... too quiet," she murmured, her voice barely above a whisper. Her eyes darted around, searching for any sign of movement. "It's like they're waiting, watching us."

George gave a slight nod, glancing at the shotgun in Adrian's hands. "We've got what we came for, though. Maybe that's why it feels so... different. Maybe they're just waiting for us to make the first move."

Adrian tightened his grip on the weapon, the cold metal grounding him in this surreal moment. It felt strange to be standing in the open after so long, exposed under the vastness of the sky, without the looming shadows of Catherine and her echoes. The very absence of their presence was a reminder of how relentlessly they'd been pursued up until this point.

"It's like the world has taken a breath and is holding it," Adrian said, his voice quiet but laced with conviction. "But we know they're still out there. Catherine... she won't let us go this easily. Not without a fight."

They stood there together, united in silent resolve, letting the quiet of the outdoors seep into their minds and souls, offering them a brief respite they hadn't realized they'd needed. For a moment, they could simply be. No running, no hiding, no fear driving them forward. Just the open air and the solemn stillness.

Mia tilted her head to the sky, her gaze searching the clouds as if they might hold answers. "So... this is the calm before the storm, isn't it?"

Adrian nodded, a slow, deliberate motion. "Yes," he replied, his eyes steady. "But we'll be ready when it comes."

And with that, they stood together in the open, feeling the weight of their mission settle into their bones, knowing that soon enough, they'd have to step back into the darkness. But for this one fleeting moment, they found a small piece of solace, a reminder of what they were fighting for. They had the shotgun, the gunkey, and each other.

The soft rustling of the wind seemed to breathe life into the silence, but it was the weight of their unspoken thoughts that hung thick in the air. They stood on the edge of the grounds, looking out into the distance. The world stretched out before them, and yet, the weight of their journey lay heavier than the sky above. The shotgun in Adrian's hands was both a comfort and a reminder—of how far they had come, and of how far they still had to go.

Mia was the first to break the silence, her voice laced with a mixture of weariness and reflection. "Do you ever wonder," she asked, her gaze distant as she stared out at the open land, "if it was all worth it? I mean, we've been chasing this... this weapon, this *key* to stopping everything, but what if we're just one step behind?"

Adrian's grip on the shotgun tightened instinctively, the question hanging between them like a fragile thread. "It's hard to think about *what ifs*," he said slowly, his voice steady, though there was a flicker of doubt in his eyes. "We're here now. That has to mean something."

Mia turned to him, a faint smile tugging at the corner of her lips. "I know, I know. But you've gotta admit, it feels like we're always chasing something. Like there's this endless horizon that keeps moving farther away the closer we get."

George, who had been unusually quiet, shifted and cleared his throat. "Maybe it's not about the destination," he said, looking down at the ground, almost as if the words were being pulled out of him. "Maybe it's about how we've come together in all of this." He glanced up, meeting Adrian's gaze. "We're not just fighting echoes or Catherine. We're fighting for each other. That's what makes it worth it. Right?"

Adrian let the weight of George's words settle in his mind. He had always known their bond was strong, but now, hearing it voiced so plainly, it struck him in a way that words alone couldn't capture. They had been through so much, each of them pulling the others through dark times, facing fears they hadn't thought they could overcome.

"It's more than just the mission, isn't it?" Adrian said quietly, turning the shotgun over in his hands as if it held all the answers. "It's about us. About how far we're willing to go for each other. Even if we don't know what's ahead, we know we're not alone."

There was a pause, a moment where the wind seemed to still around them, allowing the truth to settle. The echoes of their past struggles, the laughs, the fears, the near misses—they all seemed to coalesce in that one moment, painting a picture of everything that had led them here.

Mia exhaled softly, her eyes finally meeting Adrian's. "Sometimes, I think I'd be lost without you guys. We've been through things I don't think I could have handled alone."

"You don't have to," Adrian replied, his voice low and steady. "We're here for each other. Always."

George nodded in agreement, his eyes softening. "That's what matters most. Not the gun, not the echoes, not Catherine. It's this—this moment, right here. The fact that we've made it this far together."

Adrian took a deep breath, feeling the weight of the moment settle over him, a quiet acknowledgment of everything they had endured and everything they were still willing to face. "We're stronger than we know," he said, almost as if reminding himself as much as anyone else.

Mia smirked, her usual sharpness returning. "Well, let's hope we're strong enough to stop Catherine."

That simple statement broke the lingering tension, and they all shared a brief, knowing smile. It wasn't that they had all the answers. It wasn't that the storm ahead would be any less fierce. But in that moment, amidst the vast, empty land and the uncertainty of what lay ahead, there was something unwavering that none of them could deny.

They had each other.

"We'll figure it out," Adrian said, nodding resolutely. "One step at a time."

As the conversation dwindled into quiet, the weight of their unspoken resolve hung in the air like a subtle, unbreakable thread. They weren't sure what the future would hold, or if they could defeat the echoes or Catherine. But whatever it was, they would face it together. They always had, and they always would.

The wind picked up again, ruffling their clothes, and for a fleeting moment, the world seemed to stretch out before them in all its terrifying beauty. But they were no longer just the travelers, lost and running from the unknown. They were the ones who would stand their ground.

In the quiet aftermath of their conversation, Adrian's heart steadied, and he finally allowed himself to feel what he hadn't fully allowed himself to acknowledge before.

They were ready for whatever came next.

As the last whispers of their conversation faded into the thickening silence, the weight of their resolve settled within them like an anchor. There, in the vast expanse before them, all the dangers of the past seemed to have faded away. The shotgun was heavy in Adrian's hands, a tangible reminder of their purpose. For just a moment, the world seemed to hold its breath, as if time itself had paused to acknowledge the monumental journey they had endured.

But the calm did not last long.

At first, it was a faint tremor underfoot. The ground seemed to shudder, the earth whispering some ominous foretelling. Adrian felt it first, a subtle vibration that tickled the soles of his boots. Then Mia, her eyes narrowing, turned sharply to scan the horizon.

"Do you feel that?" she asked, her voice laced with an unsettling tone.

Adrian's heart began to race. "Yeah... something's not right," he muttered. The hairs on the back of his neck stood up, a feeling of dread sinking into the pit of his stomach. It wasn't just the landscape that had changed. It was as if the air itself had grown thicker, charged with a sudden, unseen force.

The tremor intensified, growing into a low, rumbling growl that seemed to rise from the very heart of the earth. At first, it was barely perceptible—an eerie hum, like the sound of an approaching storm. But it was not the wind that howled. It was something else. Something darker.

And then, just as suddenly as the tremor had begun, it grew louder. A low, grinding sound of footsteps reverberated through the ground, like the march of a thousand warriors. It wasn't the wind. It wasn't the sea. It was something else entirely.

"Get ready," Adrian said, his voice low, almost a whisper. He gripped the shotgun tighter, feeling the weight of their task shift. Whatever was coming, they were not prepared for it. Not like this.

Then, from the distant horizon, they saw it. A cloud of dust, rising in thick, oppressive clouds that swirled with an almost deliberate rhythm. It moved like an army—thousands upon thousands of shadows, indistinguishable from one another, their forms blending into one massive entity. Their approach was slow but deliberate, each step in unison, like a vast, unstoppable machine.

A wave of panic surged through Adrian, his breath quickening as the scale of what they were facing became painfully clear. The echoes—Catherine's army—were no longer a scattered, unseen threat. They were here. And they were marching towards them with purpose.

"By the gods," Mia breathed, her eyes wide with disbelief. "They're not just coming. *They're everywhere.*"

Adrian turned to look at his friends, his heart pounding. "We need to move. Now."

But before they could even think of retreating, the sound of footsteps grew deafening. The ground itself trembled beneath their feet as the legion of echoes continued their advance, their collective force rippling through the earth like a tidal wave. The very atmosphere seemed to change as they drew nearer, charged with an unnatural intensity.

Adrian's mind raced. How could they fight back against something so vast, so relentless? Their mission had always seemed so clear: get the shotgun, face Catherine, stop the echoes. But now, with the enormity of what stood before them, that clarity began to blur, replaced by the gnawing sense that they were outmatched.

"Where do we go?" George asked, his voice frantic as he scanned their surroundings. The museum was far behind them now, and the open land offered no sanctuary. The path they had walked seemed more like a dead end than ever before.

"We don't have a choice," Adrian said, his jaw set. He looked toward the oncoming army, his thoughts racing. "We stand our ground."

The march was now unmistakable. Adrian could see them clearly, the echoes taking form before his eyes. They were not people. Not really. They were fragmented shadows of humanity—bodies without souls, eyes empty and cold, faces twisted into grotesque masks of despair. The echoes were uniform in their appearance, their movements synchronized as if they were bound by a single force. Their faces were featureless, their clothes ragged and torn, their bodies impossibly gaunt, as though they had long been emptied of life.

It was as though time itself had collapsed in on them, turning them into mere vessels for something darker, something far more ancient. Their march was steady, unyielding, and the sound of their boots hitting the earth was like the drumbeat of an impending catastrophe.

Adrian's heart thundered in his chest as he watched them draw closer. For the first time since this journey began, doubt gripped him tightly. What if they weren't strong enough? What if Catherine had planned for this—this very moment—and they were walking right into her trap?

Mia, too, could feel the weight of the impending battle pressing down on them. Her hand trembled as she gripped the edge of Adrian's coat, her voice quiet but fierce. "We can't just stand here. We need to—"

But before she could finish, the air shifted. The whispers of the echoes, barely audible at first, began to grow louder. Adrian could hear them now—soft, mournful whispers, calling out from the depths of the army. It was as though the echoes were speaking to one another, a shared voice that filled the air with their collective sorrow.

The echoes had no eyes, no faces, no real identity of their own. Yet their presence was suffocating, their existence a mockery of everything that had come before them. It was a reminder of the destruction they had brought into the world—a world already on the brink of collapse.

"Get back!" Adrian shouted, snapping out of his thoughts. The echoes were now mere steps away, their hollow eyes locking onto him, their voices rising in a cacophony that shook him to his core. They were here. And they weren't stopping.

"Adrian..." Mia's voice trembled as she looked at the approaching army. "What now?"

Adrian's hand clenched around the shotgun's handle, the weight of the moment settling in his chest. The air was thick with the echoes' presence, and the sounds of their march made it feel as though the earth itself was collapsing under their collective weight.

"There's no turning back now," Adrian said, his voice quiet but resolute. "We face them."

The echoes were upon them now, their voices rising in a twisted harmony, drowning out all other sound. The whispers grew louder, filling the air with their mournful dirge, their twisted memories of a world long lost. They were the forgotten, the forsaken—the echoes of what had once been. And now, they had come to reclaim what they had lost.

With a deep breath, Adrian raised the shotgun, his fingers curling around the trigger. His heart was racing, but his mind was clear. This was it. The culmination of everything they had worked for, everything they had endured. There was no going back. They would either face the echoes or be consumed by them.

And then, in the distance, he saw her.

Catherine.

She stood at the head of the army, her figure dark and commanding. The echoes parted before her like a wave before a storm. Her eyes were cold, her face expressionless as she watched them, her lips curling into the faintest of smiles.

"Did you think you could stop it?" she called, her voice carrying across the battlefield. It was as though she spoke directly to them, her words reverberating with an unsettling authority.

Adrian tightened his grip on the shotgun, his entire body tensing. "We're not done yet," he muttered, his voice low and filled with the weight of everything they had fought for. "We'll stop you. No matter what."

Catherine's smile only deepened, and with a single motion, she raised her hand. The echoes shifted, their movements now even more synchronized, more deliberate, as though they were an extension of her will. The air crackled with tension as Adrian and his friends prepared for what they knew would be their final stand.

The echoes were here. Catherine was here.

And now, it was time to face them.

The sight of the army of echoes drew closer, and the very air seemed to shift, growing thick with an unnatural dread. As they marched, the ground beneath their feet seemed to tremble with each step, their movements impossibly synchronized—each echo moving with a silent, deadly precision that made their presence all the more horrifying.

Adrian's pulse quickened, his grip tightening on the shotgun. The echoes weren't just a threat; they were a nightmare made flesh, a horrifying reminder of everything Catherine had unleashed. They were death, the very embodiment of destruction, walking toward him with a cold, inevitable purpose.

But it wasn't just the way they moved that made Adrian's stomach twist with unease. It was what they were doing as they advanced.

Some of the echoes had fallen behind, lagging just enough for Adrian to see what they were doing. The disturbing, stomach-churning sound of gnawing filled the air—a sickening, wet sound. As the echoes slowed their march, Adrian caught sight of the grotesque scene unfolding in front of him.

A group of them had stopped to feast.

They were hunched over the carcass of a deer, the once graceful creature now nothing more than a mangled heap of flesh, its bones exposed as the echoes tore into it with unholy hunger. The flesh was raw, glistening red in the dying light of the day. They tore into the carcass with grotesque, unnatural fervor, their faces twisted with savagery as they gnawed hungrily at the raw meat, devouring it as if it were nothing more than sustenance for their insatiable hunger.

The echo's eyes—if they could be called eyes—were hollow, black voids that glinted in the dim light, empty of all emotion except for the stark, animalistic greed with which they consumed the flesh. The sound of their chewing, the wet slurping of their jaws, was deafening, drowning out everything else. Their hands—twisted, clawed things—gripped the torn remnants of the deer's body with an unsettling ferocity, ripping and pulling as though they were nothing more than wild animals themselves.

Adrian's stomach churned at the sight. He had seen brutality before, but this... this was something else entirely. The echoes didn't just destroy. They devoured, as though they were consuming the very life force of everything they touched. The rawness of it, the violence, it was more than just physical—it felt like something deeper, something primal, like the echoes were feeding on the very essence of life itself.

The others had noticed too, and their faces reflected the horror that was slowly creeping through their veins. George's breath hitched in his throat, his eyes wide in disbelief as he saw the horrors unfolding before them. Mia's hand trembled against his arm, as though the very sight of the carnage had rooted her to the spot.

"There's no turning back," Adrian murmured, his voice tight, throat dry. The whispers of the echoes grew louder, louder still as they continued their feast, oblivious to the living, to the world outside their ravenous hunger.

And as the last of the deer's body was consumed by the echoes, the grotesque display of savagery concluded with the same eerie silence that had marked their arrival. The echoes stood there for a moment, faces smeared with blood, their hollow eyes turning toward the group. And just like that, they began to move again, as though nothing had happened, as though the grotesque display of brutality was simply another step in their endless march.

The horror of what they were—the mindless, insatiable hunger that drove them—was now all too clear.

They weren't just an army.

They were something else entirely.

Adrian stood frozen, his mind reeling, the revolting image of the echo's feast burned into his memory. In that moment, he realized just how deadly they truly were. They were not just a force of destruction. They were predators, hunting, devouring everything in their path, without mercy or hesitation.

The air felt colder now, heavier, as if the very weight of the echoes' hunger had consumed the world itself.

And as Adrian stood there, watching the army move forward, he knew that this was only the beginning.

The echoes moved closer, the air charged with an oppressive weight that pressed down on Adrian and his friends, suffocating them in the overwhelming sense of inevitable doom. The once-quiet landscape had transformed into a living nightmare, filled with the sounds of gnashing teeth and the whispering murmurs of those who had long ago given up any claim to humanity.

The echoes, like a tidal wave of darkness, surged forward. Their collective march was almost hypnotic—an eerie harmony of relentless movement, their hollow eyes locked forward, their faces twisted with hunger and a thirst for destruction. The ground trembled under their feet, the earth itself seeming to quiver in anticipation of what was to come.

Adrian stood rooted to the spot, his heart hammering in his chest. The shotgun was heavy in his hands, but it felt strangely cold. His fingers curled around the handle, his knuckles white with the force of his grip. The weight of the moment pressed on him like a vice, every breath feeling like it might be his last. The shotgun was their only hope, the final piece of their puzzle. But would it be enough? Could it really end this nightmare?

"Adrian..." Mia's voice was strained, a mere whisper in the storm of their thoughts. Her eyes were wide, filled with fear and uncertainty. "What do we do? They're everywhere..."

Adrian didn't answer immediately. His gaze remained fixed on the advancing army, his mind racing as the reality of their situation sank in. The echoes were closing in, their footfalls deafening now. They were almost upon them.

He looked over to George, who was shaking his head, disbelief written across his face. “We don’t have a choice,” George said. “We fight. We have to.”

Adrian’s chest tightened, his throat dry. He could feel the fear gnawing at him, threatening to overtake him, but he fought it back. They couldn’t afford to fall apart now. They had come this far. They had faced the darkness before, and they had to face it again. But this time, it felt different. The echoes were not just a threat. They were a force of nature—unstoppable, unyielding. The weight of the gunkey in his hand seemed to pulse with an energy all its own, a reminder of the task ahead.

"Get ready," Adrian said quietly, his voice barely audible over the sounds of the approaching army. “We fight to survive.”

The echoes were close now—too close. Adrian could hear their whispers, the haunting murmurs that seemed to seep into his mind, filling it with a cold, unsettling sensation. They weren’t just mindless creatures. They were something more. Something darker.

And then it happened.

Adrian, driven by a mixture of terror and determination, raised the shotgun. His hands trembled slightly, but his resolve held steady. He aimed at the first of the echoes—its face twisted in a grotesque grimace, its hollow eyes locked onto him—and he pulled the trigger.

The blast from the shotgun was deafening, a raw, explosive sound that split the silence like a crack of thunder. For a moment, everything seemed to slow down, the world stretching as the blast of the gun rang through the air.

But when the smoke cleared, something was wrong.

The echo—the one who had been directly in front of Adrian—didn’t fall. It didn’t even flinch. It didn’t move.

Adrian’s heart skipped a beat. The echo’s gaze remained locked onto him, its empty eyes boring into his soul. Then, something even more horrifying happened. The bullet—after striking the echo—seemed to warp in midair. It curved, twisting unnaturally, as though guided by some invisible force. The bullet continued on, away from the echoes, and struck the ground far behind them. The sound of its impact was distant, almost muted.

Adrian stood frozen, his mind struggling to process what he had just seen. His grip on the shotgun tightened, his breath coming in short, shallow bursts. What was happening?

He fired again, aiming at another echo, this one farther away. This time, the bullet barely left the barrel before it veered off course, changing its trajectory with terrifying precision. It struck the mountainside, the sharp, echoing impact reverberating through the air as a cloud of dust erupted from the cliffside.

"What the hell?" George muttered, his voice shaking with disbelief. "It's like the bullets... they're being pulled off course."

Adrian's pulse raced, panic beginning to claw at him. He fired again, this time at a group of echoes standing in a cluster. The shotgun's roar echoed through the valley, but once again, the bullets didn't hit their intended target. Instead, they veered sharply to the side, striking the rocks of the island with violent force.

"Why isn't it working?" Mia cried, her voice trembling as she watched the scene unfold. "This doesn't make sense."

Adrian's mind raced, the fear in his chest threatening to overtake him. This wasn't just a normal fight. The echoes weren't merely flesh and bone—they were something more. Something far more insidious. And the shotgun, the one weapon that they had believed would end it all, was useless against them.

The echoes didn't even flinch. They kept marching forward, their dead eyes locked onto Adrian and his friends. Their presence was like a suffocating fog, slowly closing in, inch by inch, until there would be nowhere left to run.

And then, in the midst of the chaos, Adrian realized something even more terrifying.

The echoes were not just immune to the shotgun's power—they were *manipulating* it. They weren't just mindless beings. They were controlling the very fabric of reality around them, bending the laws of nature to their will.

Adrian felt the weight of that realization settle on his shoulders like a ton of bricks. The echoes were not bound by the rules of physics or logic. They were a force beyond understanding, something born from the cracks between worlds, from the places where light and shadow blurred together. They weren't merely enemies to be defeated. They were the very embodiment of chaos, of destruction, of something ancient and unknowable.

The air grew thick with the whispers again, their voices rising, merging into a collective hum that felt like it was coming from all directions. The ground beneath Adrian's feet trembled, and he felt the unmistakable shift of power. He raised the shotgun again, but this time, the weapon felt heavier, as if it were filled with lead.

The echoes kept coming, relentless, uncaring. They were like a tide that could not be stopped, each step bringing them closer to their goal.

And then, Adrian heard it.

A voice—low, cold, and haunting.

"You can't stop us."

It was Catherine.

Adrian's blood ran cold as he turned toward the source of the voice. Catherine was standing there, her eyes glowing with an eerie light. She wasn't standing with the echoes, but she was watching them. Watching them with the same cold, calculating expression that had haunted his every step.

"You think a weapon will stop us?" Catherine's voice was smooth, filled with an unsettling certainty. "You think you can stop the inevitable? We are beyond the reach of your feeble tools."

Adrian's breath caught in his throat, his mind scrambling for a way out. They had come so far. They had fought so hard. But now, with the echoes under Catherine's control, the very laws of nature were working against them.

"You were never meant to win," Catherine continued, her smile widening. "The echoes are not your enemy, Adrian. They are your fate."

Adrian's hands trembled as he lowered the shotgun. The weight of his failure pressed down on him like a vice. There was no way out. The echoes were too powerful. Catherine had won.

And as the army of echoes closed in, their footfalls drowning out everything else, Adrian realized that the battle had already been lost.

The echoes were coming. And there was nothing left to stop them.

Adrian's mind raced, his thoughts a tangled mess as the echoes inched closer. The weight of the moment pressed down on him like a crushing tide, suffocating every breath, every thought. His hands gripped the shotgun with an intensity that left his knuckles white, his fingers trembling as he fought to steady the weapon. But the fear—raw, primal, and unrelenting—choked every ounce of logic and clarity from his mind.

The echoes moved in perfect unison, their hollow eyes fixed ahead, the eerie whispers of their voices rising into a cacophony of haunting murmurs. They weren't like any enemy Adrian had ever faced before. They weren't just beings, they were a presence—an unnatural, overwhelming force that bent reality itself to their will. Each step they took seemed to distort the very fabric of the world around them, twisting the air and the ground beneath their feet.

Adrian tried to focus, tried to block out the rising panic in his chest. *We can still do this*, he thought, but the words rang hollow in his mind. The echoes were closing in, their hungry, hollow eyes locked onto him and his friends. They were relentless. *There has to be a way*. But as he turned the shotgun over in his hands, the same thought kept nagging at him: *What if there isn't?*

His breath hitched as he looked at the barrel of the weapon, the cold metal now feeling like a weight of pure desperation. The gunkey had powered it, it had ignited it, but it had failed. His first shot had missed its target entirely, the bullets veering off as though they were being manipulated by an invisible force. The shotgun hadn't just failed; it had been powerless. And now, the air around them seemed to hum with an unnatural energy, as if the world itself was pulling away from them, distancing them from any hope of victory.

Adrian's grip on the shotgun tightened as his heart pounded in his chest. *I can't let them die. I can't let them—*

He didn't finish the thought. His finger was already on the trigger.

In a desperate attempt, driven by a surge of adrenaline, Adrian swung the shotgun around and fired again.

The blast echoed across the valley, its force rattling the air around them. The recoil hit him hard, but he barely felt it. His eyes were locked on the advancing echoes, his heart hammering in his chest. He watched as the blast erupted from the barrel of the shotgun, the shockwave tearing through the air, sending a deafening roar that should have shattered the calm. It was supposed to work. It *had* to work. The echoes had to fall.

But once again, the same horrifying thing happened.

The bullets didn't hit their mark. The air seemed to twist around them, pulling the shots away from their intended target, sending them careening off into the distance. Adrian's breath caught in his throat as the sound of the impact echoed through the valley, but the echoes did not waver. They didn't even flinch. They kept moving forward, their march unwavering and relentless.

Adrian stood there, the weight of failure sinking into him like a stone. His hands shook as he lowered the shotgun. This couldn't be happening. *It has to work*, he thought desperately. *This has to work.*

"Adrian..." Mia's voice was barely a whisper, hoarse and filled with fear. She took a step toward him, her eyes wide and full of panic. "What's happening? Why isn't it working?"

Adrian didn't answer. He couldn't. His mind was too clouded, his thoughts too scattered. There was no answer to give. The echoes had rendered the shotgun useless, and with them advancing, there was nothing left to fight with.

He looked over at George, whose face had turned pale, his body tense with fear. George took a step toward the edge of the cliff, as though trying to put some distance between himself and the advancing army. "There's no way we're getting out of this," he muttered, more to himself than to anyone else. "There's no way..."

Mia turned to him, her voice shaking. "We can't just give up!"

But George shook his head. "What choice do we have? They're not human. They're not like anything we've ever seen. The gunkey didn't work. Nothing's working. We're as good as dead."

Adrian's heart sank. He knew George was right. Every instinct in him screamed to fight—to find some way, anyway, to stop the echoes. But nothing was working. He could feel the ground beneath him quaking as the echoes continued their inexorable march forward, and it was becoming painfully clear that there was no force, no weapon, no power they had that could stand against them.

And then, as though to confirm the dread that had been mounting in his chest, a voice cut through the air. It was cold, smooth, and utterly devoid of empathy.

"You're wasting your time."

Adrian turned toward the voice, and there she was—Catherine, standing among the echoes. Her eyes glowed faintly, an otherworldly light dancing in them. There was something almost serene about her, as if she were watching the unfolding destruction from a distance, detached from the horror she had set in motion. But it wasn't just her appearance that filled Adrian with dread. It was her words.

"You've already lost," Catherine continued, her voice carrying across the distance. "You think a weapon will stop the inevitable? You think the shotgun—your pathetic, feeble weapon—can end what has already begun?" She smiled, a smile that was both pitying and chilling. "You were never meant to win."

Adrian's blood ran cold as her words sank in. The echoes. They were beyond them. Beyond everything they had thought they could do. They were a force of nature, unstoppable and unyielding, and they had no place in this world of flesh and bone. They were the dark tide that consumed everything in its path, and now Adrian and his friends were just part of that tide—helpless, hopeless.

"Catherine..." Adrian's voice was thick with emotion, his words coming out in a rasp. "Why are you doing this? Why?"

Catherine's gaze softened for a moment, as if considering his question, but then she shrugged as if the answer was obvious. "Why?" she repeated, her voice dripping with disdain. "Because I can. Because I *am* the echoes. I am the one who gives them purpose. I have the power to command them." Her smile grew wider, more dangerous. "And you? You're nothing more than an obstacle. An annoyance in the grand scheme of things."

Adrian's pulse quickened as she stepped forward, the echoes parting to let her through. Her gaze locked onto him, cold and unfeeling. "You think you can stop me? You think you can stop this? You're too late. The world is mine now, and there is nothing you can do about it."

Her words struck like a blow to Adrian's chest, but it wasn't just her words that crushed him. It was the realization that, deep down, he knew she was right. The echoes were not just some army to be destroyed. They were a force that had existed long before any of them had come into being, a force that would outlast them all.

And now they were helpless in the face of it.

Adrian lowered the shotgun, his fingers numb as they rested on the barrel. The world seemed to fade away around him, leaving only the sound of the echoes' march and the quiet, ominous certainty that they were beyond saving. No matter how hard they fought, no matter what they did, the echoes would keep coming. They would never stop.

And Adrian knew, deep in his bones, that this was it.

They had failed. The echoes had won.

Adrian's shoulders slumped, the weight of failure bearing down on him with an intensity that made it feel like the very air around him had thickened to the point of suffocation. He could feel the eyes of his friends on him, their faces etched with fear, desperation, and disbelief. They had come so far, fought so hard, only to be met with a force they could not comprehend—let alone defeat. The echoes had proven to be beyond their wildest nightmares, and Catherine, the leader of this horrific tide, had revealed the cold truth. There was no way out. No weapon, no plan, no hope left.

His fingers tightened around the shotgun, the gunkey's weight heavy in his hands, but even as he gripped it with a sense of finality, it felt like a relic—a symbol of how small and powerless they were against what had come to pass.

Adrian closed his eyes, the realization settling in like a slow, painful ache. It was over. He had known, deep down, that it was only a matter of time before they reached this point—the point where resistance ceased to have meaning, where defiance was nothing more than a futile cry into the void. The echoes had already won.

With a deep, shaky breath, he let the shotgun fall to the ground. The sound of it hitting the earth seemed deafening, echoing across the silent, desolate expanse. The group had tried everything they could think of, and yet now, standing on the precipice of annihilation, there was no fight left in them.

Adrian turned to face Catherine, his heart pounding in his chest, his voice barely a whisper as he spoke the words that had become inevitable.

"We surrender," he said.

The words hung in the air like a death sentence, each syllable heavier than the last. It felt as though the earth itself had stopped turning, as if the moment were frozen in time, suspended in a space between life and death, between hope and despair. It wasn't just the surrender of his team, of their bodies, but the surrender of everything they had believed in—their belief in humanity's ability to fight back, to overcome the odds. The world they had known was gone. What remained now was something darker, something unrecognizable. The echoes had swept through it like a storm, leaving only ruin in their wake.

Catherine watched him, her gaze cold and distant, as though she had been expecting this moment all along. She had no need for words to express her victory. Her silence, her mere presence, was enough to confirm that the battle was over. The echoes didn't need to fight anymore. They had already won.

Adrian's thoughts flashed to the lives they had tried so desperately to save—his friends, the innocents they had encountered along the way, and those far beyond the reaches of their journey. In his mind's eye, he saw the devastation spreading across the globe—cities falling, civilizations crumbling under the weight of the echoes' advance.

And then, as if to punctuate the surrender with an undeniable finality, the earth trembled beneath their feet.

The ground split open with a deafening roar, the sound of the earth itself splitting in two, as if the very planet were reacting to the approaching apocalypse. Adrian's heart lurched in his chest as he watched, helpless, as the oceans far in the distance began to churn violently. Waves crashed against each other, rising to impossible heights, while strange, ominous shapes formed beneath the water, glowing with a fiery red hue. The water began to boil, sending plumes of steam into the sky. *What was happening? What is this?*

The world was tearing itself apart.

Adrian's eyes widened in horror as the oceans—the vast, seemingly eternal oceans—burst into flames. It was as if the sea itself had become an inferno, the water turning to fire, scorching the very skies above. The once calm and life-giving waters, the waters that had carried them through their journey, were now transformed into a furious blaze that consumed everything in its path. The heat radiated across the landscape, even from a distance, and the scent of smoke filled the air, mixing with the acrid stench of burning saltwater.

In the distance, he heard a sound, faint at first, but growing louder with each passing second. The sound of a scream. Of hundreds—no, thousands—of voices, all crying out in agony. His mind struggled to make sense of it, but the desperation in those voices was unmistakable. The desperate, panicked cries of innocent people, far away from where they stood, caught in the same storm of destruction that was now consuming the earth.

The cries were haunting. A cacophony of despair that seemed to come from every corner of the world—people running, fleeing, screaming, helpless in the face of a force they could not understand. *It's too late*, Adrian realized, his heart sinking into the depths of his stomach. *We failed. We couldn't stop it.*

And yet, it wasn't just the destruction that gripped him—it was the profound sense of futility, of helplessness. Adrian and his friends had come this far. They had crossed seas, deciphered ancient codes, faced unthinkable challenges—and they had lost. The very earth itself seemed to weep for them as the screams grew louder, rising into a fever pitch.

Far off in the distance, the light of a thousand cities flickered and died. Fires broke out, explosions rippling through the horizon, casting the land in a hellish orange glow. What had once been a bustling, vibrant world was now a landscape of destruction. And in that devastation, Adrian saw a reflection of their own hopelessness.

They had done everything they could. And now, the world they had fought for was crumbling, one piece at a time.

He heard the voice of Catherine again, distant yet close, echoing in the emptiness of their shattered world.

"Do you hear them?" she asked, her tone quiet and devoid of emotion. "The screams. The desperation. The destruction. It's only the beginning. You thought you could fight it. You thought you could save them. But this is the reality now. This is the world you've made."

Adrian looked at her, the full weight of her words sinking into him like a crushing blow. There was no denying it. This was their fault. They had set this course in motion. The echoes were just the beginning, and now, they would watch the world burn.

But as he stood there, feeling the tears burn in his eyes, his heart shattered by the sheer magnitude of their failure, there was one final, piercing thought that cut through the numbness that had taken hold of him.

He had surrendered. But that didn't mean he had to give up.

Even as the ocean burned and the cries of the innocent rang out across the land, Adrian stood, holding onto the remnants of his shattered hope. He didn't know how it would end, or even if there was any chance for redemption left. But one thing was certain: He would never stop fighting.

Even in the face of this unimaginable destruction, even as the world tore itself apart around him, Adrian vowed that he would never stop fighting.

But for now, all he could do was watch, helpless, as the earth collapsed into chaos. The echoes had won. And the world would never be the same.

As the smoke from the burning oceans curled upward, the world around them slowly dissolved into an eerie silence. Catherine, standing tall amidst the devastation, observed the chaos with a detached calmness, her gaze unwavering as if the destruction were just another victory for her—just another page in a story she had already written.

Her voice, when it came, cut through the stillness like a blade.

"You see," she began, her tone sharp, dismissive, and full of an arrogance that burned just as fiercely as the fires consuming the sea. "All of this... this was always inevitable. You never stood a chance. You think you could stop the inevitable? You think you could stand against what was always meant to be?" She laughed, a harsh, bitter sound, as if mocking not just Adrian and his team, but the very idea of resistance.

"You were always just pawns," she continued, her eyes cold and unblinking, sweeping over Adrian's defeated form. "You thought you were heroes. You thought you could save the world, save *yourselves*. But it was never about saving anything. It was about power. It was always about *control*."

Adrian felt a cold knot tighten in his chest as Catherine's words hit him like a storm, her contempt for everything they had struggled for wrapping around him like an iron vice.

"You had no idea what you were dealing with. None of you did. The echoes were never the enemy. They were merely tools. You were never meant to win. You were just meant to play your part." She sneered. "And now, here you are. Broken. Pathetic. Watching as the world you once knew is devoured by the very flames you tried to extinguish."

She stepped forward, her steps deliberate, each one echoing ominously across the devastated landscape. "You thought you had the power, didn't you? You thought you could stand against me, against everything I've built. But you never understood that you were always... *insignificant*." Her voice dropped to a whisper, as if the finality of it all needed no further emphasis. "You're just a part of the past, now. And this world... this new world... will have no place for you."

She turned away, walking toward the horizon, her silhouette stark against the burning sky. Her parting words lingered in the air, heavy with scorn, as if she had already moved beyond their existence.

"This is my world now. And you're nothing more than a forgotten memory."

With those final words, she disappeared into the chaos she had wrought, leaving Adrian and his friends to stand in the smoldering ruins of everything they had tried to protect.

And in that moment, Adrian knew. It was over. She had won. But something deep within him, some small, unyielding part, refused to give up. Even if it was just a spark—flickering, fading—it was all that was left.

And somewhere, in the depths of that destruction, he found a sliver of hope. No matter what Catherine had done, no matter what had been lost, he would not be forgotten.

As the words of Catherine echoed in his mind, relentless and cruel, Adrian stood frozen in the aftermath of it all, the heat from the burning oceans pressing against him like an invisible weight. He could feel the weight of the world pressing down on his chest, suffocating him, as if all the life had drained from the very air he breathed. The screams in the distance, the chaos, the fire—everything that had led to this moment crashed over him like a tidal wave.

His hands trembled, still holding the shotgun, but now it felt like an extension of his own failure. He wanted to shout, to scream, to do something—anything—but the world felt... still. Static. There was no fight left, no hope.

And then, in the midst of the quiet that followed Catherine's departure, something shifted.

Adrian felt a sudden tug in his chest, a spark that cut through the fog of his despair. A whisper of something, something forgotten, something buried deep within him. *The old man.*

Without thinking, his eyes shot to the horizon, scanning the scene, the destruction, the echoes moving like shadows in the distance. And there, standing just on the outskirts of the chaos, was the figure of the old man.

The same old man who had guided them once, who had told them of the gunkey, who had warned them, but then had vanished into thin air. The old man who had seemed so out of place—his presence so fleeting, yet so profound. Adrian's heart skipped a beat as he locked eyes with him.

The old man stood there, unmoving, his weathered face calm and collected, as though nothing had changed. His eyes, wise and knowing, held a quiet understanding that somehow pierced through the terror around them. He stood alone, untouched by the flames or the echoes, while chaos raged around him, unscathed, as though the violence of the world did not touch him. The echoes, too, seemed oblivious to his presence, as if he were invisible, like a ghost who had slipped through the fabric of this collapsing world.

Adrian's breath caught in his throat as the man turned his head, as if sensing Adrian's gaze, and nodded once, ever so slightly, in acknowledgment.

Without a word, the old man raised his hand, and for a fleeting moment, time seemed to slow. The echoes, marching forward in their deadly procession, were oblivious to him, continuing their march toward destruction, unaware of the figure standing just beyond their reach. It was as if the old man were shielded by some force, some invisible barrier that kept the chaos at bay.

Adrian's pulse quickened, his heart pounding in his chest. This was not a trick of the mind. The man was real. He was standing there, somehow unaffected by the horror that surrounded them. A thought tugged at the back of Adrian's mind—had the old man always known? Had he been part of this from the very beginning, a silent witness, a protector, a player in a game that had already been set into motion?

The old man's figure flickered for just a moment, as though time itself could not contain him, before he became solid once again, his presence firm and unyielding against the sea of destruction.

Adrian couldn't tear his eyes away from him. The world around him had been reduced to flames, to an apocalyptic vision of burning skies and shattered hopes, but in the old man, there was something unbreakable, something that did not bend or yield to the storm that raged. It was as though he had stood against the world itself and had come out the other side untouched, and Adrian felt a strange mix of awe and confusion grip him.

Without warning, the old man began to walk, his pace slow but purposeful, as if he knew where he was going, as if he had always known. Adrian's mind raced. What did this mean? Was this his last chance? Was there still something left to be done?

"Wait!" Adrian called out, his voice raw, desperate. But it was as if the man had heard the words before they were even spoken. He did not stop. He did not turn around. Instead, he continued to move, his steps steady, unwavering, as if the world around him could crumble into dust and he would not be swayed.

Adrian's mind raced to make sense of what he was seeing. What was this man doing? Why was he here, untouched by the very destruction that had consumed everything they had known? And why couldn't the echoes see him?

As if sensing Adrian's thoughts, the old man's head turned slightly, his eyes meeting Adrian's once more. There was a flicker of recognition there—an understanding. And then, in a voice that was barely a whisper, yet carried with it the weight of years and truths unsaid, the old man spoke.

"You've done what you could, boy," he said, his words a gravelly murmur, as though every syllable was a weight lifted from some ancient burden. "But this world was never yours to save. Not all battles are won."

Adrian felt the words resonate deep within him, like the toll of a distant bell that rang far beyond the reaches of his understanding. The old man's gaze softened, just slightly, before his lips curled into a faint smile, one that was both knowing and sad.

"You are not alone," the old man continued, his voice fading as if carried by the wind. "But it is time for you to find your own path."

Adrian's breath caught in his throat. "What do you mean?" he asked, stepping forward, unable to tear himself away from the man who seemed to hold all the answers—answers he had been chasing for so long, only to now find them slipping away like sand through his fingers.

The old man's gaze never left him, but his form began to shimmer, to fade, as if his time in this world had come to an end. His figure was dissolving into the very air, becoming one with the winds, the fire, the chaos.

And with that, he was gone. Just as suddenly as he had appeared, the old man vanished, leaving only a lingering sense of wisdom, a presence that still seemed to hover in the space where he had stood.

Adrian stood there, his heart pounding in his chest, a thousand questions swirling in his mind. What had he just witnessed? Had the old man been a guardian? A messenger? Or was he something even greater—someone who had watched the world spiral into ruin from the very beginning, guiding those who had come before, and now those who would follow?

The echoes continued their march, oblivious to the moment of silence that had passed between Adrian and the old man. But for Adrian, the world had shifted. There was no turning back now. He didn't know what the future held, or if there was even a future left to fight for.

But as he stood alone amidst the devastation, there was a small flame in his heart—a flame that had not yet been extinguished.

The old man had gone. But perhaps, just perhaps, there was still something left to be done.

As Adrian stood in the ruins of what once felt like his world, a sense of dread wrapped itself around him, thick and unshakable. The old man was gone, leaving behind only cryptic words and that lingering, hollow feeling of unfinished purpose. The echoes moved in the distance, the oceans burned, and the sky looked like the bruised aftermath of some god's wrath.

He stared out into the destruction, the fires that seemed to eat away at the very soul of the world, and a dark thought took root in his mind, creeping into the quiet corners of his psyche like a poisonous vine: *What would happen if he died?*

Adrian felt a shiver roll down his spine. He imagined the void, the emptiness that would come if he simply... stopped. The weight of that silence—absolute, eternal—pressed on him like an invisible hand squeezing his chest. A pit of dread opened up inside him as he pictured the world without his existence. Would it even matter? Would the darkness and violence simply continue, spiraling without end?

He closed his eyes, trying to imagine his own absence. But instead of stillness, instead of peace, he was haunted by visions that rose from the depths of his mind, each one more horrifying than the last.

In his mind's eye, he saw the world continuing without him. But it wasn't the world he knew. It was a broken, ravaged landscape—echoes roamed free, darkening every corner, devouring life itself. Cities lay in ruins, hollow shells that echoed with the cries of those left behind. Shadows crept over the remnants of human civilization, and the earth itself seemed to shudder under the weight of relentless decay. There were no children's voices, no laughter, no life—only the hollow cries of the echoes, moving like specters through empty streets.

He could see it so clearly. The people he had fought to protect, the friends he had risked everything for—they would fall, one by one, until there was no one left to remember that there had ever been a fight, or a cause, or hope. The echoes would fill the void, claiming every inch of space, every remaining soul, until nothing remained but endless shadows, feeding on the last scraps of memory.

He imagined his friends—Emma, Mia, George—all of them lost to the darkness, their faces fading, their spirits snuffed out. He could see them struggling, caught in a whirlwind of despair, surrounded by these monstrous beings who consumed life itself, leaving only a blackened shell of existence. And he would be gone, unable to lift a hand to help, unable to stop the horror that would unfold.

Adrian's mind spiraled deeper into the nightmare, picturing the world through Catherine's twisted vision. *She would reign*, he thought bitterly, *and no one would be left to defy her*. With him gone, the echoes would flood the lands, and Catherine would stand as the ruler of a world that was nothing but shadows and death. Her laughter, cruel and mocking, would be the only sound that pierced the silence of the graveyard that the earth had become.

Adrian gritted his teeth, his fists clenched so tightly that his knuckles turned white. The horror of it all filled him, his heart beating with a desperate urgency. *If he failed, if he died*, it would be as if he had never existed, as if every struggle, every sacrifice, had been meaningless. The world would dissolve into an endless night, a void from which there was no escape.

His breathing quickened, each breath ragged as the weight of that bleak reality bore down on him. His mind screamed against the thought, against the idea of surrendering to this fate. He felt as though he were teetering on the edge of a cliff, staring down into the endless abyss, his very existence hanging by a thread.

And yet, in that dark moment, something flickered within him. A faint, stubborn flame, a quiet defiance that refused to be snuffed out. Adrian knew, deep down, that he could not let this vision come to pass. He could not allow this world—*his* world—to end like this.

The thought of surrender, of simply giving in, was unthinkable. Because even if he were to die, he would not leave behind a legacy of darkness. He would fight to the very end, to his last breath, until he had given everything he had to stop this nightmare from becoming reality.

Adrian opened his eyes, his gaze hardening, his resolve settling within him like steel. The future might be dark, the odds might be insurmountable, but he was not done yet. The echoes could roar, the oceans could burn, and Catherine could laugh in the face of his defiance—but he would not go quietly. He would not let this world fall without a fight.

He was Adrian. And if the world was to end, he would ensure it would end with him standing, unbroken, until the last breath escaped his lungs.

The realization that his world could crumble without him had sparked a fire in Adrian's heart. All the despair, all the fear—it transformed in an instant, solidifying into a fierce resolve. This was his fight, his world, and he was not going to stand by and watch it fade into darkness. With a newfound strength, he pushed himself up, shaking off the weight of uncertainty, his heart pounding with a furious rhythm. Every fiber in his being called out to him: he couldn't back down. Not now.

With a roar of determination, he sprinted toward Catherine, her figure framed against the smoldering ruins of the horizon. She stood tall and indifferent, her expression cold as if she knew she held all the power. That mocking look on her face fueled his rage further, and he charged forward, ignoring the aches in his body, ignoring the odds stacked against him. In his mind, he was unstoppable. He was ready to confront her, to put an end to her twisted control, to save what remained of his world.

But just as he closed the distance, something struck him. Hard.

The force knocked the wind from his lungs, sending him sprawling back, his body hitting the ground with a harsh thud. His mind whirled, trying to process what had happened. He coughed, the taste of dirt and blood in his mouth as he struggled to regain his senses. When he looked up, disoriented and breathing heavily, his heart nearly stopped.

There, standing between him and Catherine, was Wren.

The sight hit Adrian harder than any physical blow could have. Wren—his friend, the one they'd lost, the one they'd mourned. The sight of him, alive and standing, filled Adrian with a strange mix of shock and hope. But the relief was fleeting, fading into a chilling realization as he took in Wren's expression.

His face was blank, his eyes distant, cold. The warmth, the loyalty Adrian remembered was gone, replaced by a hollow emptiness that made Adrian's stomach twist. This was not the friend he'd known. This was... something else. His heart clenched as he forced himself to accept the brutal truth: Wren was an echo. Wren was on *her* side.

"Wren..." Adrian's voice cracked, thick with disbelief and grief. He could hardly get the words out, his voice a mere whisper. "What... what happened to you?"

But Wren only looked at him, that vacant expression never shifting. He moved closer, his presence almost ghostly, and for a moment, Adrian saw a glint of something familiar in his eyes—a shadow of the friend he'd known. But it was gone as quickly as it had appeared, swallowed up by the dark emptiness that now filled him.

"What happened?" Adrian asked again, his voice shaking with a blend of anger and despair. "You... you're one of them now? You're with her?"

Wren tilted his head slightly, as though Adrian's words meant nothing. His eyes flicked briefly toward Catherine, who watched the exchange with a faint smile, her gaze as sharp as a knife. She seemed amused by Adrian's torment, relishing in his confusion, his pain.

Adrian's chest tightened. "Wren, it's me," he pleaded, desperation seeping into his tone. "It's Adrian. We've fought together, bled together! Remember that! You don't have to do this."

But Wren's face remained cold, unmoved by Adrian's words. He was like a shadow of the friend Adrian had once known, an empty vessel, a puppet under Catherine's command. The realization was like a knife twisting in Adrian's heart. His friend—the one who had been his brother in arms, his confidant—was lost to him. And there was nothing he could do.

"Don't waste your breath, Adrian," Catherine's voice cut through the air, smooth and venomous. She stepped forward, her gaze fixed on Adrian with a cruel glint. "He's mine now. Whatever he was to you, whatever memories you shared—it's all meaningless now. He serves a higher purpose."

Adrian's hands clenched into fists, his heart pounding with both fury and grief. He wanted to scream, to demand an explanation, to make her understand the cruelty of what she had done. But

Catherine only smiled, a twisted satisfaction in her eyes as she watched him struggle with the truth.

"Wren, listen to me," Adrian said, his voice rough with desperation. "You're stronger than this. You don't belong to her. You don't have to do this!"

But Wren remained unmoved. And then, with a deliberate, mechanical movement, he raised his hand, his fingers curling as he took a step closer to Adrian. It was clear—he wasn't just standing in Adrian's way. He was ready to attack.

Adrian's heart shattered as he watched Wren, his friend, his brother in all but blood, approach him as an enemy. Memories of their shared battles, their laughter, their struggles flashed through Adrian's mind in an agonizing rush. But now those memories felt like they belonged to someone else, a ghost of a life that had been stolen from him. The Wren he had known was gone, lost to the darkness, twisted into a shadow of his former self.

With a heavy heart, Adrian braced himself, fighting back tears as he prepared to face the one person he had never thought he'd have to fight.

As Adrian stood there, paralyzed by the weight of what was unfolding before him, a memory surged to the forefront of his mind. The words of the old man, cryptic and unsettling, echoed in his head, louder and clearer than ever before.

"To save the world, you must first destroy it."

The old man's voice had been filled with a strange sort of finality when he said it, like he knew the sacrifice that would come with those words. Adrian hadn't fully understood at the time, hadn't grasped the depth of what it meant. But now, staring at the ruined world around him, with Catherine standing like a cold, omnipotent force and Wren—his friend—lost to the echoes, everything clicked into place. The answer was there, hiding in plain sight, waiting for him to realize it.

"To destroy the world, you must first shoot to the sky."

The shotgun. The gunkey. Everything had led him to this moment, this singular point in time where the only choice left was one that would tear apart everything they had fought for, everything they had dreamed of.

Adrian's breath caught in his throat as his gaze flicked upward to the sky. The clouds above were heavy with dark storm, swirling in an unnatural dance. The earth below was trembling as if it knew the truth—that nothing could be saved unless it was undone. It was the final sacrifice, the destruction of everything in order to rebuild it from the ashes. The weight of it pressed on him, a suffocating reality that gnawed at his heart.

He glanced down at the shotgun in his hands. It was heavy, both physically and symbolically, its ancient design gleaming with an ominous energy. It had been the key to everything—the only weapon that could defeat Catherine and the echoes. But what if it wasn't just a weapon for destruction? What if it was the instrument of rebirth? The thought was both terrifying and awe-inspiring.

"To save the world, you must destroy it."

The words repeated in his mind like a mantra, a guiding principle, yet their true meaning remained elusive. What did it mean to destroy the world? What would he have to sacrifice to make that destruction worthwhile?

His gaze flicked back to Catherine, her eyes glittering with malevolent amusement, as if she already knew what was coming. She had already made her choice, had already cast her lot with the echoes. Adrian had never felt more isolated in his life. His friends—his team—had been torn apart by this nightmare. But now, in this single, breathless moment, he knew what had to be done.

Adrian's heart pounded in his chest, the weight of the decision weighing on him like a mountain. He had spent so long fighting, so long trying to protect the world, trying to save his friends, but now the only choice left was to tear it all down. To obliterate everything to save what was left.

Slowly, as if the air itself were thick with tension, Adrian raised the shotgun, the heavy metal cool in his hands, and pointed it toward the sky. For a moment, everything seemed to freeze—the winds ceased, the echoes halted, the world itself held its breath. He could feel the gravity of the moment, the immense pressure of the choice he was about to make. Would this truly save them? Or would it doom them all?

"Adrian..." Wren's voice, hollow and distant, called to him, but it barely reached his ears. The figure of his friend seemed so far removed now, as if they were worlds apart. His eyes locked on Catherine, her smug expression turning into one of calculated malice. She knew, too. She understood exactly what was happening.

"You're too late," she said, her voice ringing with an icy certainty. "There is no saving what's already been lost."

Her words struck like a blade, but Adrian didn't falter. He could feel the power in the shotgun, the strange energy that seemed to course through his very veins as he held it. His eyes narrowed, the weight of the world on his shoulders. This was it. This was the moment that would change everything.

Without a second thought, without hesitation, Adrian pulled the trigger.

The sound of the shot echoed through the air, deafening in its intensity. For a moment, time seemed to slow as the bullet tore through the sky, a brilliant streak of light that pierced the clouds. The earth itself trembled, as if the very foundation of reality was being shaken. Adrian's heart raced in his chest, the force of the blast reverberating through his entire body. The sky seemed to break apart, the darkness splitting open like a wound in the fabric of existence.

The world was being torn asunder.

Above them, the sky lit up, the clouds parting like a curtain of night, revealing a vast expanse of light. It wasn't the sun—it was something else. A blinding energy, something ancient and primal, surged through the heavens, cascading down in a shower of sparks and light. The earth trembled again, but this time it was different. This wasn't the shake of destruction—it was the tremor of something new, something unknown.

Adrian felt it in his bones. The change. The beginning of something unimaginable. The world was breaking, shattering into pieces, but in that destruction, there was rebirth. The echoes froze in place, their eerie stillness unnerving. Even Catherine, that unshakable queen of shadows, seemed to falter, her expression twisting with confusion and something else—something Adrian couldn't place.

And in that instant, as the shotgun's blast echoed through the sky, Adrian realized the true meaning of the old man's words.

To save the world, you had to destroy it first. But in that destruction lay the seed of something new, something better. The death of the old world was necessary for the birth of a new one—one where the echoes would no longer reign, where the darkness could finally be washed away.

Adrian lowered the shotgun, his body trembling with the weight of the decision. He had done it. He had destroyed the world, but he had done so for a reason. And as the light continued to pour from the sky, he felt a strange, bittersweet sense of hope rising within him.

This wasn't the end. It was the beginning.

Catherine, the echoes, the devastation—they were all but shadows now. And Adrian, standing amidst the wreckage, knew that he had done what was necessary.

Now the world would be reborn.

The world, once vibrant and filled with life, had become a fragile shell—a delicate creation on the verge of its own unraveling. Time seemed to stretch, a silent countdown to an inevitable catastrophe that no one could escape. Adrian stood there, his heart pounding in his chest, his body trembling with a mixture of fear and anticipation. He had made the choice, the decision that could either save them all or doom them forever. He had pulled the trigger. But now, as he stared at the sky—now transformed by his action—he realized that even his greatest sacrifice might not be enough.

The clouds above them churned with unnatural force, a swirling mass of darkness that pressed down on the earth like a thousand crushing hands. The wind howled with the ferocity of a dying beast, ripping through the trees, the ground beneath them trembling as if the very core of the planet was waking from a long slumber. The sky was no longer a canvas of blue or gray—it was a nightmare, blackened and twisted, as if the heavens themselves were rebelling against the world below.

Adrian felt it in his bones—the impending doom that was rushing toward them, a wave that would obliterate everything. In that instant, he understood the true meaning of the old man's words. The world, as it was, had to be destroyed. There could be no rebirth, no second chance, without the utter annihilation of everything they had known.

Wren, standing just a few feet away, was as still as a statue. His expression was unreadable, his face marked by the same sense of helplessness that Adrian felt. He knew, too. They all knew. The echoes had been unstoppable. Catherine had been an immovable force. And now, the very fabric of existence was collapsing around them.

The ground beneath their feet cracked, a deep rumble shaking the air, and the sky itself seemed to respond, the swirling clouds turning even darker, as if to swallow the last remnants of light. And then, just as Adrian thought he might lose his grip on reality, the first tremor struck.

It wasn't a small shake. No. It was as though the earth itself had been torn apart from the inside. The ground cracked wide open, fissures running like deep wounds through the landscape. The sound was deafening—an earth-shattering roar that drowned out everything. The trees, once standing tall and proud, were torn from their roots, flung aside like insignificant toys in a child's tantrum. Rocks the size of houses were lifted into the air, swirling in the violent winds that now whipped through the land.

And then, as if to answer the earth's fury, the sky cracked. The dark clouds above twisted and contorted, splintering like glass, until a single, blinding light erupted from the center, a blast so powerful it seemed to tear apart the very fabric of reality itself.

Adrian and the others could do nothing but watch, transfixed by the sheer magnitude of it all. Time seemed to slow, as though the universe itself was holding its breath. The light grew brighter, expanding, consuming everything in its path. The world was coming apart, piece by piece. There was no escape. The explosions were not just physical—they were metaphysical, the unraveling of everything that had ever been.

The oceans boiled and rose, giant waves crashing against the shorelines, swallowing entire cities, devouring everything in their wake. Mountains crumbled like sandcastles in the tide. The earth's crust broke apart, revealing the molten heart of the planet, a searing mass of fire and chaos.

Adrian, for a brief moment, felt weightless—disconnected from the world around him. He looked at Wren, who stood beside him, his eyes vacant and distant. There was no fear left in him, only resignation, as though he, too, had come to understand that this was the only way. The echoes, those twisted, soulless beings, had no place in the new world that was to come. And Catherine—she had been the architect of this madness. She had sought to control everything, but now, even she was nothing more than a shadow in the face of the unstoppable force that was tearing the world apart.

Adrian turned to her, just as she turned to him. For a fleeting moment, their eyes locked, and there was no hatred, no animosity. There was only understanding. They had both chosen the same path. They had both brought this upon themselves.

In a final act of defiance, Catherine raised her arms toward the sky, as though trying to grasp the very essence of the destruction that was unfolding around them. She screamed, but her voice was swallowed by the howling winds, her words drowned in the cataclysm that was now consuming everything. She knew, as Adrian did, that this was the end. The world would crumble, but it was a necessary destruction, one that would burn away the corruption and bring an end to the reign of the echoes.

The light that filled the sky grew brighter, the explosion of energy now so intense that it felt like the very air was on fire. The ground shook violently beneath them, and for the briefest moment, Adrian thought he saw everything. He saw the past—the battles, the losses, the struggles. He saw the present, the choices that had led him here, the sacrifices that had been made. And in that final instant, he saw the future—a future that would never come.

The earth itself split wide open, and the sky fell to meet it.

The explosion was deafening.

The world shattered into a million pieces, like a glass window breaking in slow motion. The air was filled with a deafening roar, the winds howling as everything—every living thing, every memory, every trace of existence—was ripped away and consumed by the overwhelming power of the blast. The ground crumbled beneath them, the buildings, the forests, the oceans—everything was swallowed by the abyss.

Adrian felt his body being pulled apart, the force of the destruction overwhelming him, as if his very atoms were being torn from each other. His breath caught in his throat, and for the briefest moment, he felt a peace, a quiet understanding. He had done what was necessary. The world had to be destroyed to be reborn.

And then, in the blink of an eye, everything went black.

THE ECHOES OF THE DESTRUCTION would never fade. The last remnants of a world that had once been were scattered like ash on the wind, leaving behind nothing but the emptiness of space. The oceans were still, the mountains now nothing but rubble, and the sky, once dark with storm, had become a void—an endless, silent expanse that stretched on forever.

In that silence, Adrian, Wren, Catherine, and all the others who had lived, fought, and died in the world they had known were no more. The destruction had consumed them all, leaving only echoes of their existence in the void.

And as the last remnants of the old world faded into nothingness, there was only the silence of an empty universe—waiting, perhaps, for something new to emerge from the chaos.

Written By Hiflur Rahman (The Visionary Voyager)

Don't miss out!

Visit the website below and you can sign up to receive emails whenever HIFLUR RAHMAN publishes a new book. There's no charge and no obligation.

https://books2read.com/r/B-A-WXFQC-QIDHF

BOOKS 2 READ

Connecting independent readers to independent writers.

About the Author

Hiflur Rahman is the author of the XEL series. Currently residing in Asia, he has written his first book, XEL -1. The XEL series is set in a fictional realm that includes some real-world locations. Although he began writing in 2020, he did not release any books until XEL -1. Hiflur also has plans to explore a different genre, distinct from the mystery genre.